Rose Star Runners:

And The Universe Princess

By Alex Benitez

Story by
Alex Benitez

Illustrated by
Israel Benitez

Technical Assistance
Joshua Nierodzinski

Special Thanks To
Laura Callender

Thanks Guys!

To all the men who have ever felt controlled by the women they love.

Sincerely,
A fellow victim

Table of Contents

The Time of Rose Star

Ten thousand years in the future, interstellar space travel has become a thing of the far past. Getting across a planet is as easily achieved as driving around town in our time, and traveling from one planet to another can be arranged like flying in our time. Every comfort has a number of grand technological achievements to accommodate them, as the future is mainly a paradise. Every city on every colonized planet is a metropolis of business and modern technological beauties, and skyscrapers that reach heights previously unimagined. It is a promising future, but there are still some who teeter on the brink of poverty due to their own laziness. One such man is Ky Gracen. You might wonder why a person would choose to be so relaxed when he could put forth some effort and live a much better life. All Ky would say to you is *If you are put through half the stuff I'm put through, you'd wanna take things easy too.*

Ky Gracen

A man of his time. Ky prefers, and is use to, the fast pace life of the future. He's happy to do as little as possible to get by in life. Scraping by for a living is a position, a man like Ky, is all too familiar with. In and out of custody since a teenager, this mediocre mid-twenties pilot takes odd jobs to support himself. Since he works only when he needs to, this leaves this self-proclaimed playboy with frequent nights off. His hobbies include, partying, drinking and taking naps. His happy-go-lucky attitude is maintained through even the darkest scenarios.

William A. Treyu

The young prodigy hacker. This cute blonde haired freckled face boy has a more serious deposition then his youthful frame lets on. Born an orphan, this lonely child of nine made up programs in his computer to act as friends. After being caught hacking into a government system at age six, he bounced around in juvenile detention centers until he was enrolled in a type of *big brother* program. The person that Will was inevitably paired with was Ky, who voluntarily enlisted himself in the program to find an easy way around some community service. Will sees himself as the parent of the two, and is far too serious for his age. His hobbies included, computer games, hacking systems, and bubble gum.

Jina

The poisonous flower. This young lady is only nineteen years old and as beautiful a girl as could ever be, but sadly, no one is to know her beauty. She is the deadliest woman in the galaxy when wielding her thin metal six-foot long staff. Barehanded, she can easily punch through solid cement blocks, but with the pipe, her attacks cause a string of vibrations with the impact. The vibrations cause a secondary, sometimes explosive like, strike. For a five-foot four inch girl with long black hair who dresses in various kimonos, the sight of her fighting is quite absurd looking. Although, when she stares at you ready for battle, you can feel death simmering in the air. This deadly blossom does have one severe weakness; gambling. In one very high stakes bet, the femme fatale lost a vast sum to Ky and now continuously aids him when she can until her debt is fully repaid. Besides gambling, nobody knows much about her hobbies. She is a shroud of feminine mystery and power.

I

Enter Lili

A boy laid spread out on a grassy field in a park in Gohanesse City. The park was beautiful, with acres upon acres of lush green grass and prosperous trees. It had stone trails circling the entire park for the few Gohanesse civilians who enjoyed leisurely walks. The park was dotted with clean ponds that had various ducks and geese sitting on the water's edge waiting for breadcrumbs that the elderly may disperse. Squirrels scurried among the trees hastily harvesting acorns and an assortment of nuts before the season became too cold. The park smelled of the sweet scents of pinecones, fresh cut grass, and blooming flowers. The park was a wonderful getaway from the usual hustle and bustle that consumed the overly busy city. It was like a safe haven for any city dweller who appreciates the feel of nature every now and again.

The boy was none other than William A. Treyu lying on his back with his face to the sky. His hands were tucked behind his head as he felt the warmth of the sun's rays kiss his smooth youthful skin. The excellently complex boy was content in his simple moment of calm. He looked up to the skies behind closed eyes, seeing nothing but a pink canvass content in his simple moment of calm. He looked up to the skies behind closed eyes, seeing nothing but a pink canvass of light passing through his fleshy eyelids. A tiny smile cracked in the corner of his mouth while a warm breeze rolled through. The wind gradually pushed the thick cotton clouds across the bright endless blue sky. The day was perfect, and that was the day it all began.

Suddenly, the boy became slightly colder while the pink hue of his eyelids turned black as if something had blocked his sun. He opened his eyes expecting to see a cloud obstructing the sun, but that's not what he saw. His eyes were greeted with a little girl's face staring right down at him. Will flinched in surprise when he saw the girl. The girl stayed there looking at him with a wildly huge smile streaked across her face. Both of them waited quietly in that position for a moment that could only be summed up with the word awkward.

The girl looked to be about nine, the same age as Will. She wore an odd, clean, white robe that appeared to be used in some tribal ritual. Even though the robe screamed of simplicity, it also had an important regal appearance. Her shoulder length black hair was sloppily dressed into a bun with crossed chopsticks holding it together. Though the boy would never have admitted it, her face was the cutest thing he'd ever seen. The boy was a little nervous, but he felt he had to say something.

"You're in my light." Will pointed out to the girl.

"Yeah!" She energetically agreed.

They remained silent for another awkward moment before Will requested. "Could you move?"

"Oh sure," She eagerly responded. The girl did as she promised and moved out of the way of Will's light. She daintily took a seat on the soft grass beside him. With wide eyes, she glared a hole through the boy's face. She purposely stared at him without blinking. The girl was very

Will adjusted himself on the grass and tried to relax again. It wasn't easy. He closed his eyes and attempted to resume his moment of peace, but he could feel the girl just staring at him. He opened an eye every once and awhile to see if she was there, and no matter how long he waited, she was. She was just innocently sitting beside him and looking at him with a grin from ear to ear. Why did Will let it bother him so much?

"Can I help you?" Will questioned, while sitting up and raising a brow to the girl.

The girl answered with an adorable little chuckle. Her cheeks swelled thick as her smile grew longer. It seemed as if she was just toying with the boy.

"What's so funny?" A bothered Will said.

"Nothing," She replied. "I'm Lili."

"That's cool." Will laid back down and tried his best to ignore her.

She giggled again.

"What do you want!?" An angered Will burst up and yelled.

"You," She chuckled. "You're too cute."

"What?" Will blushed and turned his head to hide the redness in his face. "Would you leave me alone?"

"No," She hastily reacted. "I'll never do that." Her smile remained printed on her face throughout the entire conversation.

Will leapt to his feet and announced. "Well, if you're not leaving, then I am."

"Okay,"

Will turned his body away from her and started walking off. He tried to put the weird encounter behind him, but the girl was too cute. Will twisted his head around to take one last look at the girl before she was out of his life for good, but what came as a shock to Will is that he saw the girl walking right behind him; she was only a few steps away.

"Are you gonna leave me alone?" An infuriated Will shouted in the middle of the peaceful park.

"Maybe,"

Will stopped and rapidly turned his head from side to side quickly scanning the park for something. "Hey, where are your parents?"

"I could ask you the same thing." Lili cleverly said.

"Urrgh," An annoyed Will grunted. He turned back around and began to storm out of the park with an excitable Lili nipping at his heels. When he first met her, Will didn't want to hurt her feelings, but as she steadily grew more irritating, that concern went right out the window. Will rudely and repeatedly bellowed *go away* while stomping out of the park, and she just as often repeated *no*. This carried on the entire time it took Will to walk out of the park. The two of them passed underneath a gorgeous rock arch that represented the park entrance. They headed left on the cluttered five-foot wide sidewalk and made it to the bus stop. Not a word was uttered between the kids as Will sat at the bench at the bus stop with the other riders. The massive silver bus rolled near the sidewalk and a few people trotted off it, then on it. Will stood up and lined up to the rear of a couple civilians and Lili motioned to follow him. Did she really mean to follow him on the bus as well?

Will jolted his whole body around in a second and bluntly ranted. "Look girl! I'm going home! You're NOT going to follow me! I want to see you turn around and head down the street."

"Okay," She recited with a bright smirk. Lili skipped down the street the same way she came.

Will followed her with his eyes until he saw her disappear when crossing under the stone arch at the park. He then blew a sigh of relief and entered the bus. The boy swiped his account card through a slot next to the driver to pay for the bus fare. He heard the driver giggle as he was heading back toward the seats. The boy halted a moment and gave a queer face to how easy-going the driver was.

Will sat somewhere in the middle of the right row and started watching the small television protruding from his seat's arm rest. No matter how much the boy changed through the stations, absolutely nothing was on. It wasn't the type of nothing your friend tells you when they're not interested in any of the programs; there wasn't anything broadcasting on the television at all. The only actual program being shown was a local news broadcast, but something was weird about it. Instead of the usual serious demeanor that the news team portrayed while informing the public, they were acting all loopy and no valuable information was being relayed to the masses. It was just the entire news team in front of the cameras horsing around with each other. The fully-grown news team shamelessly acted like a group of grade school friends who were meeting up at recess. Will was boggled by what he saw on the screen. *How could they be allowed to do all this?* Will thought to himself. The anchorman was shoving the meteorologist while the field reporter threw poorly constructed paper airplanes at the sports caster. They were all flush in the face from laughing wildly like a pack of hyenas. "It seems like news 6 kept the cameras rolling after hours." Will said to himself.

Will turned the television off out of frustration. He scrolled his eyes around at the passengers in boredom. The passengers would habitually shoot an inconspicuous gaze at the boy, and then they would turn their heads as if they were childishly trying to hide the fact that they were looking at him. Even though the bus was only at about half its full capacity, the boy still found it weird that every single passenger was doing it, as if they knew something he didn't. Will decided to ignore them for the duration of the ride.

Will peered out the bus' window gazing upon Gohanesse's beautiful commercial district, which was the area that the park was located. The commercial district's buildings stretched to the edge of the sky like monuments of metal, cement, and glass. The buildings in the commercial district of Gohanesse were easily the most appealing to the eye in the prosperous city. They were sleek and flashy and invited the masses to enter their establishments and empty their accounts. The latest and hottest fashions hung on mannequins in the first floor windows as well as advertising the newest and trendiest technologies. The wealthiest of folks roamed its streets with their noses held high up in the air. The commercial district was a chaotic jumble of consumerism.

The commercial district slowly blended into the industrial district. The stylish buildings were swapped with less attractive structures that spewed smoke out of pipes in their roofs. The buildings appeared worked and focused more on functionality. The shopping windows were traded for massive delivery trucks that shipped the very same products. The bustling crowded sidewalks were switched for blue-collar workers who were heading home after a busy day. This district was the backbone of Gohanesse's thriving economy, and strangely enough, where Will lived.

It would make sense for a boy Will's age to live with his parents in the residential district, but Will's living arrangements were a little more improvised than most. For one, the boy had no idea who his parents were, and then he's been stuck with a guardian too lazy to get off his ass, get a steady job, and move out of the industrial district. Will had some complaints about these developments in his life, but all in all he was growing accustomed to his lifestyle. It wasn't long ago that the boy ventured out on an exhausting journey to save the universe. So Will was looking forward for his life to switch gears and get nice and boring. Unlucky for Will, the peace would not last.

The bus pulled up to a studio styled warehouse sandwiched between other warehouses. The studio/warehouse was where Will lived, as its contents had been converted into a large apartment. The bus usually drove all the way to the bus stop three blocks down the road, but for some reason, the bus waited in front of the boy's place. This struck the boy as odd, but he wasn't about to look a gift horse in the mouth. He quickly made his way off the bus.

The driver uttered. "Good luck," before shutting the sliding door closed to Will's back.

Will watched the bus speed away with a perplexed expression on his youthful features. He then shrugged and brushed off the events of his out of the ordinary day. He took long strides to the plain front door of the large apartment and opened it.

The interior of the studio/warehouse was an accurate testament to the boy's humble lifestyle. To the immediate left of the entrance was a small round white dining table with four matching seats. To the right of the entrance was a room crudely constructed of flimsy sheet metal and cardboard walls. A skeleton frame of metal rods bound together the aluminum and board walls. The room looked as if it could be erected and torn down in the same hour. That room was the private living space of his laid-back guardian, Ky Gracen. Will had rarely ever been in that room, but the few times he had, what he saw could be labeled as official pigsties. Farther down on the left was a small television propped up on a makeshift entertainment stand that faced the dirty white couch in the center of the apartment. Only the small shabby wooden coffee table set on a throw rug separated the television from the couch. Past the couch and television was a set of collapsible stairs that led up to a room suspended in the air. The room resembled Ky's in construction, but was supported in the upper right corner of the apartment by a stilt system of metallic rods. That room dangling in the air was Will's room. Along the right side of the wall ran all the kitchen essentials conveniently placed in a row. It had an industrial-sized three-tub sink next to a counter, which then met a stove. The next two links in the chain were a frigerator and the stacked washer and dryer; that actually rested beneath Will's room. Past all that was a long collapsible wall much like the one making up the rooms. It was set there by Ky to create some sort of privacy for their sorry excuse of a bathroom. Beside the white dining table was a small iron ladder that if climbed, led to a narrow fenced balcony. The wall of the balcony was huge panes of glass making for a wonderful view. Sadly, the view wasn't absolutely magnificent because the backdrop was Gohanesse's smoggy industrial district. Will and Ky had set futons on the balcony so that they could relax and enjoy the view. The floors in the studio/warehouse mainly consisted of hastily installed smudged pearl tiles and a few stained and filthy throw rugs. The apartment was littered with the stench of beer and bubble gum. By the overall feel of the apartment, it was evidently clear that the inhabitants of the large apartment were a pair of mismatched male bachelors.

Will's gaze slid to the left where the dining table was, while he closed the door behind him. As his eyes set on the table he saw two familiar figures seated there.

The first person was his lousy choice of a legal guardian. The lazy man sporting disheveled hair and a five o'clock shadow answered to the name of Ky.

The second person was godly in her sheer beauty. If ever a person was attractive enough to blind someone, that person was Jina. Her skillfully proportioned figure was daintily swathed in a kimono. Her face also added to the gorgeous image of the woman bearing a button nose and crystal green eyes as wide as a clear day. Jina's straight midnight black hair drooped over her shoulders and shined like threads of the finest silk. She raised a mug to her full lush lips before sipping its contents. Her body smelt of the sweet fragrance of a field of flowers that never ceased to surround her body like a shield. Her allure was great enough to knock the sense right out of the best looking of men, but it appeared Will and Ky had grown accustom to her beauty.

Both Ky and Jina immediately darted their attention to the boy as he entered. The duo at the table also wore giant smiles, which was contradictory to both their personalities.

"Hello stud," Ky sarcastically remarked before giggling. Jina also joined him in the chuckles.

Will ignored Ky's comment without suspicion before sternly interrogating. "Did you look for a job?"

"Nope!" Ky rang with an odd confidence.

"And why not?"

"Trust me, NO ONE is hiring."

"That's not important!" Jina interrupted with so much energy she sprang up from her seat and nearly knocked over her six-foot long metal staff she set on a wall to her rear. "Tell us about Lili!"

"Who?" Will questioned as he neared Ky and Jina.

"Li-li," Ky repeated slowly only a few inches from Will's face.

Will didn't respond. He actually started smelling the air, then Ky's breath. He then took the mug that Ky was drinking from and examined the contents inside. It was an orange liquid that the boy didn't hesitate to sniff. "This isn't a mimosa. Ky are you okay?"

"Why do you ask?"

"Well, because it's like 2:40 in the afternoon and you don't reek of booze."

"I guess it depends on your definition of the word *okay*."

"What about Lili?" Jina said pressing the issue as she slapped her hand down on the table.

"Who's Lili?" Will finally asked.

"Your girlfriend," Ky answered.

An astonished Will bellowed. "My girlfriend!? I'm nine."

Jina announced. "It's all over Headscript!"

"Wait, wait, wait!" Will yelled with his hands in the air attempting to kill the excitement of the moment. "For one, I DON'T have a girlfriend. And second, you guys know I don't have a stupid Headscript account."

Headscript was a communication tool to keep in touch with friends across the cosmos. It was a website where one can acquire a free account and create a profile page. The page could be filled with your interests, hobbies, self-taken photos, along with a multitude of opportunities to say whatever you want. Others could browse your page to become your friend, drop a public comment, send a photo, give a private message or block the user entirely. Billions upon billions of socialites check their Headscripts daily, including Ky. As for Will, he just saw Headscript as a dumb fad and refused to ever make an account.

"Oh yeah," Ky said with wide defiant eyes. He got out of the seat and grabbed Will's laptop off the coffee table. Ky sat back in his place at the dining table as he opened the laptop and booted it up. As soon as he could he commanded. "Computer, show me my Headscript."

"Affirmative," Vibrated out of the small speakers in the laptop. A moment later, the laptop's monitor changed to Ky's Headscript page. Ky's profile picture was one of him face down on a sandy beach with his butt in the air as if he was dead. A can of beer was clutched in his hand carefully set in the sandy floor right side up. Even when unconscious, Ky didn't waste a drop of alcohol.

"Computer, go to William A. Treyu's profile under my friends." Ky ordered.

"Affirmative," The laptop droned.

Will confidently folded his arms together. He knew in about a second that laptop was going to say *file not found*, and that alone would clear up the whole mess. That did not happen. Will's nonexistent page popped up on the screen. Will's heart sank along with his arms and the features on his face. He couldn't believe what he was seeing.

It was, in fact, Will's Headscript page. The profile picture on his page was one of him blowing a giant gum bubble, and was taken by Jina months earlier. All his profile information had been filled out and placed in their corresponding areas. His headline read *ILY LILI LOL*.

"I don't talk like that." Will angrily added as he looked to his headline. The boy then saw something that truly startled him. About half way down on a quick synopsis of Will was a section that read *is going out with Lili*.

"See?" Jina said as she hunched over Will, also looking at the screen. "It's Headscript official."

"Would you be quiet." Will assertively insisted. The boy's eyes were guided to a section of the page that had a cheesy flashing envelope graphic next to some text. The text read *387 new comments*. "Three hundred and eighty-seven new comments?" A bewildered Will read back. Will pushed the envelope symbol on the screen with his tiny bare finger. The comment portion of Will's Headscript page swallowed up the laptop's monitor. Will immediately realized an eerie fact about all the messages. They were all from Lili. Will's comment page was flooded with messages like *ILY ;)* and *HAD A BLAST!!!!!!!!! LUV YA!* and *can't wait until 2morrow XD* and other such nonsense.

At that moment, Will's curiosity was tumbling out of control. He touched Lili's name on the screen beside one of her messages with his finger. When Will saw the next profile picture that came up, his entire world was twisted inside out. It was her, cute face, weird robe, and chopsticks in her hair bun, the girl from the park. Their encounter suddenly played back in his head like a car crash. *She DID say her name was Lili* Will thought to himself. He had completely forgotten that she had told him that. He must not have been paying attention. Looking deep into her photo and her monstrously big grin, Will became for a split second genuinely frightened of the little girl. Unable to coherently piece together the next things he was going to say, one word was able to sneak by the boy's lips like a reflex. "Lili,"

A muffled *yeah* was suddenly heard. It originated from inside the apartment. The door to Will's suspended room swung open and Lili herself stepped out onto the set of collapsible stairs. She looked at Will and gave a big smile accompanied by an enthusiastic hand wave. She said. "Hi Will,"

Will could not believe her audacity to actually show up where he lived, in his own room no less. You'd think after all the weirdness that occurred throughout the day surrounding Lili, that it would keep Will petrified of her, but her actually standing there was all too surreal. His fears left him when he looked upon her small harmless countenance. Will had a unique opportunity to confront the source of the madness. He looked up at Lili with a face of extreme prejudice.

"You!" Will roared in an unstable tone. "What are you doing here?"

"Oh Will, what exactly do you mean?"

"That's it! I ain't talkin' to you anymore. I'm sick of your goofy vague answers. I'm going to talk to someone who has a grip on reality." Will shifted his eyes to Jina and asked. "What is she doing here?"

Jina answered. "What do you mean?"

Will lifted a brow at Jina. "Are you okay? I mean why is she in our apartment?... In my room of all places."

"Because you two have been sharing that room since you moved in, idiot." Ky revealed.

"Since I moved in?" Will argued. He pointed a hate filled finger at the cute smiling girl at the top of the staircase. "She doesn't live here."

Jina and Ky looked at each other quickly in an exchange of confused faces. The pair then erupted into a wave of laughter. Their laughter echoed and reverberated throughout the walls of the studio/warehouse. The sound deafened the overly confused boy's thoughts and chilled him to the bone with an impending sense of loneliness. He didn't know what else to say. He could only stand there and listen.

As Jina and Ky's obnoxious laughter died, Ky stated. "Will, Lili has been living here longer than you have."

Will knew this was a complete falsehood. He had only met her that day, and he decided to say it.

"This is a complete falsehood. I only met her today."

"Where'd you meet her?" Ky sharply snapped back.

"At the park." Will honestly answered.

"Not a bad first date, especially considering your age and stuff."

"It was nice." Lili added.

Ky and Jina simultaneously let out a long exaggerated *awwww* after Lili spoke. They smiled at Lili and Will reveling in the thought of them going out on some cute little kid date.

Will interrupted their *aw* with frustrated howls. "No! It wasn't nice and it wasn't a date! That's the first time I met her EVER!"

"I know," Ky agreed. "That's the first time you ever met her on a date."

Will simply stared at him in disbelief. Could they have seriously have been brainwashed by that bright faced little girl? Will then did something very unexpected. He had finally figured out what was going on, or at least that's what he convinced himself. The boy decided to let the cat out of the bag.

"Okay, okay." A then confident Will said. "Ha ha, very funny guys, but your little joke is over."

Ky, Jina and Lili traded confused faces with a feeling of perplexity in the atmosphere.

"Come on," Will insisted adamantly eager for them to let go of their practical joke. "She has to be…like… Jina's little cousin who was coming down and ya'll decided to screw with me. You gave me a phony-bologna Headscript account and acted like she's been here for years. I gotta admit, you guys had me going for a while, but your major mistake was you wore your dumb joke out too long. So quit it guys." As his eyes reflected all three faces he scanned them to view their expressions, and the resulting looks truly disheartened the boy. They all looked at Will as if he was crazy and their authentic concern was noticeable in their body language. It all hit Will like a ton of bricks. He wondered if he could be losing his mind.

Ky got up and placed a caring hand on Will's shoulder. "Hey man, are you feeling all right?" Ky worried.

Will feverishly smacked away Ky's hand. "Stop it! Just stop it!" His angered gaze locked on to Lili. His eyes narrowed in size as they were set on her before he growled. "You," He slowly made his way to the true source of the problem, the sweet little girl at the top of the collapsible steps. He ran up the stairs and shoved Lili aside as he entered his room. "Outta my way!" He shouted back at her. As the boy entered the sanctuary of his room, he exploded.

"AHHHHHH!" Will shrieked like a little girl fearing for her life. He was so mad that his hands were tightened into small vibrating fists by his cheeks when he screamed, and the sound was faintly heard in the busy neighboring warehouses. The blood-curdling screech was invoked when Will had witnessed the horrors that had befallen his room. His room had been transformed into a girl's room. The walls were atrociously coated in runny hot pink paint. A small white vanity set with pony prints stamped all over it had been moved in, and sitting on the vanity was a picture of Will framed in a gold heart. An assortment of brushes, half-empty perfume bottles, and make-up kits littered the floor. A picture of a fluffy white kitten hung half way down a wall. Another bed had crudely been welded on top of Will's, making an improvised and flimsy bunk bed set. Even his bed sheets had a pink and purple flower print on it. Will's anger had struck its boiling point and the boy had no choice but to release his rage.

"What have you done!?" Will yelled.

"What do you mean?" Lili calmly asked trotting back into the room.

"Well, what I mean is this." Will pointed at the painted walls. "What's this? These walls weren't designed for painting that's why it's all streaky. Now I got ugly pink paint clumps on my walls!"

"Our walls," Lili corrected.

"Don't push it." Will warned. He then directed his finger to the adorable picture of the fluffy white cat. "And what's this? Why would I want this? Or that..." Will pointed at the vanity set. "...or this..." Will grabbed a fistful of sheets and held it up for her to view. "I want all this crap out." He ordered dropping the sheets from his hand.

"But that's all my stuff." Lili sadly argued.

"Well then why is it on my bed and in my room?

And what the hell is that smell?"

"Our room, and I'm sorry if I changed your dirty smelly sheets for you, and that smell is called potpourri, dewy meadow."

Will's thumb propped up against his chest, and he forcefully explained. "I'm not a dewy meadow kind of guy." He then bypassed her, making sure not to touch her at all, and stormed out of the room. He stomped downstairs like a raging bull.

Ky and Jina, who had returned to their seats at the dining table, silently followed Will with twin gazes. A thick tension pulsated from the boy's little body so potent that even Jina respected it. They watched as an infuriated Will headed to a cabinet near the kitchen area and went rummaging through it. They saw Will pull out a shiny black cylinder. It was a full roll of big black trash bags. Will ripped off two bags from the roll and neatly folded them over his arm. After putting the trash bags back in the cabinet, he marched back upstairs.

When the boy slammed the door to his bedroom behind him, Ky twisted his head toward Jina and said. "Lover's quarrel." Jina nonchalantly took a sip of her mug while nodding her head in agreement.

When Will got back to his room, he saw that Lili was still there. "Get out!" He shouted with an index finger to the door.

She reluctantly complied and took soft steps out the door.

The moment she left the makeshift room, Will closed the door behind her. The boy fully opened the bags and went to work. The picture of the cute kitten was one of the firsts to be thrown in. He took her things off the floor and stuffed it into one of the huge plastic trash bags. All her makeup and loose clothing got haphazardly chucked in. He tore the sheets off the bed and even shoved the hearted photograph of himself into one of the bags. Will was on a rampage and he was not going to stop until he dumped all her belongings into one of the two bags. It took Will about fifteen minutes to gather up all her things into the black garbage bags.

Will then very deliberately walked out of his room holding the two trash bags, two arms underneath one with the other stacked on top. Will struggled with the hefty bags of Lili's possessions as he carried them to the front door. By that time, Lili had joined Ky and Jina at the dining table. All of them quietly watched as Will placed the bags on the floor, opened the door and shoved Lili's stuff outside. Will vanished out the door as he continued pushing the bags. Ky, Jina and Lili arose from their chairs and stepped to the door so that they could clearly see Will outside. They saw Will push the bags near the sidewalk where they would usually put the trash then turn around to face all of them.

Lili looked at Will with huge eyes and a deeply saddened face before she was just able to utter. "Will...why did you do this?"
Will stood at the edge of what could only be described as their front yard and screamed at the top of his lungs while staring right at Lili. "This is ALL your stuff!" He then kicked the bags as hard as he could. "It's MY room now, got it!?"

Lili's tiny lips began to tremble and her big brown eyes glossed over heavily. Her head dropped but was caught by her hands cupping her face. She then started sobbing her little heart out. Her shoulders shook due to the ferocity from which she cried into her hands. She bolted out the door and ran down the street with a red face drenched in tears.

Will's overwhelming hate was suddenly drained out of him as if by some giant moral plunger. It was replaced with a hefty load of guilt. It was only then that Will realized he had done something very mean.

Jina glanced at Ky and rolled her eyes in a silent complaint of what had just transpired. She then informed Ky. "I'll go after her." Jina then jogged down the street after Lili.

Will's head traced Jina down the street while his logic wrestled with his newfound guilt. Ky walked up beside him while the boy stood there speechless.

"You know, I'm not the nicest person in the world and I don't claim to know that much about woman either, but...man, that was a real dick move." Ky advised.

"Crap," Will said to himself before rolling his eyes and running back into the studio/warehouse. He grabbed his laptop from the kitchen table then dashed upstairs and into his room closing the door behind him. Will, as well as his laptop, flopped back first on his sheet-less bed, and the boy pulled a naked pillow over his face to hide his shame. He never meant to make her cry. He just wanted someone, just one person to believe him; a person to tell him he's not insane. Only when he was in juvenile centers had Will ever felt a sense of loneliness that deep. It wasn't his fault. Why did she come? Why did she have to cry? Will felt like a jackass and tears started escaping the corners of his eyes. Will secretly cried under that pillow for what he had done. That only lasted for about five minutes before Will regained his composure.

Will remembered that there were big questions about all this that weren't being answered. Like, if his memories weren't lying to him, why does no one realize that Lili had shown up only that day? And if everyone else was correct, why couldn't he remember her? It was then that the boy decided to stop crying about it, and do some investigating. H sat up in his bed Indian-style sporting puffy bloodshot eyes. Will picked up the laptop next to him, opened it and handled his business.

The evening rolled into night and Will confined himself in his room with his face pressed to the laptop. His fingers were a mesh of clicks as he roamed the net gaining all the data he desired like a true virtuoso. In the computer realm, Will was a god, and he intended to use his powers to the fullest to get down to the bottom of things. The seclusion only gnawed at the boy's mind once when he poked his head out the bedroom door surveying the area. He saw Ky casually watching television while Lili appeared to be baking something in the kitchen area; she had a large wooden mixing spoon inside a big blue plastic bowl she clung to her chest swirling its contents around. She wore a dough-spattered apron over her robe and the bowl seemed to contain the very same dough. She was humming no song in particular and had a childish smirk with the tip of her tongue sticking out. He assumed that that face was her *I'm busy doing something* face. Will didn't even notice how well he analyzed her in that short period of time. Will slowly tucked his head back in the room and shut the door softly so that no one would witness him peeking. A tiny smile was drawn on the boy's face before he jumped to the laptop and got back to business.

The night continued on and eventually the entire apartment was filled with the sweet scent of cookies. Even the enticing allure of cookies didn't budge Will from his post. It was only ten minutes later that Lili came up and paid him a visit.

She creaked the door open and stuck her head in before asking. "Can I come in?"

Will sighed from behind the monitor. "If you must,"

The door flung open and Lili stepped in the room holding a silver tray of fresh baked cookies. The awesome smell of the cookies amplified as she neared him.

Will nonchalantly asked. "Where's Ky?"

"He went out."

"Oh,"

"I know you're upset, so I brought some cookies I baked." She offered holding the tray out to him.

"What kind are they?"

"Well, I wanted to make chocolate chip, but we don't have any chips, so they're chipless chocolate chip cookies."

"Chipless chocolate chip cookies?" Will repeated back in a queer manner. "You mean like a sugar cookie?"

"No, like chipless chocolate chip cookies." She reaffirmed. "Want one?"

Will eyed her for a minute then groaned. "Sure," He knelt up and plucked a warm one from the tray. He put the cookie to his mouth and took two big bites. While he chewed it, confusion became his face.

"Do you like it?" She anxiously wondered.

"It's weird." Will murmured while chewing. "I expect to hit a chip at some point in time, but it never comes."

"Is that all?"

"They're all right." Will assured taking another bite.

She smiled. "Oh good," Lili placed the tray of cookies at the foot of the bed and sat at the corner of the mattress. She was intrigued at Will's fingers blazing so intently on the computer. "Whatcha' doin'?" She curiously inquired.

Will calmly revealed shoveling the rest of the cookie down his throat. "First, I deleted the fake Headscript account then set their system with an undetectable glitch that makes it that no one can ever create an account under my name."

"Oh my God." She gasped genuinely impressed. "How did you do that? I didn't even give you the password."

"Aha, so you did set it up." He deduced. "I'm a pretty good hacker, so all that was easy."

"So what are you doing now?"

"Looking through every data bank there is to see what I can find out about you."

"What have you found?"

"Surprisingly nothing so far on a Lili matching your description. Is that your real name?"

"Mmmm-hmmm,"

"I suppose you could be lying to me."

"Tee-hee," Lili giggled. "You're the only person I'd never lie to."

"Whatever that means."

"So you're really good at hacking, huh?"

"I can do whatever I want with a computer."

Lili slyly cooed. "I know exactly what you mean."

Will curiously inquired. "Oh, so you must know something about computers."

"Heck no! Do you know how long it took me to set up your account?"

Will boasted. "Well I am, so if there's anything to find on you, I'll find it."

"Good luck with that then." She said while getting up from the bed and heading to the door. "I'm leaving the cookies here okay?" She added, at the door.

"Thanks,… I still hate you, you know."

"No you don't." She leisurely rang from the other side of the door.

Will continued his online investigation and his pursuit was not faring well. No matter how complete or top secret the data banks he broke into were, nothing came up on Lili. Either she had never done anything to prove that she existed or she just literally didn't exist. He searched throughout the galactic wide web with a fever he never had before. Why couldn't he find at least one thing proving she was alive beside her Headscript? She must have been born. Why could he find no birth records? He couldn't even find proof that she ever had an account or bought anything. His search only baffled the young boy and mounted a building sized pile of questions in his head.

The door opened again and Lili waltzed into the room. "Hi," She shyly said.

"Hi," Will droned.

She headed over to the improvised bunk bed set and noticed a white powder haphazardly brushed on its legs. Lili examined the powder by touching it, and rubbing it between her fingers. She even smelt the powder, but couldn't deduce what it was. "What is this?" She held her powdered fingers out to Will.

"I dusted for your finger prints." Will explained. "I wanted something else to go off of rather than your name, which you could have easily lied to me about. Speaking of which, has anyone ever talked to you about your finger prints?"

"Nope, why?"

"Because your prints are sets of perfectly straight vertical lines going up and down."

"Is that strange?"

"Yes, very strange." Will addressed shooting Lili an astonished expression. "Everyone's finger prints are their own set of distinct swirly lines, but always swirly; never straight."

"What can I say?" Lili boasted with a gloat filled shoulder shrug.

"With a set of such peculiar prints, I thought finding something on you was gonna be simple, but I haven't found anything. Nada, zilch, zero, nothing, the big fat goose egg." Will ranted personally damning himself. Before Will could come up with any more clever synonyms for nothing, he heard the corner of his bed creak as if weight was being placed on it. He pulled his eyes away from his laptop and looked out toward the edge of the bed. He witnessed as Lili started climbing the bed heading for the top bunk. "What are you doing?"

"What do you think I'm doing?" Lili shot back.

"I'm going to bed."

"Here?"

"Well, this is my bed Will, if you haven't noticed."

"Look, I thought I made myself perfectly clear earlier. This is my room, go sleep on the couch."

"This is my bed and I'm gonna sleep in it, and you're not strong enough to drag it to the sidewalk, and Jina won't do it for you, so I suggest you just deal with it." She proclaimed as she got in her sheet-less bed and draped the plush comforter over herself.

"This is too weird for me." Will admitted.

"Come on," She nagged from under her covers. "It can be fun. We could talk all night."

"Not interested,"

"Fine Mr. Grouch," Lili grumbled slamming her head to the pillow. "You can stay up all night hating me if you want. See if I care."

"If you're not leaving, I am."

"Fine,"

Will stayed good to his word and ripped the blanket and pillow from his bed in a way that perfectly illustrated how furious the boy was. The maturity level in the collapsible stilted room had dipped dramatically. They bickered much like nine-year-olds would as Will headed for the door.

"Don't let the door hit you on the way out!" Lili nagged as Will left.

"I won't!" Will shouted back to her not giving too much thought in his response. He stormed out into the dark empty apartment with his sleeping gear in hand. Will showed excellent balance as he skillfully ascended the ladder to the upper catwalk while holding his pillow and blanket. He curled up in one of the futons and tucked himself in. The boy's mind flowed like a raging waterfall that night. The events of the day churned around in his brain and inevitably led to vows of vengeance against the arrival of a certain little girl named Lili. His revenge brewed in his head and eventually lulled him to sleep.

Will's youth filled eyes had an image of a bright light. The light just had to be the sun. There might have been another smaller sun next to the big one. The omnipresent sun beamed its rays down on Will carrying a comfort with it nearly foreign to him. The sun had a warmth to it that allowed him to stare directly at it, and let him know, deep down in the back of his mind, that this was really just a dream.

The mighty light cast down upon three figures that stood in front of Will. The sun lit up the edge of the figure's silhouettes in a glow of holy radiance, but in turn, it created a shadow on their bodies and faces of pure black. It was impossible for Will to make out who they were.

Two figures were significantly taller than the third and they appeared to be the adults of the threesome. One of the adults was male while the other was female. The third was also male but was shorter than the adults as if it was the child of the other two.

Will stared up at the three figures absolutely speechless bearing a sense of comfortable displacement. From Will's point of view, he was much smaller than even the child figure, giving the boy the feeling that he either shrunk or was supposed to be younger than he was. He could hear the three talking among themselves, but they spoke as faint as soft whispers. Will struggled to make out their words.

The female figure innocently asked. "What happened?"

The boy figure replied. "Some kids made fun of him then one hit him, then he started crying."

"You were crying?" The female figure wondered.

"And what were you doing the whole time?" The male figure interrogated with an accusative tone.

"I don't know," The boy figure responded holding a tad amount of fear in the words.

"Oh, Will," The female figure sympathized with a love that Will didn't know of.

"You're supposed to take care of him." The male figure ordered. "He's much smaller than you so you're supposed to look out for him."

"I'm sorry." The boy figure apologized.

The female figure added. "You're supposed to protect him…"

That is all that Will would remember from that dream.

II

"Will's Working With Wes!"

A hardy breakfast, mixed together and roamed about the open studio/warehouse. A home cooked breakfast was a rarity in that apartment and his eyes bugged open from the excitement of having one.

When he opened his eyes, Lili was leaned right over in front of him while balancing a plate of food in his face. Lili did it again. She nearly gave Will a heart-attack. The sudden shock of seeing her as he woke up pumped gallons of adrenaline into the boy's system at once and made him jump up in the futon. He sat back up in the futon breathing heavily as he tried calming his nerves. He shot a disapproving gaze at Lili for her crazy antics.

"Oh my God!" Will shouted. "Do you need to be all up in my face every time I wake up!?"

"Sorry," She sincerely said. "I brought you some breakfast." She offered with a smile while pushing the plate closer to Will's face.

"It's probably poisoned."

"Of course not!" She defended. "Eat it, you'll like it."

Will reluctantly took the plate of food as he fully sat up. He hesitated to take the first few bites, but in no time, he was inhaling the meal. Lili watched him intently with a loving grin. It seemed she liked when Will enjoyed her cooking, but Will was once again feeling awkward due to her presence.

"Now I don't want to seem rude, but could you not watch me like that." Will requested.

"Sure," Lili began to head for the ladder down the catwalk-like balcony.

Before she was able to reach the ladder, Will complimented. "It's good, thank you."

She showed him a cute appreciative smile before she descended down the metallic ladder.

Will sat up with the sun beating on his face through the giant windows. He could hear the other household members conversing and carrying on below as he enjoyed his breakfast in mild peace. He listened in as Ky and Lili goofed off downstairs in an oddly lighthearted fashion. He could also hear Jina as well; which was an extreme rarity for her to be there that early in the morning. He tried to ignore the threesome's shenanigans as much as he could. He found it annoying that Ky and Jina foolishly bantered on with her without suspecting a thing. How come they couldn't realize the truth? She was a total stranger.

Suddenly Will heard something that slightly perked up his spirits. He heard Lili say *Bye guys* followed by the sound of the front door slamming shut. He darted off the futon (chucking the plate of food scraps across the catwalk) and looked out the window down to the street. He saw her gleefully skipping down the sidewalk away from the apartment. He cracked a smile and hurried to the ladder. This was his chance. If he was going to show Ky and Jina the truth, this was the moment, while she was gone. He slid down the ladder into the large apartment's main room with the intent of convincing his friends, but when he saw the absurdity going on downstairs, it made him momentarily forget his coaxing.

Jina was sprawled out on the couch watching

television. Jina never watched television, but at that moment, her eyes were glued to some cheesy soap opera re-run. Will still found Ky's actions much more bizarre. He was cleaning the dishes with a grin on his face. The boy did a double-take to accept what Ky was doing.

"What are you guys doing?" Will instinctively questioned.

"Nothing," Ky and Jina rang in unison.

Will took a seat at the white dining table as he further investigated. "Why are you here so early?"

Jina twisted her head to Will and argued. "What? My visits are time restricted now?"

Ignoring her response Will continued. "Where'd Lili go?"

"I don't know," Ky and Jina said at the same time once again.

"Oooo-kayyy, what do you mean *you don't know*?"

"It means just that, we don't know." Jina answered. "Maybe she went to work?"

Will chuckled a bit. "Very funny, but seriously, where'd she go?" Will's eyes shifted from Ky to Jina and back again. They didn't need to say a word; their faces said it all. They were serious. "You guys gotta be kidding. For one she's a girl, and two she's probably younger than me."

"Ummm, I think she's older than you." Ky disagreed.

"Yeah, she's at least three or four years older than you." Jina concurred.

"What the hell are you guys talking about? Have you looked at her?" Will reasoned.

"She's way older than you." Ky insisted.

"And prettier," Jina added.

"Yeah, she's way older and much more pretty than you." Ky concluded.

Will roared. "This is SO STUPID!"

Ky and Jina giggled to themselves.

"And why aren't you looking for a job?" Will demanded to know asking out of blind anger.

"It's like I told you yesterday." Ky said with a wide satisfied smirk on his face. "No one is hiring."

"So you're trying to tell me that there isn't one job in all of Gohanesse that you're qualified for?" Will spoke exaggerating the words in disbelief of Ky's implication.

"No, there isn't one job in Gohanesse what-so-ever."

"Boo-hockey!" Will blurted assuming that Ky was just being lazy and lying to him. The focus of Will's voice then shifted from Ky to the laptop on the coffee table just in front of Jina. "Computer, find a job for Ky. Anything he's qualified for."

"Affirmative," A comforting female voice blared out of the tiny speakers on the laptop.

Will crossed his arms, puffed out his nine-year-old chest and bore a face brimming with confidence. He knew in a few moments his trusty computer was going to literally post a massive list of jobs from which Ky could choose. Slowly the boy realized something was wrong. The *few moments* it would have taken for the list to upload had long passed, leaving nothing but a doubtful silence in its place. Five, six seconds had elapsed without Computer giving any response. A total of ten seconds passed before the laptop gave the odd reply *No such job available.*

"Seee," Ky dug deeply into his youthful friend.

A soft-spoken *that can't be* crossed Will's lips as his eyes and arms sank as if suddenly weighed down. Will then shook his head and barked at Computer. "Computer, you're telling me there isn't one job out there that Ky is qualified for?!"

The speakers blankly repeated. "No such job available."

"Don't you get it? So just calm down, kick back, and

enjoy yourself." Ky advised.

"I don't wanna enjoy myself!" Will cursed as his eyes darted about the studio/warehouse for his coat. He found it on a neighboring seat at the dining table and threw it on.

Ky and Jina shared expressions of concern toward Will's drastic actions. As their eyes followed the boy, Ky asked. "Hey buddy, where you goin'?"

"I'm getting a job since you won't." Will said adjusting his sleeve.

"You?" Ky called out baffled. "You're only ten."

"Nine actually," Will corrected. "And I got to."

"How?" Ky questioned. "You saw what Computer said."

"I once read once that people used to get jobs other ways besides using a computer." Will ranted like some wise old sage. "They went from business to business and directly applied there. I believe I can exercise that right."

"Fine by me then." Ky finally gave. "You try and make sense of what's going on out there."

"Fine, I will." Will forcefully agreed and huffed his way up to his room. He grabbed his satchel. The bag was a leathery brown and could hold his laptop perfectly as it hung comfortably across his chest and over his shoulder. He returned back downstairs and nestled his laptop into his bag before heading for the door.

Right as Will was leaving, Jina wished him an honest. "Good luck,"

Will exited the large apartment and headed to the bus stop a few blocks down the street. He saw that the bus stop was utterly desolate but he sat at its lonely bench and waited patiently anyway. He looked around for the bus but couldn't see one in sight. Will just sat there, silently waiting for the bus as minutes crawled by. Will began to become worried that the bus wouldn't be coming and waited for fifteen more minutes before he totally convinced himself of that fact. Will squirmed off the bench and walked away from the bus stop defeated yet again.

Will strolled past the countless factories and warehouses that made up Gohanesse's industrial district. The factories weren't bustling with the usual fervor they did on most days and actually most of them seemed abandoned. The few people in the factories that Will did see were engaged in activities that could be described as anything but constructive. Basically they were just horsing around.

The towering dark and dirty factories that use to spew thick black smog sort of scared the child side of Will. The boy was well aware of the backbreaking labor involved with getting a job at places like that, and knew that that particular job field is in no way suited for a nine-year-old boy. Will knew he'd have to hit a more casual and accommodating part of the industrial district before he started applying places.

It was a twenty-three minute walk before Will found the type of street that he was searching for. The street was a designated pit stop for the blue-collar industrial worker's heavy schedule. It was lined with convenience stores, fast-food restaurants, little café's and any other kind of establishment the average man uses to unwind during their breaks. Will figured it would have to be a place on that street. With the transit-system out of commission, it was the only place close enough to walk to with a workload a boy could handle. Optimism filled the boy as he neared the street corner.

He eyed down the peculiar people roaming its streets. The citizens were acting ridiculous. They choked the street laughing and fooling around like if they were on some schoolyard playground. A huddled mob of twenty or thirty people suddenly burst into a spontaneous synchronized and choreographed dance routine. Full-grown men bantered back and forth like girls while painting each other's nails. Songs were being sung, jokes were being told, and hair was being braided. Someone broke a fire hydrant and a huge group of people played in its gushing water. They were the type of antics children would choose to do at some kid's birthday party in third grade.

"What the hell is going on with the world!?" Will screamed out to the afternoon sky. Why was all this happening? It was like the boy was plagued with this unsolved riddle that inevitably drove him to the point where he stopped asking questions. Will had resorted to just trying to find a sliver of sanity no matter how remote in his new found topsy-turvy world.

The boy shouldered his tiny frame through the idiotic masses that made up the crowds. He decided to start his search at the first building on the block. He read its quaint sign dangling above the entrance. It read *Co-z Café*. It was a small corner coffee shop that catered pastries and bagels to wannabe yuppie aristocrats and snooty businessmen. Will confidently stepped inside seeking employment.

The place was a wreck. It appeared that a herd of stomping elephants had trampled through the coffee shop. Tables were turned over, chairs were broken and the walls were stained with coffee smears and icing splatter. Everything that seemed breakable had been destroyed. No professional business had ever been left in such disarray during working hours. The patrons and employees played around the café's interior like members of an amateur circus. A few people swung from lines that connected the low hanging light bulbs to the ceiling. Some people coveted expensive mugs while they ran around the shop keeping them as their own. One man had flipped over the bagel-slicer and held it like a gun. The man would then pick up day-old bagels off the floor and yell *bombs away* before loading the hardened bagel into the slicer and launching it across the shop like a torpedo. It was a complete madhouse, but Will didn't let that discourage him.

Will's feet crushed raw coffee beans that had been spilled on the floor as he approached the register. Will looked up at the giggling, sloppily dressed cashier. The cashier's uniform was heavily stained and wrinkled as well as his shirt not being tucked in. This sight was an accurate clue to the hospitality that the boy would receive at the Co-z Café.

"Excuse me sir," Will respectfully called out to the disheveled cashier.

"What do you want?" The cashier rudely asked.

"Bombs away!" The slicer-wielding employee yelled out before firing a stone-like bagel through the slicer that slammed against the roof of the café. A roar of laughter echoed out of the mouths of all who witnessed it.

Will strained to pull his attention away from the bagel-shooting maniac before he humbly requested from the cashier. "Well, I wanted to see if the Co-z Café needed any help, sir."

"Help?" The cashier mocked with confusion for a face. "Does this place look like it needs help to you?"

Will stood there silently to fully ingest the cashier's ridiculous question and its obvious answer. The boy shot quick glances at the broken furniture, food-stained walls, and the crushed coffee beans beneath his feet. Was the cashier serious? The place looked like it needed a fleet of new employees to straighten the mess up.

Not sure how to answer the attitude filled question, Will said. "Ummm well…"

"Bombs away!" The nut with the bagel-slicer screamed out again. He then loaded a bagel into the slicer and launched it across the café. The bagel was flung at a shaded light bulb that exploded on impact. Another round of laughter soon followed. Will's nerves jumped as the bulb blew up and his focus was instantly yanked away from the cashier.

"Look, my advice is get out of here, go home, and relax; got it?" The cashier advised, not giving Will a chance to finish the sentence he started before being interrupted.

"I just wanted a job, dude." Will defended.

"Hey Harvey!" The cashier disrespectfully called out to some guy in the back of the house.

A manager type figure walked out of the back. "What is it?"

"This little kid wants a job." The cashier told the manager while pointing at Will.

The manager took a gander at Will, and then a huge smile creased across his face. The manager then burst out in loud chuckling. The cashier joined in and soon enough, the two of them were blatantly laughing at a nine-year-old boy. Modesty seemed to be a foreign idea to the employees, because they didn't hold back their cackling out of a sense of manners. The angered boy headed toward the front door of the café with the vicious laughter following him out.

As Will left, he heard another *bombs away* along with the sound of something shattering. The boy exited the café.

A thoroughly heated Will rustled through the moronic crowd that littered the boulevard. He was slowly making his way to the store across the street from the Co-z Café. It was a small convenient store, or more precisely, it was a *Park'n Drive*.

The first thing Will noticed was the huge glass panels that acted as the front wall of the Park'n Drive had been smashed to bits, and people freely moved in and out of it as if it was the entrance. When Will entered the Park'n Drive, he saw that the place was also left in shambles. The merchandise, snacks, bottled drinks, and cigarettes, had been spread out on the floor. People rushed into the convenient store simply grabbing what they wanted and running out. Will couldn't believe what he was seeing.

Will assertively approached the man behind the register. The man seemed exceptionally carefree for a guy who was obviously being robbed blind. He was sitting in a chair with his arms behind his head and his feet resting on the counter in a laid-back fashion.

"Are they gonna pay for that stuff?" Will accusingly asked the cashier.

The cashier picked his head up and gave the consistent flood of entering and exiting marauders a long hard gaze. He then sunk back into his previous position before sighing. "Probably not,"

"So, they're stealing."

"You could call it that."

"Aren't you going to call the police?"

"Why?"

Will's eyes grew three-times larger, utterly baffled that he'd literally need to explain why to this man. "Well, because you're an employee of the Park'n Drive convenient store, and as such, you have an obligation to manage the store. That includes making sure you aren't being looted."

"Maybe," The cashier answered.

"No! Not maybe! Yes!" Will argued.

The cashier reasoned. "The way I see it, people are mainly good at heart..."

"What!?"

The cashier continued. "So everything they're taking is something they really need or they wouldn't resort to stealing it, and stealing is bad."

"This is ludicrous!"

"Hey, it's not my stuff. I'm not losing money." The cashier mumbled before closing his eyes and taking a nap.

A flabbergasted Will stood there on a bed of candy

bars and broken glass just staring at the sleeping cashier. Anger rose up in the boy's face and he shouted. "Has the entire world lost its mind!?" Will then left the Park'n Drive getting a strange notion that his attempts to find a job were purposely being stifled.

As Will continued to search for a job, a young man sat behind the counter of his self-owned and operated store. The man was the very definition of relaxed while he sat back on his chair tuning a guitar and chewing on a toothpick. He was a man at the mere age of nineteen, and yet he found himself the proprietor of an antique store under mysterious circumstances. His vibrantly long blonde arrow-straight hair was slicked back and sat about an inch above his shoulder blades. The man was as slender as they come, but not to the point where it seemed unhealthy. A tight pinstriped vanilla colored vest rested behind his cool maroon jacket. The man's aura gave off a sense that he was the slyest man alive. The only feature about him that didn't fit that persona was a lengthy scar that ran from the upper portion of his forehead's right side and penetrated deep into his hairline. The man's name was Wes Vega.

Will walked to each shop and store along the street with similar experiences. The places were always complete catastrophes and no one was taking their job seriously. Some places he went to didn't have a staff whatsoever. They just lay open and bear, inviting looters to come deplete their stock with no consequences. Every time an employee was present he was told to go home and relax. This zany world Will found himself in was taking its toll on him, but he continued to press on fully determined to claim a job. Will then found himself standing in front of one of the last shops on the street.

Will's spirits brightened as he examined the place.

The first thing he noticed was that the place was not broken into. The store's merchandise was neatly sorted in its displays safely guarded behind the clean glass viewing windows. The windows were filled with old artifacts and dusty pottery. Will's eyes rose up to the banner that hung over the store's entrance. The banner wasn't anything spectacular, but it wasn't the type of poor quality that the other places oozed. The banner just gave the idea that the store hadn't been there long enough to have an official sign installed yet. The banner read *Wes Vega's Antiquities and Nic-Nacs*. His gaze fell back on the viewing windows and the boy saw something he hadn't noticed before. It was a small black sign with big orange lettering that read *HELP WANTED*. Will was amazed he actually saw one of those signs. He had only read about one or saw one in a movie about ancient times. The sign must have been an antique in itself. This boosted Will's confidence and as he slapped a wad of nerve calming gum in his mouth, he was convinced his search was over.

Wes' store was cluttered with antiques and old furniture. An outrageous multitude of glass tables dotted the store and their surfaces were swamped with useless aged artifacts. Wooden animal sculptures took up most of the remaining ground space. Marionettes, dream catchers, and chandeliers dangled from the ceiling and had to be closely watched to make sure one wouldn't accidentally damage one. The store was packed with junk, and it felt like if you tripped and fell you'd break half the merchandise in the process.

Wes coldly sat behind the counter tuning the guitar, seemingly not worried about his lack of customers or the wacky outside world. All of a sudden, a boy walked into the store. The boy seemed to be about twelve, and had long frizzy black hair that poofed out and nearly ate his face.

Acne dotted the boy's face with red patches. He was chewing on gum obnoxiously like a cow and wore a smile from ear to ear. The boy walked up to the counter still chewing loudly.

Wes leaned the guitar on the counter beside him and slid his sunglasses down slightly to catch a good look at the boy. Once his eyes had their fill, he slid the sunglasses back up his face. He cleared his throat and bluntly asked. "What do you want?"

"Hi," The boy greeted cheerfully. "Your sign outside says you need help."

"What are you chewing?"

"Uh, gum sir,"

"Mmmm," Wes hummed with a hand to his chin as if he was deep in thought about the answer. "That's not a good sign."

"Am I being interviewed?"

"Sort of," Wes admitted as he grabbed at something behind the counter. He slammed the object on the counter with enough force to rattle his merchandise in the display case below. The object was a small adobe tribal warrior. The sculpture was outstandingly graphic. They even sculpted the rib cage on the warrior's skinny and tiny chest. He held a skull in one hand and some crude cutting implement in the other. Its inch long face was masked in a seriously pained expression that would make one cringe. He also had several bone piercings in his face including along his nose and in his ears. It was poorly painted, which only added to its unattractiveness. The sculpture was only six inches tall but packed enough ugly to overload the store. "What do you think of this?"

The boy's eyes melted along with his heart as he glanced at the tribal sculpture. The boy cooed. "Awwww, it's sooo cute…"

Wes then immediately put the sculpture back behind

the counter cutting off the boy mid-sentence. Wes then roared. "No! It's not *cute*. It's hideous. It's probably the ugliest thing in this store. You fail. Get out." He pointed at the entrance.

"What?" The boy said completely submerged in confusion.

"You're not welcome here. Get out."

"But..."

"Out!"

The boy timidly headed for the front door and opened it. Right as the frizzy headed boy left, another boy walked in. This boy had blonde hair and was only nine-years-old. The new boy was Will anxiously trying to inquire about a job position. Will approached Wes' counter in a much more sedated manner then the previous boy.

Wes had enough time to seat himself again before he turned his head toward Will and asked. "What do you want?"

Will had been told that phrase a bunch of times throughout that evening, but something was different about how Wes said it and his mannerisms. Unlike everybody else, there was a certain seriousness in his voice. He wasn't acting like an immature child or an angry preteen. His actions appeared to be his own. Whatever was afflicting everyone outside was not affecting him for some reason and Will secretly welcomed the thought. "You have a sign out front saying you need help." Will honestly answered. The boy was becoming nervous, so he chewed his gum more intensely.

Wes noticed the mad chewing and gave a disapproving glare at the boy. "What are you chewing?"

"Gum,"

"Uh," Wes Vega sighed. "That's not good." He began to reach for something behind the counter.

"What?" Will defended. "I like gum."

Wes ignored Will's response and proceeded to place the horrid tribal warrior back on the table.

"Oh my God!" Will instinctively blurted out at the sight of the sculpture.

Wes questioned. "What do you think about this sculpture?"

Will paused for a long moment unsure what to say. He took a few seconds before finally answering. "Uhhh... it's not my favorite piece here."

"Do you think it's *cute*?"

"Uh, no. I actually think it's VERY ugly. I just didn't want to hurt your feelings." Will remarked in disbelief that anyone would ever describe that thing as cute.

A smile cracked in the corner of Wes' mouth. He looked over at Will with a whole new interest before placing the ugly sculpture back behind the counter. He then leaned back in his chair and casually said. "So what's your name?"

"Will Treyu,"

A certain life was drained from Wes at that instance. The cool invisible shield that he had set around his body had quickly crumbled away. Something Will had said struck an incredibly personal chord in Wes' heart. He slowly removed his sunglasses as he faintly whispered. "Treyu," Wes' eyes carried signs of endearing feelings and a deep sadness. He tried to soak in the image of Will as much as possible. Every inch of the boy he quickly examined.

"Yeah!" Will agreed, not very sure what was going on. "William A. Treyu."

Wes then snapped back into reality and put his glasses back on his face. "Yeah, yeah, yeah." Mr. Vega hurried his words out. "Nice to meet you Will."

"So how does this work?" Will inquired while rubbing his hands together and the ever so subtle lip lick.

"Do I need to go online or talk to a manager or something?"

"I'm the owner. I'm Wes Vega."

"You're the owner?" Will interrogated sounding unconvinced.

"Yeah," Wes retorted. "The owner; why? Is that a problem?"

"Well, you're like...a teenager." Will began to explain.

"Yeah,"

"And you own an antique store?"

"Yeah,"

"And you don't think that's a little out of the ordinary?"

"Out of the ordinary?! Have you been outside?"

"You must really like antiques." Will persisted.

"Yeah, I love'em kid." Wes Vega monotonously droned.

"How did you get this venue?"

"Do you always ask so many questions?"

"When did you know you wanted to own an antique store?"

"Do you want the job?"

Will cheered. "Yes, I'd love it."

"Then stop asking all those questions."

"Okay,"

"Thank you," Said Wes as he melted back into his seat relieved that questions had ceased.

"So you're saying I have the job?" Will asked.

"Yeah, sure kid." Wes assured with his body as limp as a blanket on a chair.

"Woo-hoo!" Will celebrated jumping up and down like an idiot pumping a fist in the air between a mass of hanging junk. Will danced around for a moment in a state of pure glee. The excitement wasn't so much caused by the

attaining of the job, but because this was his first victory
since Lili showed up. He was determined to celebrate it no
matter how small the achievement was. As Will began to
calm himself, he faced Wes with a much chipper demeanor.
"Yeah! So, uh, when can we start?"

"How 'bout now?"

"Really? Don't I need to fill out some paperwork or
link accounts or something?"

"We can do that later. I'll just keep track of your
hours."

"Cool, so what do I do?"

"Shipments. Come with me." Wes instructed. Mr.
Vega's body creaked out of his chair. He went to a door in
the back of the store that blended into the dreary bluish-
gray wall. The door had a white sign that had *EMPLOYEES
ONLY* generically written on it. Wes took a key from his
vest, unlocked the door and opened it. Wes disappeared
into the back room and returned with a sizable cardboard
box. There was a long white strip sneaking out of the fold of
the box. Wes placed the box on the floor by Will's feet.
"This shipment needs to be stocked. Check it out." Wes
Vega yanked the long paper out of the box. Wes held out
the long paper so Will could clearly see it. The paper had
dozens of similar stickers on it. The stickers were item
prices complete with prices, barcodes, and serial numbers.
Wes peeled off a random sticker and pointed at the last four
digits of the serial number located just below the barcode.
"These are the numbers you use to identify an item." Wes
then opened the box on the ground and rummaged through
its contents with one arm while he held the sticker in the
other. He pulled out piece after piece checking the bottom
of the antiques for something before putting it back in the
box. After a while, he grabbed one and said. "Here it is." He
showed Will the underbelly of the antique to reveal another
sticker. The sticker was similar to the ones on the paper

except it had no price. It only had a barcode and a serial number. Wes held up the lone sticker to Will as well. "Notice how the last four digits match up?"

Will squinted at the stickers. "Yeah, I see it."

Wes continued. "After you match up the numbers, just put the item on a shelf or display… wherever you have room." Wes placed the item on top of a glass display case. "Then put the sticker underneath it." He then literally slapped the sticker on the sill of the glass display case just below the item.

"That's it?" Will said utterly boggled at its ease.

"That's it."

"Cool,"

"So get to it." Wes delegated before taking his place in his chair. He reclined as much as he could then silently watched the boy. Even though the process was pretty simple, Will wasn't doing that good a job. When Will would pick a sticker, it took him God knows how long to find the matching item in the box. He realized it was taking young Will approximately fifteen minutes to put up two items. Will was in the middle of looking for an item in the big box with a certain serial number when Wes decided to come over. The boy was about to throw another piece back in the box that failed to have the correct number, when Wes gently placed his hand on the one Will was using to grasp the antique. "I find it easier to grab the antique first then match its number with the sticker." Wes flipped the item Will had in his hand to view its serial number. Once he memorized the last four digits, he scoured the sheet with his eyes, finding its corresponding sticker in a much more orderly and less time consuming fashion.

Will chuckled at his boss' helpful hint, it was so obvious, and he wondered why he didn't think of it. It made more sense to go searching on the paper rather than constantly rummaging through a load of crap. It was one of the timesaving techniques only a person with retail experience would immediately figure out.

With his new organized stocking method, Will went to work with a new found confidence. Will steadily emptied the box neatly on the shelves while Wes sat behind the counter occasionally strumming a few notes. About two hours after his arrival, Will was nearing the bottom of the box. Will put up the last few items truly proud of the job he had done. It wasn't easy arranging all the stuff that was on the shelves to make room for the new stuff in the box, but the boy managed to do it.

An accomplished Will marched over to his boss thirsty for a new assignment. Will approached a relaxed Wes and announced. "I'm done."

Wes' head perked up in attention as he glanced over to the empty box and assumed from the glimpse he caught that it truly was empty. "Oh, okay, good." Wes remarked climbing out of the seat. He headed to the rear room once again with Will following close behind. Wes swung the EMPLOYEES ONLY door wide open revealing a room consisting of nothing but pitch-black darkness. Wes nonchalantly flipped a switch near the door in the black room.

An ordinary light bulb clarified the room and what Will saw made the boy gasp. Although it was a rather small room, (10ft long, 8ft wide, and 12ft high) the floor and the shelves fixed to the walls were choked with boxes that all had similar sheets jutting from them. Will's jaw dropped.

"Now you can start on these." Wes handed down like a death sentence.

Will sighed and got right to work. He'd pull out a box, sort it on the displays, and then go for another. He packed the merchandise together shoulder to shoulder trying to move the monstrous amount of boxed product onto the already full shelves. There was too much stored product to fit in the limited space. Will hadn't even scratched the surface of the box pile and he had absolutely run out of room. Will's frustration had been growing as the shelf space dwindled. Finally, he marched over to Wes holding a tiny porcelain white elephant with gold trim, and a half used paper sheet of stickers. Will barked. "Hey, there's absolutely no place I can put this thing."

"Oh," Wes murmured as he caught attention of the situation. He backed off the counter that he was leaning against and surveyed the shelves and displays. What Will had said was indeed true. There was not enough space to fit anymore of the boxed junk. Wes then explained. "Some of this stuff is old, and hasn't been selling. So you can get rid of some stuff to make room for new stuff, got it?"

"Yes," Will agreed. He then grasped an adobe clay monkey with its hands on its head off the display case next to him. "Can I get rid of this?" He inquired about the monkey.

"Yeah, that's cool." Wes easily gave in.

Will shifted his head around wondering what he should do with the clay monkey. Will then cleverly chucked the monkey into one of the boxes he had already emptied. The boy then tore the sticker off, slapped on another and lastly, put up the white porcelain elephant.

Will continued to scour the inventory for the shabbiest pieces to discard. Every time Will asked if he could throw away a piece, he was given the go ahead. No matter what it was that Will suggested, he was told to trash it. As the night rolled on, it became so common that Will stopped even asking. He began just throwing away stuff to save from the hassle of asking his boss every time he needed to. While Will carried on with his stocking duties, Wes mainly lounged around the shop as the day transformed into night with relative peace.

As night began to set in, Wes received a phone call

that made Will suspicious. He noticed that before his boss answered it, he made sure to scurry into the back room. Seeing this piqued Will's interest and it wasn't long before the boy had an ear to the door. The boy was unable to decipher any specific dialogue for the heavy door muffled Wes' voice all too well. The only thing about the conversation Will could determine was that tensions were getting high. The steadily rising tone in Wes was a clear sign of the mounting animosity. Will suddenly heard footsteps nearing the employee door and Wes' talking had ceased. Will rushed back to his box filled with antiques to hide his eavesdropping. Wes exited the back room much more calm and cool than was revealed to Will while he listened in.

"It's getting late." Wes admitted. "How about we call it a day."

"Are you sure?" Will questioned. "I haven't even gotten close to emptying all the boxes."

"Well aren't you just the regular little worker bee." Wes complimented in his own suave way. "That pile wasn't intended to be finished all in one day."

"Oh good," Will sighed as an overbearing obligation was instantly lifted off his shoulders.

"You can just leave that stuff where it is. I'll take care of it when I open shop tomorrow." Wes instructed.

"Cool," Will grunted as he slowly stood up with a body aching from an honest day's work.

As Will headed for the door, Wes said. "I'll see you tomorrow bright and early at 11:00."

"Okay,"

"Be careful on your way home."

"Will do. See ya,"

"Peace,"

The boy left and Wes locked the door. Wes leaned against the door with something troubling his mind. His encounter with Will had hit him personally for some reason. The whole time Will was there he made sure to disguise that feeling well. Wes breathed an overwhelmed sigh. Wes' phone began to ring and he was quick to answer it.

Wes answered the phone with a simple. "Hello?"

A powerful male voice on the other end of the line assertively asked. "Is he the one?"

"Most likely, he doesn't appear to be influenced."

"That's her target, no doubt about it."

"Why'd you put me on this?" Wes forcefully investigated to the voice on the other line.

"What do you mean agent Vega?"

"What do you mean what do I mean?" Wes argued. "If this was anyone else, you know they'd be taken off the assignment for being personally involved. Why haven't I been?"

The voice on the other end of the line sighed. "You're wrong Wes. It is like we told you when you agreed to take this; your personal experience in this issue is why you've been picked. It being him is another reason why you fit perfectly in this situation."

"I won't do it." Wes concluded.

"Perhaps," The voice reasoned, giving into Wes' defiance a little too easily. "Although, if you went through with this, the wellbeing of your many remaining years will be assured. It's time we find out where your allegiance lies, in your past or with us." The phone went dead. The voice had hung up signifying that it was the final word on the matter.

Wes placed the phone back in his pocket while lost in a storm of complication.

The night slowly blackened as Will leisurely walked home. The streets seemed vacant and the boy welcomed the peaceful stroll. He was unsure if he could handle any more weirdness in the world. At least he met Wes, a guy who appeared unaffected by Gohanesse's growing oddities. The encounter had reassured Will that he retained his sanity. It was a big relief that was taken off the boy's shoulders. He actually looked forward to his next day at work just so he could be around someone who still had all his marbles. It was an odd thing for a nine-year-old boy to look forward to.

Eventually, Will found himself in front of the studio/warehouse and he casually walked in. He saw Ky at the kitchen cleaning dishes and doing other such domestic chores. The boy saw Ky cleaning twice in the same day. He started wondering if Hell was freezing over. The boy had almost no choice but to address the issue. He stomped over to Ky and inquired. "What are you doing?"

Will was interrupted by an enthusiastic *Hi* that he followed to the other side of the apartment. He saw Lili sitting knee first on the couch turned completely around to face Will. Her eyes contained love that hung over a wide smile that expressed her genuine excitement and glee that came over her when he entered.

Will gave a quick wave before he said. "Hi," He was trying to show a civil politeness towards her, but the greeting still came out rather rude. His attention shifted back to Ky. "Why are you doing the dishes?"

"Because they were dirty, silly."

"Silly?" Will mocked. "That was weak. Are you sure you don't have any plans or something?"

"Why?" Ky asked putting a few dishes on a rack to dry. "Should I?"

"How should I know? It's just the few times I've ever seen you doing dishes and it's never been this late. You're usually out and about at this time."

"Really?" Ky said with a baffled tone and a jerk of his head. "But I just went out yesterday."

"And?" Will laughed off.

"Hmmmm," Ky hummed as if he had just come to some realization. "Maybe I'm more of a party animal than I think I am."

"Can I ask you a question?" Will said in a volume just above a whisper.

"Shoot," Ky bellowed while going to war with stubborn pan grime.

"How do you get a girl to leave you alone?"

"Pssh, I don't know. Girl's don't leave me alone, they flock to me." Ky joked.

"No, but I mean…" Will began to explain. "Sometimes I see you with a girl in the morning and they ask for your number, and you give it to them, then I never see them again. How do you do that?"

"Ohhhh! I give them Red's number, and boy does he get pissssed!"

The man by the name of Red that Ky referred to was one of his best friends. They met when Ky answered an ad online for a rental space accommodating a galactic cruiser (The Guider). After Ky had been parking his craft (a commonly used abbreviation for spacecraft) there for a few months, he ran into him again at a bar and they found out they had a lot of things in common, mainly partying. Since then, they had been joined at the hip and have acted as each other's *wingman* on many occasions.

His full name was Red Marrado, and he was a muscular, bald dark skinned man about four inches taller than Ky. Red was the son of a well-rounded craft mechanic and was practically born with a wrench in his hand. When he was just a teenager, it was obvious that his mechanical skills were to surpass his father's and he was soon offered a lucrative government job, which he didn't hesitate to take. When he accrued a small fortune, he quit and purchased a sizable portion of open grassy land. He cleaned up his acres upon acres of land creating a spacious valley. He filled the valley with craft-hangars that people could pay to rent for storage or repairs. Ky's galactic cruiser, the Guider, was parked there. In addition to Red's already low parking prices, he eventually gave Ky another discount for being so tight with him. The duo were partners in crime, and as thick as thieves.

"That doesn't really help me." Will mumbled leaning his arm against his chin that was planted on the kitchen counter. He slouched his back and released a defeated sigh.

At that moment, Ky's phone rang. He flipped the phone out of his pocket and gazed down at the name on its wide lit up screen. He voiced a command to his phone. "Show text message." The screen lit up again with a virtual fragmented sentence written on it reading *Yo! We out!* He closed the phone and sheathed it back in his pocket. "All right, I'm out of here." Ky dropped the dish in the sink that was only half washed and trotted thoughtlessly to the front door.

""Hey! Where you going?" Will questioned picking his head up from the counter utterly dumbfounded by Ky's impromptu plans.

"I'm going out with Red." Ky informed closing the gap to the door.

"Now? I thought you were gonna finish the dishes."

"This is what I normally do, right?" Ky said with a tilted head and a hand on the door. Some strange honesty was in his eyes that seemed to mildly imply that it was a real question. Ky left, leaving the two small children home alone.

Will's head twisted to face the couch and gave the person sitting on it backwards a terrified look. It was Lili who released a devilishly wide grin when Will set his pupils on her. She was ecstatically happy when Will acknowledged her, but he didn't share the sentiment. He rolled his eyes back and whispered to himself. "Oh God,"

"How was your day?" An overly energetic Lili politely asked.

"Fine," Will droned as he trudged loudly up to his room.

Lili jumped off the couch and followed closely behind the young boy. "Really? What happened?"

"Nothing," A disinterested Will said approaching the set of collapsible steps.

"Really? Did you find a job?"

"Yes," Will revealed in the same uncaring monotone voice half way up the stairs.

"Really?" She uttered a bit different bearing a sense of true confusion. "That's crazy! With who?"

Will stormed into his room and flopped on his bed face first before blurting out with his mouth pressed to the mattress. "I don't know, some guy."

"Really? What's his name?" Lili continued her questioning while hovering over Will's bed.

"I don't know." An annoyed Will said. "Wes... Wega, Vega yeah! Wes Vega."

"Wes," Lili gasped.

"Yeah, you know him?" Will interrogated while pulling his head from the bed in a slight interest.
Lili slowly shook her head horizontally from side to side with a playful expression

"Oh," Will dropped his head back to the bed.

"Do you like it?"

"Why do you care? Did you forget I hate you?" Will snipped perking up his head again. "But Will," A slightly saddened Lili sighed. Her sentence paused as she sat on the edge of Will's bed. "Haven't I been nothing but sweet to you?"
"Well, yeah," Will confessed. "But that's not the point."

"What is the point?"

"Well, obviously…uh…" Will was stuck. He began to wonder why he was showing such animosity toward her. There was no doubt she arrived there under extremely suspicious circumstances, but she hadn't done anything to harm him. It was quite the contrary. She had only shown him unbridled affection. This little man had no idea how to answer her simple question. His head defiantly slammed against his pillow before he belched. "Shut up."

Lili leaned back on the edge of the bed supported by her arms and started speaking to Will in a warm and comforting tone. Will instinctively picked up his head once again in a rare moment where he was willing to listen to her side. She sweetly said. "Will, look, I just want…"

Before she could finish her sentence, both of their faces turned to stare at the wall opposite the bunk beds. It was there, they saw it; a hand-sized figure stuck smack dab in the center of the wall. The figure also resembled a hand with an additional three digits, a thin layer of fur and a round butt. Their eyes widened in terror as panic took over their tiny bodies. Will wasn't even more scared when he was being held at gun-point. Lili and Will screamed out for their lives simultaneously. "SPIDER!"

Ten minutes later, both the children were perched side by side on top of Lili's upper bunk. They were both bent over on their knees keeping all four eyes glued to the motionless spider on the wall. Even though the insect filled them with terror, they watched it to make sure an even more horrifying reality didn't occur; that the spider would crawl away and they'd have no clue to its whereabouts. They intently and quietly kept an eye on the small fuzzy beast.

It was right about then that Jina lazily came trudging through Will's bedroom door. She sported bags beneath her eyes and an annoyed grimace as if she was abruptly awakened during a deep sleep. It was only a few minutes earlier that Will used his wristwatch communicator to call Jina's phone. He pleaded with her in the dead of the night to come deal with their arachnid problem. She dragged her six-foot long metal staff at her side, which was constantly scraping against the floor, as yet another piece of evidence to just how tired she was. Her sleepy beautiful emerald green peepers shifted to the spider on the wall. As soon as her eyes caught sight of the eight-legged fiend, her staff twirled around in her left hand and rushed toward the insect at supersonic speeds. The blow came so fast that the spider with all its eight eyes couldn't see it coming until it was too late. The end of her silvery staff blurred across the room and crushed the arachnid under merciless pressure. The attack had punched a circular dent into the hard aluminum wall and was covered with what remained of the spider's frame and entrails. The spider's guts had instantly oozed out the sides of its body and its numerous furry legs slowly coiled up as all life was drained from the insect.

Jina then pointed the end of the long staff at the top bunk to address Will and Lili. The arachnid's bodily fluids were still visible on the end of her staff. "I'm taking off at least ten dalaz from my debt to Ky for waking me up at such a late hour." Jina commanded to the children.

"Okay," Will conceded, willing to do anything at that moment for the person who killed the spider for him.

Jina lowered her staff and pulled a handkerchief out of the end of her large kimono sleeve. As she wiped the spider guts off her staff, she added. "And I'm grabbing that turkey leg I saw in the frigerator."

"Okay," The boy repeated.

As Jina turned around, she said. "Have a goodnight kiddies."

Lili shot back. "Goodnight,"

While Will showed his gratitude by saying. "Thank you Jina."

Jina then sluggishly left the studio/warehouse with a staff in one hand and a turkey leg in the other.

Will blew a sigh of relief as he and Lili timidly crawled down from the top bunk. "Thank God."

Lili began to tend to the mess of the crushed spider on the wall as Will nestled into his bed with shaky nerves. The little girl shifted her eyes around noticing Will settling in the bed. "You're not gonna sleep on the futon tonight?"

"Well, I was thinking of what you said last night." Will explained without so much as removing his head from the pillow. "That might be your bed, but this is rightfully my room, and I'm not just gonna stand by and let you have it."

"Yay!" Lili celebrated as she tossed a handkerchief filled with the spider's remains into a small plastic trash receptacle in the corner of the room. A bright-excited energy bloomed around Lili when she got word that Will would be bunking with her. She bounced over to the bunk bed set and began climbing up it with a long smile traveling clear across her face. She enthusiastically ascended the bed. "We can talk and..."

"We're not gonna talk!" Will roared from his bed interrupting Lili nearly immediately.

Lili's cute little girl face turned as serious as it could possibly get; not much. "Why do you gotta be like that Will!?" Her body waiting in mid-hike up the bed set.

"Because I want someone to see the truth about you." He honestly answered.

"But you say you don't wanna talk to me and you're talking to me right now."

"..."

"... Will?"

"..."

"Will?"

"..." Will thought he started understanding her

game.

"Well fine, whatever, goodnight Will."

"..."

Lili then tucked herself in and faintly whispered. "Lights off,"

The lights in the room instantly turned off and both the children eventually drifted to sleep.

Will was once again in the same scenario in his dream state; a big bright sun over overshadowing those three strange, yet somehow familiar figures. This time around, the dream seemed more vivid and the boy was able to remember a little more.

The mysterious female figure had finished saying to the shadowed child. "You're supposed to protect him, he's your brother."

"I-I'm sorry," The boy figure repeated carrying a much heavier load of shame.

"And what about you, Will?" The grown man turned to Will. It was the first time in this weird dream in which Will was directly addressed.

Will stood in attention to the man, and yet was unable to speak. What had transpired later in the dream would be forgotten to the boy once he woke up.

Will woke that morning to the aroma of a well-cooked breakfast. He woke up with his eyes still closed, and a thought crossed his mind. This was all too familiar; the dream, then the smell of breakfast. Will was certain when he opened his eyes Lili was going to be right in his face with a plate of food. The boy braced himself for her face and he opened his eyes. Lili wasn't there. In fact, she wasn't in the room at all. Will casually yawned and sat up in the bed. His head twisted to the right and Will saw on top of Lili's vanity a plate of eggs, toast and bacon set out for him. It had a small note in front of it. Will got up and grabbed

the small note. It read *I know you don't want me 'in your face'
anymore so this card will have to do. Have a good breakfast.*
Signed *Lili* accompanied by a happy face. Will consumed
the breakfast without thinking twice and let its
nourishment fill his little belly.

Will then dressed himself and got ready for work.
He wanted to take a shower, but he promised to meet Wes
early and if he didn't start walking, he'd be late. He exited
the flimsy aluminum door to his bedroom and sprinted
down the set of collapsible steps. Down in the living area,
Ky was watching television accompanied oddly by Jina. Lili
was fixing something else in the kitchen. She was again
mixing some batter in a big bowl with a content smile on
her face. As soon as Will reached the bottom of the stairs, all
six eyes darted at him.

"Good morning Will." Lili sincerely greeted.

"How are you Will?" Jina lovingly asked.

"Hey Will." Said Ky.

"I'm going to work." Will blankly commented in
reference to everybody. The boy headed for the door with
the other inhabitant's heads following him out. Will wasted
no time and started walking toward Wes' Antiques. He
passed by the usual peculiar people doing the usual
peculiar deeds that were beginning to become all too
routine to the boy. He started closing in on the corner of the
street where Will had found his job. It was the same street
lined with numerous businesses to which Will tried
applying to the previous day. In the corner of the street to
his immediate right was the *Co-z Café* that Will had been
laughed out of as recent as yesterday. Will found himself
sleepy and he was making good time, so he decided to go in
and order a latté.

As he entered the café he secretly wondered if there
would be any problem serving a child his age caffiene. At

Ky's place, Will drank coffee all the time, but it wasn't like his lazy guardian was wrestling with the moral issue, so he brewed it as he pleased. Now at an actual establishment, he was curious if its employees would huff and puff at him for being so young. Soon enough, Will brushed off these worries. He remembered how loopy everyone had been acting and plus, why would the business turn away a paying customer? By the time he passed through the door his mental dilemma had vanished from his mind.

Inside the *Co-z Café*, the place was still in disarray. This time, the boy was use to the mess and didn't hesitate to step directly on top of the spilt coffee beans when he approached the register.

"Hey!" Will shouted at the same rude sloppy employee that laughed him out the day before. The employee stopped mid-giggle and looked down at Will in attention. "Get me a latté my man." Will ordered brimming with confidence.

"Ha, what's a latté?" The employee joked.

Fed up with the horrible service, Will growled. "Hey! Guy! I know things are crazy around here right now, but I asked for a latté. I have the money on my account so I demand to get one."

An eyebrow lifted to the employee's forehead in a slight interest in Will's rant. "How about this deal? You make it yourself and you can keep your money."

A baffled Will replied. "Are you serious?"

The employee lifted his arm in a comforting gesture toward the café's expensive equipment. "Yeah, of course. All the stuff for it is right there; help yourself."

"Okay," An unsure Will chimed back.

He motioned to the back of the register to serve his own coffee, but once he got behind the counter, Will suddenly got a new idea. Some of the registers were entirely unmanned. All the registers had to be wired to the business' main computer giving each one certain data including customers' account information. Greedy mischievous thoughts flashed in the boy's head and he sneaked over to an abandoned register. Will effortlessly guide himself through some of the company windows with a few keystrokes applied to its touch screen. With that alone, Will basically understood how its computer system was structured. Hacking into the *Co-z Café's* main computer and recovering the confidential and hidden files regarding customer accounts would've been a moderately difficult task for any ordinary hacker, but Will was no ordinary hacker. He was a superb hacker and within moments, Will was looking down at a window listing every customer's account numbers. With those account numbers, a hacker like Will, could hack in and pay for anything he wanted online and it would simply charge those accounts; Will found himself a wealthy person when he printed out the long list of account numbers onto a receipt paper.

Will's pupils grew three times their normal size as he looked over the receipt paper he held delicately in his hands. "Oh my God! I can't believe it! I don't even need a job anymore! I'm set for life!"

Will watched to see if anyone was looking at him as he secretively shoved the long receipt paper in his back pocket. He quietly shimmied out the door like a sneaky assassin without even fixing his latté. The boy didn't notice a few of the café's patrons follow him out.

Will continued leisurely strolling down the street with a new brightness and an old purpose. He presumably was heading to Wes' Antiquities and Nic-Nacs to formally quit, but it didn't take Will long to spot the couple of people tailing him. They appeared to be everyday civilians except they were eying down the boy with devilish gazes and obviously following him. Will's head turned back around and he tried to ignore those people, but his pace still quickened slightly. Just a moment later, curiosity got the best of him and he shifted his head back around a bit to see if they were still in pursuit. Not only were the people even more blatantly following Will, but also their small crowd seemed to have grown. Will's speedy walk transformed into a light jog as a suspicious worry formed inside the boy. His head twisted around again and the crowd had become significantly larger. Panic took hold of the little boy, as he started full-blown running away from the crowd. As Will dashed down the street, pedestrians who weren't involved in the situation in any way would lift their heads to the boy and also give chase. The small crowd inevitably turned into a giant mob hunting down Will. Will sprinted down the street fearful of his own life.

As Will ran full force down the boulevard, he didn't have time to stop or breath. At the rate he was going, the large gang of people would eventually catch up, so he had no choice but to keep it up as long as possible. He even galloped right past Wes' Antique shop without so much as even looking at the building as he zoomed by.

Wes witnessed the situation from his shop window.

Will continued booking-it down the avenue, but exhaustion was rearing its ugly head. His face was red, his breathing was heavy and his feet clanked against the ground determined to find some way to escape the enormous crowd. It wasn't long till the road came to an end and Will found himself running directly toward a small grocery store. The store, like most of the places around there, had been left destroyed with all its huge windows busted out. The boy ran for the store in desperation; maybe he could somehow lose the crowd inside there. As Will's tired body knelt down to leap right through one of the grocery store's broken windows, something bad happened. It was too late, the crowd had caught up to the boy and one of the people grabbed him. He struggled to break free from their grips but it was no use. The multitude of people wasted no time in surrounding the boy and restraining him from all sides. They ripped at and grappled the boy from every angle and fear completely took over Will. His finger jerked to his wristwatch communicator out of reflex as he frantically pushed a tiny button on it. A circumference of the massive group around Will spanning ten people outward instantly dropped to the floor. Countless rows after that were stunned as Will fired fifty-thousand volts of electricity through the gang like lightning through water particles when striking an ocean. When the rest of the large crowd came to, they sifted through the limp electrified bodies in search of Will. They couldn't find him.

Will had given them the slip. He had wiggled through the electrified bodies as they fell to the ground and rummaged his way into the travesty of a grocery store. Will was already in the back of the warehouse area of the store by the time the mass of people had realized what happened. He was trying to locate a back exit to the building. Will had found his exit in the form of a steel shutter that led to the loading dock. Will had to summon all his strength just to creak it open. Will somehow managed to pry the shutter open enough for him to lay flat and slide through. The boy fell down a four-foot drop to a cement ground before he started pumping his legs away from the building.

A false sense of relief rushed over the boy as he fled from the abandoned broken grocery store. At that instance, no one was around him and he was truly convinced that he had escaped the overwhelming mob. He kept this positive attitude even as a few people came whirling out of the back alleys between the grocery store and the neighboring buildings, and they were still advancing toward him like hawks to their prey. Sadly, soon enough, the group regained their incredible numbers and continued to chase the boy down through the complicated network of back roads in Gohanesse's industrial district.

Will's body was becoming tired once again as he came to the realization that his attempts of escape were futile. It wasn't going to be long until the gang reached the exhausted small boy and then it'd be over. The energy cell that powered his electrified under-vest wasn't even close to being recharged, so that was out of the question. The boy had run out of ways to buy time, so he turned around in the middle of a shipping truck parking lot to face his fate. Fifty yards away from Will, the mob charged him like a football league. Their feet roared towards the petrified Will as they clapped against the pavement. Will just stood there in awe of the sheer number of people who had shown up to hunt him down.

Suddenly, there seemed to be an explosion of people among the large crowd. Bodies flew every which way in the center of the horde. It appeared some sizable vehicle had rammed the group of people from the other side with no regard to human life in any such way. The vehicle unforgivably plowed through the masses, forcing aside or running over anyone who got in its path. The vehicle was racing directly at Will. As the vehicle slammed out of the crowd, Will could clearly make it out even with a few people dangling off of it.

The vehicle was designed much like a motorcycle even though it was significantly bigger. There were three wheels on the vehicle; a small one in the center of the vehicle's nose that freely swiveled, and two much larger wheels mounted in its rear. There was a raised passenger seat behind the driver and both were encased in a capsule-like pod. Most of the face of the pod was a clear hard windshield and popped open to gain access to its interior. The three-wheeler was sleek and seemed extremely modern even in those times. Will watched helplessly as the vehicle closed in on him.

The vehicle passed by Will and skidded around to face him, going from eighty to zero miles per hour in mere seconds. The vehicle halted inches from the boy as a trail of kicked up dust mirrored the large motorcycle's path. The clear windshield popped up hoisted by a piston system revealing its driver. Wes reached out a hand to the boy from inside the open vehicle.

"Come with me if you want to live." Wes stated coldly from behind the wheel of the vehicle.

Will took a glance back at the ever-growing crowd people that was still gaining ground on him. After an eyeful of that mess, Will gladly stretched up and took hold of Wes' hand. Wes helped yank the boy up to the vehicle's passenger seat and the pod's lid closed around the guys. Wes didn't think twice about screeching the maneuverable stylish vehicle in the opposite direction of the mob and speeding off. The inside of the vehicle shook and rocked furiously due to Wes' reckless driving; it was so bad, that poor Will could barely keep his balance.

"Oh my God!" Will reacted lost in a field of panic.

"Things have gotten too serious already!" Wes loudly remarked out of nowhere.

"What!?" Will assertively inquired. "What are you talking about?"

Wes sighed then spoke in a slightly calmer manner as he ran over people as needed. "I regret to inform you, Will, that I'm going to be forced to take action for this."

"Action for what!?" Will yelled trying to maintain stability.

"Look around, Will. This has gone on long enough."

"Dude," Will commented finally becoming steady in his seat. "You're straight out of an online comic book."

The large vehicle smeared the mainly vacant streets it traveled with rubber as it made its way to the outskirts of

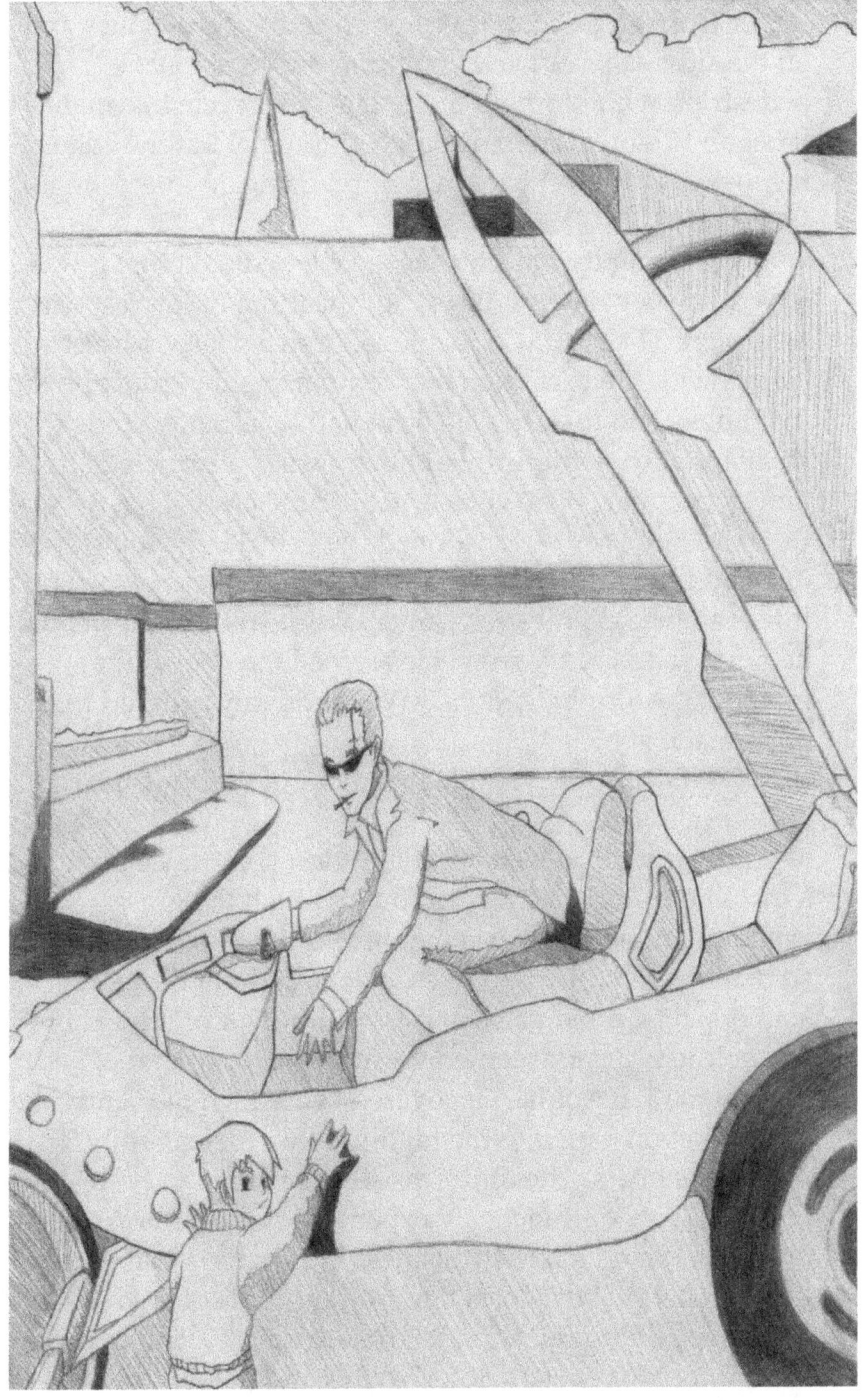

Gohanesse City. It veered through the avenues and on the sidewalks as needed, hitting the occasional pedestrian who ran right at the big motorcycle like maniacs. It began to slow down in a large grassy field at the edge of the lost city. The vehicle was approaching an interesting spacecraft.

Judging by the craft's size Will deduced that it was most likely a galactic cruiser, but the thing of interest was its design. The craft was fashioned into a nearly perfect sphere with the exception of a compartment planted on top that housed all its thrusters. Will had seen many crafts in his life, but something about how it was constructed struck him as peculiar. Wes' vehicle neared the craft.

When Wes Vega stopped the vehicle, the top shifted open and the mysterious man exited in an orderly fashion. It was as if he didn't even care about the numerous people he must've killed that day. He seemed too cool at the moment. "All right, get out." Wes suddenly ordered from outside the vehicle.

Will complied and crawled out of the stylish large motorcycle.

The craft opened a hidden sliding entrance door and a metallic walkway stretched out to touch the grass. Walking out of the craft came three or four soldiers. These soldiers weren't dressed like Galactic Federal Bureau soldiers; they must've been from a different organization. The soldiers' armor seemed vastly superior to that of any ordinary G.F.B. soldier. It covered every inch of their bodies and was even joined to the highly technological, fully masked helmets. The uniforms also appeared very flexible, just like a few outrageously expensive space suits Will had once saw. Being a boy of business Will judged that each uniform had to be at least tens of thousands of dalaz each. What type of organization felt it necessary to fork over that kind of loot for every soldier? Will knew something fishy was going on with all this.

"Hey! What's going on?" Will questioned Wes as he simply watched the soldiers advance toward them.

Wes Vega turned around to face the boy and said. "What I'm doing, I can't tell you. All you need to know is that this little ride you've been taken on is going to end soon."

One of the soldiers approached Wes' side while the two others headed over to the large motorcycle. The soldier that neared Mr. Vega whispered. "What's our course of action?"

"We'll be moving out soon. The situation has just gone from lighthearted to hostile." Wes commanded to the soldier.

"Right," The soldier agreed before heading back to the odd craft.

"I don't understand." The confused boy let escape from his lips.

"You don't need to show up for work anymore Will. It won't be there. Not now that I know she's controlling you."

"No," Will disagreed in a near whimper somehow knowing whom Wes was talking about. "She's not controlling me. I don't think she can. I'm pretty sure she's controlling everyone else."

"No," Wes vaguely foretold as the soldiers climbed into the motorcycle-like vehicle. "That's only what it looks like. She's probably controlling you easier than everybody else."

Will stood there unsure what to make of Wes' words as the soldiers drove the vehicle into the craft.

Wes scratched the back of his head. "I'm truly sorry to indirectly inform you that you're out of a job, but a day's work is a day's work, right?" Wes reached into his vest pocket and pulled out a small card. He handed out the card to Will between two fingers. "Here, take it."

Will took the card examining it.

Wes informed. "It's a temporary account card. It has two hundred dalaz on it that you can deposit in your account. Not bad for a single day's work." Wes turned around and started walking to the craft. Mr. Wes Vega departed with a final from-behind hand wave. "See ya around."

As Wes took his final steps into the round craft, Will analyzed the card. The card was as blank white as could be. It bore the usual black magnetic strip on the back, but had none of the traditional text beneath it. The front of the card was all white with only an inky black *IO* printed directly in the center. Will would eventually use that card even though what he had stowed away in his back pocket was a guaranteed fortune. The boy gave the card a good two or three looks over as the unusual craft lifted into the air.

Will gazed onto the craft as it bolted into the sky kicking up a vicious wind. The boy was blown away by everything that had transpired that day and silently looked out to the sky trying to absorb it all. He was left speechless until minutes later he said. "I guess my career in antiquities is over."

Later that day, Will got in contact with Ky to come pick him up, whom was oddly cool about doing so. He didn't even ask why Will was out there. Will tried to relax the rest of the day and locked himself in seclusion while he rolled the encounters with Wes around in his head.

III

The IO

A few days passed with little headway forming in the Lili and Will situation. Lili stayed just as cheerful while Will's anger toward her only grew greater. One morning Will woke up with expectations of a Lili-cooked breakfast, but there wasn't one. Actually, absolutely nothing was going on that morning. It was much quieter in the studio/warehouse then it had ever been before. Will sprang up with the feeling that something was wrong. He leapt out of his bed and headed out of the room.

With his first gaze downstairs, he immediately came to the realization that Ky and Lili were gone. This perplexed the boy, but Will almost welcomed the moment of calm. He lounged on the couch with a content smile on his face. He stayed there for a while, but soon enough, the boy became bored with the uneventful day. He tried television, but all the networks were out. Then he tried the Internet, but all the servers were down. He had already beaten all the video games he owned, so there wasn't much for him to do. The only friend he had there was Computer. Will tossed and turned on the couch shooting the occasional question at Computer.

"Computer?" Will hummed out of boredom while lobbing a small ball to the sky and catching it.

"Yes Will?" A soft comforting female voice echoed out of the laptop's tiny speakers. There are hundreds of different voices one can choose for the program Computer to speak in. Will chose the soft female voice titled *kind older sister* often. Although, when the boy heard the voice, he didn't think of it as an older sister, he thought of her as a more caring and omniscient figure. It was more motherly to him.

"Do YOU think there's something wrong with the world lately?"

"Following the social behaviors of humans is as task I cannot perform, but economical exchange patterns and the average purchase rate of the world has been extremely irregular recently."

"So, I'm not crazy." The boy commented at a near whisper.

"Judging your sanity is also a task I cannot perform."

Will sat there for a few moments deep in thought. He was trying to mentally chart his next course of action. He was taking his time and treading carefully with his upcoming move, because everything he tried so far since Lili arrived had blown up in his face. The boy knew he had to do something to unmask all this madness, but how was he supposed to do that if everyone was in on the joke? Still, he was convinced that the problem was the world and not him; Computer corroborated that fact. The only person who seemed to know what was going on had days earlier shot off into the sky in a peculiar galactic cruiser. Will figured out right then that he had to speak with Wes Vega again. The mysterious young man had told Will that if he returned to the shop that it wouldn't be there, but he just had to see for himself. All his other options had been depleted. Will jolted his body off the couch.

He unlocked the front door and walked outside. "I'll be back later."

After he locked the door behind him, he walked down the sidewalk toward Wes' Antiques like he had previously done twice. The boy mainly kept himself in seclusion since he had almost been ripped apart by a mob of civilians, but something was telling him that that wasn't going to happen this time around. Plus, the boy had taken some extra precautionary measures in case it did. The boy walked down the street that sunny afternoon carrying excess artillery and confidence, but he still kept an eye on his back.

Will was in front of what use to be Wes' shop without incident, but sadly, the words Wes spoke were true. The door was locked and the glass viewing windows had shelves that lay naked and bare of any former merchandise. Even the shabby banner that flimsily hung over the entrance had been removed. Will sighed in disappointment as he peered into the empty building. Will scanned the area surrounding him to see if anyone was watching, then he realized everyone was still acting like goof-balls. Will casually picked up a chunk of dislodged sidewalk. He lobbed the slab of cement at the viewing window and the glass gave no resistance under the cement's pressure as it shattered to bits. Will crawled inside and over the shelves, making sure not to cut himself on the shards of glass. Once inside the boy saw that the shop was completely barren. The hefty displays and the clutter of junk on them had all been taken away. All the crap that was hanging from the ceiling was missing too. The only things left were the dirty counter and an aluminum fold out chair. The interior appeared to be four times larger with all the stuff gone, but also a lot lonelier. They even took the *Employees Only* sign off the back door. After noticing that, Will headed to the back room, which was for some reason ajar. He easily pushed the door fully open and flicked on the light switch. Just like the rest of the store, its empty white shelves stared at him absolutely exposed. The boy found no evidence that the antique store had ever been there in the first place.

Miles away, Ky was inside the Guider (his galactic cruiser) ready to take it somewhere. The Guider's virtual monitors and indicators turned on all around him in that stuffy cockpit, but something was obviously not right with Ky. With wide unblinking eyes he expressionlessly stared out into nothing. He was looking straight ahead, but something was weird about it. He seemed to be gazing past the holographic charts and windows, past the shade adjusting tempered glass windshield that coated the room, even past the flush forest backdrop that met the windshield. He seemed to be looking out into nothing. The Guider's engine began to kick on.

The back door to the cockpit opened as little Lili trotted in. She sat herself on the armrest of Ky's pilot seat, which would be very dangerous during actual flight, and rested her head on his shoulder. She huffed to herself then whispered in Ky's ear. "It's time to go."

The Guider lifted off the ground, flew out of its hangar and into the bright blue sky.

Will walked home feeling as if he had lost another battle. Nothing was adding up and one answer was just leading to a thousand more questions; Will felt trapped at that instance. He had no other leads to work off of, so he felt that his fate rested on the will of that oddly gleeful girl. He made his way back to the studio/warehouse hoping that no one was home.

His wish came true as he stepped into the large empty apartment. He had skipped breakfast, so he reheated a doggy bag filled with Ky's leftover sloppy bar food. The to-go container it was in was clearly marked *Ky's don't touch*. Will didn't follow the instructions. He sprawled himself on the couch mowing down a hot plate of soggy cheesy fries. Suddenly Jina just walked in simply turning the locked knob to the point that it opened anyway.

"Hi Will," Jina greeted with a wave of the hand that was not holding the staff.

"Hey," Will monotonously blurted in an uncaring tone.

The beauty twisted her head to examine every corner of the apartment. "Where's Ky and Lili?"

"I don't know," Will shrugged.

"Well, I just wanted to..."

A slight ground rumble interrupted Jina's words. They both looked to the floor curious about what was occurring. The rumbling gradually grew more intense, and as it peaked, it was accompanied by a consistent booming sound like a vehicle with an outrageous amount of bass. Their minds started piecing together patterns in the sounds until they were both able to conclude with certainty that the noises were composing a musical beat. Will and Jina bolted outside to see what was going on. The sounds were indeed music. It was a very aggressive techno-dance song that rang out loudly throughout Gohanesse's entire industrial district. What was causing the rumbling came as more of a surprise to the boy.

It was hundreds of tanks rolling into town. Some crazy army was invading Gohanesse. The tanks were definitely not G.F.B. vehicles; they were larger, equipped with a better arsenal and overall more technologically advanced. Each tank was also fitted with enormous dual speakers fixed to both sides that pumped out the deafening music. The music was synchronized so the same song blared all throughout Gohanesse. The tanks veered through the district's roads taking over the area and trampling people if they had to. The screams of horror the civilians released as they fled were drowned out by the music.

The soldiers were even more peculiar than their vehicles. They littered the roofs of the tanks, some coming dangerously close to falling off. The fully armored soldiers danced to their music atop of the tanks, and they were really good. Some pop-locked like true experts, while others floor-rocked and flipped about like seasoned B-boys. They tumbled and twirled, twisted and boogied as they nonchalantly invaded the city. Will instantly recognized their high-tech uniforms. They were the same as the soldiers that accompanied Wes before he left.

Will tossed up his hands and admitted. "All right! That's it! There is way too much to even start explaining now!"

Jina's sensitive ears picked up on Will's words through the loud music. "They're the IO!" Jina began to explain at a decibel high enough to reach Will's eardrums.

"What!?" Will yelled while covering his ears trying to block out the music. "You know them!"

"Yes! IO stands for the Invisible Organization! They are a very real and very powerful organization, but as for being on paper, they don't really exist! They only show up to face problems that can devastate galaxies!" Jina shouted.

"Well, how do you know them!?"

"They were once assigned to kill me!"

"Oh! Well how did that go!?"

"I'm still here, aren't I!?"

"Well, what's with all this dancing and the music!?"

"The dancing keeps them nimble, strong and flexible! The music keeps them dancing!"

"Well, why are they here!?" Will wondered.

"I think they've come to harm you!"

Fear ripped the strength out of the boy's body as his

hands dropped slowly away from his ears at the news. "W-why?"

Jina's ears sifted through the music and found Will's question. "No time to explain! Go inside!" She ordered.

Will jumped at Jina's command and her sincerity ingrained a heavy worry in the boy's heart. Will fled inside and his head darted over every inch of the studio/warehouse frantic to come up with what he should do. There was too much adrenaline flooding his brain for him to think straight. His eyes combed the entire apartment for the perfect hiding spot, but he knew deep down it'd be futile. Based on the way the soldiers were fitted and by Jina's description, he could tell that they were professional and no matter where he hid they'd find him. His head was lost in frenzy.

"Oh my God! Oh my God! Oh my God! Oh my God!..." Will nervously kept repeating in the middle of the studio/warehouse while shaking his hands wildly in front of him. Will had officially panicked.

Out of nowhere, a mild calm came over the boy as something clicked in his head. It was something Ky was trying to tell him a while back. At the time, Will wasn't very interested, but as the seconds rolled on, Will was desperate to recall every detail.

Will remembered that Ky was calling out to him from somewhere in the apartment. The boy was barely listening because he was too busy with computer games.

"Yo! Check this out!" Ky's voice echoed through the studio/warehouse.

"What is it?" Will courteously said back from the couch with his nose in the laptop.

"It's, like, some type of compartment... Holy crap! We have a basement!"

"Really?" A disinterested Will blurted back with his focus on the screen.

"Geez! It's huge! Its gotta run under the entire building."

Will snapped back to reality as he formulated a plan. He had to pinpoint where Ky was yelling at him from that day. It obviously wasn't Will's room or the second story balcony because Ky mentioned a basement. He also ruled out Ky's room or the main open living area because Ky's voice sounded too far away. So what place could be left? Then it hit Will like a bag full of bricks. He called it out as his thoughts came to their final conclusion. "The bathroom!"

Will rushed to the bathroom's flimsy door and nearly ripped it open. Will's pupils performed a speedy scan over the bathroom in pursuit of any strange compartments. His quick once over came up with nothing. He peered into the tub and still came up empty handed. Next, he bent over and opened the bathroom cabinet beneath the sink. He tossed out the toiletries from the cabinet to further investigate inside. The boy threw all types of items on the ground. Cologne, toothpaste, a plastic brown jug of hydrogen peroxide, and a plunger were all chucked out of the cabinet. Will then grabbed a small dark tube with a prescription label on it. The label was filled out for a one Ky Gracen, and Will read out loud what the prescription was for. "Fungicide! Gross!" Will also discarded the tube and wiped his hand that touched it off on his jacket.

Will shoved aside the rest of the items and Will discovered a little knob on the back wall of the cabinet. The knob easily slid to the side revealing a new compartment. It was dank and dark inside and Will was certain he found the basement Ky was talking about.

"Bingo!" Will remarked with a growing smile.

Outside the studio/warehouse, Jina stood in front of the entrance door absolutely still. She was a stoic angelic statue guarding the apartment with the dedication of a Minotaur protecting his labyrinth. The only evidence proving that she was not a real statue was her perfectly straight hair that delicately danced in the wind. Her staff was ready, tucked in her right hand under an airtight fist. She was a deadly warrior blatantly challenging the army with her stance and making no attempt to hide that fact.

Two of the IO's tanks slowed down in front of the large apartment and quite a few fully suited soldiers descended off of them. It was ten to fifteen soldiers that filed off and out of the tanks, and they confidently marched toward the femme fatale to the beat of the drum. Each of them had fully automated miniature machine guns mounted to their armor on their right arms. As the screens on their high-tech helmets analyzed Jina's face, their machine guns flipped into their hands ready for battle.

The soldier closest to Jina stopped as his helmet listed all the specifics the IO had about her on their system. "Halt!" He commanded to the rest of the men with his gunned arm in the air. The arm was an official militaristic hand signal for the rest of the soldiers to stop in their tracks. "Switching music to internal speakers!" With a click of a button at the base of the soldier's helmet, the music blaring out of the tanks was muted, but you could be sure as the rising sun that the techno-dance tune was still loud as ever in their helmets. "Well, if it isn't Jina."

"Seeing those IO uniforms sure does bring back memories." Jina reminisced, still not moving a muscle.

"Sir," A soldier behind the one talking to Jina said. "If these reports are accurate, we're going to need backup."

"We're going to need a lot of backup." The first soldier corrected. "Go ahead and call it in."

The second soldier took a step back and pressed a button around the neck of his helmet. He was most assuredly calling for more IO soldiers as backup.

The soldier in the front carefully took a few steps forward. "We are going to be searching that building Jina."

"On what grounds?" Jina assertively questioned.

"Ha," The soldier laughed. "What do you think?"

"The case on me was closed years ago." Jina revealed.

The soldier inched toward her as if he were approaching a ravenous dog or a wild bear. "I understand, but you need to see this from our perspective. You must admit, finding you in this backwater planet is really suspicious."

"Be careful Phil!" One of the soldiers called out to the one who was nearing Jina.

"Don't worry," Phil the soldier assured. "I was actually shipped out on her case all those years ago so I know exactly what she's capable of."

"Perhaps," Said calm and collected Jina.

"Look Jina," Phil negotiated. "We have no quarrel with you personally, but we will be searching that warehouse and we will engage you if you do not comply." As Phil the soldier explained the situation to the deadly woman, four more tanks arrived on the scene. The IO soldiers riding those tanks joined the small crowd and pumped the soldier count to well over fifty.

One of the soldiers who had just got there yelled. "Phil! Get away from there!"

"My experience automatically makes me commanding officer in this matter!" Phil screamed back to his cautious comrade. He shimmied closer, little by little toward Jina. "So that's how it's going to be Jina. You either move or we fight."

"And I'm telling you." Jina testified taking her chance to speak. "Once you get close enough I'm going to hit you."

Phil slowly walked across the lawn getting all too close to Jina. "Come on Jina, move aside then we…"

BANG!

Jina slammed the end of her long metal staff against Phil's abdomen so fast that none of the soldiers trained eyes could follow it. Phil's body went careening across the lawn like a bullet in a perfectly straight line. Amazingly, the other soldiers in the trajectory of Phil's shooting body easily dodged it, but as for Phil, he crashed against the side of a tank. He hit the tank with such unbelievable force that the tank immediately fell on its side and cracked the cement road underneath it. Phil the soldier was wedged into the side of the tank and the injuries he sustained from that blow would haunt him for the rest of his life.

"Fire!" Some anonymous soldier hollered.

The front line soldiers took their mark and pointed their mounted mini-machine guns directly at the heavenly Jina. They mercilessly fired their weapons in a barrage of bullets that threatened to assault the beauty. Before the high velocity bullets made impact with her features, it appeared as if her body was instantaneously encased in a dome of metal. The walls of bullets ricocheted against the metallic dome and were sent sailing back at the army. The stray bullets should have devastated a sizable fraction of the army, but most of the nimble soldiers were able to leap out of the way like professional acrobats. Only two soldiers were injured in Jina's magnificent display of skill. The dome disappeared and Jina's hair ferociously kicked around in a small windstorm.

Jina did not miraculously create a metal dome around her body. She actually twirled her staff around herself at such an outrageous rate that the image of the staff blurred together forming the illusion of a dome. Jina's abilities were vastly superior to any one of the IO soldiers, but as a collective the army had a very real shot of taking her down. She still had lots of work ahead of her.

The IO soldiers formed a safe perimeter around Jina, far enough that her six-foot staff couldn't possibly reach. The dangerous woman held her staff at eye level in a fighting stance as if daring the army to attack her. Five of the soldiers charged at Jina from all sides. They made sure not to have too many people engage her at once because the commotion of twenty soldiers trying to fight her at the same time could actually work against them. They cleverly chose to rush her from all directions to increase the chance that she wouldn't be able to notice or address all of them before at least one managed to land a blow. Battle tactics and strategies were constantly being streamed to the hard-drive of their headgear as they were being updated as the fight progressed. The IO were no ordinary soldiers.

In the blink of an eye, Jina took her staff in one hand and it came down on the soldier right in front of her in a silvery flash. That soldier was squashed to the ground like a bug. With her free bare hand, she punched another soldier square in the face with the speed of a lightning bolt. The impact of her fist immediately snapped his neck. In the mere milliseconds it took her to perform those two strikes, the other three soldiers had got dangerously close to her. Two were on opposite sides of her and one was dashing at her back. Jina bounded high off the ground and administered a strength packing split-kick to both of her sides. The kick successfully connected to the two soldiers advancing at her left and right flank and aggressively knocked them back into the growing crowd. The man to Jina's rear hobbled under her due to the momentum of his own punch. Jina planted an overhand thrust downward with her staff to the soldier's open back that was strong enough to bounce him against the grass. Jina landed back on her feet in the middle of the front yard completely unharmed.

A crafty soldier to Jina's right was waiting for the exact moment when she was too distracted with the battle to make his own strike. He did a Capoeira style sweep-kick to her right leg with the power of a famous home run hitter up to bat. His hopes were that even if he didn't hit her, the kick might knock her off balance and leave her open for a later attack. Little did the soldier know that Jina had spent two days standing on a two-inch wide pole during her training years to perfect her balance. She simply lifted her right leg up and the soldier's kick passed safely beneath it. The end of her staff met the wily soldier's chest and launched him through the air like a boulder from a catapult.

Frustration mounted in the hearts of many of the IO soldiers. The IO were highly trained killing machines who were more than proficient at their job, but they had been engaging this girl for over two minutes and have not been able to touch her yet. Most of them had never faced Jina before or seen her in action, so they couldn't accept it. A large mass of them ran straight at her fully ignoring the strategies being uploaded to their helmets by the second. They were being led by anger.

Jina systematically batted away the numerous forwarding soldiers with ease. The soldiers' swelling aggravations compromised their formidable skills and Jina did not hesitate to take advantage of their faltering. IO soldiers began raining from the sky. They were still unable to land a single blow on her.

Lots of IO men had forgotten that they were there to search the warehouse and not to face Jina. A particular soldier did not forget his main objective. He took eighteen men and moved them to the large apartment's entrance while Jina was too focused on battle to do anything about it. Though the IO was in no way winning the bout with the female warrior, they were that much closer to accomplishing their true mission. One soldier ordered to the small platoon of others. "Get in the warehouse!"

The IO soldier kicked in the door with one sturdy thrust of his leg. They flipped, twirled, rolled and tumbled into the studio/warehouse with their arm-mounted machine guns pointed in various directions. It was a precaution for the chance of some other devastating warrior waiting inside for them. Lucky for them, no one was there, and that placed the soldiers at ease.

"This is definitely illegal housing." One soldier commented.

"Why is she protecting this shabby apartment?" Another soldier wondered.

"Jina isn't protecting this place," The soldier who seemed to be in command explained. "*she* is. We must be getting close. Search the place."

The platoon scattered. They scoured the apartment in search of someone or something. One man somersaulted over the couch and checked the cabinets in the kitchen area. Another soldier dragon-kicked Ky's room wide open and searched his personal quarters; that man coincidentally took the longest time looking in one area because of Ky's overwhelming mess. A third soldier did a backhand spring onto the set of collapsible stairs and raced up to Will's room. He shoved open the door and checked the boy's room in vain. Two soldiers bounced off the walls like tennis balls and landed on the upper balcony area. They all rummaged along the ground to the ceiling still coming up empty handed. Apparently what they were looking so hard for wasn't there.

"She's not here sir." One man reported to the commanding soldier.

"It would seem so." The commanding officer discussed. "Judging by Jina's speech patterns…"

"Sir!" A soldier interrupted running up to him from the bathroom. "I think I found something."

"Show me,"

The entire platoon instantaneously converged on the center of the large apartment and somehow piled into Ky's small bathroom. The soldier opened the bottom cabinet beneath the sink. The commanding soldier bent down and took a gander inside. On the back wall of the cabinet was a compartment left gaping open; Will had forgotten to shut it on his way out. The soldier managed to wedge his head and gunned arm inside the opening. He turned on a flashlight, which was housed next to the mini-machine gun, to get a better view of the hidden room. He saw that it was a huge dank cavernous basement meant for additional storage to the warehouses above. Although, there were more cobwebs in the massive room then boxes. The soldier removed his head and arm from the compartment and stood up.

Another soldier questioned. "What is it sir?"

"It's a basement. It must run under the entire building." The commanding officer informed.

Some other soldier interrogated. "Does it lead anywhere?"

The commanding soldier confessed. "There must be an exit/entry point in every warehouse in this building."

"Do you think the room's a clue?" A different one asked.

"I believe the boy must've escaped through here." The commanding soldier theorized.

"Why?"

"Because it was left open?"

"We should go after him." An eager one hailed.

"All of us are too big to fit." The head soldier reasoned. "And we don't have the kind of time frame to knock down this building, so..." His words led his mind directly into thought.

An entirely random soldier inquired. "What about the girl?"

"She's nowhere around here."

"So what do we do now?"

The lead soldier stood silent for a moment contemplating what their wisest move would be. "We'll request a search party and have them comb the surrounding area. He couldn't have gotten far, he's only ten."

"He's nine sir." Some nameless soldier corrected.

"Whatever! Point being is he couldn't have gone far, it's not like he can drive."

"Understood," A more sensible soldier agreed.

"Our work here is done, let's help with the efforts outside." The commanding soldier commanded.

The IO left Ky's apartment. The information that the platoon had recovered in their search had been relayed to the rest of the army within seconds.

Back outside, The IO made little progress in their efforts to defeat Jina. She easily thwarted any wave of advancing enemies. Two soldiers posted on her sides believed they had devised the perfect plan to land an attack on her. Like chess, they planned out a series of resulting moves before even executing the first one. It was foolproof, or at least that's what they believed.

The soldier to Jina's right threw a battle knife to her head while the one to her left threw a similar knife at her legs. Jina slightly jumped up raising her legs avoiding the lower knife, while she placed her metal staff right in the way of the one aimed at her head; the knife pinged off the staff. The men's plan was not finished; the purpose of the knife throwing was to create a ruse. The soldiers lunged from their corresponding sides while she was too busy avoiding the knives to dodge their upcoming attack. The one to her right launched a fist at her gorgeous face, and the soldier to her left prepared a drop-kick to the lower half of

her body. Jina's staff zoomed down on the head of the man to her right. Her staff was already directed at him, and the blow shot him to the floor so fast that he actually got pegged with the knife that was aimed at her feet. She simultaneously delivered a split second sidekick to the advancing soldier at her left. The soldier flew back into the heart of the IO forces.

As Jina landed back on her feet, another brave soldier charged right at her with a sliding sweep to her legs. She effortlessly skipped over that guy and came down with a blow of her staff at the soldier behind him. Then something happened that amazed Jina for a long time. The soldier she intended to crush with her staff actually blocked it. The soldier by chance had his knife in his hand and had been able to lift it up before the staff made contact with his face. The cracked knife held her mighty staff at bay just mere millimeters from the tip of his helmet.

"I think my arm's broken." The soldier remarked in a wince of pain. The soldier was indeed correct. Jina's strike had broken his arm in seventeen different places.

At that instant, a lone soldier amidst the army decided to implement one of the overlooked tactics that his helmet suggested. The soldier put his hand to a disc-like object on the back of his equipment belt. The disc had a small white ball wedged in the center of it, and five finger-sized holes arranged in it. The holes were purposely placed in specific spots so it could be grasped quickly and easily. He unhooked the disc from his belt and slid his fingers inside the holes. He hurled the disc object toward Jina. The soldier's aim held true as the disc sliced through the air and speed toward Jina's breathtaking visage.

Jina first noticed the disc darting at her face from two-feet away. The disc gained another foot by the time Jina took a swing at it with her mighty long staff. The soldier had counted on Jina deflecting the object, and as her staff met with it, his plan came to fruition.

The object was a bomb that had several different interesting ways of being triggered. One of the ways is a touch sensitivity feature that allows the bomb to explode with any slight touch after being activated.

The scene was lost in a loud cloud of flames and debris as the explosion tossed the front line of soldiers around like popping kernels. The noise and the dust settled leaving nothing but an ashy destroyed sidewalk.

Nobody had noticed Jina was missing until her body came down feet first on some poor anonymous IO soldier's shoulders. The soldier's body immediately gave way and slammed to the cement hard. Her unrivaled speed allowed her to leap out of the way of the blast as it was blowing up. The soldiers that all of a sudden found themselves around her attempted to jump back to a safe distance. Her staff danced in a wide fast sweep that spanned all three hundred and sixty degrees around her. The tremendous strike should have connected with approximately twenty soldiers, but it only hit ten as the other soldiers dodged and darted out of the way.

She could feel their forces closing in on her, so she knelt down and held her staff above her head with both hands. She began twirling the staff over her body horizontally and the metal rod started gaining speed. In no time flat, the staff resembled a helicopter propeller spinning madly above the beauty. She wanted to keep them off of her while she plotted out her next course of action.

Jina looked down and realized that two of those peculiar discs had been slid down by her feet. Another way that those bomb-discs can be triggered is if they are set to a timer. The two white spheres in the middle of the discs lit up like light bulbs. Jina could only speculate to what that meant.

BOOM! BOOM!

Dual explosions erupted and ignited the street in flames and smog. This time around, some of the soldiers were able to keep their eyes on Jina. Jina's body appeared to elongate like a spaghetti strand as she rocketed into the sky and out of range of the bombs. The few IO soldiers who kept up with the speed demon aimed their guns at her in midair as she descended back to the planet. They shot at her repeatedly but their bullets continually missed her plummeting body by mere centimeters.

Jina's body flipped and twisted in a dazzling show until her falling body landed on a tank. A single soldier positioned on the tank looked at Jina in a surprised gesture as she landed on her feet beside him. Jina facilely swatted him away with a simple swing of her staff. The soldier flung through the air and bashed into a distant building, busting a hole into its thick concrete wall.

Jina surveyed the scenario around her to gauge how much of a problem the rest of the battle was going to be. During her reign of havoc, many other tanks had arrived on the scene. Every inch of the street was cluttered with hundreds of IO soldiers. She looked over at the apartment realizing that the skilled army had ample time to have searched the apartment. She knew somewhere Will was in danger and she had to come to his aid. Jina also knew lingering around there was going to be a huge time consuming headache so she had to resolve the engagement quickly.

Before the soldiers who were cautiously climbing the tank could reach her, Jina drove her staff downward into the heart of the highly mechanical war machine. She skewered the tank with the ease of a hot metal rod into a marshmallow. The staff subtly and yet rapidly shook from side to side. A low-pitched tone resonated from the long slender metallic rod for a moment before the entire tank blew apart from the inside out. It appeared as though some grand invisible explosion occurred from the center of the mammoth tank, effectively ripping it to shreds. Chunks of the tank and metal shrapnel littered the sky and the IO soldiers kept an eye on the dangerous falling debris. Most of the soldiers were able to dodge and avoid the broken tank parts as it assaulted them. Only two men out of the entire IO force were injured by the falling tank pieces. As the excitement simmered down, the soldiers realized Jina had fled the scene.

Fifteen miles away, the only mobile car in the city of Gohanesse was speeding away from Ky's studio/warehouse. The car had already entered the commercial district as it tried to create as much distance as it could between itself and the large apartment. The only occupant of the accelerating vehicle was William A. Treyu. The soldier who searched the apartment wasn't entirely wrong. Will didn't know how to drive, although the boy did know how to hack into a car's system with his laptop. Will quickly discovered that he could control the automobile much more fluently with his computer controls, so he sat in the car's right driver seat using his laptop to guide it. A multitude of wires trailed from his computer device to a panel beneath the wheel that Will had popped off. That was where the boy hooked his laptop up to as he performed the marvelous hack job.

As Will zoomed passed the streets of Gohanesse it became apparent to him that the city was deserted. Nothing except a few IO tanks and about a billion abandoned vehicles remained on the avenues. For some reason, every citizen felt it necessary to hide from the army. It also appeared the bulk of the forces were dealing with something else. Will was able to race down the roads unhindered.

All of a sudden, Will saw that a shadow was cast

above his stolen vehicle. He remotely veered the car dramatically to his left and a huge craft slammed to the ground. If the boy hadn't reacted so fast, he definitely would've been crushed under the tremendous weight of the galactic cruiser. Without stopping for a second, Will continued driving passed it, but he noticed in his rearview screen that the spherical craft belonged to the IO. Many more IO crafts started dropping all around the boy and he did his best to weave the car through the mounting obstacles. The vehicle was hastily approaching a two-way fork in which the street he was driving on met a dead end. The car was going much too fast to make the sharp turn on the horizontal road, so it simply plowed through the guardrail and into a grassy plain. The crafts ceaselessly fell around the car, causing block-wide tremors as they pounded down to the grass. Will tried to keep his wits about him among the mayhem, but the small grassy field was coming to an end. With every passing moment, the car kept speeding toward the great Keona River, one of Gohanesse City's borderlines. The vehicle made a harsh stop at the river's edge, coming all too close to diving right in. Will killed the engine, locked the doors and waited.

A few more crafts descended to the ground before platoon after platoon filed out of them. The soldiers took their time walking over to the stolen vehicle because they weren't sure if Will had run out of tricks. They surrounded the car without arming themselves then one soldier approached the driver side. The soldier's hand stretched out to the door's handle as he tried opening it, but he realized it had been locked.

"Open the door." The soldier ordered to Will bearing a forceful tone.

Will glanced up at the mildly frustrated soldier then back down to his useless laptop. An expression of deep melancholy formed on the boy's face as he blatantly ignored the soldier. Will was a child capable of many things, but still a child nonetheless. When that fact, or anything else that reminded him of his own limitations was thrust in his face, he hated it. His helplessness made him feel even more like a small kid.

"I'm not going to tell you again. Open the door!" The angered soldier reiterated pointing down to the lock.

Will didn't even raise his head that time. He just blankly stared at the floor with the sadness still gracing his youthful features. He then sniffled twice.

The soldier drove his fist straight through the driver side window. The glass shattered under the mighty pressure of the soldier's balled up armored hand. The boy jumped in his seat as the flailing glass shards inflicted minor cuts across his face. The soldier grabbed Will with both hands tightly by his collar and rustled with him. He was trying to drag the boy genius out the broken window.

Will wrestled with the soldier's strong arms showing as much pride and character as any full-grown man. Will pushed a button on his wristwatch communicator and a massive amount of electricity surged through the soldier's arms. Sadly for Will, the soldier's armored uniforms acted as lightning rods as the immense dose of electricity traveled along the edges of his suit and safely into the ground. The soldier was completely unharmed by Will's attack.

The violent soldier sliced the boy up more as he almost yanked him out the glass-ridden window. Before he had the chance, someone of importance yelled. "Let him go!"

"Sir!" The hotheaded soldier argued.

"You heard me! I said let him go!" The male voice repeated carrying an obvious load of authority with the words.

The soldier unhanded Will and the boy flopped back into the seat. The soldier took a step back and crossed his arms watching Will like a hawk.

Will glanced into his rearview screen and saw that Wes Vega was steadily heading to the car. Instead of going to the broken window, Wes motioned to the passenger side. He then bent over and lightly tapped on the glass with his index knuckle a couple of times. Will's eyes slid to Wes' welcoming face for a second then back down to the floor. Wes tapped on the glass again and Will's entire face twisted to look up at him. Will clearly saw Wes silently mouth *Can you let me in?* Will's hesitant hand slumped over to the armrest and unlocked Wes' door.

Wes casually opened his passenger door and sat in the seat. He then reclined back the seat seeming rather relaxed considering the situation.

"You know, you gave us a run for our money back there." Wes conversed. "We never thought you'd be in a car. We were looking for you on foot."

Will shook his head up and down in acknowledgment to Wes' statement. He still appeared very sad.

"You know, you must be one crazy hacker to get into a car's system so fast." Wes claimed in an attempt to pick up Will's spirits.

"Yeah,"

"Yeah!? Is that all you got to say about it?" Mr. Vega chirped still trying to lighten the mood. "I consider myself an awesome hacker, but that still would've taken me at least a half an hour. You did it in minutes."

Will didn't respond. He just stared outside the windshield sniffling occasionally.

"Look, Will," Wes comforted trying to relate to the boy. "I know all this must be real confusing to you, and I wish I could tell you what's going on, I really do. But, all I can do is give you a piece of advice. Don't be fooled by her."

"…" Will remained quiet.

"She's really cute isn't she?"

Will confessed in a volume so soft Wes didn't catch it. "Yes,"

"Sir!" The soldier stationed right outside Will's window yelped interrupting their little talk. "I think we have a problem." The soldier pointed somewhere far behind the car.

Wes turned his head around to glare past the headrest and out the back windshield. On the city horizon, planted somewhere in the middle of the street, he could see it. It was a gorgeous girl with jet-black hair wrapped in a baby blue kimono. She was also holding a hefty staff longer than her whole body in one hand like it was nothing.

Wes remarked as he smiled and opened his passenger door. "I guess that means it's our time to go." Wes began to exit the vehicle.

"Sir!" The soldier complained voicing the word rather rudely. "We should apprehend the boy right now."

"We're not here to fight a full-scale war at the moment." Wes said half way out the car. He did a slight jerking of his head to refer to Jina whom was walking toward them all slowly.

"With all due respect sir," The soldier persisted. "A beacon has been activated meaning we take immediate action."

"And need I remind you we're not here for the boy. We came to locate the girl."

"If we have the boy the girl will come for him."

"Not necessarily," Wes reasoned. "Jina seems to be retaining a lot of her original memories. That means she's most likely far away from here."

"But sir…"

"We're pulling out and that's it!" Wes interrupted in a loud and threatening manner. "We have enough accumulated info to file an official report and keep my higher ups happy. So do you wanna back talk me again and be court-martialed or do you want to follow orders?" Wes Vega flexed his authority.

The soldier remained silent for just a second. "Understood, sir." The defiant soldier marched back to the swarm of the IO's impressive fleet shouting *Pull out! Pull out! Move! Move!* The IO's army flipped and danced their way back into the crafts.

"See ya around." Wes said as he walked out of the car.

Will sat there not speaking a word.

Wes joined his soldiers as a few of the crafts started warming up their thrusters. The crafts began gradually ascending into the heavens one by one. The grass rattled back and forth due to the power of multiple thrusters igniting. The army had fully left the scene as Jina neared the car.

Jina busted open the passenger side window before climbing into the car.

"Jina! Could you NOT be crazy!? What the hell!?" Will yelled out in surprise at Jina's needless violence.

"Is that what you call gratitude?" Jina asked as she shut the passenger door. "You should be safe now. Let's go back to the apartment."

"Yeah, thanks. Thanks a lot." Will said fortified with sarcasm.

way. It seemed they were allowed to do as they pleased for the time being. One thing they didn't notice was a tiny floating camera high in the sky.

The camera was implementing a helicopter-like system of propellers to stay in the air and relayed live feed to a pair of high-powered binoculars.

Over forty miles away, there was a large hill. The hill

had grown in popularity for being a perfect spot to take a date and lounge under its one huge lone tree. A lot of people would picnic with their date, enjoy the wonderful view of the city, or carve their initials into to the tree's bark. It had become so widely known for that that people unofficially dubbed it *Lover's Hill*. Four entities stealthily camouflaged themselves inside the hill's big tree, and their reasons for being there were a lot less romantic. One of the people's eyes was set behind the binoculars receiving the camera feed. The image of Will and Jina were being streamed to his oculars by the second.

The man looking through the binoculars was the one you'd be most astonished that he was actually hiding in a tree. He was a mountain of a man peaking at nearly eight-feet tall. Though he was relatively slender for his size, his body was outrageously toned. His muscles were etched into his body with the precision of an ancient roman sculpture. His hard sharp facial features were set under shaggy black hair. Everything about the man projected an image of strength, and the giant stone club that rested on the branch beside him further amplified this.

"The IO already made their move." The mountain-man detailed. "That's going to make getting her out of here that much more difficult." His voice was as deep as a bear's and just added to his strong persona.

"Let me have a look, Baloe,"

Baloe gave no resistance to handing the pair of high-tech binoculars over to the other man. While Baloe was sitting on a branch, this other guy was standing on the same branch beside him. The man reached down and took the binoculars from the gracious Baloe.

The other man had an average build, probably just a couple inches shorter then Ky. The man had an abnormally smooth face for a guy and his brown hair was pulled back into a small ponytail. His clothes were also rather peculiar for their unnecessarily high level of formality while Baloe was suited like a true warrior. Also, the interior of his traveler's jacket glistened with the magical sparkle of numerous concealed firearms.

The well-dressed man brought the binoculars to his eyes and commented. "Can you believe the people she has chosen to chaperon her? Not fitting company for a princess."

"Did you see the female fight, Byne?" Baloe asked. "My club is tickled with excitement for a chance encounter with her."

Byne casually lowered his hand holding the binoculars by his side. "All of us together, she would not even be a formidable foe."

"Guys!" An unidentified member of the foursome shouted. "We're not here to fight anyone! Our only purpose is to protect her and bring her back home!"

The shouting man was leaning against the thick center bark of the tree. He was an extremely skinny fellow with almost snow-white skin. Though he was a young man, his hair was gray like an old man and it flowed down his back. His eyebrows were silvery as well and overgrown, prompting him to curl them at the ends. He wore basic street clothes and had no signs of a weapon whatsoever.

"Okay Doc, calm down." Byne soothed trying to put the gray-haired Doc at ease. "You are correct, and if we are able to accomplish our duty without resorting to battle, that is the course we shall take."

"Why don't I believe you two?" Doc mentioned.

Byne ignored Doc's sentence as he stated. "You know there is another person who accompanies the boy. It's a man."

"Yeah, but in comparison to that female, he's nothing." Baloe voiced his opinion.

The last member of the group was kneeling on a

branch separated from the rest. A portion of his wild dark hair was covering his creepy face. Only one eye was exposed and constantly kept moving around as if he had an extremely severe case of attention deficit disorder. His eye flashed to all his surroundings quickly examining all of it. An insane psychotic smile was on his face at every moment and let you know right when you met him, that his mind wasn't stable. He was dressed in an assassin's traditional tactical gear, but he carried with him an unusual amount of razor sharp swords and knives all over the suit. He had nine full sized swords on him including three strapped to his back alone. His head consistently twisted to face any slight movement in the tree, completely incapable of keeping up with the other three's conversation.

"Hey guys!" The crazy one blurted out of nowhere. "Have you ever felt like you were just introduced in a book?"

"Shut up, Riftkin." Baloe moaned dismissing Riftkin's nut-ball question.

"We need to tread lightly from here on in." Doc suggested getting back to the point.

"Well, I believe that's something we can all agree on." Byne concurred.

Baloe nodded his head up and down unconvincingly.

The four of them stayed disguised in the tree, but you could be sure that these entities would surface again before this little riddle would be completely solved.

The car pulled up near the large studio/warehouse. They weren't able to get in front of the door because there was a gigantic hole in the center of the road. They couldn't mount the curb either because there was a somewhat smaller hole in the sidewalk. There were huge chunks of robotic debris all over the place and the front wall of Ky's converted apartment was lined with bullet holes. Will was left stupefied as he fully absorbed the mess.

Jina did a slight nod of her head as if she was impressed before saying. "Wow, they cleaned up pretty good; especially all the bodies."

"What the hell happened here?" Will grumbled at Jina as the vehicle was set into park.

"What do you think happened? I defended myself. You should've seen this place before." Jina answered.

Will sighed before they both got out of the car.

The boy started trudging to the front door already sick and tired of the day. After a few seconds, the boy realized he was walking to the apartment alone. His face swiveled around to the road and he witnessed Jina trotting down the sidewalk away from the apartment.

"Jina!" Will screeched at her. "What are you doing?"

"I'm leaving,"

"What if they come back?"

"Uhhh," Jina was obviously stalling to think up a good reason for her not to stay. "I really don't think they're coming back today."

"Jina, could you stay until Ky gets back please?" He sweetly questioned with big sourdough puppy-dog eyes.

Jina's head dropped backwards as if it was unhinged and she released a big breath in the air. Her elbows also fell a level before she groaned. "Huh, fine."

Will skipped to the apartment while Jina followed behind, dragging her feet. Will perched himself in a seat at the kitchen table impatiently waiting for Ky to get home. Jina had spread out on the couch willing, but not eager, to comply with the boy's wishes. She became so bored, that she even drifted off to sleep a few minutes at a time. Will stayed wide-awake in the seat as the day turned to night like a pissed off mother hen. Dreadful thoughts raced in the boy's head of what Ky and Lili could be doing together. He waited like an aggravated and concerned mom staying up until her daughter got home. The anger that had been welling up inside the boy almost exploded as the clock rolled past ten.

Suddenly, the door swung open as Lili and Ky came barreling and giggling their way inside.

"Where have you two been?" Will investigated as if it was imperative for him to know. "Do you know how late it is?"

"Calm down Will," Lili reasoned as she began relaxing in the apartment.

"What were you guys doing?" The boy forcefully persisted.

"Will," Lili laughed off. "Ky just gave me a ride on the Guider. That's all."

"Yeah, chill Will. It was just a ride." Ky corroborated.

"For ten hours!?" Will scolded.

Lili shot back. "Well sor---ry, we lost track of time."

"Shut up. I don't believe a word you say."

Jina sprang off the couch and commented. "All right, I'm out of here." Her angelic body trotted to the door and escaped out of it before Will's lecture had time to form.

"What's wrong man?" Ky asked.

"Look around you Ky!" Will furiously tried to bring to light. "That's what's wrong."

"Awwwww," Lili cooed while making a sweet face and butterfly eyes at Will. "Are you jealous?"

Will didn't even think about it like that, but that didn't stop him from blushing. He twisted his head the best he could to hide his rosy face. "No!"

Ky laughed out loud and casually strolled into his room shaking his head at the boy.

"You know I only have eyes for you." She smiled as she approached the embarrassed boy playfully tickling at his stomach as she passed him.

"Like I care," Will insulted as he followed her toward the collapsible steps leading to their room.

"Well, if you don't care so much, why are you in such an uproar?" She pointed out climbing up the stairs.

"Because there's something up with you and this army showing up. I'm not sure how, but I know you're involved."

"What army?" Lili inquired.

"Don't play dumb with me." He continued nipping at her heels. "The army behind every tank at every street corner; the army that jacked my face all up."

"I wondered what all that was." Lili sincerely panted nearing the top of the stairs.

"I'm serious," The boy growled as they entered the room.

Lili turned to face Will, smiled and remarked. "You're so talkative when you're jealous."

"I'm …not… And I'm…not…" Will stammered at her double-edged comment. He gave up, huffed over to his bed and proceeded to plop himself into it. He just wanted to ignore it all once again.

"Awww, Will." Lili affectionately moaned as she too began climbing up to her second bunk. "One of these days it's gonna be you and me out there."

"Mmmm-hmmm," Vibrated between the boy's lips in an annoyed sounding buzz.

"And that's gonna mean so much more." Lili continued.

At that moment, Will's eyes wondered in a sad longing. He thought deep down, that a day with her did sound like a fun idea. He also knew his own stubbornness might hinder him from ever doing that.

"Don't you think?" Lili asked to the person in the lower bunk not expecting an answer. She didn't get one.

"I think so." She said as she started tucking herself under the covers. "So next time, *YOU* gotta take me out on the Guider, okay?"

"…" Will tried not to respond.

"Okay, goodnight Will."

"Goodnight," Will fired back without even noticing he said it.

Lili's ever-present smile expanded tremendously before she whispered. "Lights off." Will would never know how much joy that *goodnight* made her feel.

The automatic electronic lights dimmed until the room was pitch black. It wasn't long until the kids were asleep.

"And what about you, Will?" The full-grown mysterious man figure turned to Will in his dream.

Will stood still facing the male figure lost in a daze and yet beaming with confidence. The boy found himself unable to speak. He was once again in his reoccurring dream, being able to recall just a little more this time around. His eyes were fixed to the shadowed man's words.

"Did you stand up for yourself?" The grown male figure probed. "Or did you just stand there helpless and let yourself get hurt?"

Will stood there still not speaking a word. The gaze Will placed on the three figures remained one of confusing affection, even as the male figure's voice was growing with tension.

"Well? Answer me?" The man ordered at Will.

"Oh Terry." The female figure interrupted succeeding in breaking the tension. "Leave him alone. He was the one that was hurt."

"And crying from what I hear." The male figure shot back to the female trying to invoke a sense of shame in the boy.

"Oh Terrence…"

Will woke up to no breakfast for the second time in a row. Since Lili had shown up, she had been fixing him a morning meal every day, but the last two mornings she had failed to do so. For some reason, Will didn't seem surprised. He also appeared to be expecting the next tiny detail that came to light. Lili was missing again. Will absorbed the inconsistencies of the morning much more fluently this time. He was also a lot less depressed than the day before, a lot less helpless. Maybe the boy had formed some kind of plan.

He tucked his laptop into the brown leathery satchel and hung it around his body. He exited his room and onto the stairs and stared down at the apartment. The only other occupant was Ky lounging on the couch still sleeping. This was a much more common way for him to find his guardian, and it reminded him of how things use to be. He slowly made his way down to the apartment floor pumped full of some mysterious confidence.

Will nonchalantly looked around the apartment for someone or something. "Is Lili not here?"

Ky yawned still waking up at the time. "Huh, I guess not… if you even need to ask me that."

"I bet if I tried to get in contact with Jina, she'd be gone too. Funny, I thought she'd take you again." Will predicted out of nowhere.

"Uh huh," Ky agreed for absolutely no reason.

"Is that weird army still around?" Will investigated while beaming his eyes down Gohanesse's avenues through the window.

"Uh, yeah," Ky answered.

"Good, I was counting on it." The boy said as he scoured about for certain items in the apartment that he tossed in his satchel as he found them. "I'm out of here. I'll see you later." Will got ready to make his departure by opening the front door. He then looked back at Ky with a slight smirk. "You know, you seem a lot like your old self."

"Thank you." Ky moaned not hesitating to accept the compliment.

Will left the studio/warehouse all by himself.

One hour and thirty-seven minutes later, an IO tank sat unmanned on an overpass above a highway. The tank was illegally parked on the sidewalk of a large main street that bridged over interstate 130. I130 was eight lanes wide on both sides, making it one of the most massive roads in Gohanesse City. The overpass was a street three lanes wide on both sides; proving it was a fairly major boulevard. Both roads were much busier a week or so ago, but by that time, they were reduced to vehicle graveyards. Automobiles of all shapes and sizes were left abandoned or even crashed on the streets' pavement. The lone disheveled roads emitted an eerie feel.

Two IO soldiers walked back to the tank in the day's intense heat. Both of the soldiers were carrying pouches of beef jerky with them as they headed toward the tank.

One soldier nagged to the other. "Man, I wish just a few of the civilians would wake up. I can't keep living on these snacks we keep stealing."

"Yeah," The other one agreed marching to the tank at a much steadier rate than the nagger.

"Oh, and trying to use one of these fast food restaurant grease-baths myself!" The complaining soldier ranted. "Forget about it. I always end up burning everything to a crisp. How am I supposed to get a decent set of fries around here?"

"Yeah," the other soldier said climbing into the tank. He didn't really seem interested in his partner's food concerns.

"Man, I can't wait to liberate this city." The soldier whined as he too got into the tank with his upsetting packs of jerky.

The men squeezed into the tank's interior like they had countless times before. A cramped walkway was the only thing that connected the pair of soldiers to their respective seats just big enough to accommodate the two. The tank's limited interior was a big reason why the majority of the IO army rode on top of them, as opposed to inside. One of the two control seats is used for the tank's driver who would also overlook the status of the tank's defenses and engine. The back seat was designed for the soldier operating the tank's impressive cannon. That soldier was also in charge of aiming and firing the rest of the tank's arsenal with professional precision. No more than those two people could securely ride inside the tank.

The soldiers closed the lid on the tank and wiggled through the tank's narrow deck to their control seats. They fastened themselves in with numerous safety belts, straps and bars. It was as if they were getting ready to ride a mountainous roller coaster or blast off into space. The soldiers were then set to go about their business and enjoy their snacks.

"Ready?" One asked the other as a precaution.

"Everything is go here."

Suddenly all the men's safety belts unfastened and their seats safety bars were undone. The engine died as they heard the lid of the tank lock automatically. The second soldier immediately dropped the bags of jerky.

"What the?" The soldier in the driver seat reacted. He attempted to use the controls to manipulate the tank, but his efforts gained no response.

"What's going on?" The soldier manning the weapons questioned to his comrade.

The engine then miraculously kicked on and the tank

started moving on its own. The driver tried to regain control of the tank, but no matter what he did, his actions had no effect.

The tank backed up into the middle of the overpass, shoving aside a few cars littering the street. The tank stopped then drove forward right toward the bridge's edge. The tank drove clear off the bridge and the cement guardrail instantly crumpled by the force of the tank as the monstrosity sailed through it. Pieces of cement and dusty debris hit the hard floor of I130 like a precursor to the giant tank that was about to sink itself halfway into the street. As the tank slammed into the highway below, the soldiers were flung around in its tough compact inner quarters like coins in a tumbling jar. The tank met the floor with a deafening crash and crushed a few abandoned cars in the process. The barrel of the big cannon on the outside of the tank was instantly shoved to the side as the tank made impact with the ground. The cannon was then facing the tall walls of the highway. The armored vehicle was in pretty bad shape.

The soldier at the weapons seat pried himself from the tank's wall, which he was savagely thrown at during the fall. He searched quickly with his eyes to locate his comrade. The other soldier had been left mangled on the other side of the control deck obviously unconscious. The still aware soldier gradually crawled back to his seat. He reached aside to a console to the overturned seat's right. He was trying to push a distress signal to effectively radio for help, but he didn't realize the added danger he put himself in as he stretched to the button. He was placing his body in the kickback trajectory of the interior portion of the tank's massive barrel and hammer. Soldiers were taught to stay clear of the barrel's track at all times to prevent serious injury or instant death from the cannon's deadly kickback. This soldier forgot his protocol in his desperation for help.

Something fired the tank's cannon and its kickback struck the wounded soldier with the incredible force of a moving jet. The shell exploded out of the barrel and ferociously tore through the highway wall leaving a cloud of smoke and dust in its wake. The soldier was immediately knocked out without having a chance to push that blasted button.

Little Will looked down on the whole scene on top of a three-story building overlooking the overpass. Will had his fingers to his open and active laptop as he occasionally surveyed the crash through a pair of binoculars he didn't forget to grab.

"Gotcha!" Will gladly remarked as a satisfied smile streamed under his nose.

Will had been staking out the overpass for just such an opportunity. He watched as the soldiers in the tank left it to get a bite to eat. The boy then hacked into the tank using a self-made program, which locates and scans any electronic devices within a certain proximity of his computer. Fifteen minutes later, a rather lengthy hack for Will's standards; the boy had absolute control of the tank and all its workings. All Will had to do was wait for the perfect time to trap some IO soldiers.

A few minutes after the crash, the lid of the tank unlocked and swung open. Since the tank was wedged into the pavement, the lid was at ground level, easy enough for any boy to enter. Will crouched into the tank's narrow lopsided interior and examined the unconscious soldiers. He unhinged their helmets and removed them from the soldiers. The boy noticed when he took off the helmets the soldiers made identical soft whines before they were rendered unconscious again. He left the tank in an orderly fashion and headed back to his scouting spot on the roof of the building with the helmets.

Once back on his scouting spot, where the boy for some reason felt comfortable, he wasted no time getting to work. He pulled out all types of bare crude wires, strippers, crimpers, wire heads, and widgets. He created his own cords and started programming wire functions as he prepared to connect the helmets to his laptop. He hooked up the complex system of wire cords and lines to the helmet as if he was planning to do so the entire time. Will, armed with the almighty power of his keystrokes, began clicking his way into the IO's wealth of information. Will suspected that the mysterious army came on account of Lili for some reason or another. If he wanted to uncover anything about her, their data banks were the obvious source. Will had been formulating the entire night how he could gain access to the IO's information. That's the plan that had been boosting the boy's confidence that day. Will broke down the vast array of protective barriers and guard programs one by one; even their superior technology was no match for the boy.

Will looked past their main case filled with files and headed straight for their cryptic *ghost* files, the real meat of secrecy. Will visually scrolled through endless folders that all dealt with some planet threatening event. It was sort of humorous how Will so nonchalantly breezed past files dealing with such cataclysmic and shocking moments, but the boy was singularly focused on information dealing with the weird girl. During his file cruising, he suddenly hesitated on one certain file he came across. He took a second look at it in interest.

"Holy free-holies!" Spilled out of Will's mouth in surprise. "They have a file on Jina." Will clicked on the file out of curiosity. He read a lot about Jina's past that only a handful of people in all of existence were aware of. Though, the only fact the boy ended up remembering was the only one that made him chuckle. "Ha ha! That's Jina's real name?" Will held a hand over his grinning lips to silently contain his laughter as he exited out of Jina's file.

Will searched the files a little while longer before he came to one titled *Lili*. When he opened that file, a lot of unexplainable questions that Will sought were answered. A section was subtitled *Abilities* and that's where Will decided to start. He had a sneaking suspicion of what he might find out, but he more realistically thought he'd be reading up on dumb things like she could speak several languages or she takes ballet. Never did he dream that his worst fears would so boldly unfold on the screen.

Most of the long paragraph rattled on with medical jargon that the boy couldn't possibly understand, but he read aloud what his mind could grasp. "She is capable of controlling the minds of intelligent beings on a worldwide scale. The phenomenon is called ladameric-phonlitisis hyvithrosis when the medulla oblongata is swelled... yada yada yada... let's see..." His eyes scoured the screen for the fragments he could decipher. "Her powers can be measured by the proximity to her victims; the closer you are to her, the stronger her mental hold will be." Will also recited. "Her brainwaves can emulate multiple other brainwaves while her own remains active. The trans-mental occurrence is known as telepathy and vastly... whatever whatever, blah-blah... She can delve into her victim's memories, recall their thoughts, or manipulate them all together." Will gasped in amazement. "She really IS controlling everybody." His eyes once again glued themselves back to the laptop's monitor. He wished to further unwrap this mystery. "We have discovered a few individuals throughout the universe who are unaffected by her abilities. There are certain brain frequencies that Lili cannot emulate or control. It is the research we accumulated on these individuals that have helped us develop the program *Lili Blocker*." Will then shot the monitor an odd and curious gaze as he repeated. "Lili Blocker?" The boy just had to read on. If this was what he thought it was, it could be the answer to his mounting problems. "The program *Lili Blocker* emits a *scrambler* frequency that camouflages the users natural brain wave frequency, effectively rendering the user immune to Lili's mind manipulation abilities. All IO helmets have *Lili Blocker* pre-installed along with IO crafts and vehicles." Backing away from the screen for a moment and with a hand to his chin, Will commented. "Hmmm, very interesting." His eyes next peered down at a section titled *Biography*.

Will's eyes rapidly roamed the paragraph, reading out loud as he followed her story. "Lili's origins begin in uncharted space and she is known as the *Universe Princess*." The boy then pulled back from the screen and rang in disbelief. "Wow, the uncharted region of space!? I wonder what she is?"

In that time period, civilized man had made leaps and bounds when it came to matters of space travel, it still had many mysteries lingering in its infinite beyond. The civilizations of man, and the few alien civilizations man was aware of, had only accounted for a very small fraction in comparison to the entirety of the limitless void that constructed outer space. The ninety-eight percent of unexplored universe was known as uncharted space. The beings, anomalies, and life that resided in that vast portion of space were yet to be discovered. Apparently, that was where innocent-looking Lili was from.

Will continued to read on, eager to find out what else he may discover. "The title *Universe Princess* is at the moment being classified as an unofficial title, for no other regal entities or royal family members in relation to her have yet to be identified." Will skipped past a huge amount of the biography paragraph. "Most peculiar about Lili's genetic makeup is that her DNA is constructed of over a fifty percent *perfect* gene-strand. This would allow her certain abilities that most could not achieve. Her unique genetics is the basis of the theory behind her remarkable abilities of mind manipulation." Will had already come to that conclusion but he also remembered her perfectly straight fingerprints. Her untainted gene pool was a reasonable explanation for her fingerprint's odd pattern. Will skimmed the paragraph for further information of interest. "She has four guard entities that protect and have titled themselves as *Knights*. These four *Knights* are skilled and very dangerous. They should be engaged with the utmost caution. Little else is known on their identities." Will backed away from the computer to throw in his own thoughts. "Knights huh? They must be worried sick about her."

His pupils were next drawn to a portion of writing below the title *Objective*. He read. "Her highly influential abilities are too powerful for such a young girl to wield so freely. Since Lili's location has been classified as *unknown* she has been deemed hazardous to the universe. For this reason, she must first be located then neutralized." His head jerked back in surprise. "Oh my God! They're gonna kill her!" A genuine level of worry awakened in the boy's heart. Did Will feel a sincere concern toward Lili's well-being?

With his thirst for top-secret knowledge quenched, he packed up his laptop and started heading back home. Will did not forget to take the two IO helmets with him.

Back at the studio/warehouse, Ky was halfway finished with a pile of dishes as Will came waltzing in.

Ky heard the door close to his rear. "What's up, Will?" Ky graciously asked not turning around to see the boy.

Will slowly, and more importantly, quietly advanced toward Ky's back as he answered. "Nothing,"

"Where'd you go?"

"No place in particular." Will crept mutely to Ky's

unsuspecting back.

"What'd you do?"

"Nothing," The boy blankly retorted as he closed the gap between Ky and himself.

"Well, I've been cleaning all day. I…"

Suddenly, Will leaped to Ky's back holding one of the IO helmets, which Will placed over Ky's head and forced down in mid-jump. You can be sure that the program *Lili Blocker* was fully activated in the helmet.

Ky screeched as if he was dying and wildly flung around his body. Ky dropped to his knees while clawing at the helmet as if it was inflicting intense pain upon him. Ky released another loud cry before fainting. Ky's body fell limp and slapped against the hard tile floor like a fish out of water.

Will was baffled. He didn't expect that drastic a reaction. He wasn't sure if he caused Ky serious damage. A new worry formed in the boy as he approached Ky's motionless body. What had the boy done? He didn't expect that to happen in the least. Actually, Will wasn't sure what was going to happen. He leaned over Ky concerned about his friend's wellbeing.

"Ky?" Will whispered nearing his fallen comrade. Will so desperately wanted Ky to respond and take the guilt of killing his friend off his shoulders.

Will didn't notice as Ky balled up his right fist. When Will leaned close enough, Ky let him have it. Ky drove his fist as fast as he could into the boy's stomach. Ky began to stand as Will fell flat on his bottom from the punch. Ky stood erect and for the first time in a while, something about him had returned.

"What the hell is going on!? Why do I have this crap on my head!? And for God's sakes why do I have this crazy-ass headache!? I feel like a part of my brain was just ripped out!" Ky raged demanding to get some immediate answers.

Will stayed on the floor cradling his stomach from the pain of Ky's blow, although that didn't really matter to him. Will sniffled on the verge of tears. "Ky, it's you, it's really you."

IV

The Day the World Woke Up Pt. A

Will had finally restored his friend to his former glory. The boy held no detail back as he reenacted all that had been transpiring since Lili had shown up. He went on and on about what the overly chipper girl had been doing to them and what she was capable of. He also recounted everything he knew about the IO. Will told Ky about Wes Vega and how the IO had been watching them. He fully described how the outside world had been reduced to a bubbly band of school kids and how everyone was being tricked. It was finally his chance to explain himself to a person who would listen to him, but more importantly, a person who would believe him.

"...so that's about it. For the past week and a half you've been being controlled by a little girl." Will concluded laying out the entire situation to an overwhelmed Ky.

Ky simply sat there absorbing the fantastic story that Will had unveiled. Ky's expression was camouflaged by the IO helmet sitting around his head, but you can be assured he was none too happy. He remained silent for a few moments before his voice bumped out from behind the helmet. "What about Jina?"

Will wasn't too sure what Ky's question was driving at, so he responded. "What do you mean?" the boy threw on a slightly bewildered face.

"Well," Ky fortuitously headed to the fridge explaining. "Having Jina under that so called little girl's spell could be a big problem. She's way too destructive." Ky illustrated while retrieving a beer.

"Yeah, I know." Will contemplated with a hand to his chin. "We need to have her wake up or be contained all together. It's too dangerous having her on Lili's side."

"Getting a chance to do that will be no easy task my friend." Ky confided as he sat at the small dining table twisting off the cap of his glass bottle. The drink's carbonation fizzed as the lid separated from the bottle's lip.

"Don't worry, I think I got a plan." Will assured, seemingly still in thought.

"Cool," Ky said in a manner that fully expressed his relief. He put the Jina dilemma out of his mind as he raised the bottle up to take a sip. The glass clinked against the flashy metallic helmet that completely engulfed his head. "Oh this sucks!" Ky slammed the beer on the table as he realized just how much the helmet did indeed *suck*.

"Sorry," Will sincerely apologized. "That's the only way I know that you're really you."

"How am I supposed to eat?" An aggravated Ky questioned. "Tell me how I'm gonna eat?"

"It's only till we resolve all this, so chill out."

"Fine, then let's set up to catch this broad."

"Now you're talking." An evil smile grew across the

boy's cheeks. "Let's do this."

The guys set up for Will's supposed plan. How did they plan to best the greatest warrior their planet had ever known? They had quite an undertaking on their hands.

Hours later, closing in on nighttime, Lili and Jina had finally arrived. Lili walked in first. Lili's eyes met only with little Will. Will was just standing in the middle of the apartment. He wasn't holding or doing anything, he only stood there.

Will waved at Lili and smiled much like she had to him many times before. "Hi!"

Lili threw up her hands a tad confused. "What's going on?" She began to approach Will heading deep into the studio/warehouse.

"Oh nothing," Will voiced appearing at that moment as the more playful one.

"Where's Ky?" Lili honestly asked.

"Don't you know?" Will cleverly shot back at the girl.

Right about then, Jina passed the threshold of the door. As she came in, she was obviously dazed from Lili's mental hypnosis, which ended up working against the little devil. Something started falling toward Jina's head. It was Ky. He had been holding onto the metal guardrail on the balcony above the entrance and had been waiting to get the drop on Jina, literally. He made sure to drop and not to jump to ensure the most minimal amount of noise. He also made sure to plummet at her from directly above so he could go undetected. In all honesty, if Jina was her normal self, she still would've noticed and dealt with him accordingly, but luckily for him she was not. With Lili in such close proximity, her mental grip on Jina was very strong, and that caused Jina's sensory skills to be compromised. Lili didn't notice Ky, therefore Jina didn't either.

Ky was holding the other IO helmet that Will had confiscated in his other hand. He shoved the masked helmet over Jina's head until it locked into place down by her chin. The gorgeous warrior let out a blood-curdling scream as the helmet made contact with her perfect head. Ky's body collided with Jina's and they both hit the floor. Ky began to get back up, but Jina remained on the floor as the program *Lili Blocker* rearranged her memories.

Then something happened that wasn't part of Will's plan. Ky slipped on his compact photon cannon as quick as he could and pointed it at the little girl with incredible characteristics.

Will's accomplished face was switched with one of worry as he watched Ky pull a powerful gun on a little girl. "Ky!"

"Get out now!" Ky forcefully ordered at Lili. Lili was caught in a debilitating fear. She was frozen as the elaborate charade she had put up around them came crumbling down. She was like a deer in headlights and had instantly been reduced to the normal little girl she appeared to be. "I-I," She stuttered.

"Ky! What are you doing!?" Will shouted in a horrified amazement at his guardian's barbaric actions.

"Shut up Will! Get out now or take a photon blast to the face." Ky blankly threatened as he pushed the massive barrel closer to her nose.

The tears started flowing from her eyes as she informed. "I-I...have no place to go."

"Like I care,"

"Ky! Stop it!" Will demanded.

"What's wrong with you Will!?" Ky argued. "You told me what she can do. This is what she deserves. I thought you'd be happiest of all."

"Not like this Ky!" Will rebutted. "She's just a girl."

"No," Ky reasoned. "She's from uncharted space with crazy mind powers. She could be anything."

Jina started coming to. Her body slowly grew taller as the tension-filled situation was reaching its climax. As Jina awoke, it was as if her mind had awakened as well. The slate in her memory banks of the past week and a half had been wiped clean. She had emerged as her old self, with the exception of a technologically heightened helmet that masked her angelic face. She placed a hand on her head as if something inside her cranium was bothering her.

"Awww," She moaned from a pulsating sore in her skull. "What's wrong with my head? What's going on?" Her neck swiveled to her left and she spotted Ky pointing a photon cannon at a seemingly innocent girl. She also noticed Will a little more centered in the room behind the girl appearing rather worried. "Ky, why do you have a gun drawn on that small girl?"

"Stay out of this Jina." Ky barked in a way that respected Jina's power and yet let him hold onto his masculinity.

"No Jina, stop him." Will ordered off on the sidelines.

If anyone had been able to peer through Jina's helmet they would've seen an image of instant conflict grace her visage.

"She has been controlling you and me for the past week or so. She's too dangerous and she needs to be gone." Ky ranted stating his case to the feminine warrior who could easily tear every person in the room apart if she so chose to.

"I wasn't entirely controlling any of you!" Lili cried out in a last ditch effort to save herself.

The cannon's charge began to hum as Ky coldly tossed out an ultimatum at the frightened little Lili. "You got one second to go before I shoot a hole through your cute baby face."

Will slid between the barrel of the cannon and Lili. His arms were stretched out as if he was protecting her. An insane fearless determination was spread across his face. Whether it was a bluff or not, it was clear that Will was not just going to stand by while Ky killed her. Will had been watching her eyes from time to time and he kept catching glimpses of a scared lonely expression that the boy was all too familiar with. Will figured no matter what she did in those eleven days, she did not deserve such a cruel fate.

Only one of Ky's eyebrows lifted inside the helmet due to the interesting move Will made. He was certainly not going to fire with Will in the way, but he didn't want to lose control of the situation, so he kept the gun directed at the children. Ky's voice growled inside the helmet. "Will, get out of the way."

"No!" Will defied. "This has gone too far!"

"Will," Ky began to explain in a calming tone. "She's too dangerous, do you understand? The farther away she is from here, the better off we are."

"Are you really gonna shoot a kid?"

"We don't know what she is. She screws with minds, remember? She could just be making us think she looks that way."

"Impossible!" Will began to elaborate his reasoning. "Since she got here I've been immune to her, and now that you have that helmet, you are too." Will shook his head and slightly stepped aside putting his hands out as if he was showcasing the terrified puffy-eyed Lili. "You see? She's still a little girl, so she has to be a little girl."

"I don't care," Ky insisted.

Jina chimed her opinion from the side using context clues to get her up to speed. "I must agree with Will. Whatever she's been doing to us, we're still here and in one piece. So I don't think she should be shot in the face with a cannon."

"But that also doesn't mean we should keep her hanging around." Ky said back to Jina trying to get his point across.

"Do you know what that army is going to do to her outside!?" Will squealed. "They're gonna kill her Ky!"

"That's not our problem." Ky plainly stated bearing a logically harsh heart.

"Come on Ky. Lighten up." Jina proposed. "Why not sleep on it and figure out what to do in the morning."

"But Jinaaa…" Ky whined.

"Kyyy," She mocked back at him.

The hum of the cannon gradually ceased as the gun rested at Ky's side. Ky finally gave in to the other two's wishes, but he resented his decision. "Fine! But she is out of here in the morning, got it?"

"Yeah," Will hastily concurred with a satisfied childish grin on his mug.

Ky stormed off to his sheet metal shack of a room. Ky spout out his mouth before slamming his bedroom door shut. "I'm gonna TRY and go to bed with this stupid contraption on my head. Hope she chokes you to death in your sleep."

The moment died down leaving the remaining three in an awkward silence. The kids looked up to Jina in a longing unsure gaze. They didn't know what to do and searched Jina's shielded face for guidance. She could sense the little one's feelings by the expressions they were delivering to her.

Jina cleared her throat. "Ahem, I'm gonna spend the night here on the couch. Why don't you guys go upstairs and try and get some rest. Tomorrow we all need to sit down and figure out what to do with her."

"Okay," Will and Lili complied seeming somewhat saddened.

Lili was still sniffling. Her face was red and moist, her heart was racing, and her eyes had flushed out too many tears. She was still shook up from the confrontation and as Jina took her place on the couch, Will could read the worry plastered on Lili's face. He had felt that same thing before in the past. The feeling carries a crippling uncertainty to what the next day will bring. Will knew that fear well and had learned to cope with it, but he was afraid that Lili might not have been as fortunate. Will gently grasped Lili's hand certain that all she wanted at that second was someone to lead her.

"Come on, let's go." He whispered to Lili in a soft confidence. He slowly led her upstairs by her hand in a way that conveyed his compassionate side.

Lili quietly sniffled as she was being walked up to the stilted aluminum room. Her demeanor took a complete one-eighty from the way she was when she arrived. Her carefree fun confident disposition was instantly replaced with a sad crying vulnerable little girl. She could feel the citywide facade that she had constructed falling to pieces around her. The party was over and Lili was taking it hard.

They went inside the room and Will flopped onto his bed dead tired. He spread out for a moment and shut his eyes, but then he remembered Lili was in the room and sat up. He saw Lili still by the door with her head hung down in shame. A few last tears squeezed out of her eyes and she rubbed them away with her sleeve. She was obviously distraught and Will felt like he was the only one who could make her feel better. He trotted over in a playfully annoyed manner and started nudging her toward the bed.

"Come on. cry baby," Will joked trying to pick her spirits up. "Get into bed."

Lili didn't give a response; she just let Will shove her over to the beds. She timidly ascended the crudely built bunk bed with her own guilt weighing her down. She finally made it to the top bunk and laid in it like she had before. Unlike the previous nights, she wasn't trying to talk to Will. She was too traumatized by what had happened to be her usual chipper, lively self.

Will wasn't sure what to say to her. He wanted to make her feel better, but he had no idea how. For so long he wished someone would see the truth about her, but ever since his friends were awakened to it, Will had been feeling bad for her. He got what he wished for, but the end result was not what he bargained for. He deeply contemplated what to tell her, but consistently kept coming up with nothing. His thoughts tired his brain and he began to doze off.

"Will," Lili said loud enough to snap the boy's eyelids back open in a flash.

"Hmm?" Will grunted as an invite for her to continue.

"Do you hate me?" She wondered.

"No. I don't hate you. I just hate what you're doing." Will calmly explained.

"Why? I'm just trying to make everyone have fun."

"Yeah, but people can't have fun all the time or nothing would get done."
"Really!?"

"Of course, this world hasn't been able to function since you took away its free will."

"Oh," She sighed as if the words hurt her like a sharpened dagger. "I'm sorry, I've just been lonely since I left home."

"Why'd you leave home anyway?" Will curiously questioned.

"My gift isn't as effective there as it is here. Everything there is so expected, so planned, so…what's the word I'm looking for?"

"Prearranged?" Will guessed.

"That's it, prearranged, thank you. I just don't want my entire life scheduled for me. Did you know my husband has already been chosen for me?"

"Wow," Will sympathized. A tiny hidden hatred of that particular piece of knowledge mixed into the boy's emotions.

"I just wanted a few surprises in my life, so I disguised myself as a commoner and set out on the next craft off my planet. I've been hopping Universal Trekkers ever since. Now, I'm here, and with you, one of the only people I can't control in any way." She felt comfortable enough with Will to divulge her life story to him.

"Your parents must be worried sick about you." Will remarked.

"I don't know about that." Lili revealed. "My mother, the Queen, is too busy ruling the planet to pay attention to me, and I don't have a father."

"What do you mean *you don't have a father*?" Will inquired.

"I mean just that. My father is the energies of all there is or ever will be. I was birthed with no actual father. That's why the majority of my gene strands are pure."

"Whoa," Will said absolutely astonished. He shook his head then decided to press his previous point. "Still, she loves you. She's just busy. If she didn't she wouldn't have sent those knights after you."

Suddenly Lili jumped up in her bed and her speech became hysterical. "The knights!? Where!? Did you see them!?"

"Wow! Calm down! I didn't see them." Will assured. "I only read about them in the IO data banks."

"Oh good," Lili whispered with relief as she rested her body flat on the higher bunk again.

"But they are looking for you." Will warned. "That's what the report said."

"I'd rather die than have them escort me back

home." Lili didn't hesitate to admit. "That planet doesn't need me anyway."

"Are you kidding?" Will blurted out holding a heavy honesty. "The planet is probably lost without you."

"You really think so?"

"Yeah," Will rang with his words as sure as a bell. "Lili, the things you can do…" Will paused for a second scouring his brain for the perfect way to prove his point. "…the things you can do, some can't be done. You're a very special person Lili."

Lili blushed deeply and was thankful that Will couldn't see it. "Thank you Will."

The conversation had grown sentimental and Will forced it back to a playful discussion when he said. "So what's it like? You know, cruising through people's minds?"

"I think I can best describe it to you as hacking."

"No kidding,"

"Yeah, some files or functions of the brain I'll use and some I won't. It all depends on the situation."

"That's amazing." Will complemented.

"Yeah, I don't like to delve into too many memories or intentions. Some peoples' are very dark and scary."

"Yeah, I bet." As Will said that, his mind traveled to thoughts of Ky.

"Yeah," She agreed in a soft tone.

Will laughed. "Ha, you can control the real world and I can control the cyber world. We'd make a pretty good team."

"We would, wouldn't we."

"Can I ask you something?" Will graciously asked.

"Yeah,"

"Well, it's a favor really."

"Go ahead."

"Could you stop controlling people?" The boy

requested to the girl with the outrageous mind powers.

"Why?"

"Because I want things how they used to be. Because I wanna look a person in the eye and not wonder if it's just a third person you…Because I wanna be able to talk to my friends without him wearing a metal head."

"Hmmm?" She pondered the pros and cons in her head. "I never thought of that. I do it so fluently I never thought of just shutting it off all together."

"Please," Will pleaded. "For me?"

Lili smiled. "Sure Will, for you."

"Well goodnight Lili."

"Goodnight Will."

"Lights off," The boy commanded.

As the lights dimmed to black, the kids drifted off to dream land. Even with Ky's savage and vicious threats, it didn't take them long to fall asleep at all.

Will's reoccurring dream came to him anew. It was all the same: the bright blinding sun shining between the cracks of three somehow soothing figures. Two of the figures seemed parental in nature while the significantly younger one was implied to be their child. All three were blackened by an intense shadow that was cast by the white light high above them. It was getting to the point that whenever the boy slept he was locked in that moment.

This time around, Will didn't remember much more in ways of dialogue. Later, when he awakened, no new events would stick out in his memories. Although there were a few clues that Will picked up on that he hadn't noticed before. The first thing of some significance that Will realized was that he was standing in a large grassy field. The next thing was dealing with the face of the fatherly figure. He focused intently on his mug and found it to not be as shrouded in shade as he previously assumed. He could clearly make out the features of his masculine face.

Something about the man was eerily familiar. He knew the man's countenance was that of a stranger's, but it did closely resemble that of a person he was acquainted with. Will just couldn't put his finger on who. His look seemed like a more rugged version of someone he knew. It was the man's short brown hair cut that impeded Will from figuring out who the mysterious guy looked like.

When Will awoke, this advancing development would secretly swirl around in the boy's mind.

The next morning, nothing was the same. The entire planet was released from Lili's trance; she had granted Will's favor. They had awakened with no knowledge of the eleven days they spent in a giddy child-like anarchy. Everyone had their lives flipped on its head at that moment, unsure of what to do or even what day it was. That day was a sloppy, but first step toward the world regaining order. It was not a joyous day for anybody.

Early that morning, about fifty miles north of Ky's studio/warehouse, was a large town called Buckton. A massive building in the middle of nowhere was alive with activity. The building had remained nearly undamaged for those eleven days due to its lonely discreet location and the lack of people occupying the building when Lili took over. That well-guarded building was the liveliest place anywhere that day.

The building was the Galactic Federal Bureau Department Building and its surrounding fields were swamped with IO crafts and tanks. As G.F.B. federal agents woke up that morning, the presence of the IO forces were quickly realized. Not knowing where the army was from or what it was doing, The G.F.B. formally requested that all the IO forces be summoned to the closest federal office for interrogations and to give them a chance to explain themselves. Rather than breakout in an all-out war between the G.F.B. and the IO, the Invisible Organization simply complied. The G.F.B. was attempting to unravel the mysteries behind the world's lengthy slumber and the arrival of the dangerous dancing army. The proceedings could either have ran smoothly or erupted into a gruesome blood bath.

G.F.B. soldiers dashed about the loud, rambunctious offices inside. Secretaries and office workers hurriedly filed paperwork, made phone calls, and clicked computer keyboards like mad, trying to get to the bottom of everything. The G.F.B. that retained the most authority was left stressed and baffled by the day, and was burdened with the hefty task of explaining what had been going on. IO soldiers crowded the halls and the waiting rooms, sworn to secrecy by their superiors. They lingered in any space available like stone statues, while heads of both forces tried straightening things out in the most covert meeting the planet had ever known. Yelling and rage-filled bickering became routine that day and a lot of people from both parties were slowly growing convinced that nothing would ever go back to normal.

In mid-evening, a G.F.B. detective burst into the double-door entrance like he owned the place. A few of his most loyal G.F.B. subordinates followed behind the detective retaining a respectful distance. Every eye that fell on him as he entered felt the thick block of tension that accompanied the detective. He marched down the hall like a vengeful bullet and every head swiveled to follow him as he passed. He hiked in like an uncompromising demon about to exact his deepest and most hated revenge. People could basically feel the aggressive energy projecting from the detective. The detective was intimidating enough under most circumstances, but that particular morning, he was really pissed off.

The unyielding man was known as Detective Lee. He was among the most bold, respected, and revered detectives that the G.F.B. had ever produced. Detective Lee preferred to stay in a commanding *in charge* position, so the recent incidents they faced were especially difficult for him to take. The hardened federal agent epitomized the idea of a slick, fast talker. Coupled with his borderline cocky attitude, wherever he went, he could never simply be ignored.

He stood a mighty five-foot nine inches, but don't be fooled by his lack of stature. Detective Lee had more testosterone in his left hand than two six foot men. The detective had short wavy thick black hair that was usually tucked under a fedora hat. A wide smoggy cigar could be found crimped between his lips at most times, and his chiseled cement slab of a chin rested right beneath it. His medium build had a trench coat draped around it that was reminiscent of the detectives of the distant past. His tactical gear and weaponry were hidden behind very outdated clothes, giving him the feeling that he was straight from a long lost era. Every aspect about the man was a true testament to his ridiculously high level of intensity and professionalism.

Detective Lee beamed through the halls of the G.F.B. building like a purpose-filled juggernaut. It was as if some unstoppable spirit was driving him as he charged into the heart of the building.

"Sir?" One of Lee's following soldiers timidly addressed the detective.

"What!?" Lee roared back.

"Excuse me for saying this, but I don't think this is such a good idea." The scared soldier warned.

"Like a give a flippin' freak about that." The detective noisily chattered. "Nearly two weeks drop off the face of the planet, then some bizarro army is miraculously around and I'm not supposed to ask any questions? Nun-uh! I'm not putting that can of beans back on the shelf and calling it kosher. Am I right?"

"Right," The soldier complied to not further aggravate Lee.

"You bet your ass I'm right."

The detective and his men sifted through the bustling crowd catching many curious eyes along the way. His determined stroll walked him up to an encased office with a glass door. Plain white writing was scrolled across the simple blinded glass door. The official text written on the door read *Superior Director Gerald S. Parabus*. The small office was filled with six or seven G.F.B. bigwigs along with an IO representative. The discussion taking place in that room would determine the future relationship between the G.F.B. and the IO: either it would be one of cooperation or they'd take a less favorable stance towards each other. To keep the security of the important meeting fair, one G.F.B. soldier was stationed outside the door on the east side and an IO soldier was posted on its west side. Detective Lee waltzed right up to the office and motioned to the door as if he was going to briskly walk in.

The G.F.B. soldier stationed at the door placed a sturdy arm to Lee's chest to halt the detective's advancement. Detective Lee's pupils zipped down to the man's hand on his chest in absolute astonishment that the soldier had the gall to touch him without warning. Lee vacantly threatened to the soldier. "Unless you wanna pull back a stump, you'll get your hand off me now."

"Sorry detective," The soldier apologized as his hand dropped back down to his side. "But no one is to be admitted inside accept for directors and secretaries."

"Okay chum," Detective Lee played along stifling his aggravation for a moment. "I'll bite. Who gave you that order?"

"Parabus himself sir,"

"Superior Director Parabus, huh? So you shouldn't have any big to-do if I go in and ask him myself." Lee figured as he headed to the door again.

This time, it was the soldier's words that stopped the detective in his tracks. "Sorry sir, but I was given explicit directions to keep you out especially."

"Well." Lee backed away from the door. "I don't like the way this sits in my stomach." The detective didn't hesitate to confess. "So, what am I supposed to do out here, huh? Sit on my hands till they fall asleep?"

The soldier didn't need to answer the loaded question. Right then, the door to the office creaked open and a bunch of men in suits casually walked out. In G.F.B. circles, all the men leaving the room were very important people. All of them were secretaries that headed several different branches of the G.F.B. security force. They all had much more authority than Lee did, but the detective didn't recognize any of them. To Lee, they were all bureaucrats and smooth talkers who had forgotten how it was to be a soldier on the battlefield. Even though they were technically his bosses, Detective Lee had far less respect for them than his loyal soldiers that wouldn't think twice to follow him into certain death. The secretaries silently passed by Lee acting as if they didn't see the intimidating detective that stood directly in their path like an angered statue.

"If I knew which one of these guys was the commanding officer of this kooky army, I'd strangle him here and now." Detective Lee whispered to one of his subordinate soldiers behind him.

"That would be me!" A voice projected out of the small group of suited men heading away from Parabus' office.

The men continued sauntering out of the department

building while one remained standing there. He just stayed there eying down the detective, ready for his verbal assault as the other men walked around him. He was the only man in the small crowd that had no ties to the G.F.B.; he was IO affiliated. The man was Wes Vega, and he stood there as stoic and cool as ever.

Detective Lee marched up to the brave young man examining every inch of him along the way. Lee posted himself inches from Wes' face and insulted. "This is the head of this so called Invisible Organization? I didn't know they allowed babies to run armies."

"I'm not the leader of the IO, genius. I'm just the head of this assignment." Wes bantered back.

Lee smoothly probed, attempting to indirectly gain more information on the subject. "And which assignment would that be, Boy Scout?"

"Come on," Wes laughed off. "You're going to have to be sneakier than that soldier."

"That's detective to you punk." Lee corrected.

"Really?" Wes further instigated. "Aren't you a little old to be a detective?"

"Aren't you a little young to be such a wise-ass?" Detective Lee instantly fired back.

The heated conversation was very high profile. G.F.B. soldiers, IO soldiers, and the department's pencil-pushers alike began to attract to the rather loud discussion. It was just like children in grade school hallways. As the apprehension mounted, more people flocked to Lee and Wes. The growing tension lit the air with the electricity of an impending fist fight.

"Look old man," Wes Vega continually pressed his luck. "Your rank is beneath me sir. I don't need to waste my time talking to you."

"Let me tell you something Boy Scout." Detective Lee lectured while pointing a forced finger up to the young man's nose. "You have no real connection to the G.F.B. therefore, I can turn you to a pretzel where you stand."

"Well actually, with the agreement we're making, I will have immunity. So you will lose your job if I'm touched." Wes forewarned while staying calm and collected.

"I have chunks of punks like you traveling through my intestines."

"Are you saying you wanna dance grandpa? I'm right here."

"You may wanna shut your flappers before you find yourself on the receiving end of a back door whistle maker."

"What the hell is that?" Wes truly wondered breaking the intensity for just a moment. A queer expression was slapped on his face.

A G.F.B. soldier behind Lee in the middle of the forming group interpreted the detective's cryptic metaphor. "Uh…that means he's gonna punch you…Uh…in the teeth with uh…the back of his hand." The soldier accepted a few smiles, cheers, and high-fives from his comrades for his well thought out translation of Lee's confusing words.

Lee and Wes faced each other again and immediately snapped back into their argument.

"Look old-timer, I gotta go for an important meeting with your bosses, but I'll be back, so try and not die from old age till I return." Wes humiliated the detective nearly twice his age.

The veins in Lee's brow popped out of his head as his rage reached its pinnacle. The detective's short temper was all used up as his right fist instinctively flew through the air toward Wes' unflinching mug. A G.F.B. soldier caught Lee's arm below the elbow before it had a chance to make contact with agent Vega. His other hand motioned for a blow, but was again stopped before it could rise too high.

It took a total of four soldiers to completely subdue the enraged detective. It wasn't because they felt Wes was right and Lee was wrong, but because they didn't want their superior officer discharged due to one moment of blinding anger. They were looking out for him.

"Let me go! Let me go!" Lee screeched as he wrestled with his own men in the middle of the building.

One of the soldiers said while holding back his commanding officer back. "With all due respect, no sir."

"Lee! Get in here!" Roared out from behind the open office door.

Detective Lee rustled out of his men's grip and jerked his arm free of them. Still a little red in the face, the detective adjusted his coat with a manly tug to his collar. He made a hand gesture as if he was telling Wes that he wasn't even worth bothering with. Before walking away, Lee grumbled at the much younger Wes. "You better keep one eye aimed at your back, Boy Scout."

Wes Vega's only response to Detective Lee's threat was a cocky half-grin. Wes watched Lee disappear into Superior Director Parabus' office with the hem of his long trench coat dancing behind him. Wes remarked on his first impression of the memorable detective to one of the IO soldiers. "Wow, isn't he a little ball of ruggedness." Wes then turned around and headed out to a meeting deemed too important for the likes of the detective.

Detective Lee entered the office to find the place left in the same condition as it usually was. Waiting in front of the cold hard wooden desk were two lonely matching chairs. Government files and papers were strewn on the desktop as if they were of little importance. The rest of the desktop was cluttered with official junk like a small laptop, pens, paperweights, and framed family pictures. There was even an old time lamp set there even though the room was already well lit. The back wall, which was the only wall not made up of glass, had a capacious bulletin board on it. The bulletin board had musty profile pictures or descriptions of the most wanted criminals in the tri-solar area pinned to it. About half of the profiles had an enormous black *x* on them to indicate the felons that had been captured or killed. The paper profiles were sloppily arranged having no real order to them. The only other object in the barren office was a three file high, light blue filing cabinet in the corner.

The man seated behind the desk was *the man* himself, Gerald Simon Parabus, the top man of the G.F.B.'s militaristic force. He was a rather chunky fifty-two year old man with a face as serious as a tumbling cement block. His head was balding on its peak, but his black frizzy hair was grown out a few inches on the side and back. His pores were the size of hubcaps and his arms were hairy; he just wasn't the prettiest thing to look at. But you could tell by the gaze in his eyes that he was a man who held a lot of weight.

Parabus was dressed in a white business shirt that had its first button undone, no tie, and sleeves rolled up to his elbows. His big belly slightly hung over a leather belt that wrapped around a pair of dress pants. The pants led to Parabus' worn out dress shoes. The pants, shoes and belt were all a matching boring brown color. Even though his attire could correctly be described as *business casual*, it was all just too disheveled to seem professional. As Lee walked in, Parabus blew out a plume of smoke and flicked a cigarette head into an ashtray on his desk.

Detective Lee slumped into one of the waiting chairs ready for whatever speech Parabus was going to dish out. They both sat in the office for a moment without a word between them; they were just sizing each other up.

Then Detective Lee threw up his hands and bellowed. "All right, what did I do now?"

Parabus sat their calmly taking another drag from his

smoke while he mentally formed exactly what he was going to say to the impatient detective. As he put his cigarette out, he asked the detective. "You know, there are only a small handful of detectives I actually know. How come I'm talking to you at least once a month?"

"Because I'm the one who gets the most results." Lee answered with confidence.

"You're also the one who does his own thing the most."

"Let me know if I've broken any codes or bylaws, sir."

"Not recently!"

"Well, there you go."

"You don't need to break any rules to be a pain in my ass, Lee!" Parabus howled. He then began ranting to further prove his point. "Like today, you're here on a routine case update and it almost ends up in a fist fight in the most prestigious federal building. What's that all about?"

"There's something happening on this planet that needs to be addressed and I don't think we should leave it to that army that no one has ever heard of." The detective said articulating his true feelings as well as he could.

"I know how you feel." Parabus sympathized. "I'm not a big fan of it either, but all their stuff checks out. I have no choice but allow them to carry on with their investigation without interference."

"This rooster ain't sittin' well in my hen house. I can't just ignore this Parabus." The detective persisted.

"You can, and you will. You see, this is what I'm talking about Lee! Your gut might be right most of the time, but this is something that I'm ordering you not to get involved in!" Director Parabus yelled imposing his authority on the detective.

Detective Lee sat quietly for a second before his soft

rebuttal. "Maybe I wouldn't have to if I was allowed access to more information."

Parabus instantly denied. "That's classified. I may have been able to tell you if you didn't turn down those numerous promotion opportunities we gave you."

"To be frank, sitting at an office desk all day hasn't exactly thrilled me to the bone, no offense. Plus, I'm no good with computers." Detective Lee explained.

"Be that as it may, that's the reason I can't help you now."

"This is a load of crap." Lee said barely relieving any bit of the mountain of anger that had manifested inside him.

"Look! I want you to chill out, finish your follow up investigation, and get on the first craft off this planet." Parabus ordered.

"But Parabus..." Groaned out of Lee's mouth like a reflex.

"I mean it Lee!" Crowed Parabus forcefully. "You better stay in your jurisdiction or you're out and that's no joke! NO NOSING AROUND!"

Lee calmly took the scream that his boss delivered. He got up and stepped to the door without speaking a word. The detective nonchalantly grabbed the office doorknob and opened it to leave. He then turned back to Director Parabus and droned. "Yes sir, whatever you command sir; will do sir."

"One complaint and you're out." Parabus summed up with the sincerity of a car crash.

Detective Lee slammed the glass office door shut behind him before he started barreling out of the building with the same fervor as when he entered. The detective's face was balled up into a scrunched tight knot of frustration. As his soldiers followed him once again, it was easy to determine the massive level of anger rising to the surface of Lee's rosy face. The detective had just received a lecture from one of the only people in the galaxy who he couldn't give lip back to and he didn't like it. Lee was the type of man to go against the grain if he felt it was right, and sometimes that meant going against his own superiors.

About halfway out of the building, a compassionate soldier following the detective said. "I heard what happened in there. So are we wrapping up this follow up investigation and going home, or are we checking out all these bizarre events?"

"You bet your ass we're checking out the weirdness." Detective Lee declared projecting out a defiant vibe. "This is what I have on this unofficial case..." Without Director Parabus realizing it, Detective Lee was closely studying the top secret documents spread out on the desk while being lectured. The detective knew back then what he was called into the office for, and he knew the Director's decision before even one word was uttered. Lee went along with the *bad cop* conversation to spend as much time in that office as he could gaining information. "It has something to do with a little girl and mind powers, whatever the freak that means"

"But...sir..." Fell out of the soldier's mouth stumbling all over the words, worried about the authoritative implications Lee's illegal investigation may cause.

The soldier was ignored as Detective Lee spewed out more facts he came across during his covert analysis. "Also, I want this number checked out." He demanded so unbelievably fast that his men could barely register what he said. "Seven, five, five, oh, oh, oh, oh, oh, two, three, two, six, two, two, two, seven, nine, five, six, two, oh." He recited as clearly as if he was reading it off a sheet of paper in front of him. One of Lee's soldiers scrambled for his cellphone as Lee called out each number. Luckily, the man was able to punch in the numbers real quick before his hurried mind forgot it. The soldier was glad to have averted the severe repercussions that accompany asking Detective Lee to repeat something.

"Uh," The soldier who got the number stalled. "What is the number?"

"Not the faintest clue," Lee had no problem admitting. "But that's what I want you pack of jackals to find out."

"Sir, I hate to bring this up." Another soldier pre-apologized. "But what if your superiors get wind of us snooping around?"

"They won't." The detective confidently assured. "If they want me to stay in my jurisdiction, then that's exactly what I'm gonna do."

"What do you mean?"

"We're officially here to finish the follow-up report on the Diamond of Faith case. My three key witnesses in that case live in Gohanesse, the same place where the bulk of the IO have been hanging around." Detective Lee explained dropping hints of his plan.

"Oh, I get it." One of the soldiers behind Lee thought he figured it out. "So we go down to Gohanesse, using interviewing the witnesses as cover for us being there."

"Negative," Lee chimed disagreeing with the soldier. "You're only half right. We are actually going to interview them."

"Why?" One of the confused soldiers reacted. "Do you think we'll come up with some clues from them?"

Detective Lee theorized. "I think they're directly involved."

"How do you know?"

Lee lit a cigar in the middle of the federal building as he slyly replied. "Something in my gut is telling me."

"What about Parabus and the other higher ups?"

Lee answered like a true cool warrior for righteousness. "We leave them like cockroaches, in the dark."

Lili's eyes cracked ajar much slower and with less vigor than they ever had that morning. Her body took its time as it set itself into a sitting position. Her face was a slab of pure worry that couldn't be wiped away. Something was obviously bothering her down to the deepest reaches of her carefree soul. Perhaps she worried because her whole charade was unmasked, or she was saddened because she knew she was going to be forced to leave, or even maybe she was scared to meet a world that wasn't being influenced by her. Whatever the case, it was very apparent that she was extremely reluctant to face that day. But like anyone else who ever confronted a day built of panic, she knew she had to.

Lili dragged herself off the top bunk and inched toward the door. She patiently twisted the doorknob, opened the door, and set foot into the unsure and frightening day. Her pupils fell down to the main living quarters of the studio/warehouse, trying to figure out the overall mood of the large apartment and its roommates. She was somewhat relieved to find the guys downstairs acting quite mundane, as if the intensity of the previous night had vanished. Will was sitting Indian-style in the middle of the couch, using voice commands to change the television channels. Ky had his head shoved in the fridge as he rummaged through its contents in search of something. The surreal atmosphere calmed some of her edgy nerves and it wasn't long before she gathered enough courage to venture on the ground floor and meet her fate. She stood in the center of the expansive room silently, too ashamed of herself to even greet the boys.

"Channel up," Will commanded to the television as

it instantly switched to channel one seventy-three. He watched the programming for a moment before he repeated. "Channel up," The television then changed to station one seventy-four and the boy carried on with this.

"I had a turkey leg in here, where'd it go?" Ky whined with his head buried in the fridge, which still had the mechanical IO helmet wrapped around it.

Will informed with words that lacked any type of enthusiasm. "Uh, Jina took it and ate it while you guys were, you know...being influenced."

"Are you serious!?" Ky shouted. "I was saving that thing."

"Are you for real?" Will bantered putting some emotion to his voice this time around. "That turkey leg was over two weeks old."

"I still would've ate it."

"No big shocker there."

"What about my leftovers from the bar?" Ky further complained.

"I ate that."

"Well, what am I supposed to eat?"

"I don't know. You're a big boy. Make something."

"Fine," Ky finally gave in as he pulled a half full gallon of milk out of the fridge and he lumbered back around facing the apartment interior. That's when he caught sight of Lili standing there with her head hung down in shame. "Hey," Ky blankly said to her while closing the fridge door behind him. He headed over to the cabinets and explained to the girl while fishing for a spoon, a bowl, and some cereal. "Look, I'm sorry I threatened to shoot you in the face with a hand cannon. I may have overreacted a little."

"A little?" Will remarked from the couch.

Ky simply ignored Will and continued. "But in all seriousness, I need you to be out of here by the end of the day. You're too much heat that I don't need to carry."

Will pointed out while turning his upper body around on the couch to face the others. "Ky, have you seen what she can do? Maybe throwing her out isn't the wisest decision."

"Whatever," Ky easily dismissed. "Whether having her here would be good or bad doesn't matter. Either way it's going to come with a butt-load of drama that I don't need to deal with."

"The IO is gonna kill her when they find her. Can you live with that?"

Ky sat down at the white dining table and fixed his bowl of cereal as he said. "Don't even try and lay that guilt-trip on me. The IO is gonna be tied up all day in federal tape, so today is the perfect day to find a new hideout." He smoothly motioned to lift the mouthpiece of the IO helmet away for the bite. He then directed an accusative spoon at the little quiet princess. "Don't you even think about it." He then proceeded to pull the lip of the IO helmet up passed his mouth.

Will slumped back into the couch a little angered, because he couldn't come up with anything else to defend his case. He then glanced at Ky as he suddenly remembered. "Oh, by the way, Ky, that milk went bad a couple of days ago."

As Will was saying that, Ky had just placed the very first bite into his hungry mouth. Will and Lili's eyes were simultaneously glued to Ky, curious as to how he was going to handle himself. Ky delayed and elongated his bites, judging the integrity of the milk and the cereal. Ky's adam's apple bobbed down then back up as he swallowed the stale cereal and the sour milk. Ky dropped the helmet back over his face and concurred. "So it has." Ky, spiteful of a ruined breakfast, threw a rage filled spoon back at the bowl. "That's it! I'm out of here!" Ky quickly got up out of his seat.

"Where you going?" Will inquired.

"I'm gonna go check that my stuff hasn't been tampered with while the warlock-princess over there was mucking everything up."

Will then made sure to clarify to Ky before he exited. "You know, Lili promised not to control anyone anymore. You can take that helmet off."

"I'll keep it on thank you very much." Crossed Ky's lips along with a thick layer of sarcasm spread all over it.

"Suit yourself."

Ky then dictated. "I'm not gonna be gone that long. By the time I come back, I want her out."

Will and Lili's playful expressions both turned empty and quiet. They didn't say a word as Ky left the apartment.

Right after Ky left, Lili dashed up to Will on the couch. "What do I do Will? What do I do?"

Not even really reacting to her, Will just said as he gestured to the television. "Look. Look at everything that's happening because of you."

Lili looked at the television and made herself comfortable on the couch. Her virgin eyes gazed on the carnage that her playing had caused.

"It's on every channel; even the ones that have absolutely no news." Will added.

The broadcast was of a certain news team that only eleven days earlier, were acting like monkeys on the air. As the children watched them on that fateful day, it was all back to business. Their suits were pressed, their hair was neat, and their broadcast was serious and sharp. That news team and the entire world had only been talking about one story that full day. Of course, it was about trying to unravel the mystery of the eleven day time fade.

Lili had caught the well-dressed anchorman in mid-speech. "…and WLGN is committed to give you more details as they develop. Now, back to Kent Kind in the field, Kent!"

The image on the screen changed to a plump man with smooth skin and thin blonde hair that could have been a wig. He held a microphone in front of his nice suit and had a white earpiece that squiggled down his back and away from the television. He was standing on the sidewalk of a popular avenue of commerce that was left devastated. Windows were broken into, and valuable merchandise was strewn about the cluttered street. Walls of all types, even those of pure granite, had holes smashed into them and were riddled with webbed cracks and fissures. A few G.F.B. soldiers roamed into view of the camera trying to keep some type of order. People in the background rummaged through the vast mess, desperately trying to salvage anything they could find from their past lives.

Kent stared straight into the camera for a second as the cue fed into his earpiece. "Thank you, Ron. This morning has been a horrifying mix of emotions. Everyone wants to place the blame on someone, but no one is sure who. Some believe this was all some freak accident; others are looking to the government for an explanation, while others are taking their aggressions out on the arrival of this mysterious new army. Out of all this confusion, one thing is certain, everyone will remember this as a day of crippling travesty."

Suddenly, the footage went into a discouraging montage of emotionally destroyed Gohanesse civilians. Kent Kind's voice narrated the montage, but the tone was slightly lower as if it were prerecorded. The video broadcast showcased ordinary people whose lives were ruined by Lili's horseplay. The broadcast clearly illustrated the horrible aftermath and how it affected the people. Some were business owners with their establishments left vandalized and burglarized, others were being rushed to the hospitals for serious unexplained injuries. Some cried hysterically grieving for lost loved ones. It was a gut-wrenching scene that Lili's wide eyes had a hard time digesting. Will hoped that a certain moral thread was penetrating her brain. The narration purposely coincided with the images on the screen.

Kent narrated. "In every house, on every street corner, on every street, and in every store, there is only one question on everyone's lips. *What happened?* Eleven days vanished off the face of the planet without an explanation, and has left the world looking like a warzone. Some people came to their businesses to find them in shambles, the places left absolutely destroyed. This morning, they come to find their merchandise looted and their walls vandalized. Their dreams, like their goods, have been left dashed and broken on the floor. Maria Walton woke up to find her house in a similar condition, but she's not the only one. Recent information suggests that over eighty-eight percent of all Gohanesse civilians have experienced this, and much more worldwide. Some unfortunate souls like Emanuel Gramatakakis woke up today with a broken arm. A total of three million people got up this morning and realized they needed immediate medical attention, and that number is rapidly growing. Although, none of this is as close to as sad as the news that was broken to Mariebelle Marrano this evening. She found out that her brother is dead. Thousands of heartbreaking stories like this are pouring into the newsroom with seemingly no end in sight. I believe it's safe to say, no one will have any closure until we find out what happened those eleven days. Kent Kind, Gohanesse News Six, Gohanesse."

The news feed flipped back to the anchorman, Ron Jordan, in the newsroom. It seemed Ron had a few questions for field reporter Kent Kind. "Thank you Kent, now what do people think happened in that lost time so far."

The image on the screen changed back to Kent in the field. "That's a mixed bag, Ron. Some people honestly believe it was all some freak accident, while others will go so far to say it was divine intervention from God as a prelude to Armageddon."

The camera feed continually switched back and forth between the two men as the conversation progressed. "Are there any less..." Ron's hands floated around in front of him as he contemplated the precise word usage. "...farfetched theories?"

"Certainly Ron, in fact the major consensus is that this was all caused by the mysterious army. People are getting angry, and everybody is doing their best to prevent a city-wide riot."

"That's some scary stuff, Kent. Now, is anyone blaming the government or the G.F.B.?"

"Oh, absolutely Ron, absolutely." Kent gave one more affirmative head-nod before they cut away from him for good.

Will shifted his head to face Lili. He then said. "You see what you caused? Do you understand now why it was wrong?"

Lili finally pulled her eyes off the television that had completely glossed over and were on the verge of tears. Her overly shiny eyes closed in on Will's face as she pleaded. "I...I was just trying to get people to have fun." Her head fell forward and hung down in shame.

Will watched her unsure how to remedy her growing amount of guilt. They both stayed on the couch silently with a horrid feeling seeping into them.

Lili slinked off the couch and moaned. "I guess I'm gonna go pack."

"Hey, let me give you a hand." Will politely insisted

like a true gentlemen.

The children ran upstairs to fill bags with Lili's belongings, so that she'd be set to find a new home. Will was glad to assist her, but not because he wanted to see her go; he just honestly wanted to help her out in her current situation. They both reluctantly packed.

Thirty-seven minutes later, a cab drove off a dusty dirt road leading to a clearing in a field. The clearing was a five hundred square-yard grassy field that was surrounded by dense green forest. The clearing was located so deep in the forest, that sturdy pine trees towered over and choked the hidden path leading to the field. Once the vehicle reached the clearing, it skidded to a stop and a thin layer of kicked up dust floated around the tires. The cab's passenger side rear door opened and a man with an odd helmet planted his foot onto the perfect grass. The man finished exiting the car and faced out toward the field.

The cab driver rolled down the passenger automatic window and held a card out the door as he said. "And here's your account card Mr. Gracen, and again, thank you for your business. I really needed it; especially today."

"No problem," Ky graciously replied as he retrieved his card from the desperate cab driver. He then watched as the driver wished him a good day and turned the taxi around to head back down the same dirt path they used to arrive there.

Ky's mechanized head turned to face the field once again. The clearing was not a totally barren grassy yard. Peppered in the massive expanse of land were various sized craft hangars and storage houses. Cargo boxes, heavy greasy tools, and giant unappealing vehicles designed for labor were stacked against the walls of the hangars. Some of the hangars housed lavish crafts while others did not. At the far end of the field, just sitting there without a hangar, was a Zenon7 M; one of the newest and most magnificent galactic cruisers at the time. Only a business tycoon or a person of incredible wealth could afford the craft.

As Ky casually walked through the field, his eyes were set on the Zenon7 M. As he continued his stroll, Ky let out a loud envious whistle that accurately portrayed how impressed he was by the grand galactic cruiser. He then commented. "What a sweet ride."

As Ky made his way into the heart of the clearing, he'd peer deep into every hangar and storage house he passed by. He was looking for someone, but the estate seemed abandoned. After a few minutes, Ky's simple plan succeeded as he spotted two people working in one of the hangars. They both appeared to be official grease monkeys. They had on either denim overalls or stained blue pants. They also wore heavy-duty leather worker gloves and small black safety goggles. Everything about their attire screamed that they were mechanics. One was a fat man with short black hair and the other was a near twig with tight curly dirty blonde hair.

The men were focused on checking the engine of the craft in the hangar and didn't even notice Ky stop in the doorway. Ky knocked a couple of times on the hangar's flimsy sheet metal wall to gain the men's attention. The men simultaneously pivoted their heads to look at the man in the doorway.

The scrawny gentlemen took a few steps forward and wiped his oily hands off on a rag as he asked. "May I help you, sir?"

"What are you talking about Cid?" Ky remarked in a tone dripping with confusion. He remembered then that his head was still encased in the IO helmet. "It's me guys, Ky."

They both smiled and harmonized. "Ky!" They happily approached him as friends.

The overly chubby man questioned Ky as he

removed the greasy goggles from his eyes. "Why do you have that helmet on?"

"That's a long story, Vince." Ky answered. Ky then deliberately and hastily changed the subject. "So Red allowed tweedle-dee and dumb to work on the same day?"

As the guys turned back to the craft to resume their work, Cid, the skinny fellow, joked. "Yeah he did. Crazy, ain't it?"

Vince explained as he grabbed his familiar tools. "Yeah, he called us both in this morning to give all the engines a good look over. I guess he's making sure nothing funny happened during that whole crazy time elapsing thing."

"I can hear that." Ky agreed. "Speaking of which, where is the big guy?"

"Uhhh…" Cid thought to himself

"I think he's checking out the Xela26 Hawk." Vince quickly informed with his body already lost in the underbelly of the craft's hull.

"That's right," Cid concurred. "That's over in uhh…hangar twelve."

"Thanks guys, take it easy." Ky said heading out of the hangar.

"See ya," Vince echoed from under the craft.

"Don't get lost out there machine-head." Cid goofed as Ky left.

Ky once again made his way around the open field. He checked the large black numbers painted onto the high walls of the hangars. He was trying to locate the number twelve and a friend. As he continued climbing the hangar number chain, Ky realized that the hangars were not arranged in any particular numeric order. They just seemed randomly numbered; finding Red was proving difficult. Though lucky for Ky, his search wasn't that hard. Red was standing outside of hangar twelve awaiting Ky's arrival. As

Red's features started to become visible in the distance, he saw that Red was cackling at him hysterically. The wild loud giggling did not cease even as Ky neared within mere feet of the man.

It was truly none other than Red Marrado, the widely famous craft mechanic. Red laughed as Ky approached him. "Haha! Man! Why the hell is that on your face?"

"You never know who's trying to get inside your head."

"Cid and Vince told me you had some nutty contraption on your head, but that's just ridiculous." Red continued.

"Yeah, yeah, enough of that," Ky hurried the conversation along.

"Well, how about this then?" Red playfully proposed. "Nina,"

"Nina?"

"Yeah, Nina." Red assured. "She called me this morning looking for you."

"Oh yeah!" Ky recalled with a devilish sound hidden in the words.

"Do me a favor and next time you pick up a piece of tail at the bar, just make up a number, or one day you'll come here to find the Guider in pieces." Red jokingly threatened.

"Does that mean I wouldn't have to pay you anymore?" Ky capered on.

"Hey, I never said I was gonna move the pieces out of the hangar."

"About the Guider, I came to see that it was all right since all that weirdness happened." Ky calmly informed.

"It's fine, I checked it earlier today. Tell you the truth; I didn't even wanna mess with it too much. It purrs like a kitten and works better than ever since you got back

from Arlia."

"Good to hear, that's a load off my mind." Ky articulated.

"So did you bring the sandpaper?" Red inquired.

"Of course," Ky retorted pulling a wad of sandpaper out from his back pocket.
"Well let's get to it."

Back at the studio/warehouse, the children had just finished packing Lili's things. They piled the few bags of luggage near the front door and the moment grew a little awkward as the two good friends prepared to say goodbye.

Will tossed the last bag by the door as he said. "Well, that's it."

"Thank you," Lili said softly and appreciatively. "I guess I better get going."

"Yeah," Will hesitantly uttered in compliance.

Lili intimately spoke her goodbyes accompanied by a friendly punch to the shoulder. "It was awesome meeting you Will."

"It was quite a trip meeting you." Will helped Lili slip one of her bags on her shoulder.
Lili grasped a smaller bag in her tight right hand. Words of pure melancholy left her mouth. "Bye Will."

Will then opened the door for her. As Lili was halfway out the door, Will bantered. "Wait. I just wanna say I'm sorry for how I treated you the first few days. I wish we became cool with each other much sooner."

"It's okay," She reassured.

"Good luck out there and be careful, okay?"

"Okay,"

"Bye Lili,"

"Goodbye Will,"

She stepped out into the small shot-up yard heading toward the blown-up sidewalk without looking back. Will watched her walk away for a second carrying a backpack, a sizable gym bag over her left shoulder, and a smaller bag crimped in her right hand. She headed out into the dangerous world bearing the strength of a full-grown independent woman. As her body grew smaller in view, Will reluctantly closed the door.

The boy would never have admitted it, but he was a ball of mixed emotions. He was getting all choked up about her leaving and he didn't know why. Ever since she showed up, his main goal was to get her out, but when it was actually happening, it cut to the boy's heart like a sharpened razor. He looked over at the metallic ladder before he sluggishly climbed it. He gazed down at the sidewalk from the second story windowpane as Lili gradually walked away. He secretly wanted her to give one last look back so he could wave to her, but she didn't. She just kept heading down the sidewalk with her head held high until she disappeared from the window's sight. Will pressed his forehead against the window after Lili escaped his view.

Will quietly murmured to himself. "Man...this just sucks." The boy stayed in that state of depression for just a couple of seconds as he started to think. Suddenly a new exciting energy rushed into the boy's body as he removed his head from the window and ran downstairs as fast as he could. Will rapidly picked up his satchel containing the laptop and dashed out the door. The boy swiftly locked the door behind him, and sprinted down the sidewalk toward Lili's direction. She was only a tiny speck on the horizon, but Will could still see her. Will shouted at the top off his lungs. "Wait!... Lili! Wait!"

Lili faintly heard her name and stopped to turn around to see who it was. She then caught sight of Will charging at her full speed. His face was red from the incredible intensity from which he was running. It seemed tremendously important, so she halted. The boy slowly stopped in front of her and bent over, placing his hands on his knees and breathing heavily from exhaustion. Lili bellowed with a surprised expression. "Will!?"

Will squealed between long exaggerated breaths. "Lili…hold on…wait."

"What is it?"

Will's heartbeat began to calm down, so he then stood erect. He let out one powerful gust of air from his lips before he revealed. "I can't let you do this. I can't let you leave, not like this."
"Will,"

"I gotta make sure you end up somewhere safe, so I'm gonna make sure you find a good place to stay."

"Thank you,"

Will took Lili's large gym bag off her shoulder and placed it over his own like a true gentlemen. Will then slyly suggested. "Are you hungry? Do you wanna go get something? I know this place not too far away."

"Sure," She gladly accepted with her usual smile once again featured on her young face.

"It's this way." Will led trotting further down the sidewalk.

They headed down a very familiar route for the boy. They maneuvered through the same avenues Will had those two days he worked for Wes. The landscape primarily remained the same, but the atmosphere bore a different attitude from when Lili was in complete control. The industrious factories were buzzing with busy employees. The factories were the first things to get up and running because, for some reason or another, factories received very minimal structural damage to their buildings and machinery. That odd fact was most likely true because factories seemed scary and unappealing to a nine-year-old girl, therefore they would be unappealing to a world being manipulated by a nine-year-old girl. It took the factory's staff only a few hours of checking over equipment before they determined they were all in good working order. By the time the two children had passed by the factories, they were nosily churning out goods at the same speed they had a few weeks before.

A little less than a half hour later, the street that Will and Lili walked met an intersection. Once the gifted princess followed the sidewalk's bend around to face the new road, her suffocating amount of guilt got that much denser. She saw similar images on the avenue that she had seen in the news broadcast, but in person. People were crying as they witnessed their once thriving businesses left in shambles while others comforted them. Teams of goodhearted volunteers brought their own cleaning supplies to help put the ravaged street back in order. They had worked so hard to undo the damages caused by Lili's reign and the child felt the responsibility of her actions. Her eyes were drained of a certain life as the terrors she had produced had met her face to face.

Will almost kept walking until he noticed Lili's pace waned. He saw that Lili was confronted with a great sorrow as she watched the hardworking citizens. Will wanted Lili to get the message, but at that point, he felt it was just beating a dead horse. He softly took her hand accompanied with a warm gaze. "Come on," he helped her along.

On the corner to the kids' right was a small bakery café that Will had visited several times. The little place Will had been talking about earlier was the Co-Z Café. The establishment was still utterly destroyed, but the overall mood of the café had transformed into something much more professional. The first thing Will noticed about the place was the broken glass, coffee beans, and whatever else was on the ground had long been swept up. It looked as though every employee had been called in, although the actual restaurants functions of the small café were being performed by the least amount of workers possible. The rest of them were scrubbing the walls, vacuuming the carpets, and tidying up the joint as best they could. If Will wished to apply for the job at that moment, perhaps they wouldn't have simply shunned him away.

As Will and Lili entered the Co-Z Café, they thoroughly observed their abundance of scrambling employees, and their lack of customers. There were two exceedingly loyal patrons occupying the establishment, and they were sitting together. Rows upon rows of booths and tables lay open, trying their hardest to invite paying guests. For most people that day, it was far too sad and busy of a day to stop for some coffee or soup. Most places were closed due to that fact, and because they felt they needed some time to renovate. Still, some companies like the owners of the Co-Z Café felt they needed to try and make their money back from the worldwide disaster as quickly as they could. For that reason, it was not absolutely impossible to find certain places open and running.

They threw Lili's luggage by a small table they intended on returning to and headed up to the man behind the register. It was the same sloppily dressed rude cashier that Will had dealt with before, but this time it seemed he had turned over an entirely new leaf. His haphazardly placed work shirt had been neatly ironed and tucked into his pants. The employee's old *don't give a damn* attitude was replaced with a smile conveyed by a warm and welcoming *Hello*.

Will walked up to him fully acknowledging just how the man changed . "Hi, hold on a second." His attention had right away diverted to the cute girl to his side. "What kind of bagel do you like?"

"Bagel?" Cloudiness became Lili's face over the word.

"Nevermind, uh…" Will thought of the quickest means for her to make her choice. "Do you like sweet or savory stuff for breakfast?"

"Sweet'"

Will then veered his head back to the cashier. "Um, let me get a blueberry bagel with strawberry cream cheese toasted, and a toasted onion bagel with a garlic and herb shmear."

"Will that be all?"

"Two lattes both with cream extra sugar and extra foam."

The cashier fired a suspicious leer at the children as he wondered if the kids were too young for coffee. He then remembered the sorry state the company that gives him a job was and decided to let it slide. "That'll be four seventy-three."

While another employee was fixing the lattes, Will rummaged for a small sheet of receipt paper in his pocket as he explained. "I seem to have lost my account card so…"

"That's fine, do you know your account number?"

"Uh, yes..." Will retrieved the receipt paper from his back pocket and read off a long list of numbers on top of the sheet. At the end of their transaction, Will's bill was unsuspectingly paid for by a one Darrel Rydell. Will walked the trayed bagels to the table while a nice employee handed Lili the lattes whom then followed the boy.

They returned and took a seat at the small round finely polished wooden table designed for two in the center of the restaurant. Lili passed Will one of the coffees while he slid the tray with the blueberry bagel on it to her. Lili carefully examined the hot bagel with a queer expression while staring at it, then picking it up, and finally sniffing it. Her mouth reluctantly trembled before she took a tiny bite from the fruity bagel. Her mood immediately changed while her taste-buds were lost in a pleasant surprise. As her face transformed, she put down a few more scrumptious mouthfuls.

Will sipped his coffee and watched Lili's bagel discovery with wide eyes. "Wow!" Will quickly squealed in awe of Lili scarfing down the bagel. "I guess you like it, huh?"

"I love it!" She loudly screeched with full cheeks. "These are awesome!"

Will commented as he took his laptop from the satchel and placed it on the table. "Good,"

Suddenly, Will's wristwatch communicator began to ring a low-pitched electronic jingle. Will wasn't expecting a call, so he looked at the name on the communicator curiously.

His curiosity faded as he remarked. "Oh," Will hit the button on the communicator to answer. He raised the mechanism on his wrist near his lips and barked. "Jina!"

On the other end of the line was Jina, who was standing in front of Ky's studio/warehouse. Her face, which was still hidden by the IO helmet, was gazing down at her cellphone screen. It was receiving live feed of Will in the café.

"What?" She replied at a decibel high enough to reach her phone's speakers.

"Where'd you go?" Will complained at his wristwatch communicator. "You were supposed to help me convince Ky to let Lili stay."

"Oh no sir," Jina argued with the boy. "I said no such thing. All I said was we were going to figure out what to do with her, and I left to check on my personal affairs to make sure they haven't been tampered with, thank you very much."

"Well, it's too late now anyway. I'm out with Lili trying to find her a new home."

"Too bad," Jina sympathized in a very uncaring and

empty way. "What about Ky?"

"He's out doing what you were doing."

"Oh, do you mind if I crash at your place for a while?" Jina requested.

"The door's locked." Will warned.

"Please," Jina droned. Will should have known as well as she did that in no way could a small door lock keep her out.

"Yeah, whatever I guess." Will granted.

"See you when you get back."

Will then questioned. "Haven't you seen the news?"

"I don't watch TV." Jina reminded.

"Well, Lili isn't controlling people anymore so you can take that stupid helmet off."

"Oh, cool,"

"Later,"

"Bye."

Jina flipped her phone shut and tucked it deep inside her large sleeve as Will ended the call on his communicator. Jina entered Ky's apartment as the kids resumed enjoying their breakfast. Will and Lili laughed and goofed off while they slowly ate their bagels like two best friends. It was an odd brand of perfect.

V

The Day the World Woke up Pt. B

Ky found himself strapped to the nose of his craft, the Guider, rubbing it with a worn out strip of sandpaper. One of the reasons that Red didn't really mind giving Ky his extra discount was because the hangar the Guider was stationed in was too small for the craft. Since the craft was too big for its hangar, the large shutter doors were always ajar with about two feet of the Guider's nose poking out of it. Those two feet of the craft were completely exposed to the forces of nature; including rain. Since it occasionally got rained on, those two feet would end up rusting at a rapid rate. Rather than simply paying a little more for a bigger hangar, Ky would head out to Red's about once a month with sandpaper to sand off the accumulated rust. This eventually became an excuse for the two to hang out and shoot the breeze. It was one of those times.

Ky finished sanding off the last bits of rust on the Guider while hanging from the nose by a simple system of straps and buckles. Red Marrado sat on the platform portion of a vehicle much like a cherry-picker. A spacious platform accordion-ed up near Ky, and Red just sat on it conversing with him.

Red interrogated. "So, Ky, what do you make of these missing eleven days?"

Ky's face froze for a second, though Red couldn't recognize under his mechanized head. He was stuck. He would've loved to have blathered on and on about Lili and what actually happened, but he couldn't. If he divulged any information to him about that, he knew he'd end up receiving an earful about it from Will. He was uncomfortably wedged between his own wishes and Will's. Ultimately, Ky decided not to tell. He just wanted her out, he wasn't about incriminating people; he didn't want to be a rat.

"Oh, I don't know. How does anyone even really know it happened?"

"Oh, it happened," Red assured. "All my files and junk wouldn't be all screwed up if it didn't."

"Oh," Ky sounded feeling rather empty. His eyes stayed planted on a small area he was overly sanding.

"But, I mean, how do you think it happened?"

"Uh, I'm not sure. I haven't thought about it too much."

"What do you mean? Everyone's been blaming somebody. Some people blame it on that secret invisible army, but I think it was something else."

"Really? What?" Ky said trying to seem genuine.

"I think it was something else powerful; something dangerous."

"Why?"

"This army seems strong, maybe even stronger than the G.F.B., but they don't seem mystical, right? Something extraordinary made everyone forget that week and a half, and that army is hunting it down."

A fake *Wow* escaped Ky's lips. He was horribly attempting to mask the fact that he knew the truth and that Red's prediction wasn't far off. He realized then that this was not going to be the end of that line of questioning. Ky then knew that anyone he was going to meet from then on would ask his opinions on the matter in passing, so he needed to get his story straight. He decided to tread lightly on the subject until he had enough time to totally get his side down.

Red then observed that Ky had been sanding the same part off the Guider for a long while. Red jokingly criticized. "Hey Ky, do you think that part is finished yet?"

Ky snapped back into reality and slowly inched the paper away from the craft. "Yeah, I'm done. Get me down."

"Yeah," Red moaned and stretched as he stood up on the platform and stepped over to the small control panel in the corner of it. Using the controls, Red positioned the platform beneath Ky as the man fastened to the craft started unbuckling his customized harness.

Ky unfastened the last strap and dropped to the platform under him like a ton of bricks. He landed on his feet as if he was a certified professional of getting out of that harness. It was then that Red slowly made the scissored platform descended to the vehicle base like a retracting slinky. They took their time getting off the vehicle with the adjustable platform and began to trot away from the hangar too small for its craft.

As they headed away from the hangar, Red persisted. "So, you don't have any theories or opinions about what happened those missing days?"

"Nope," Ky confidently bluffed.

"Man," Red croaked out of amazement. "I wish I was as blissfully indifferent as you."

"Well, you know..." Ky's gloating was abruptly cut short as something tiny rammed itself into Ky's helmet at an intense velocity. The impact was great enough to instantly knock the full grown man off his feet. It was a bullet that luckily didn't bear enough force to pierce through Ky's armored helmet, but strong enough to lodge itself into the mechanical mask. By the time Ky hit the floor, his vision was gone. The helmet's optical system, which allows the user to see as if he wasn't wearing a helmet, all had been utterly compromised. All Ky could see at that moment was a field of static like a rabbit-eared television with no reception. Every program and feature that the helmet had to offer was malfunctioning ultimately becoming useless. At that point, the mask was only acting as a blindfold truly endangering his life.

Ky then felt an arm urgently grab him, help him off the floor, and then tugging him into a forced wild sprint; it was presumably Red. Above the sounds off the failing helmet's static, Ky could hear guns being fired and even felt the wind push aside as bullets whizzed by his body. Ky's back was thrust against some kind of metal slab. His balance left him and his rear end fell on the ground. Sitting on the floor with his back to the wall, Ky decided to rid himself of the helmet, or at least for the time being.

"I guess I'm gonna have to trust the preteen black witch for a couple of hours." Ky mumbled to himself. He then reached one hand to the bottom of the helmet around the base of his jaw. Ky ripped the IO helmet off his head and chucked the damaged thing to the floor. A spot of blood drizzled down the side of Ky's cheek leading from where the bullet nearly punctured his skull. He quickly surveyed his surroundings to determine his current level of screwed. He found himself behind a large metal cargo bin; he assumed Red had placed him there for cover. Pressed next to a far off hangar, the large bin also guarded Red as he rummaged through a much smaller wooden box frantically searching for something.

Red hysterically ranted. "Where are they? Where are they? Where are they?..." He rushed through the junk in the small box, discarding item after item, desperately looking for something while his chant echoed on.

"What's going on?" Ky demanded.

"Some psycho is shooting at us... and worse, he's good." He explained with his head in the box. "Ah! Here they are!" Red pulled out two twin handguns from the wooden box. He also retrieved a long belt lined with gun-clips. The clips at first glance appeared too large for the guns he was holding, but Red slipped a clip in each one with grace. The clips protruded about five inches out of the handle. Red's handguns were fully automatic, so when he pulled the trigger the weapons would rapidly and continually spit out bullets, thus the banana sized clips. If the cartridges were regular sized, Red would need to reload much too often. "You ready to get nuts Ky?"

"I don't know, I guess."

"Let's get nuts." Red poked his head over the large metal container with his guns aimed in the general vicinity of the attack's source. He directed his firearms up toward the Zenon7 M far off in the distance. Red pulled the triggers and unleashed a battle roar. "Ahhh," A firestorm of bullets blasted out of the gun chambers and raced at their attacker.

Standing directly on top of the very expansive Zenon7 M galactic cruiser was the overly egocentric gunslinger Byne. His trained eyes precisely focused in on the small smudge that was Red far away. Lights flickered around the small black smudge as Red mercilessly shot at him. Byne has had an unheard of amount of experience with an unbelievably vast variety of guns, so he knew exactly what those distant flickers meant. His brain instinctively and hastily judged where Red's bullets would end up based upon the upward angle he was firing, the wind, and the bullet's deadliness from the mere flickers. A few blinding golden bullets streaked past Byne while he calmly just stood there. Suddenly he swayed to his side in a delicate, graceful, and fluent motion. Then a few more rounds flew where his body just was. If he didn't move, he would've been tagged. Byne then continued elegantly swaying back and forth like a unique ballet. Hot lead zipped past around the man, but none of them touched him. It was like a boy dancing in the rain successfully dodging droplets. Byne's dance concluded as Red's onslaught ceased.

"It appears they have received my invitation." Byne declared in a regal tone. "Though, to my dismay, this gentlemen is an atrocious shot. The only thing saving him is that he is so recklessly spitting out bullets. I happen to be a person who believes the true value in a firefight is quality and not quantity. If it continues this way, I will truly find no fun in this game."

Red leaned down with his back to the metal cargo crate as he reloaded his automatic pistols. He shoved the clips into the guns and cocked them back. He then looked up to Ky and asked. "Do you think I got him?"

Ky answered with a confused look and a shrug of his shoulders as if to say *How should I know?*

Red then breathed a heavy sigh and slowly got to his feet. Red twisted his head around and looked over toward the Zenon7 M. Before he could get a good look, a bullet ricocheted off the edge of the crate, mere centimeters from Red's head. A spark from the deflected round then landed in Red's eye. He dashed back behind the crate cradling his grazed pupil.

"Damn it!" He shouted in pain. "Ky! Do something!"

"What do you want me to do!?"

"I don't know! Get that one-girl-wrecking-crew you keep telling me about over here to take care of this guy!"

"Good idea." Ky's hand went for his wristwatch communicator and he pushed a few buttons.

Jina was smack dab in the middle of taking a lengthy

nap sprawled out on Ky's couch. She had long past removed her helmet, so she lay there in all her beauty. There was never a more alluring sight then watching Jina peacefully slumbering, occasionally stretching her flawless body. She would tussle around every once and awhile seeking comfort and letting out a coo that sounded sweeter than that of a newborn baby. It was like a single twinkling star in the middle of a black and lonely sky.

Her phone began to ring and the corny jingle reached the woman's gorgeous ears. Her eyelids leisurely spread apart in awareness and she released an attractive pant. The phone ceaselessly chimed as her yawn finished, not letting on to the full urgency of the call. She sat up on the couch and took the cellular phone out of her long sleeve. The constant ringing didn't stop as she examined the name on the tiny screen.

"Ky?" Jina wondered. "What does he want?"

Jina then heard a slight rumbling from outside the apartment. The very minor tremors would only last a second before occurring again. Jina curiously got up from the couch to investigate while the phone kept madly ringing. The rumbling progressively grew louder, more severe and much more rapid. As Jina lazily slumped over to the door, the strengthening quakes took mere milliseconds before the next one would transpire. Her angelic face neared the door as the alternating rumbles magnified to the point that it lightly shook a few trinkets inside the apartment. Jina's emerald green eye met with the door's peephole and what she saw called for immediate action.

Jina received an eyeful of a mountain-sized man charging the entrance like a true dynamo. The man was rushing the wall with his massive overly muscular shoulder only a couple of inches from making contact with the door. She had no time and needed to react before the man came busting through the door.

Jina instinctively leapt to her left forming into a dodge-roll. The studio/warehouse's front wall exploded, flinging slabs of cement and small wooden chips of door throughout the large apartment.

The mountain sized man known as Baloe rammed through the door like an unstoppable train, his body was lost in a heavy smog of kicked up cement soot. The dust cloud began to fall revealing Baloe's humongous frame and his equally large gravel club. Baloe roared with the intensity that would match the intimidation of a fully developed male lion. Baloe's stone face combed the apartment in search of Lili, but the low flying dust clouds he created hid the contents of the place.

To Baloe's surprise, a long metal staff swung at him from out of the clouds like a sideways catapult. It came at him so fast that the highly skilled warrior had no chance of avoiding the strike. The metal staff caught Baloe in the abdomen and launched him out of the studio/warehouse like a line drive to center-field. Baloe's body flew out of the apartment and bounced against the hard ground several times resembling a well-thrown skipping stone jumping across a pond. Baloe's body finally came to a halt as it slammed against the wall of the warehouse across the street. Baloe crashed to the ground before looking up to figure out what had hit him.

Jina slowly stepped out of the gaping opening in the apartment wall with a look on her face that told Baloe it would be her to act as his contender. She had no questions for her unknown assailant, just a built-in confidence that she was going to silence the giant man.

Baloe sluggishly got to his feet, somehow weathering Jina's devastating blow. He then smiled at her as he challenged. "So it is you. I am truly grateful that it is you that I have the pleasure of facing."

Jina stayed silent. She just stared down her opponent

with a dead serious grimace.

"I am Baloe, and it has been so long since I faced a worthy adversary." Baloe announced before taking a fighting stance.

Jina took a step forward. As for her phone, it remained ringing and unanswered on the dust-covered couch.

"She's not answering." Ky sadly informed. Ky knew what this meant, so he started loading his pistol and preparing his miniature photon cannon.

Red concluded. "You mean we're on our own?"

"Looks like it."

"Just great, all right, so here's the deal." Red planned. "You see those crates over there?"

Ky's head followed Red's invisible eye-line. He snapped his neck to his left to see a few other metal cargo bins similar to the one they were hiding behind. Those bins were also set next to a hangar wall and offered the same level of protection.

Ky answered. "Yeah,"

"Well let's make a break for them on three and keep firing on his sorry ass the entire way."

Ky cocked back his handgun and then motioned his free hand to slip into the cannon. "Got it!"

Red's adrenaline level heightened and sweat beaded down the tall dark man's brow as he patiently counted. "One... Two... Three!"

Ky and Red sprinted out from behind the safety of the metal bins with guns drawn.

As soon as Byne saw the two pop outside their cover, he began firing upon them with abnormal accuracy. Byne shot at them with an average sized pistol, yet his aim was as true as a professional sniper and without the assistance of a scope. Byne's gun savvy was beyond proficient.

There was something peculiarly customized about Byne's gun. It had two triggers and two separate barrels. The second trigger was directly below the first and his middle finger rested on it without pulling it back. Likewise, the second barrel was welded on to the gun about an inch beneath the original and had a swirled inner lining as if something could be screwed into it. It was obvious that the gunslinger had a few tricks left up his sleeves. He relentlessly shot one bullet at a time toward Ky and Red as he executed minor body leans to dodge oncoming fire.

Red shimmied across the green field toward the new set of crates leading the assault. His guns mercilessly sprayed bullets at the almost invisible dot perched on the Zenon7 M. Hot lead whistled dangerously close to Ky's and his own body as they advanced toward cover.

As for Ky, something was wrong. As he ran out from behind the crates, he pulled back on his guns' triggers, but nothing came out of them. Amidst a deadly gunfight, Ky clicked the guns several more times with no response whatsoever. About halfway to his new post, Ky gave up and simply made a break for cover. Ky and Red made it behind the crates with too many close calls to count. Their attempt to mount an offensive failed.

Byne cackled wildly atop the craft at Ky's sloppy antics. He found it infinitely hilarious watching him trying to use his malfunctioning guns then scurrying off like a scared mouse for safety. "Ha ha! This is truly pathetic."

"What the hell was that!?" An anger filled Red demanded to know.

"I don't know!" Ky apologized. "For some reason my guns aren't working!"

"Are they jammed or something!?"

"No! I just checked it! And that doesn't explain why my photon cannon is messing up!"

Red shouted. "Well you better figure out something

fast or we're as good as dead!"

Byne's patience was wearing thin. His freehand slithered inside his fine jacket and he took out a small metallic cylinder. He placed the cylinder on the tip of the gun's second barrel and spun it on in one cool motion. The cylinder screwed and locked itself into place on the barrel. Byne took his time as he pointed the customized pistol at the huge crates that the pair hid behind. Once he was satisfied with his gun's position, he squeezed the second trigger. The gun administered a raw kickback and the cylinder sailed through the air forming a tail of white smoke as it raced toward the crates.

As Ky frantically checked his firearms, Red peaked over the crates to evaluate the situation, and that's when he caught a glimpse of the speeding cylinder.

Red screeched at Ky containing the seriousness of a dead relative. "A MISSILE!"

Ky and Red were suddenly charged with a revitalizing energy and they jetted away from the metal cargo bins. They ran down the side of the hangar wall doing their best to stay alive.

The missile struck the bin in its dead center and the entire side of the hangar erupted into a ball of flames and deafening noise. The pair tumbled to the grass from the force of the explosion. Luckily, burning falling debris missed the downed duo. Gunfire skimmed around their temporarily limp bodies. The rising black smoke plumes from the explosion provided enough cover to compromise Byne's exceptional aim. The two were able to regain themselves and crawl behind the rear wall of the hangar.

Byne was only able to catch a quick look of Ky's leg sneaking behind the wall. "It is this game you gentlemen wish to play? Quite tedious, but truthfully, it may be enjoyable."

Ky and Red stayed spread out on the grass guarded

by the hangar. Their lungs expanded and contracted to their limits as they desperately tried to replenish their energy. Ky and Red were already spent in both mind and body. They knew good and well that they were outclassed and they were running out of options.

"We're still alive... right?" Red questioned between long pants.

Ky ignored Red's words but informed. "Let me call someone else."

Will sat in the comfort of the Co-Z Café giggling and socializing with the adorable and amazing Lili. Will was full on bantering with her, but oddly while he had his laptop out surfing the galactic web. He was actually checking reports around the world to see how far Lili's influenced reached. He quickly acknowledged that it was in fact a global phenomenon. The boy glanced up from his screen to look at Lili as he only half listened to what she was going on gabbing about.

She went on gabbing. "...and then my brother Doc, who so totally has white hair..."

Will then peppered the conversation with an *uh huh* blankly stated in the middle of her sentence.

"...he didn't even know how tall I was..."

Will's wristwatch communicator started letting out a high-pitched rapid beeping. Will said. "Hold on," Lili then graciously hushed herself anxiously waiting for the instant that his phone call was done to continue her story. Will looked at his communicator and realized the caller was Ky. *Probably to check if Lili's gone yet* the boy thought. Will pushed a button on the communicator and greeted. "Yello!"

"Uh, yeah, hi Will. Would you happen to know maybe why my guns wouldn't be working for me if I was trying to shoot them?" Ky mentioned to the boy.

"Yeah!" Will brightly answered. "Because I put a

lock on them."

"What!?" Ky yelled from the other side of the line.

"Be-cause...I...put...a...lock...on them." Will slothfully repeated with the addition of an annoying voice.

"Why!!??"

Even a simple pistol like Ky's, which wasn't exactly the newest model at the time, has some kind of computer chip in it. Will was telling Ky that he had hacked into his guns and shut them down indefinitely. Ky was naturally outraged.

"That little display last night." Will confidently defended. "You think I'm gonna feel safe having a loose cannon with guns around? You got kids living with you, you know."

Ky and Red started seeing bullets being shot through the hangar wall around them. The sides of the bins they previously hid behind were built sturdy enough to suffer the harshness of space, but the hangars were constructed of a makeshift sheet metal designed only to withstand the planet's elements. It certainly wasn't capable of stopping gunfire. To add to the pair's woes, that particular hangar was empty, so there was nothing on the inside that could deflect the bullets and he was allowed to shoot straight through it. The only thing they had going for them was that the wall was very wide and Byne had no clue as to where they were behind it.

"Oh yeah, well that's smart, I guess." Ky ranted on with each sound in the sentence harmoniously fused with pure sarcasm. He then urgently ordered. "Turn them on!"

"All right, all right, already, just chill." Will finally gave in to Ky's forceful demands. He began casually perusing his laptop opening new programs. "...just hold on a second."

"I'm in a deadly gunfight!" Ky yelled.

"There you go. Your guns should be good now." Will expressionlessly delivered the nerve relieving news as if Ky's desperate pleads were muted. Will then heard the line go dead on the other side. "Ky?"

Ky hastily shut off the wristwatch communicator as the number of bullet holes piercing through the flimsy sheet-metal hangar wall steadily increased. A small grin was seen on his face as life returned to his weapons. They remained stationary, their bodies spread out on the grass hiding behind the weak hangar wall, but Ky looked upon Red with a cocky confidence.

Ky readied his firearms as he adjusted himself and formulated. "Okay Red, so this is what I'm thinking. We're gonna work our way up to the Guider. Once we get in it, I don't care what kind of arsenal this nut-bag has on him, my craft will wipe the floor with him."

"Yeah," Red responded still a little overwhelmed.

"Sound like a plan?"

"Yeah,"

"All right, round two." Ky burst off the grass and dashed to the same edge of the hangar wall that they had fled for their lives behind moments earlier. He ran clear across the flames that the missile had caused with his guns drawn up. He was prepared to shoot immediately as his aim came to him. Ky's weapons then came into the fight biting-viciously.

Byne dodged the two bullets and the photon blast that Ky had sent his way, but not at all in the graceful way that he avoided Red's assaults. He dramatically jolted his body to the floor to spare being tagged. Byne looked up to the empty space where he was nearly shot.

The aristocratic gunman remarked. "Well, well, it seems this one is a decent shot." Byne got back on his feet as he further analyzed his opponents. "He also has a miniaturized photon cannon in his possession. It stands as proof of his skill. I am ecstatic that this bout may prove somewhat more amusing."

Ky and Red had successfully made it to a more reinforced spot for cover.

"Ky?" Will repeated into his wristwatch communicator even though he heard the obvious monotone hum of a cut line.

Lili finished her bagel with an expression of mild confusion. "I wonder what that was about?"

Will closed his laptop and slipped it into his satchel before replying. "I don't know."

Something savagely sunk into the wooden table that the children sat at. The force jerked the table and gave off a sudden snapping sound. Will's eyes immediately shifted to his left as Lili's veered to her right. Their eyes met with a three and a half foot razor sharp sword sticking out of the table. Their pupils followed its hilt back to the blade's origin of flight. Sitting in a chair at the cafe's back wall was a man with shabby black hair that ran over most of his face. The maniac was wrapped in so many swords that it was difficult to identify the tactical gear underneath. It was the unbalanced swordsman Riftkin.

Will watched Riftkin's one visible eye rapidly roam around the café as if he was unable to focus. The boy was paralyzed in disbelief as an eerie smile crawled across the swordsman's face.

Riftkin instructed slowly so that they grasped the full gravity of the situation. "This is the part where the little kiddies run."

The fear was evident in the children's eyes as they hastily stammered out of their chairs completely leaving Lili's luggage behind. Will snatched his satchel in one fluid motion before bolting out the door. The boy blew the swinging glass door open with his shoulder and sprinted out of the café with Lili following close to his rear. The kids jetted down the avenue fearing for their lives.

Riftkin casually stepped over to the table that was formerly occupied by the children in no big rush. The employees and the few loyal patrons stayed as still as a photograph as the unbelievable scene unfolded. With one powerful tug, he dislodged the sword from deep within the finely polished wooden table. He twirled the cleaver in his hand playfully as all eyes in the café were all at once planted on him in sheer disabling terror. "This is my favorite part of the dance." The unstable warrior then chased after the kids before anyone in the restaurant could comprehend what was happening.

As Will and Lili ran down the street, the boy rapidly started pushing buttons on his handy wristwatch communicator.

Lili hysterically blurted out. "What are you doing!?"

"I'm getting Jina over here."

Baloe and Jina's eyes locked as the solar system's most deadliest creatures faced each other determined to prove who was the better warrior. Like an unexpected thunderstorm, Baloe was suddenly around her crashing down with a mighty element of raw power. His huge club made a clang sound and bounced away out of nowhere, which was a completely foreign event to the giant brute. Jina had raised her staff in defense with such speed that her movements hadn't even triggered a defensive thought in Baloe's martial art's infused mind. Baloe didn't falter. He reflexively took another swing at her, but this one was different. He decided to deliver his most efficient blow that exercised absolutely no wasted motion. Baloe's massive cement club performed a swipe at her side so fast that pebbles were caught in the attack's wind-tail and were slightly lifted off the ground. The action met with the same fate. A clang sound rang out before his club fell off of her. The mountain-sized man then spared no time in administering a relentless combination of seven precisely placed strikes. Every time his club went down on her it chimed that haunting clang as it was briskly deflected. He then gave it everything he had in one outrageous double-handed downward thrust to her preciously adorable head. Baloe thought he had done it, for his club met with no resistance and he could see her perfect frame still behind it. He then quickly realized what he was seeing was just a shadow silhouette of her and that he had actually struck the ground. Jina had avoided the attack with a slide to her right fast enough to leave an after-image of herself where she stood. She was, in fact, standing safely a few inches to the club's side. Baloe lifted his weapon and tried the same slam of the club again. Baloe's immense strength bashed the slab of cement to the pavement and the roadway webbed out in a vast crack that cut deep into its crust. To his surprise, Baloe found Jina standing on the tip of his rock-like club like a breathtaking weightless sprite.

The end of Jina's staff streaked through space until it landed flush against Baloe's cheek. It had hit him so hard that his body was propelled through the front of the warehouse they were outside of and clear out through the back of it. Baloe's body landed with a thud spurting up a dust cloud as it pounded to the center of a work lot.

Baloe gradually stumbled to his feet and he could instantly tell that his face was partially crushed in. The portion of his cheek that had made contact with the staff had caved in and the bones beneath it were shattered. The left side of his face was swelling up rapidly and being rendered motionless. Lots of blood spilled to the ground from the man's damaged mug. Hot thick dark bodily fluids rolled out of his mouth along with a few desperate coughs. The fight seemed to be working against him, but like a true warrior, Baloe never let go of his club.

The warrior had a moment to collect and survey the area. He was in a loading dock that the warehouses utilized to move merchandise around and take in new shipments. There were a few palettes spread around with stacked raw materials like wood and steel. There were piles of huge metal pipes and compact vehicles designed to pick them up scattered around the lot. The workers stood in stunned silence at the warrior's impromptu arrival. All at once, Baloe's moment of peace ended.

A hefty lifting vehicle with the capability of hauling multiple half-ton pipes miraculously exploded. Chunks of metallic shrapnel shot outward in every direction. Baloe leaped out of the way of a man sized wheel, but was then pinned under a door that could keep an elephant immobile. The warehouse employees then shrieked and ran off in a frenzy.

Baloe tossed the vehicle door off him as if he were opening a door. His one good eye focused on where the vehicle was to discover the unscathed Jina standing in its place. Baloe knew she had simply jumped the gap between them and her reentry to the ground had demolished the vehicle.

The mountain-sized man could be heard uttering. "Well, it looks like this is not going well for me."

Jina's phone was left ringing on the couch.

"She's not answering!" Will howled at Lili who ran with him by his side.

The maniac Riftkin chased after them down the sidewalk with a smile of twisted pleasure carved on his face. He rushed past the crowded streets as innocent civilians tried to clean up their city and reclaim what was lost. Their eyes became glued to the scene of children running from a sword-wielding psycho, but none of them took any action toward it. The day was too mixed-up as it was to then start addressing that problem.

"Who is this guy?" Will wondered aloud not thinking he would actually get an answer.

"His name's Riftkin. He's one of my knights."

"One of your knights!?" Will barked back at her.

"Yeah, though I don't know why the others would have let him retrieve me alone...they must really be desperate."

"Well, if he's your knight, why is he chasing us? Shouldn't he, you know...be on our side?"

Lili explained. "My knights want to take me home and I don't really wanna go."

"That's it!?" Will yelped. "That's nothing worth throwing swords over!"

"They'll take me by force if they need to, which means he'll kill you in a heartbeat. Plus they usually supervise Riftkin."

"Where are the rest then?" Will questioned.

"I don't have a clue."

"Crap!" Will shouted with no filter. "Can't you just stop him with your...you know...powers?"

"He's been around me so long that he's grown a tolerance, but I can do something." Lili suddenly stopped running and turned around to face Riftkin's impending pursuit head on. Will also ceased, watching Lili's actions with a curious gaze. She stood in the middle of the street with her arms out to her sides and her palms open. As Riftkin neared, she slowly moved her arms until they both met in front of her. Innocent onlookers and pedestrians were locked in a debilitating trance. They all dropped their brooms, power tools, and whatever else they were using to help rebuild their community before they drowsily gathered in the center of the road. They started forming in front of the princess in a line shoulder to shoulder. The line of people spanned across the entire street and the civilians just blankly stared at the steadily approaching Riftkin. It was a human barricade that Lili was implementing to keep the knight at bay until they had a chance to escape. Will caught wind of her plan and didn't like it at all.

Riftkin skillfully unsheathed two long swords from the holsters on his sides ready to tear the human defensive line to shreds.

The boy angrily snatched the girl by the sleeve and yanked her along. "No!" He scolded as he dragged her into a sprint back down the street. The children's legs began to aggressively pump off the ground as the chase resumed once again.

The civilians instantly snapped out of the princess' spell as their heads jerked back and they moved around freely trying to piece together the few previous moments.

Riftkin barreled through the human wall. "Out of my way!" The mad knight yelled as he broke through the line shoving a couple of the civilians to the ground. Luckily, he chose not to use his blades.

"Why'd you do that?!" Lili argued as they ran for their lives yet again. "That would've bought us enough time to get out of here."

"Those people could've been killed back there!" Will lectured as if Lili's question held no weight to it.

"What...?" Her entire demeanor shifted. Her voice became softer and less forceful as the feeling that she did something wrong finally boiled in the princess.

"Those people have a mind and will of their own! You can't just use them like they're expendable!"

"Those commoners...?"

"...Even commoners have feelings."

"So what are we gonna do then?"

"Looks like I'm gonna need to take care of this." Will said with the confidence of a full-grown man. He unzipped his coat and threw it off himself revealing his protective vest underneath. The vest was littered with various high-tech lights and buttons. The boy pushed one of them and it glowed with a blue hue. He turned his attention back to Lili and instructed. "We need to stall him for about seven minutes."

Minutes earlier, Ky and Red had been pinned behind a cargo bin under heavy gunfire. Byne had realized that his handgun was going to take all day to puncture through the reinforced bin that was tough enough to go unharmed in outer space, so while the men hid behind the cargo crate, he started assembling a different weapon. Concealed under his fine jacket, Byne pulled out a giant barrel along with a shaft and a large gun magazine. He retrieved more technical pieces and put together a giant automatic rifle. It took him a mere two minutes and seventeen seconds to construct the massive customized rifle. He held the gun in one hand and fixed a circular gun clip to its side with the other. He then grasped the rifle with both hands and unleashed an overwhelmingly powerful barrage.

Byne could tell that the thrashing of the bullet marathon was bending the bin's strong metal to its will. Every time a piece of blazing fiery-red hot lead collided with the crate it created a dent the size of a silver dollar. Sparks flew as bullets pelted the crate, slowly forming it into a less symmetrical and more abstract shape. The black bin looked like a giant recorded sun-drenched prune that was being played in fast-forward. It wasn't going to be long before the defensive capabilities of the crate would be compromised.

"This guy's gonna rip us apart!" Red screamed out above the deafening gunfire.

"Ky replied. "We need to work our way up to the Guider!"

"Easier said than done!"

"Boss!" Someone called out in the distance.

Ky and Red's heads jerked to the same side in unison. It was Red's mild mannered employees Vince and Cid. They had been checking an engine on a neighboring craft and heard the sounds of a war-zone. They cowered around its hangar door unsure of what to do.

"Vince! Cid! Get your asses inside that hangar! He hasn't seen you yet! Get in the craft and stay as much in the center as possible!" Red urgently advised to them.

"Yes sir!" Vince and Cid recited simultaneously before scurrying back inside.

"Okay!" Ky mapped out. "We're gonna need as much cover fire as possible at this point! We need to wait out how many bullets this guy has, but he's gonna shoot right through this crate so we need to move now! Got it!?"

"Yeah!"

"Let's go!"

The men jumped out from the safety of the crate with guns blazing. They made their way closer to the Guider while effectively stifling Byne's assault with their own medley of assaults. They watched as Byne dipped, ducked and dove out of the way of their attacks, still managing to send waves of bullets in their direction. Byne's accuracy was being significantly retarded, but getting to the next point of cover was still like running between raindrop, horizontal golden raindrops that would drive through their flesh on contact.

The chaotic scene was more or less going according to Ky's plan until the unthinkable happened. Ky's pistol ceased firing only about half way to the Guider's hangar. His guns ran out of bullets, and even worse, so did Red's. They had forgotten to reload their weapons before they

made their valiant strike. They were left virtually naked in
the center of the grassy field with absolutely no cover. They
instinctively and desperately dashed across the green plain
to the nearest point of cover to shield them from the
impending onslaught, but Ky and Red knew the awful
truth; they were sitting ducks.

Byne silently chuckled to himself as he confidently
aimed the rifle at the simple-minded unarmed men. He had
been handed his kill-shot on a silver platter and he was not
going to let it go to waste. There was nothing they could do.

Unbeknownst to anyone on the battlefield, rocket-
thrusters started igniting at full blast. The Guider's hangar
filled up with smoke within seconds. The hangar doors
blew open as craft headed out on its own unscheduled
flight. The entirely unmanned craft surprisingly took to the
sky.

Byne pulled back on the rifle's trigger, but his melee
was intercepted by the freshly sanded nose of the ever-
rising Guider. Byne lit up the side of Ky's craft as it passed
by. Byne's rifle was usually strong enough to take down
such spacecrafts, but there was something special about the
Guider.

Ky had been hailed as a hero on the planet Arlia, and
as a gift, they lined Ky's craft with a nearly impenetrable
Arlian metal. Most conventional weapons were useless
against his craft. As Byne unloaded his entire clip on the
craft, every round harmlessly ricocheted off the side of the
Guider. The craft continued skyward and vanished into an
endless blue.

"Well, well," Byne grumbled as he dropped the rifle
on to the Zenon7 M's roof. "It looks as though I did not
bring enough ammunition. This is taking more effort than
it's worth."

Ky stood in the field motionless as he witnessed his
empty craft fly away. In that moment, the Guider's actions

had saved his life, but his ultimate plan had literally flown away with the craft. His mouth gaped open in an overpowering shock and disbelief to what had just transpired. With a clouded mind, Ky blurted. "What the hell was that?"

It was the second time that Will fled down the same avenue in a chase. The first time was by a hypnotized mob then by a sword-wielding basket case. Unlike the first time, Will did not find his way to the lot behind the supermarket; there were too many innocent civilians in the way that would be thrust into his dire situation.

Instead, the boy made a left when the road ended. He knew there was a construction site located about a block down and he thought it would make be a pretty good place to hide for a while. The boy neared the chain link fence of the site with Lili following close behind and Riftkin gaining ground. The fence had an advertisement banner lining its perimeter to shield the city from the unpleasant sight of a construction zone. Will clamped onto the bottom of the fence and yanked part of it up high enough for a small child to crawl through.

"Get in!" Will commanded with a strain in his voice from keeping the piece of fence suspended in the air.

"In there?" Lili asked with disgust. "My robe will get dirty."

"Do it!"

Lili hesitated getting on her hands and knees, but she did crawl under the fence as instructed. Will looked out to the road, checking the status on Riftkin and he saw that the knight was quickly closing the gap. Once Lili wiggled through, he dropped the linked fence with a gasp of relief.

"Now grab the bottom of the fence and let me in!" Will hastily ordered.

Lili grasped the fence and let out an *urrrgh* as she

struggled to lift it up. Will shoved his way through getting scratched up a bit and the scared pair scurried into the construction site.

It was only four seconds later when Riftkin swung a vertical slash at the fence creating a perfect, nearly invisible slice that ran the complete height of the fence. The psycho knight then easily jumped clear through the fence.

On the other side was a bright large sandy and rocky lot with heavy equipment spread around. The building was only in its seedling stages of construction, so only the metal skeleton of half a building lay exposed in the center of the lot. Steel beams and wide cement tubes were stacked on top of each other, ready to be carefully assembled in place when the time came. The site was a clutter of iron alloys and concrete and had approximately thousands of places for small children to hide.

A few workers with hard hats leaned against a mixing truck with a picturesque view as the swordsman barreled onto the site.

"Hey! What are you doing!? Are you after those kids!? You're gonna pay for that fence!..." One of the brave workers started lecturing Riftkin.

Riftkin's eyes slowly set on the worker as he pulled a small knife off his belt with his freehand and threw it at the mixing truck. The blade pierced the truck's side and thick still moistened gravel mixture poured onto the workers. They veered out of the way of the cascading liquid cement, completely aware that they would need to hurry and wash the mixture off before it dried. Riftkin dashed deep into the site with a sword drawn out while the workers were occupied.

Will and Lili hid behind a stack of enormous concrete tubes out of Riftkin's immediate field of sight. The children panted endlessly and loudly as they tried to recuperate from their lengthy sprint. They were utterly drained.

Will squealed between long exaggerated heaves. "We gotta keep him busy for about five more minutes."

Lili responded panting equally as deep. "...Why?"

A sinking sound of a long sword that was skillfully swung abruptly occurred. The children's heads twisted up toward the top of the tube pile and they saw Riftkin leap on it in a single bound.

He landed on the giant cement tubes and informed. "I could hear your wheezing."

The top portion of the tube gradually slid away from the bottom creating mirrored half-pipes. It was a delayed reaction from the knight's previous sword slash. The top half of the tube tumbled down to the kids with Riftkin riding it the entire way. Will and Lili miraculously became reenergized and booked it for safety. The cement half-pipe crashed against the ground kicking up dust and shaking the area below their feet. Terror rattled Will and Lili's nerves.

Riftkin jumped off the half-pipe as it hit the ground and continued his pursuit for the children.

Will's wristwatch communicator then rang out. He never stopped running as he gazed down at the tiny monitor to see that Ky was calling him yet again. What could he possibly want?

"What?" Will answered the call in an annoyed and forceful tone.

"Uh yeah," Ky investigated. "Do you have any idea why the Guider took off all on its own?"

"Yeah! I need it!"

"No! I need it!" Ky furiously bickered. "I gotta kill this crazy-ass gunslinger before he blows mine and Red's head off!"

"Well, now I got this lunatic with a billion swords hunting us down!" Will revealed.

"Us!?" Ky remarked. "Are you still with Lili!?"

Will explained. "Look, I was gonna help her find a place, but the point is, this guy is trying to kill us and I don't have any guns like you."

On the other end of the wristwatch communicator, Ky rolled his eyes. "Fine, whatever! So what am I gonna do about my guy!? He's better than me!"

"I don't know!...I guess you gotta outsmart him!"

"Outsmart him?!? You know I'm no good with that!"

From far behind Will, the boy heard Riftkin roar like a battle cry. "Dance of a thousand slashes!" The cry was quickly followed by the sounds of a ridiculous amount of speedy sword strokes being executed. All around the kids, equipment, construction materials, and heavy trucks began getting sliced apart with expert precision. Will couldn't see any swords or even Riftkin for that matter, it was some sort of special technique he was using to cut everything around the children to ribbons.

"Hey, I gotta go!" Will concluded before rudely hanging up on Ky.

"What's going on?" Lili desperately asked jogging alongside Will while everything was being diced around them.

"Ky's apparently facing some guy with a bunch of guns." Will didn't hesitate to inform.

"A bunch of guns?" Lili repeated with a ring of vague recognition. "That sounds like Byne."

"Byne?"

"Another one of my knights,"

"Another knight?" Fragments of what must have been going on started piecing together in Will's mind. He began to devise a hypothesis for a reason behind the simultaneous attacks. An important revelation hammered at the boy's brain. His eyes went wide. "Wait a minute..."

Ky and Red were hunkered down behind a wall of the hangar that was housing the Guider before it took off on its own. It was a moment of relative calm as both parties involved in the deadly shoot-out took a minute to figure out the best course of action.

Red anxiously asked. "So what did the boy wonder say?"

"We need to outsmart him."

Red threw up his hands and his pupils rolled back into his head as he ranted. "That's it. That's it! We're screwed."

"Give me a piece of your shirt." Ky requested as he pulled a knife from his belt.

"Never on the first date."

"I'm not asking you to undress stupid, just rip off your sleeve and give it to me."

Byne unholstered another peculiar handgun. His previous gun was still in hand, (the one with two triggers that could also fire a missile) but his current predicament called for a different weapon. The new weapon was a miniaturized rotary gun with three tiny spinning barrels that could be used with a single hand. The gun's magazine was considerably larger than even Red's guns and the bullets were much more deadly. The specialized firearm also spit out rounds at a more rapid rate than the mechanic's. His plan was to spray the entire hangar with bullets so that no matter where they were behind it, they'd be hit. He knew he could riddle the hangar with hot flaming lead in seconds with his recently drawn weapon. It was checkmate.

Gunfire whizzed at Byne from the left corner of the hangar. The firing was devastatingly sloppy and Byne barely had to move to keep from being tagged. The gunslinger then deduced that the duo had to be huddled in that corner of the hangar. He cracked a game winning smile as he aimed the hand held Gatling gun at the left side of the hangar.

Ky popped out of the right side of the hangar with his photon cannon directed at Byne. His diversion had worked and Byne was too focused on the decoy gunfire to notice him. First, he drove the knife into the ground at the edge of the hangar's left corner. He tied Red's strip of cloth to the knife around the trigger of the gun so that it was constantly firing. He then positioned the gun at Byne's general direction and switched the safety off. The firearm wildly lobbed bullets at his assailant while Ky hurried to the other side to take advantage of a clear shot. The nameless gunfire had successfully grabbed Byne's attention and Ky sent a wad of positively charged neutrons sailing up at the distracted gunslinger.

Byne only realized the ruse at the sound of the cannons blast, which was too late. His eyes swerved to his right to face the dangerously close photon charge. There was no time to dodge it or even raise a gun. Ky became noteworthy in Byne's mind.

The photon charge thrashed against a wall of light between Byne and the blast. Before the gunslinger was struck, a protective blinding ball of light surrounded him. It absorbed the cannon blast and immediately disappeared, leaving Byne unscathed.

Byne held up his left arm and his long sleeve fell away. On his left wrist was a metallic armband. In the center of the band was a circular, mechanical pattern that housed a small glowing light.

"These peasants came up with a clever plan, and now there isn't much hope for my shield. Though to stay optimistic, I didn't expect the shield to weather a photon cannon blast so well. It seems my luck has not run out. Well then, no more underestimating them." Byne said to himself in analysis of the situation. The glow of the little rock in the middle of his armband faded and fizzled out.

Ky ducked back behind hangar. He leaned against its sheet metal wall and cursed. "A gamma shield. Are you serious!? How did he get a freakin' gamma shield!?"

The device Byne had used to save his life was indeed a gamma shield. It's a device that automatically surrounds its user whenever a projectile of any type gets within range. A very useful defense, however gamma shields have been outlawed for nearly a century. At one point in time, every G.F.B. soldier had been issued one because they were incredibly effective and inexpensive to manufacture. Sadly, the gamma shield's life was short lived. Even though preliminary tests had shown that the amount of gamma radiation a person would be exposed to when the shield activated was safe, people started getting sick. Gamma shields had caused a vicious string of cancer cases and other severe complications. Anyone who had ever been equipped with a gamma shield that had activated even once eventually died from a related illness. Yet despite the weapon's high level of danger, Byne had been using one.

Chunks of perfectly filleted construction gear flew about the children's area and chilled them to the bone.

"Do you have any more knights?" Will interrogated.

"Yes. Baloe, the most powerful, and my brother Doc," Lili promptly responded.

"They must be with Jina."

"What are you talking about?"

"I think your knights are keeping my friends busy," His eyes then fixed on Lili with a brewing seriousness. "So this one can get to you."

Lili's head faced forward and slumped over with guilt in her gaze. She felt the weight of the blame at its heaviest that day. She truly didn't mean to be the cause of that much carnage.

Will wasn't particularly paying attention to his

footing and he accidentally stumbled over a sizable rock. The boy tripped flat on his face, meaning he would be the first to suffer their impending doom.

Lili paused for a moment in shock of Will's nasty tumble. She gasped with eyes as wide as the sun and her hands covered her mouth.

"Run! Keep going! Run! Hide!" Will loudly ordered with a ferocity that drove a stake to the middle of Lili. After that, she did as she was told. Lili turned back around and darted deeper into the construction site.

Will flipped his body around and was about to get up, until he caught sight of what was standing over him. It was Riftkin, with a sword already by the boy's nose. The boy was caught like a deer in headlights as his body was rendered motionless with fear.

Riftkin cracked a wild smile as his one visible eye wiggled at the boy. He whispered. "Dues ex machina."

"What?" The boy's seven minutes were up.

Suddenly Riftkin heard a very familiar sound. It was the sound of a craft's rocket thrusters roaring intensely. As his eyes searched the sky he saw a craft that was heading a little too close to the ground. The craft was flying down so fast that everyone on the site was convinced that it was going to collide with a crane. Riftkin relaxed his grip on his blade for a second and Will instantly took the opportunity to make his escape.

He ran about nine yards away from the mesmerized knight and placed his fingers inside ten corresponding circular hooks that were neatly organized on his vest. He pulled his fingers away from his chest, revealing thin, practically invisible, wires that tightly threaded from the hooks to his vest. The boy smiled confidently and chuckled. "This is over." Will then systematically twitched his wired fingers up and down.

Will was implementing two other features of the vest besides the electric pulse. The first was how the genius hacker was able to make the Guider come to him with no one driving. This era did have the kind of technology to accurately guide a craft somewhere with no driver, but that was only certain important registered areas like space-ports or government buildings. If you wanted to get around in your craft to any normal place, having someone piloting is the only real practical way. What Will did when he pushed that button on his vest earlier was virtually register the area around him as a landmark and then sent a piloting request to the Guider. The Guider was the only craft the boy genius could pull off that trick with because it was the only one that was registered to his landmark's frequency.

The second feature was only a dream until his trip to Arlia. Some of Arlian's finest technological engineers helped the boy perfect his programming. It was a program to manipulate the Guider through the wires on his vest. Every time Will twitched a finger, he was sending a specific command to the Guider's system. This was the first time he was using it since the reprogramming. He hadn't had a chance to test it yet.

The nose of the Guider skimmed across the dirt ground, missing it by mere inches as it raced at the immobile Riftkin. Dust and wind raged on in a fight as the tip of the Guider thundered at the knight. Riftkin very methodically shifted his body to face the charging spacecraft with a sword pointed directly at it. Once the immense craft was close enough, Riftkin took a very fast swat at it with his sword. It seemed as though his intent was to actually cut through the craft. The lunatic's razor sharp blade landed on the Guider's unbreakable shell with a loud clink. Ky's craft plowed straight into the knight. The craft crashed into the building under construction, launching Riftkin's body through a thick steel beam and into the frame's interior.

Will ran along the construction site to adjust and improve his field of vision, but also to make sure he was witnessing all the action. His fingers continued to twitch like a master puppeteer on his favorite marionette.

The Guider backed away from the building showcasing the dented, deformed metal frame caused by the craft. The craft leveled out, hovering about twelve feet off the ground. The full sized twin photon cannons that Ky illegally installed slightly swiveled before relentlessly blasting charge after charge into the skeleton half building. The photon waves bombarded the dense metallic support rods and exploded into its interior. A swirl of dust and flaming ash mixed into the air as the building began to topple and collapse.

Riftkin burst out of the side of the building in a blazing flurry of sword slashes with three blades. One sword was gripped normal in his right hand and two were in his left in an awkward angle held between his fingers. God only knows what the unbalanced man was doing in there to defend himself, but with the addition of two more unsheathed blades, it appeared as though he was kept quite busy. Riftkin landed against orange dirt ground with a thud, got up, and kept running. His movements were less fluid and graceful. It was evident that the Guider's attacks had caused him bodily harm.

The Guider slowly oscillated, attempting to keep the deranged knight inside the trajectory of the continuous photon fire. Riftkin was literally staying one step ahead of the devastating photon charges.

Riftkin then dramatically stopped and faced the Guider as its attack was inevitably set on him. He was going to try dodging the photon charges blast by blast.

Rather than the obvious dangers of staring down the barrels of two photon cannons, those weapons posed more of a threat than Ky's miniaturized hand held version.

The technology that was involved in the construction of photon cannons can't help but be big and bulky. A person strong enough to carry around a photon cannon is a rarity, so the concept of even a two-handed photon weapon was a farfetched idea. That was until an engineer by the name of Dedrick Matierre tackled the impossible task. This genius engineer was the only person to create a reliable miniaturized version of the photon engine with special parts he titled *disc-gears*. The engineer reached fame status when he patented both *disc-gears* and *the mini-photon engine*. Matierre successfully built a little over a hundred single-handed photon cannons before he died, dragging his highly sought after secrets to the grave with him. That sparked an entire generation of hunters and collectors who wouldn't think twice about killing a person to just to get one of those photon cannons in their possession. They gradually stretched across the known universe as many died coveting and searching for those weapons. Some estimate there must be an average of three in each industrialized solar system. The miniature cannon Ky had was the seventy-second one that Dedrick Matierre built and was a much rarer piece than even Byne's gamma shield.

With how impressive the history of the one handed photon cannon may have been, it actually just wasn't as powerful as a regular sized cannon. Even though both used identical power-cells, the smaller parts resulted in less potency in the charge. Riftkin was lost in a display of his true madness as he simply waited for photon blasts to shoot straight at him. If Riftkin didn't dodge each swirly mass of neutrons just right, he could end up with a beach ball-sized hole in his chest. The first cannon blared, and exactly how the knight had planned, he quickly dashed to his left at the last second. He then found himself facing another photon charge, so this time, he jolted into his previous position;

making sure it was after the last blast had blown through the ground. He did that again and again, infuriating the boy whom was trying to neutralize his assailant. Little did the kid know that Riftkin was grabbing another blade off his body every time he shifted. In a few seconds, the maniac had taken all his swords in his hands, simply wrapping his fists around the multiple hilts. A couple more seconds passed before the photon cannons ceased firing completely.

Calm returned to the scene momentarily. The landscape hissed with the sound of the eye of the battle. The cannon's power-cells had been all used up. There was an automated system installed on the Guider that reloaded the photon cannons, but it took a while. It was time that Will didn't have. He knew Riftkin would be able to reach and kill him within that time. His little wired fingers wiggled like mad.

The knight looked far off in Will's direction and smiled. He very haphazardly tossed all his swords straight up high into the air above his own head. He then called out. "Dance of the guards!" He knelt down in place.

A pair of hidden gun turrets just beneath the nose of the Guider rapidly discharged devastatingly massive bullets out of its calibers. Will had truly outdone himself, for the swarm of bullets was heading directly at the kneeling psychopath. The gunfire had nearly smashed against Riftkin's face until it met a metal slab of compressed titanium instead. One of Riftkin's swords sunk itself into the soil in front him when it fell, saving him from the gun's barrage. All his other swords soon followed, each one landing at a specific point that only added to his defense. The blades dropped so close to his body, that it seemed like he must have been getting sliced apart. In the end, Riftkin was in the middle of an impenetrable cocoon of swords surrounding him.

Bullets continually pelted against the knight's

cleverly formed shield, but it was no use. Riftkin's swords were well wedged into the dirt and were impregnable. The blinding gunfire ricocheted and bounced everywhere, tearing up the site around the blade-barrier into little pieces.

Dust, piles of gravel, and dirt covered the sky, but Will kept on firing his guns. The boy was convinced the turrets' onslaught would break through his defenses, so he just kept on shooting.

High up in the sky, a tiny black floating camera spied on all three battle sites.

G-Web station XGNN, Gohanesse News Network, broadcasted its emergency signals that day like all other web stations did, but more trouble lurked on top of its building. A man was sitting on the tip of the metal scaffolding that the station used to broadcast its signal. The man had a peculiar set of binoculars pressed to his eyes. The binoculars relayed images of the fights as they happened. He knew everything that was going on.

The white-haired Doc pulled the binoculars away from his face and commented. "You guys wanted to fight sooo bad, now you got what you asked for. It looks like you guys will be needing my intervention after all." Doc stood up on the scaffolding's slender iron bar demonstrating his exceptional sense of balance. Doc hung the binoculars around his neck by a leather strap, shut his eyes, and placed his hands together as if lost deep in prayer.

Ky had retrieved his pistol and reloaded it. He and Red were still pinned behind the hangar and Mr. Marrado was becoming delirious. He started shouting at the calmer Ky out of frustration.

He noisily complained. "Well that didn't work at all! Do you have any more bright ideas Matierre?"

Ky yelled back. "Be quiet! I'm trying to think!"

Byne looked down upon his own frame. His body had begun glowing a golden hue. It was a mystical sight to behold.

"It seems as though Doc does not believe we can handle this on our own steam. Well it does not matter. There is not a thing I can do about it now." Byne remarked about the strange phenomenon.

Byne pointed his gun down toward his opponents, but that time, something was different. The gunslinger's eyes focused more accurately than humanly possible. It was as if he was only half the distance away at that moment. He aimed his pistol at a small portion of Red's arm that poked out of the side of the hangar several centimeters. Byne sent a single bullet at it.

A bullet plugged Red in his arm and he fell forward. The mechanic then crept to his knees and gauged his injury. "I've been shot? Oh my God! I've been shot!"

"Shhhh..." Ky hushed.

"Easy for you to say, you haven't been shot!"

"Shut up!" Ky frantically ordered. "I'm trying to figure something out here!" Ky then speedily started babbling some incoherency. It seemed as though he wasn't thinking straight. "Okay. If I shot at his left, he'll dip right. Then if I shoot at his head, he'll duck. If I shot again, he'll jump. Then if I shot him in the air...that's it...I got it." Ky's face brightened up when the ladder portion of his sentence had passed his lips. Ky happily darted out from behind the safety of the hangar's wall. Red watched him as if his friend had truly lost his marbles.

Ky popped out of the side of the wall looking up at his skilled assailant. One of his eyes was covered by the barrel of his drawn weapon. Ky intended to best Byne with his pistol alone and he holstered his photon cannon. Ky showing himself so suddenly took Byne by surprise, giving our hero the single chance to fire off the one round he so

desperately needed.

Ky shot at his left and Byne dipped right. At that instant, Ky then discharged another bullet at Byne's skull. The gunslinger ducked underneath the hot lead. Ky fired again at his foe, but Byne jumped at the right time avoiding the strike. Ky let out another round aimed directly between Byne's eyes, but gravity started taking affect and pulled him down just enough for the bullet to fly right over his head. The gunslinger wasn't landing back on the roof of the Zenon7 M, but instead, his descent continued down to the floor of the grassy plain. Ky shot at him once more as Byne's body dropped like a rock in front of the expensive craft. Ky then let loose another bullet from his gun's chamber that also missed Byne. It seemed like a last ditch effort, because the shot was sloppily administered and had not a chance of hitting the plummeting fiend.

Byne's feet met with the grass. He jolted into a standing position and directed his firearm at the defenseless Ky. Byne hesitated his game winning shot as he witnessed Ky's expression. A sinister grin was planted on his face. He investigated. "For what reason do you bear a smile?"

Something splashed against the knight's back unexpectedly. A thick bronze liquid continued to ooze on him and inevitably found its way into his firearms, jamming up their tiny mechanics. The confused gunslinger shifted his vision skyward to find out what it was that was gushing all over him. It was propulsion fuel. Ky's last few wild shots had no intention of hitting him, but rather he planned to pierce the Zenon7 M's fuel tank. The fuel cascaded upon Byne and dripped the oily substance everywhere. The highly flammable goo made its way through the blades of grass and trailed by Ky's feet.

Ky casually knelt down and put his gun's barrel at the end of the fuel trail.

Byne knew at that time he'd been bested. His

weapons were all but useless and even if he could escape the fire-stream that Ky could spark at any time, the fire's intense heat could ignite his fuel-drenched body without direct contact. With no other logical action to take, Byne dropped his weapons and raised his hands in the universal symbol of surrender.

With his pistol still at the fuel trail, Ky sighed deeply and admitted. "Man, that sucked."

Smoke and fire plumes grew and surrounded the construction site as the Guider's barrage of gunfire began to slow down. Will was still determined to break through Riftkin's sword barrier but, so much dust had been kicked around by the boy, he couldn't tell if the craft was hitting its mark, so he halted his assault for a moment until he could see clearly.

"Will!" The boy heard Lili call out with urgency. Will maneuvered his head to face the direction of her voice.

Lili was standing safely off in the distance, but there was something different about her appearance. A divine golden glow was emitting from her countenance. Despite the benevolent occurrence, her face was ruled by despair. She warned. "Be careful! He's much stronger now!"

Lili's worry began to infect Will and his eyes went back to check on his adversary. The smog lifted enough so that Riftkin's sword shield became visible. The compressed titanium cocoon was still in place, but swords were missing from the bunch. The absent scimitars made Will able to peer inside the barrier and he saw the enclosure was empty. The unbalanced knight had fled from the protection of his swords.

Riftkin exploded out of a cloud of dust wielding the two missing sabers in his hands. He, like Lili, was glowing with the mysterious golden hue and felt a new surge of strength and confidence. He fiercely dashed across the area, sprinting at more than double his previous top running speed. His image streaked along his path similar to a long marker stroke. He scurried around the construction site like a pesky mouse at hyper speed.

Will made the Guider swivel to the side in an attempt to better face the speed-demon. The craft unleashed a volley of bullets at Riftkin's direction once again, but it was no match for the knight's new found speed.

Riftkin bravely advanced at the galactic cruiser, easily crisscrossing between its oncoming gunfire. The psycho truly meant to meet the giant craft head on. An enormous dust-tail followed behind the knight as he reached the Guider's face without a scratch. Riftkin swung a silvery upward slash at the Guider and its left photon cannon separated from the craft.

The unbreakable Arlian alloy that covered the Guider was difficult to weld, fashion, and mold small intricate moving parts and gears, so the cannons and weaponry of the craft was much less durable than the majority of its body.

Riftkin leapt into a double-flip with a twist and landed on the roof of the Guider; it was an awesome display of his acrobatics.

The knight knelt on one knee and uttered. "If this doesn't work, nothing will." He then gave it everything he had as he drove one of his long blades down at the shell of the craft. The sword instantly snapped in two upon impact with the Guider's tough hull. Riftkin examined his hilt and sword stump in sheer astonishment.

All ten of Will's little wired fingers lifted at that moment, and the Guider's hull was filled with a hefty electrical current. Much like his vest, it raced along the craft's outer edge and Riftkin fell victim to its unseen attack. Fifty-thousand volts of electricity ripped through the knight's body, and the fact that he was holding the swords in his hands made the charge that much more severe. Riftkin's glow faded and he fell from the craft without even trying to break his fall. He was no longer conscious. A small dust cloud plumed up as his limp motionless body plopped to the ground.

Will blew a huge sigh of relief as he removed his fingers from the hooked wires that then recoiled into his mechanical vest. His head slouched over just glad that the entire ordeal was over.

An enthusiastic *Good job!* rang out right behind the boy that put his nerves in haywire again. His body jolted around to a smiling and literally glowing Lili who happily wasted no time approaching the boy after the danger had passed.

The boy let out another large breath to calm himself then angrily inquired. "All right! What's going on!?"

Baloe just stood there. His body was so bleeding and broken that he decided to mount an entirely defensive position. He waited in the same spot and just watched her in case she attacked. Basically, his plan could succeed if either one or both of two different conditions were met. The first being that one of the other knights already won their bout and showed up as backup, and the second was that Doc would finally intervene. Baloe always preferred Doc, and on that day, he got his wish.

Baloe's broken body miraculously grew completely erect with ease as his wide chest emanated a deepened golden glow. As his bright golden hue slowly advanced toward Jina, his busted jaw formed as much of a satisfied smirk as it could muster. He halted about twenty-feet away from the still immobile Jina. He then boasted. "This game shall go differently now. One of my comrades has the ability to amplify the talents and skills of person that contains certain DNA. In my case, that would mean my strength, speed, and overall skills for battle are multiplied in an instant." The colossal knight took a fighting stance. "I hope you're ready, because now I can't afford to take it easy on you."

Baloe's outrageous swing was no exaggeration. That strike was in a totally separate league than his previous attacks. Despite all that, his thrashing was knocked back. He didn't notice that she tried hitting him at the same time and he merely deflected her blow. She was coming again, and the knight realized that he could actually see her movements, but they were still blurred. Jina was still much faster. He could not afford any mistakes if he wished to claim victory.

Baloe's gravel club and Jina's metal staff rapidly bashed against each other like a public declaration of the two titans dueling. The two titanic weapons' pings echoed for miles. The gargantuan knight started to convince himself that he could pull off defeating her. Baloe was timing her blows, looking for a pattern and a possible opportunity for a counterattack. He waited for the moment when he figured it out and came with his own undetectable counter-swing. His club still met with the end of Jina's staff, but on that particular swing, something very bad happened for the knight. His ears picked up a low-pitched reverberation immediately followed by his giant gravel club blowing up into crumbling pieces. Then a wall of wind smacked against Baloe three times harder than Jina's normal attacks, and the force applied to every inch of the front half of his body. He was tossed through the air like a rag doll.

Once the echo of the thunderous clap of Jina's technique died down, Baloe lifted his head off the busted cement below him, some forty feet away from Jina. All at once, Jina was then over his devastated form with the end of her slender long staff to his throat. Baloe's eyes rolled back before he closed them accepting his loss.

Jina's head twisted to the sky noticing huge towers of smog and dust off in the distance.

Jina stopped walking when she visually located Will and Lili on the construction site. By that time, the children had got a hold of some support straps designed for securing heavy cargo bins inside the Guider, and had bound up Riftkin with them. Their cute heads shifted away from Will's laptop when they spotted Jina's arrival.

When Jina showed up, she had a ten-inch thick iron beam wrapped around the unconscious Baloe. She carried him by the beam like a baseball at her side.

Will urgently wailed. "There's another one! I tracked him to the top of that tower." Will and Lili simultaneously pointed at the scaffolding of XGNN on the far horizon.

Jina chucked Baloe's body to the floor before taking off on foot.

Doc observed his allies' situations worsen through his binoculars. He then repeatedly checked if what he was seeing at the construction site was real. Something about the scene wasn't adding up. Doc wondered aloud. "Where'd that girl go?"

BAM! The pair of binoculars was smashed in his hands by a mighty silvery flash. The white-haired man's eyes reluctantly lurked up. There he saw Jina in all her grace and deadliness hanging by a bar with one hand and wielding her mighty staff in the other. He dropped the binocular pieces while putting up his hands and pleading. "Please don't kill me."

An agreeable smile formed on Jina's luscious lips. "You made the wise decision."

About forty-five minutes later, Doc, Baloe, and Riftkin were tied up as hostages in the middle of Ky's living room. Will, Jina and Lili roamed freely around the apartment, discussing what they were going to do with the knights a little too casually. That's when Ky made it home.

Ky walked through the gaping hole that used to be his front door with a gun stuck up to Byne's oily back. Once in the living room, he pushed down the fiend toward the other knights with his pistol. "So is this where we're dumping all the flunkies?"

Will sprang up, running to Ky with a proposal. "Ky! We need to do something!"

Ky then caught a glimpse of Lili in the kitchen. "Why is she still here!? This is all because of her. Isn't it!?" Ky motioned over to the round kitchen table and had a seat.

"That's what I wanna talk to you about..."

Ky didn't mind interrupting the boy with a finger to the wall's huge hole where the door used to be. "And what the hell is this!?"

"Ky," Will reasoned. "We all had our own fights to deal with. That wasn't even me, it was Jina's fight."

"The wall is my fault...sorry." Baloe apologized from the living room floor with his usual ruggedness in his tone.

"Don't worry, we'll get it fixed." Will resolved.

Ky grasped Will's satchel and lazily asked. "Oh yeah, and how are you gonna do that?"

Will took a seat as well and informed. "You remember? This morning? I told you I jacked these accounts numbers? I'll pay for it with that."

"You better,"

"Anyway, I think we should help them."

A brow lifted up in disbelief of Will's audacity for such a suggestion. "You mean the people who tried to kill us."

"Ky, they're knights, and they were waiting until the G.F.B. and the IO were too caught up with each other to separate us and get Lili back."

"Great!" Ky sarcastically cheered. "They can leave now, good riddance."

"They missed their window and they have no real way back to their region of the universe."

Ky slouched in his seat and roared with a pushy attitude. "Exactly what are you suggesting?"

Everyone in the studio/warehouse felt the weight of the mounting tension in the air. Jina then chose to alleviate some of the tension. The beautiful warrior walked up to the nervous Lili and said. "Lili, why don't you show me your room?"

"Okay," Lili timidly accepted. The ladies headed upstairs to see the room and escape the conversation.

Once the ladies were in the room, Will clarified. "I'm saying we help get them back home. We're bound to be showered with riches for getting their princess back."

"The rarest of jewels and wealth beyond your wildest dream would be bestowed upon you if you were to assist us." Byne elaborated.

"Hey, butt out buddy." Ky ordered to Byne. His attention then diverted to the boy once again. "So you wanna do this for money? If we have those account numbers then what good is more money?" Ky announced while removing the laptop from the satchel's pouch.

"The numbers plan isn't full-proof. Once people notice the missing money, they could have accounts shut down or traced to us. If we make our fortune through them, I don't care who's snooping around, no one would be able to trace our loot to the unknown region." Will bantered.

Ky flipped opened the laptop and switched it on. "And how do you plan on doing that? Another wormhole?" Ky laughed.

"Well..."

Ky's eyes grew. "Are you serious? You wanna

illegally go through another wormhole?"

"Well actually two," Will admitted. "One to get there, and one to get back."

"I don't care." Ky showed his indifference. "Just make sure I get a huge portion of the booty and leave me out of any of the work. I've had enough long distance space travel for one year."

"That I can do," Will agreed. "But I'd need a big favor to do my thing."

"Oh geez!" An annoyed Ky moaned. "What do you want?" He started firing up the computer.

"You see," Will negotiated. "We'd need to lay low for a while so the heat can cool down before I make my move."

Ky smiled while web surfing. "Oh Will, are you asking for a prolonged slumber party?"

"If you wanna call it that,"

"Fine, but I do nothing and get a huge chunk of the booty, AND make sure they don't bother me or get in my way."

"Yes!" A wild grin was seen on the boy's face. "Thanks man, you won't regret it."

"Yeah yeah,"

"What are you doing?" Will questioned leaning over to gain a view of the laptop's monitor.

"Get out of here. I'm checking my Headscript."

VI

The Knight Life

Only a couple of days rolled by until the knights were getting on everybody's nerves. It took the gruesome squad of four virtually no time to slide into their daily annoying habits. Our three heroes were coping with the knight's idiosyncrasies in their own way. Jina didn't technically live in the apartment, so it was easy for her just to leave. Will secretly wanted to spend more time with Lili, so he just bottled it all up. Ky was amazingly taking it the easiest. He was just too laid back to get all worked up over four strange guys crashing at his place. The only thing that truly bothered Ky was Lili. He still showed obvious resentment toward her. The days slothfully crept by with every inhabitant at the studio/warehouse aware that some type of move had to be made sooner or later.

That morning was a beehive of activity. Baloe was in the kitchen area silently brewing a boiling concoction in a giant silvery soup pot. His proud chiseled face was well-wrapped in bandages because of the injuries that Jina had inflicted upon him. Bandages were dressed around his waist and chest as well. Doc and Riftkin were hogging the television playing a video game drably titled *Bash of the*

Gods. It was a two-player fighting game in which you can play as characters loosely based off of fabled gods. Their attention was nearly cut off from the rest of the apartment as they wholeheartedly tried to kick each other's virtual ass. Byne had locked himself in the bathroom for some peculiar reason. Lili sat at the round dining table across from Ky whose head was still hidden in another IO helmet. (the helmet in which Jina discarded) He apparently didn't trust her to stop manipulating minds. Jina stood out front against the wall with her staff in hand just surveying the passing IO. She was like a guard assuring the army would stay at a distance. As for Will, he was pacing eccentrically around the apartment like a chicken with its head cut off. He was like a high-strung mother trying to helplessly manage the entire household.

"Will, sit down." Ky advised. "You're gonna stress yourself out and you're making me nervous."

"You want me to sit down? Fine, I'll sit down." The boy strangely reasoned. "After I found out what he's making." Will said with the tip of his finger directed at Baloe's well-built back.

Baloe's left eyebrow lifted a level higher than his right as Will's sentence concluded. He wondered why he was ousted.

The boy slyly glided to Baloe's side trying to seem casual but obviously being nosy. His elbows rested on the countertop as his eyes skimmed Baloe and his thick boiling brew. The huge silvery soup pot was nearly over flowing with an unappealing grayish slop. The mountain-sized man attentively stirred the peculiar mixture with a large black plastic spoon.

Will indifferently inquired. "Sooo- what is that? 'Cause I don't think we can eat it. It looks gross and smells like chalk."

"The substance that makes up my club is no ordinary

gravel." The giant knight began to explain. "I'm carefully making a batch so I can mold it to the rest of the remaining shards and forge a new club."

"Hmm," Will remarked. "Is that crap gonna be easy to clean?"

Silence fell over Baloe as his error began to process in his head. He knew a thin layer of film would most likely remain on the pot and harden to a substance tougher than the pan itself. Thoughts raced in his head of how to quell the situation. Baloe proposed. "I'll buy you a new pot."

Will had formed an angered gaze during the knight's suspicious silence and it fell on Baloe harder at that moment.

The huge man realized what he was mixing it with. "And a spoon."

Will released a disgruntled sigh before his eyes rolled away from Baloe. He knew if he barreled into a speech about his growing annoyances that Ky would be quick to come in with an "*I told you so*" comment.

Riftkin then yelled while lifting his controller skyward in celebration. "I win again."

"Whatever," A fed up Will said. "I gotta take a leak." He trudged over to the rickety sheet metal door and knocked on it thoroughly. "Hey Byne! You done yet?"

"Please accept my dearest apologies, but if you would allow me a few more moments to properly freshen up." Byne answered from inside the bathroom.

The gunslinger was at the sink leaning over it with his face pointed to the bowl. He had the faucet on full blast making entirely sure that the blood he had spat into it minutes earlier was washed out. Byne wanted to hide his secret from the others. He looked up in the mirror to see his bagged eyes and paling skin. He deeply wondered how far gone his body had become.

Riftkin then cheered from the living room with a

gratifying smile to the television screen. "I win again! This has to be the best game ever!"

"This game is stupid." The consistently losing Doc grumbled on the couch beside Riftkin. He threw his controller down in frustration.

"Hey! Watch the merchandise." Will warned. "Remember none of this is your stuff."

The way the morning was going was not only getting on the boy's nerves but someone else was having enough. Ky just had to interject. "Yeah, so Will, when is that Universal Treker scheduled to arrive?"

"Not 'til next week." Will replied.

"You know, it's funny." Ky investigated. "Last time you pulled this trick off you were able to do it with the Treker light years away, but now it's got to be in close proximity. Why is that?"

"Well, you know, with the networks and my laptop's functions and... uh..." Will incoherently babbled.

"Smells like bull." Ky commented before swiftly lifting the mask for a sip of beer then sliding it back down just as fast.

It was then that Byne waltzed out of the bathroom like royalty. He leaned against the flat side of the couch and assured. "The throne is yours young man."

"Thank God." Will sighed before promptly heading to the toilet to relieve himself.

"So what is it you're doing in there, pretty boy?" Ky clowned on the gunslinger. "You take longer than the crazy little girl."

Lili covered a light chuckle with her little delicate hand.

Byne shot back. "Perhaps I could be quicker if I was not subjected to such meager accommodations."

"Hey buddy, there's not many places around here

taking in wanted people. If you wanna try one of those, there's the door." Ky huffed back gesturing to the hole in his wall truly a little offended.

They still didn't have the gaping hole fixed yet. Will had called for repairs the next day, but so much damage had been caused in the city that it was going to be a week minimum before anyone was going to even look at it. All anyone in the apartment had done to help was crudely hang a blue tarp over the opening.

Byne further heckled. "This cement shack is no bigger than Lili's personal closet."

Lili giggled once more undeniably tickled from Byne and Ky's bickering. Both hands then came to her giant smile to mask it.

"Isn't it your snoring I hear all night?" Ky recalled.

That was true. Byne's pampered behind slept like a baby night after night on his own futon on the balcony. Baloe slept on his own futon as well, but he had to; he was just plain too big to even think about putting any place else. Doc spent his nights on the couch while Riftkin would drift asleep sitting erect on the edge of the white dining table.

"Rubbish," The knight denied. "No person associated with a royal family would snore."

By that time, Will had finished his visit to the toilet and made his way back.

Ky's attention switched to the boy. "Hey Will, can I shoot this guy's head off yet?"

"All I know is, you can *attempt* to fire at me." Byne corrected.

"All I know is, I won that last duel we had, remember?" Ky mentioned delivering a felt sting. He all too soon flubbed up his smoothness. "So, yeah!...respect."

"All right guys! Knock it off!" Will shouted charging in between them. "Ky, if you don't calm down I'm gonna tell them about the fungicide I found in the bathroom."

Everyone in the apartment let out a hearty laugh; even the completely distracted Doc and Riftkin chuckled at that one.

"Oh that's cool." Ky whined. "Why not just put all my personal business on full blast?" The pilot then sarcastically announced to the entire room. "I have occasional athlete's foot people. ATHLETE'S FOOT!"

"You also need to cease with your smart mouthing too Byne." Lili ordered finally joining in after Will said something.

"Princess, this man is a drunk and beneath me. He is assuredly hopped up on all types of dopeys and skibbys and other various drugs." Byne argued.

Ky quietly repeated with a confused disbelief beneath his IO helmet. "Skibbys?"

Jina then abruptly walked through the blue flap into the studio/warehouse. She acknowledged no one until she quickly reached Ky at the table and informed. "Detective Lee's and a few other G.F.B. vehicles just parked outside."

Will blared from the news. "Detective Lee!? What is he doing here!?" The boy questioned at Ky.

"I don't know!" Ky convincingly replied.

Will asked. "Do you think he's gonna wonder why they're here?"

"Welllll..." Ky droned as if opening the tab to his sarcasm reservoir. "Seeing it with everything that's going on in the world and the fact that we're harboring galactic fugitives, yeah; I'd say he'd have something to ask about it."

"Crap! Quick, you guy's gotta hide." Will hastily demanded to Lili and her knights.

"Where are they gonna hide?" Ky pointed out. "You know he's gonna be looking all over the place. He's gonna find them."

"How 'bout the passage in the bathroom under the sink?" The boy hysterically suggested.

"Nope," Ky said shaking his head slowly from side to side. "Only the girl can actually fit in it."

"We're screwed."

"Don't worry!" Lili suddenly called out. "Just follow my lead." She said as she got up from the chair. "Knights, lay your bodies flat against the side wall."

All four knights immediately complied and spread their bodies as flat as they could on the wall behind the television set. After all the knights lined and pressed themselves against the wall the princess' focus fell back to the apartment's true original inhabitants.

Lili oddly instructed. "Okay, now just act like we're not here." She then joined her bodyguards as she pressed against the wall as well. Her eyes drifted to a close as her head hung down. Her lips slowly formed silent words like divine chanting.

Ky, Will, and Jina simply watched as their strange house guests started implementing the vague and highly questionable plan. They were all just standing against the wall, plain as day, hoping not to be seen. It all seemed so infantile in nature that the trio was left speechless and unable to voice the numerous flaws the plan had. Unfortunately they had no more time and the plan went undisputed as Detective Lee and his men rushed inside.

Lee and his men moved the tarp aside and barged in. It was after the detective was already inside when he knocked on the broken cement wall and said. "You got company."

An overly relaxed Ky and an outrageously nervous Will sat at the dining table by the entrance. Jina leaned against the far wall greeting the detective and his entourage as they examined the place. Even though Ky and his friends could clearly see Lili and her knights against the wall, the G.F.B. affiliates failed to notice them at all. It was like the five of them were rendered invisible.

Lee's eyes instantly zipped to Ky's masked face and he suspiciously inquired. "Ky, why are you wearing an IO..."

Lili's eyes twitched slightly.

"..." The detective remained silent as the relevancy of his question vanished in a flash. A moment earlier Lee could have sworn that Ky had on an IO helmet but as the agent's gaze found him again, the helmet was gone as if it had never been there to begin with. "...uh...nothing." Lee vigorously rubbed his eyes and continued. "I must be working too hard...my eyes are playing tricks on me."

"Can we help you?" Ky tried to hurry along.

Detective Lee and his men settled into the heart of the large apartment with their eyes casually combing the apartment's walls. Lee rushed the questioning. "Yeah, I'm here doing a follow up report on the events involving the Diamond of Faith heist, do you remember it?"

"Yeah," Ky admitted in an annoyed manner.

"Good," Lee rang, taking a small notebook from his trench coat and jotting down a few notes. "Now, do you know where Hanz M. Denicci is?"

"In a shallow grave in the sands of Asteroid Q." Jina answered from her spot on the wall.

"Good!" Lee bellowed even louder then followed up with more note taking. "And the diamond... Do you know the whereabouts of the Diamond of Faith?"

Will stayed quiet for a second unsure how he should respond to the simple inquiry. "... Uh, Arlia?"

"Good," Lee said one final time before tucking his little notebook back in his coat. "So what's the story with the door?" Lee asked with an interrogating thumb to the giant hole in the wall behind him.

"Uh, well..." The boy thought up an excuse quickly. "I guess someone decided it shouldn't be there during those missing eleven days."

"Now that we're chit-chattin' about that, what do you guys make of that whole hullabaloo?" Lee gracefully transitioned to his true investigation.

The question was mainly directed at Ky for being the man of the house, but he just sat there for a minute shrugging his shoulders and commenting. "Don't look at me."

"Well... you know... we think what everybody else does. You know? Maybe a little of this, maybe that weird new army. You know? What everybody else thinks... maybe." An obviously nervous Will blathered on.

Detective Lee's suspicious gaze covered Will as the boy's odd rant rendered him speechless for a moment. The detective's deductive gears were turning in his head. "You mind if we look around?"

"Go right ahead." Ky promptly answered sounding almost like he wanted to be caught.

"All right boys, do a good once-over and let me know if you find anything suspicious." Lee delegated to his men.

"Yes sir," The soldiers chanted in harmony before they spread out to the four corners of the studio/warehouse. It was an unwarranted search so the soldiers respectfully didn't break anything or go punching holes in Ky's walls. They just scoured the apartment from top to bottom. Will's dramatically thumping heart nearly skipped a beat as a soldier passed by the wall that Lili and her knights were quietly pressed to. The soldier stared dead at the galactic fugitives but miraculously just walked away as if he had no clue that they were just blatantly standing there. One soldier rummaged through the bathroom, another reluctantly entered Ky's room, and a couple went upstairs to search through Will's room. "Sir," A soldier called to Lee while executing a head jerk gesturing to the boiling pot filled with Baloe's gravel mixture.

"What's that?" The detective immediately asked.

"Just making some stew." Ky joked knowing that the dark thick oozing substance in the pot could never be mistaken for any kind of stew.

The soldier further analyzed the contents of the pot. "It smells... delicious!" The chalky thick powdery stench romanced the soldier's nose. The soldier tilted his head over the pot and loudly filled his nostrils with the aroma.

"Well Ky, I wouldn't have pegged you as such a culinary wiz." Lee complimented in his own way.

"What can I say?" Ky bragged as he lounged deeper in his chair.

The soldier mixed together the hot gravel with the spoon as his mouth watered. "Noodles, beef, potatoes..." The soldier took a spoonful of the inedible mixture and put it to his lips. The boy's face curdled in horror as the soldier gladly ingested the gravel with a smile on his face. "It's fantastic."

Words could not form in Will's head as he wondered about the health implications that are involved with eating gravel. The soldier wasn't going to die, but there was going to be a week that he'd wish he could rip his stomach out as the gravel inched through his digestive tract. The man had no clue.

Detective Lee's eyes wandered over to the lit up television screen. "What's this?" He questioned as he marched to the monitor of the set for a closer examination.

"Umm... I was just playing the game." Will lied on the spot.

"It's set for two players." Lee pointed out.

"We were both playing." Ky covered for the boy.

"Quite a casual game don't you think? The time is still running." Lee interrogated. He was knelt down with his face to the screen soaking in all he could. Little did the detective know that just past the television stood Lili and her knights.

Ky clarified as he placed his hands behind his head. "Well, that's the kind of laid-back living we've grown accustomed to here."

"Is that so?" Lee played along. "Hey Jina, did you get down on a couple rounds of this?"

"Please," The gorgeous warrior replied. "I don't play video games."

"Of course not,"

"Hey Lee, are we done here?" Ky said obviously implying that the detective had overstayed his welcome.

"Any bum-outs should refer to me as detective and yeah, I think we got what we need." Lee said. "All right boys, let's get out of this heap."

The soldiers ceased their search and converged on Lee in the living area.

"Go on boys, start heading out." The detective ordered to his soldiers. They filed out the hole in the front one by one as Lee turned around for a few parting words. "It's pretty freaky stuff happening around town... I'll keep in touch." Detective Lee followed the last subordinates out. They all trotted back to their vehicles.

As they leisurely strolled back, one of Lee's soldiers sympathized. "Too bad we couldn't come up with anything boss."

"They were lying." Detective Lee abruptly commented.

The soldier was instantly blindsided by Lee's snappy accusation. "H-how can you be so sure?"

"Listen to me kid, I've been reading people while you were no more than a hope and a wrinkle in your old man's unmentionables. I just know."

"With all due respect sir, it kind of goes against everything G.F.B. if we continually follow your blind instinct."

The group halted at the side of their vehicles and Detective Lee stomped to the back-talking soldier's face. "What are you saying soldier?" Somehow Lee was able to make that sound like a deadly threat.

The soldier explained. "Well sir, all I am saying is we'd probably all feel better if we knew you were basing this illegal investigation on cold hard facts and not just personal emotion."

"Facts!" The detective refrained from shouting too loud but his voice still carried an aggression. "Facts? Okay big man, let's run through some facts. Fact one, the boy was a nervous wreck. I know the boy, he wouldn't act that way unless he was hiding something. Fact two, three separate activities were going on in there and nobody was doing nothing."

"What do you mean?" Remarked an unsure soldier who truly did not know what the detective meant.

"A stew was brewing and a video game with two players was on when we went in there, and everyone was just sitting around. Who leaves a game in the middle of a match with time running? Nobody! Also, you should never leave a boiling stew unattended. Ky cooking? Never." Lee divulged a little insight to his deductive reasoning.

"Still sir. Three people, three activities? It's kinda thin."

"If you remember, Ky confessed to making the stew and playing the game. My theory was confirmed a moment later when Jina said she never plays video games. Two people doing three things."

"Meaning...?"

"Meaning, they were lying." Another soldier answered for the detective.

"What else you got boss?" One of Lee's men said ignited with excitement.

"Will kept firing off looks toward the apartment's left

wall. Something was going on." Lee delivered.

A soldier noted. "But they couldn't have stashed up to three people or got them out in the time we got there. We would have noticed."

Lee said. "I think this whole mind control angle took an interesting turn."

Before the thought had time to simmer in the minds' of the soldiers, Lee's wristwatch communicator let out a jingle. He clicked the button on the communicator as he held it to his mouth. "What do you have for me?"

A voice resonated out if its tiny speaker box. "Sir, I think we're making real head way on the number code you gave us."

"What is it?"

"We're going to need some more time to answer that."

"Good work. I'm gonna finish this follow-up report and we'll check out the number in the morning."

"Yes sir," The communicator sounded before the line went dead.

"Okay, let's go." Detective Lee said to his men.

All of them neatly got in their G.F.B. vehicles with the exception of two who lingered just a moment longer. One was barbarically sticking his tongue out and rotating his jaw like he was trying to expel some rancid flavor. The other looked upon his comrade's actions with a little concern. He asked. "Hey are you okay?"

The first soldier answered. "Yeah I guess. I don't know. It tastes like I swallowed a cinder block or something." The two soldiers then got in their vehicles like the rest and Lee's entourage left.

"Are they gone?" Will asked, still a ball of nerves from the unscheduled visit.

By that time, Jina had made her way to the balcony, keeping an eye on the G.F.B. agents. She watched as they departed, then informed. "Yeah, they're leaving now. You guys can get off the wall."

Lili and her knights whipped themselves off the wall. They let out relief-filled gasps like a drowning man's revitalizing first breath. They slowly settled into the comforts of the apartment. As Byne came off the wall, he coughed behind a clutched hand and hurried to the bathroom.

"All right, let's get back to the game. I wanna whomp you some more." Riftkin teased Doc. The maniac anxiously took his place back on the couch. Doc much more hesitantly took a seat beside him.

"What the hell just happened? How did we not get caught right off the bat?" Ky demanded to know.

Lili relaxed in a chair at the dining table near Will and confessed. "I made it that they couldn't see us along with a few other tricks."

"You mean you were messing with their brains." Ky simplified with a disapproving voice.

"We needed to lean against the wall because if they bumped into us my illusion could have been broken." Lili continued giving Ky no true reply.

A thought returned to the boy that had struck his mind several times before. His head twisted over toward Doc's direction. "Hey Doc, you're Lili's brother right?"

""Yup," Blankly responded Doc with his focus mainly set on the bout with Riftkin.

"How come you don't have mind abilities like Lili?"

Doc rolled his eyes and Riftkin released a gratifying chuckle as the white haired knight lost yet another match. He then answered before starting the next round. "Lili and I have a gene structure with the least amount of imperfections which unlocks attributes lost to most. I have the ability to amplify talents of anyone who shares the blood of the royal family, but Lili, they found her genetic code to be even more flawless than mine. That's why her gift is more extravagant."

"Is that also why..." Will pressed but was quickly interrupted.

"Yes!" Doc yelped bearing a hint of anger. "That's why I'm not a prince."

Baloe had inched over to Ky's side and the masked pilot didn't notice him until he started talking. Baloe said. "Doc's ability, like Lili's, is based on proximity. The closer he is to us the greater our amplification is. He only chose such a remote location in our fights was so his influence could reach all of us."

Ky wasn't sure why the mountain-sized warrior was telling him that but he decided to converse anyway. "So that means you're all related to the girl."

"No we are not. We are the greatest fighters on the planet Verra. We have been injected with cells of the royal family so that his ability can affect us too. We have been sworn to protect the princess and we willingly guard her with our lives."

Ky again was unsure how to reply to the knight's speech. He childishly just tried to one-up the man. "You see Jina up there." Ky watched as Baloe's eyes drifted up to Jina on the balcony who was standing like a statue keeping a constant vigil. "Yeah, she owes me lots of money. She'll just stand there like that guarding the place all day if I promise to knock off some of her debt. Pretty bad-ass...huh?"

Baloe didn't answer; his eyes were locked on Jina carrying a respectful admiration. He knew she was the only true contender he had ever faced and began to view her as his rival.

"What are you thinking?" Lili asked Will.

"That you guys are something else."

"It's our skin." Riftkin noted.

"What?" A baffled Will blurted out.

"Sure," The sword-wielding knight decided to further illustrate his point. He reached into his pocket retrieving a small plastic bottle while his other hand continued mashing buttons on the video game controller. The upper half of his body twirled around to see Will showcasing the tiny bottle between his index finger and his thumb. The labeled bottle was filled with a thick creamy green liquid. "We all use Royal Family Treatment hair and body wash so our skin retains the same amount of moisture and firmness."

"I don't think that's it." The boy retorted.

"Damn it, you gotta be kidding me!" Doc yelled as Riftkin achieved victory in the bout one-handed.

He gloated. "Are you serious?! I had no clue what I was doing and I still won?! I gotta be like the best person at this game ever!"

Doc gently placed his controller on the coffee table and scowled. "Yeah well, let's see if you can do that mono-e-mono."

"Man, I'd mop the floor with you." Riftkin further bragged jumping to his feet exploding with excitement. "No one can touch me; Baloe couldn't even hold a candle to me. I can merk anybody!"

Baloe formed a face real quick convincing those who saw it that Riftkin's claim was highly embellished.

"What about Jina?" Ky calmly asked the enthusiastic nut.

"Anybody!" Riftkin reiterated to stress the point.

Suddenly Jina landed in the center of the living area like a hawk dropping from above grasping its prey in its clutches. Her angelic face jolted over at Riftkin's direction. Her body swiveled around to fit the position of her head. She proposed to the maniac. "Are you willing to bet on that?"

Riftkin wasn't expecting to be so rapidly put on the spot, but he couldn't lose face. He said. "Yeah...yeah...sure definitely!"

She detailed the specifics of her bet as she positioned her body in the middle of the large apartment. "All right we have someone count to three and whoever can strike the other first wins the bet. The wager is 1,600 dalaz, deal?"

"Deal," Riftkin agreed while firmly planting his feet in front of Jina and clasping a sword on his belt with his hand.

"Wait, hold the phone." Ky interrupted temporarily breaking the tension. "Jina you have 1,600 dalaz? Where's my cut?"

"You'll get 2,000 dalaz toward the debt when I win." Jina reasoned.

Ky responded. "So I'll count."

"Are you ready?" Jina asked with her eyes locked on her opponent.

"Are you?" Riftkin shot back while unsheathing his blade letting out a reaffirming loud ching. "You better be, because I'm gonna hit you with my fastest technique."

"Yup,"

"All right," Ky voiced and leaned over in his seat bringing the boiling anticipation to a nice simmer. Everyone's eyes were glued on the two, curious to see what would unfold. Even Byne exited the bathroom and watched. "1... 2... 3!"

Riftkin screamed like a charging train. "Velocity Dance!" His arm came up so quick that it created 5 ghost images of his arm trailing it. The madman had genuine confidence in his attack. He didn't have a clue.

Jina's staff beamed through Riftkin's sword and slammed down on top of his right shoulder before he realized it happened. The blow instantly cracked Riftkin's

shoulder blade and his body crashed to the ground like a
lead ball.

Jina walked and hovered over the broken man. "I'll
be needing your account information when you get up."
She then decided to take Riftkin's place on the couch.

Doc leaped out of his seat in intimidation.

Baloe huffed angrily at the whole scene and climbed
the ladder up to the balcony as his mixture settled.

Byne chuckled with satisfaction before heading over
to the fridge.

The night dragged on. Baloe had finished molding
and cooling his new club. Byne continued to hide his
rapidly deteriorating health, and Doc spent the day losing
to Riftkin in every video game Will had. Their presence was
trying the boy's nerves, but to ensure more time with Lili he
had to endure the turbulent household. Will's favorite time
of day was when everyone went to sleep. That's when he
got the chance to talk and laugh with the girl for hours
alone before they eventually tired out. That particular night,
they stayed up giggling about Jina's assault on Riftkin.

The boy recounted. "They were just standing there
one second, then a blink of an eye later... SPLAT!" The boy
clapped his hands together. "Riftkin slammed to the floor
like a rock."

Lili laughed wildly as she remembered the moment.
Will joined in on the round of laughter and it carried on
until it disappeared into happy content sighs. They smiled
and reclined on their respective bunks hoping nights like
that would never end.

"Will," Lili cooed ringing with a slight seriousness.

"Yeah," Will answered matching the care in her
voice.

"You don't want me to leave, do you?"

Will blushed in his bed and admitted. "No,"

"I don't wanna leave either." Said Lili before the

conversation was led into a brief silence. The princess then asked. "Can I tell you something?"

"Sure,"

"I came here for a reason."

"What?" Will sprouted up in his bed. "What do you mean?"

She drew one long breath and explained. "My ability doesn't really affect my people that well, and they are suffering badly."

"Wow," The boy echoed unable to think of anything comforting to say. "I'm sorry."

"It's okay," She assured. "But I think I know a way to save my people."

"What do you mean?" Will repeated.

"A long time ago, the gods feared a certain cataclysmic force called Omega. So they banned together and sealed it in a dimension of oblivion named the Abseninus Void. If I can get to the Abseninus Void and unlock the power of Omega, I know when I return to my people they'll have the faith in me to lead them."

"Wait a minute." Will interjected. "How are you gonna get into another dimension? Inter-dimensional travel has usually been an act of some godly entity."

"When the gods formed the planets, they placed inside each one of them four very special beacons. If you activate these beacons an altar will appear in the middle of the planet that can allow a person to travel to another dimension depending on their key. They made the beacons in case some emergency called for inter-dimensional travel. It's kind of like a... what do you call it?"

"A fail-safe program?" Will guessed.

"Yes, exactly." She agreed. "I haven't been on a planet long enough to trigger all four beacons because out of nowhere the IO started chasing me."

"Do you have the right key?" Will asked.

"I think so." She remarked in wonder. She then popped her head out from the top bunk looking down at Will. She sweetly requested. "Will, will you help me?"

"Me?...help you get Omega?" The idea rolled around in the boy's mind. "I don't know, it sounds dangerous."

"Not really," she calmly informed. "I hope you don't get mad, but I've been having your friends help me unlock beacons."

"Ohhhh," Will droned in realization. "So those days you were missing with Ky and Jina..."

"Yeah, I was having them help me find beacons." Lili finished for Will. "I only need to trigger one more before the altar will appear."

"So you want me to help you activate the last beacon and get to the altar." Will summarized.

"Yeah... I know we can do it... me and you." Said the princess.

Suddenly Will's eyes perked up and found Lili's cute face hanging off the side of the top bunk. She was looking upon him with a comforting graciousness, pleased that Will was so willing to assist her. The boy couldn't help but return her smile with one of his own. He had grown quite fond of the mysterious princess.

Lili then stated. "Well, we better get some sleep. We got a big day tomorrow."

"Right,"

Lili pulled her head back over the top bunk and snuggled inside of her sheets. "Goodnight Will."

"Goodnight Lili. Lights off,"

The lights then automatically faded to black.

Will's familiar dream haunted him again that night, but something was drastically different from the previous times the dream came to him. The sun cast no intense shadow on the three figures and he could make them out clearly. He then realized who the brown haired fatherly figure reminded him of. The figure looked like a brown headed grown up version of himself. The motherly figure had long blonde hair like he did and subtle parts of her facial features resembled a certain IO agent. The mainly silent child figure seemed to be an acquaintance he just met but only much younger. He realized that he was remembering his family. He had forgotten the image of his parents a long time ago. It had been so long that he couldn't immediately recognize them in his dreams, but on that night, the revelation was clear and his discovery consumed his inner thoughts. The dream played out exactly how it did before except bearing a newly found meaning. He watched the scene unfold as it usually did, unable to utter a word.

The dream stretched out longer than it ever had before and Will's mother continued. "Oh Terry, they're only children."

Will's father, Terrence Treyu, then said. "I'm aware Elaine, its all the more reason they learn their lesson. You know... while they're young."

The boy's mother then looked upon the father with a hesitant approval of his somewhat harsh means of dealing with the situation.

Will's dad gazed straight at him and ordered. "You need to stand up for yourself when people try to pick on you, you got it?"

Will was able to slowly bob his head up and down.

"And you need to protect your brother if this happens again, do you hear me?" Terrence barked at the boy figure.

The older boy had a blanket of guilt coating his mind that made him unable to speak.

"Do you hear me? Are you listening?... Wes!"

Will woke up in the middle of the night screaming accompanied by an excruciating headache. He was on his knees and his face fell to the ground out of some unexplainable exhaustion. His face met with a bed of long grass and the boy then realized he was outside somehow. His eyes looked up to see one of the moons was full and cast a shallow blue hue on the long white grass. He placed his right hand on his forehead to try and combat his pulsating migraine. His eyes searched the field for answers but only found Lili. She was standing a few feet to Will's side as a somber mood hovered around her.

She whispered to Will on the verge of tears. "Will... I'm sorry."

Will's head jolted to his right and was met with a sight that instantly formed terror in every cell of the boy. A giant growling mechanical jaguar was mere inches from Will ready to take a vital chunk out of the boy's face.

A heavy gravel club struck the jaguar's side. Baloe had applied enough force to send any normal jaguar soaring in the air, but for some reason the mechanical cat was only moved a few feet. Something was odd about how the robotic jaguar responded to force.

"This silver gilded jaguar is not going to make it easy for us." Baloe commented like a mighty warrior in the moonlight.

Will frantically ran away from the silver gilded jaguar until he felt he was at a safe distance. Will turned around and noticed all the knights were on the field engaging the big cat in a taxing battle. It was also the first time the boy had a chance to get a good eyeful of the silver gilded jaguar. It was indeed entirely mechanical from snout to tail and shined as if freshly polished. A vicious ten-inch drill flailed and twirled at the end of its tail like a wild rattlesnake. The precision that went into the jaguar's engineering surpassed even the technology of the advanced Arlians. Also, he had never seen a completely robotic entity acting freely on its own. Even with the boy's vast knowledge of computers and technical devices, Will had never seen anything like that silver gilded jaguar.

Will instinctively pressed a button on his wristwatch communicator before he dramatically squealed into it. "Ky, find me! We need the Guider's back up now!"

"Huh," Ky answered as if he was just waking up. "Wait. What's going on?"

"No time Ky! Just get over here now!"

"Hold on." Ky complied before hanging up.

"Let's get serious boys!" Doc confidently commanded from across the field. His hands came together as if in deep prayer. Doc's amplification ability started taking effect and the other knights, with the addition of Lili, began to glow. Doc was much closer to his comrades than he was before, so the golden hue was much more intense.

The silver gilded jaguar lunged at the nearby Baloe. The mountain-sized knight was barely able to defend from the cat with his club. The speed with which the jaguar attacked him thoroughly impressed the warrior. The only thing he had ever seen move so fast was Jina. The jaguar's head hung over Baloe's club ferociously snapping at the knight and it was taking all the man's might to hold the beast at bay. His pupils zipped down for a moment and he realized that the cat's literal razor claws had pierced straight through the club. They were locked in a power struggle.

A missile connected to the silver gilded jaguar's side that resulted in a sizable explosion. Baloe was launched back close to the man who had fired the missile, Byne. The gunslinger remained vigilant for the jaguar was not blown back from the blast. The force should have nudged anything back somewhat, but the jaguar's position was exactly the same prior to the explosion. He had two handguns drawn in the cat's direction just waiting for the smog to subside.

Baloe started getting up as he cursed. "You were not supposed to interfere."

"I had not a choice." Byne defended. "The beast's drilled tail was about to come down on your skull, but you did not notice for you are a fool." The dust began to fall and the top of the cat's arched back shimmered in the moonlight. "Clear a path!" Byne ordered.

Everyone made sure they were out of Byne's trajectory as he unleashed a hailstorm of bullets at the jaguar. The big silvery cat became a tornado of twists and dodges as it further exercised its outrageous speed. No matter how hard the gunslinger tried to peg his target, it was simply too fast.

"What's going on!?" Riftkin heckled. "I've never seen you miss so much."

"Well, it is difficult for me to shoot something that can move faster than my bullets."

The mysterious jaguar seemed to calm down and slowed to a halt. It was as though it no longer saw the assault of gunfire as a threat. Byne didn't hesitate to take the blatant opening and sent his barrage of fire dead center into the jaguar's face. The hot pieces of lead met their mark but something most peculiar happened. Instead of the bullets puncturing the silver monster or pinging off of its shiny skin, the shells would instantly stop at the point of contact and casually drop to the grass. The useless swarm of bullets continued peacefully falling off the cat as its automated eyes focused on Byne.

Byne suddenly saw the mechanized cat grow in size. The jaguar didn't miraculously grow, it only seemed that way because it actually bridged the gap between Byne and itself in a single pounce. The jaguar had a huge strong paw raised at the gunslinger's head. Everything was moving so quickly that Byne didn't have time to think. Even if he could have, he would not have been able to do anything to divert the blow. So, he kept popping rounds point-blank at the jaguar. The cat's paw came down, threatening to rip his face off but instead smacked against a wall of dense radioactive light. Only projectile fire has been known to activate a gamma shield, but something about the jaguar's physical strike triggered it.

Byne was launched in the air like a human sized pinball made of light. A lot of things have been known to break down a gamma shield, but nothing in history ever sent one airborne, especially with someone still inside it; the laws of physics wouldn't allow that to occur. Something about the silver gilded jaguar was bending all the laws of physics, force, and pressure, as if it was foreign to their reality and the rules did not apply.

Baloe found himself the closest to the mechanical beast again so he took another swing at it with his weapon. His gravel club was only half way to point of contact before the silver gilded jaguar spun around and sank its hind legs into Baloe's abdomen.

In a single moment, the robotic cat had dispatched both of them easily. At about that time, Baloe fell in the grass about 25 yards away and Byne landed to the ground with his shield still on. The gamma shield shut off as the gunslinger tried to recover from the attack. Byne let out a soft cry before his body drooped to the floor again from some hidden pain. The regal knight put a hand to his mouth as he coughed into it. When he pulled his hand away there was blood all over it.

The surrounding grass blades were simultaneously sliced off. Then a long broad sword flew up out of the tall brush before it fell and sank into the soil elsewhere. Riftkin had neared the beast and his arm was extended as if he had just thrown a heavy object. He faced the deadly jaguar with a psychotic grin, then gracefully flipped two huge swords off his back with one hand alone and pointed them at the jaguar holding them between his fingers. Riftkin forewarned. "She's coming for you." The maniac then shouted. "Dance of a thousand slashes!"

Seeing this attack from a different angle, Will could then deduce what was happening with that technique. He was actually throwing his swords fast enough that any untrained eye couldn't see it. This was an attack that involved chasing after your enemy, because you had to pick up the swords that had already been thrown so as not to run out of ammunition. Riftkin delicately balanced throwing which sword when he had to, reloading with swords he threw, and keeping the swords he had on him organized in a manner that allowed him to continue throwing. That was the level of precision that went into a technique he entitled a dance. Sadly, much like Byne's bullets, his blades were having no effect.

He was indeed chasing the silver gilded jaguar, because it seemed to retain the mentality of an actual cat, and a crazy man running right at it did catch the beast off-guard. The folly of the attack was the swords simply clinked and bounced off the jaguar's legs and sailed back into the air still spinning. It was a fruitless effort. Still, it was pretty impressive as all the grass was cut up and spreading through the air.

Riftkin seemed to maintain a psychological advantage over the jaguar until the mechanical beast decided to strike. In the middle of being chased, the silver gilded jaguar suddenly dove at Riftkin. Its paw was aimed at the maniac's chest. Riftkin was able to slide one of his large swords between the paw and his body. The beast's claw sliced through Riftkin's sword as if it was made of paper. The nutty knight had to take a large bound to his rear to ensure that what happened to his compressed titanium sword didn't happen to his flesh.

He held the hilt and blade stump he still had in his

hand at eye level and angrily complained. "Not another one."

The jaguar slowly stepped around in his position as if gauging what to attack next. Its robotic eyes then beamed far off into the distance to the new warrior who had just made her way to the fight.

Jina set foot onto the field and said. "I came as soon as I heard."

Will called across the grassy field to the glorious battle goddess. "Where's Ky?"

"He's on his way." She informed as she calmly approached the silver gilded jaguar. Everyone else, including the battle-scarred knights, took a step back as if conceding to Jina's power. It was like they did not wish to hinder her skills by getting involved. She came within ten feet of the beast before she halted locked in a deadly stare.

An intimidating grumble continuously rolled out of the jaguar's silver jaws. It trotted back and forth with its optic units glued to Jina as it prepared to attack.

Jina didn't give the cat the chance. She stepped forward and thrust her staff downward on the face of the beast in half an instant. The jaguar was not aware of Jina's blinding speed and it absorbed the blow right on the snout. The jaguar's head whipped back like a person receiving a knee-buckling punch from a professional boxer, but that was it.

As Jina pulled her staff back near her face she found herself genuinely surprised. She had grown accustom of things shattering or being instantly destroyed when she struck them, and the fact that the jaguar weathered her hit so well, came as a real shock. She knew at that moment that the cat was one of the toughest things she had ever faced.

The silver gilded jaguar jumped at the female warrior in retaliation with its claws and teeth gleaming. Its strong mechanical mouth wrapped around Jina's weapon after she administered a last minute defensive move. It was then that she realized the cat could also match her speed.

Jina kicked the silvery jaguar off her staff and ran at it ready to assault the beast with a lightning fast combo. Her attack patterns rang true as she dealt strike after strike on the overly resilient mechanical fiend. Her hits were the most effective out of the entire group but it still was not significantly damaging the beast. The pummeling was pushing the monster back but its silvery coat remained pristine. Her combination concluded and the jaguar still appeared unscathed.

A large bright spotlight showcased the beast in the field and the jaguar's eyes searched for the source. The Guider descended from the black sky and revealed itself to the cat-machine. The jaguar curiously stared up at it as if locked in a trance.

Ky's voice loudly blared out of the craft's speaker system. "Hey kitty, kitty, kitty. You wanna rock'n roll?"

The cat didn't respond, it just continued gazing at the Guider.

"Let's do this!" The giant craft announced. An invisible wad of churning neutrons bashed against the jaguar's face, but the feline stayed immobile as if it wasn't hit at all.

Ky did a double-take at his electronic viewing screen from within the comfort of the Guider's cockpit. What he had just witnessed astonished the pilot. "What the?... You've got to be kidding." His IO helmet leaned over to the microphone. "Okay," Ky said into the craft's speaker system. "Well how about this?" The Guider's gun turrets fired a volley of bullets at the silver gilded jaguar.

The cat dodged and weaved between the heavy gunfire assuring that each powerful shard of lead missed. The only thing Ky was doing was occupying the beast.

Jina just watched the scene wondering what her next

move should be. Riftkin and Baloe started walking up to the female warrior trying to confer with her the best course of action. She turned around facing the other fighters and bantered. "The cat is unbelievably durable."

Riftkin hinted. "I don't think that's it."

Jina snapped in a tone that demanded an answer. "What do you mean?"

Baloe explained. "That thing is acting strangely to any force applied to it. It's like the normal laws of physics don't apply to it."

Jina hummed as if Baloe's sentence made her ponder something. "Hmmmm,"

The jaguar continued dodging Ky's attacks looking like a silver smear swirling between hot golden rain and bursting mounds of dirt. It flipped backward and caught something it didn't expect. Jina's staff whacked the jaguar in its back in midair. Any normal organic being would've had its spine snapped in two by the force, but the cat's momentum was barely stifled by the strike. A low-pitched whistle resonated from the end of her staff then a force three times Jina's strength pounded the beast all at once. The jaguar landed on its feet only four yards away.

Jina had come up with a theory about the jaguar's ability to easily endure massive attacks. If the laws of physics did not apply to the creature, then she'd need to rely on the most basic of force principles to bout the monster. She depended on the universal rule that if you push something hard enough it will move. She decided to go all out and deal her mightiest blows in hopes that it would actually do something to the mechanical cat.

Jina bombarded the silver gilded jaguar with tremendous blows from her staff, each one followed by her authentic sound technique delivering a much stronger secondary hit. Jina and the cat clashed in an epic fight while they danced between the cascading bullets from the

Guider's gunfire. The scenario still looked bleak, for Jina was expending a lot of energy using her trump card over and over again. Fortunately, luck was on her side because she tagged the beast with her sound wave strike directly on its left shoulder. A lot of mechanized parts were joined there and the blow split a small opening in the shoulder exposing the complex machinations within. The jaguar let out a growl of pain as it came to the ground. The cat winced and hobbled on the leg as a sign that it was in fact hurt by the gash.

Everyone on the field watched the silver gilded jaguar seeing something that was technologically impossible. Tiny strands of silvery fiber no wider than a fishing lines started weaving together around its wound slowly sealing up the injury.

"No way! A self-repairing mechanical organism!? What's with this thing!?" Will blurted in disbelief of the sight.

Jina's flawless countenance grew sterner and she was determined to not allow the cat to get the advantage again. She leaped thirty feet in the air above the beast holding her staff downward with both hands. As she fell back down, she plunged her staff into the jaguar's small injury, spreading it open just a little. The familiar low-pitched tone sounded throughout the field followed by the jaguar's chest blowing apart completely. The silvery cat fell limp in the field and its red glowing optic units vanished as a testament to its defeat.

They all blew a sigh of relief as they were able to overcome their potentially fatal ordeal with nobody critically hurt. The Guider hovered to the soft grass and everyone took their turn trudging over to it.

Lili stood near the craft watching everyone file in with a worried look on her cute face. It appeared as though she was guilty of something.

Doc walked by his sister bearing an angered mug as he scolded. "Thanks a lot Lili."

Byne was next in the line and he added. "That's what transpires when you try and pull something out of the Abseninus Void prematurely."

Will didn't know what to make of the knight's words, but he saw the guilt in the princess' eyes thicken. He placed a comforting hand over her shoulder and said. "Come on, let's go."

All of them boarded the vessel and it took off for home. Little did they know that there was another galactic cruiser near the field. The spherical craft went unnoticed, hidden by the darkness of the night, but had managed to record the entire fight.

An IO soldier dragged Wes over to his monitor where he had paused a scene of the jaguar fight. Baloe, Jina, Will, and Lili were caught in the frame of monitor. The soldier feverishly pointed his index finger at the screen and stated. "You see sir? We now have video confirmation that they are harboring the fugitive."

Wes leaned over and analyzed the screen. What the soldier said was indeed true. There was no way Wes could cover it up any longer; Will was with Lili and it was his duty to act on it.

"What should we do sir?" The soldier asked.

Wes remained silent as he mentally wrestled with the moral issue in his head.

"Sir, may I remind you; this calls for immediate action." The soldier insisted.

"Fine!" Wes yelled. "We'll make our move in the morning, but do not harm the boy if we don't have to, is that clear?"

"Yes sir," The soldier agreed.

"God help my soul." Wes whispered before turning around and leaving the way he came. He wondered if what he was about to do was the right thing.

There were not many words spoken as the Guider
headed back to Gohanesse. Ky was too pissed to explode in
the craft in front of everybody, and everyone else was too
tired to discuss the ordeal. So during the ride many
questions went unanswered like, *what was that silver gilded
jaguar? And, how did they end up over 300 miles away from the
city within a few hours?* They all just accepted it so that they
could be allowed to go back to sleep as soon as possible. No
one said a word as they all entered the studio/warehouse.
They all sunk into their sleeping places and shut their eyes.
Ky gave a gracious *goodnight* as he wrapped his hand
around his bedroom's doorknob.
Will chirped back. "Goodnight,"
Suddenly Ky grasped Will by the collar and jerked
the boy's face to his mask. Ky growled in a low threatening
tone so only the boy could hear. "We're gonna talk about
this tomorrow."
A soft *okay* passed Will's lips not anxious to
challenge the man who just woke up in the dead of the
night to go save him. Ky shoved him away and went into
his room.
Will's head shifted around to find that Lili had also
already retired. The boy ascended the collapsible stairs and
walked into his room. He could hear Lili snoring on the top
bunk and cracked a small smile. Deep down in his heart the
boy was glad she was all right. Will plopped on his bed and
was ready for a long sleep.
Will never realized his long sleep because he was
nudged awake only Forty-seven minutes later. His dazed
head swiveled about and finally found Lili hovering over
him. "What is it?" Will inquired.
"Come on," She said. "It's time to go."
"Okay," Will happily complied. He took the princess'

hand and he left with her.

VII

<u>*The Great Universe Reprogramming*</u>

The day began early for many that morning. Among those people were a handful of G.F.B. soldiers. They were stationed at a small federal facility that was just a hole in the wall compared to the G.F.B. Department Building. The soldiers that were usually there to run the facility's daily operations were out dealing with the endless stream of complaints caused by Lili, so the place had the least amount of staff possible. That fact was actually why the handful of soldiers chose that particular location for their deeds. They were huddled around a computer illegally investigating a lead given to them by their superior.

"Is it ready for him?" One of the soldiers asked the federal hacker who was in on the investigation.

"Yup," The hacker assured leaning back in a plush rolling chair; finally finished with his duties after hours of work.

Detective Lee charged into the small office and asked the clerk behind the counter. "Where are they?"

Barely acknowledging the prestigious detective, the man pointed the blunt end of a pencil at a side office where all of Lee's men were cramped around a small computer.

Without another word spoken, Lee bypassed the few soldiers and pencil pushers in the facility and joined his party at the computer.

Making sure he closed the door behind him, Lee entered the small private office and asked. "Okay boys, whatcha' got for me?"

The hacker turned completely around in his chair and explained as the other soldiers made a path for the detective. "Well that number sequence you gave us is a pass code to the files of some IO agent."

Lee's face neared the computer as he looked at it and investigated. "Who's the lucky agent?"

"I don't know. Some guy named Wes Vega."

"Jackpot," The detective remarked. "Have you looked inside the files?"

"Nope, we were waiting for you." The aloof hacker answered.

"Good man." Lee said. "Let's take a little look-see." The detective hesitantly started pushing parts of the computer's touchscreen. It was obvious that Lee had no clue what he was doing.

"Just hit the enter button in the corner." The hacker instructed with a finger directed at the monitor.

Lee clicked the key and every question he had about the peculiar events around the world were answered and more. He scrolled down the page absorbing the contents. A lot of his personal theories were corroborated with just as many surprises greeting Lee's inquisitive eyes. He commented while studying the text. "Apparently Wes had to withhold the truth from his own troops in fear that they wouldn't accept the mission." His gaze continued reading; unlocking the deepest secrets of the case. With only four fifths of the report read, Lee's eyes bugged out and his body asserted in one violent jerk. He ordered. "We need to get that boy now!"

Ky woke up with his neck in pain, like it had been for the past few days, but that's what happens when you insist to sleep with an IO helmet on. His body flung up and his hand went to his masked head. He tried to fix his neck before heading to his bedroom door. Outside his room seemed a lot quieter than usual and the reason was confirmed as Ky's eyes only found Riftkin and Byne. Byne was on the balcony searching for something and Riftkin was peering under a couch cushion.

Ky asked. "What the hell are you guy's doing?"

"Baloe and Doc weren't here when we woke up. We're looking for them." Byne claimed.

"Well you're not gonna find either of them under a couch cushion." Ky enlightened as he briskly walked into the center of the apartment.

Riftkin finally dropped the cushion and probed. "We were hoping you might know something about this."

"Nope, sorry," Ky rang almost as if he was pleased to disappoint them. "Where's Jina?"

"She is outside in front." Byne answered. "She does not know anything either."

"I don't know, maybe Will knows where they went." Ky suggested. The lazy pilot then roared up at Will's stilted room. "Will get up!" Ky stood there for a few moments without a response. He then shouted. "Will!" He again waited for a reply or at least a sign that he was there. Ky let out an annoyed moan. "Huuh... Riftkin, can you do me a favor and drag Will out of bed?"

"Sure," The delighted crazy knight horned. He then merrily dashed up to the boy's room.

"Just get him out of bed." Ky reiterated to ensure the nutty swordsman didn't end up hurting the boy.

Riftkin swarmed into Will's room.

Outside moments earlier, Jina was at her usual post

like the apartment's guard dog. She diligently held her position, but noticed that she had not seen any sign of the IO all day. In the days prior, soldiers would nonchalantly walk by or tanks would patrol the block all equipped with long suspicion filled gawks at her. Jina was coming to the realization that she hadn't seen any tanks or soldiers the entire time she was out there.

Suddenly, someone was coming in her direction; someone big. Jina could quickly tell by the man's sheer girth and the fact that he held a massive club in one hand that it was Baloe. His body was dressed in long brown dirty robes that drooped everywhere. Most of his form was hidden underneath the dark robes. The concealed knight approached Jina.

Jina inquired. "Where were you?"

"..."

"Where is Doc?" Jina further questioned.

"I don't know?" The mountain-sized man responded. He motioned to the blue tarp to enter the studio/warehouse.

Jina philosophized before Baloe had a chance to head in. "You know, if you choose the path to gain power quickly, you may lose the very thing that makes you human."

"I already have." Baloe proclaimed. "I'm just wondering if you have too." With nothing else said between them, the robed knight went inside.

Ky's and Byne's eyes shot to the blue tarp in attention as Baloe walked in.

Byne hopped off the balcony area and said to his fellow knight. "Baloe, have you seen Doc?"

"No," Baloe answered. "I heard the situation from Jina. He must've left at a different time than me."

"Well where were you?" Ky questioned with his arms crossed.

Ky's answer was forgotten as Riftkin beamed out of Will's room and announced. "Guys! Will and Lili are gone!"

"Oh geeeez..." Ky groaned from under the IO helmet. "Let me call him." Ky's wristwatch communicator was raised to his helmet and a push of a button later it dialed for Will. A second later, an obnoxious high pitched signal came ringing out of the communicator's tiny speakers. "Great! Will turned off his receiver. There's no reaching him now." Ky lowered the communicator for just an instant before pressing another button.

"What in heavens are you doing?" Byne asked.

"Calling someone else," Said Ky before speaking into his communicator again. "Hey Red!"

"Yeah what's up?" Red Marrado answered on the other end of the line.

"Hey is the Guider still there?"

"Uh, nope; took off on its own at the crack of dawn."

"I freakin' knew it." Ky cursed.

"You should really get a handle on that." Red advised.

Ky whined into his communicator soaked with sarcasm. "Thanks."

"See ya later man."

"Later," Ky's arm fell to his side as the conversation concluded.

"You don't know where they are?" Riftkin wondered.

Running out of leads, Ky screamed. "Jina!"

Jina promptly entered the studio/warehouse. "What is it?"

"Will and Lili are missing too. Do you know anything about it?"

"Not a thing." She informed.

Byne raised the question. "How could those children have sneaked out with no one bearing witness?"

As Ky thought on the subject the answer suddenly hit him. He begrudgingly remarked. "Damn that secret passage."

As Ky, Jina, and what was left of the knights, disputed what could have happened to the kids and where they could have gone, the IO forces made their move. A fleet of IO tanks stealthily lined up in front of the large apartment with their music off trying to maintain the element of surprise. Hundreds and hundreds of soldiers emptied out of the tanks and cluttered Ky's front street. The sphere shaped IO crafts hovered all around the studio/warehouse claiming the advantage over the sky as well. Two peculiar reinforced vehicles joined the army on the street that was only half the size of any normal tank. The strange vehicles had what looked like a giant shiny metallic javelin loaded into a cannon sized barrel mounted on top. The vehicles were positioned to face the front wall of the apartment. Thick ten-inch metal spikes retracted from the bottom of the vehicles and sunk into the cement below anchoring them to the ground. The barrels fired the massive javelins at the apartment in two awesome blasts. As the giant javelins sailed at the apartment, a thick chain was visibly linked to the ends of both of them that fed back into the vehicle's barrels. The javelins careened at the studio/warehouse in a flash.

Everyone in the apartment heard two awesome blasts erupt from outside.

Riftkin yelped with a little worry. "What was that?"

A loud crash echoed in the apartment as something smashed straight through the upper right corner of Ky's granite front wall. A similar crash occurred a moment later as the upper left corner of the wall was struck. All eyes zipped to the ceiling as the dust fell revealing two long metal slabs poking out of the wall's high corners. Then three legs popped out of the slabs like an umbrella.

Outside, the odd vehicles started recoiling the chains back into the barrels until their slack disappeared.

As the tension on the chains grew, the metal slabs slid out of the holes until they were caught by the three extended prongs. The giant three-pronged javelins started pulling apart the wall from the rest of the apartment in a ground shaking tug of war. The tenants inside watched as the corners of the apartment began to crack and crumble. The javelins proved too much for the wall and they tore it straight off its bearings. Chunks of granite and piping broke into pieces as the wall fell to the front yard like a drawbridge. The wall had been completely yanked off the apartment, exposing its inhabitants to the overwhelming army lined up outside. Everyone's eyes slowly rolled over the army knowing that serious trouble had found them.

A fed up Ky threw up his arms and complained. "That's it... they destroyed my apartment."

A single voice vibrated out of the tanks' impressive stereo systems. It forcefully dictated. "Baloe Renault, Byne M. Dumonte the III, Riftkin Wingfeather, you have all been found guilty for the crime of aiding and acting as accomplices for a known galactic fugitive. You are to be detained for execution. Ky Gracen, Jina, you are accused of the crime of harboring a known galactic fugitive and are to be detained for questioning. How do you plead?"

The warriors, with the addition of Ky, started conversing among themselves trying to determine the best course of action. They left the massive IO force in a moment of silence ready to battle at the drop of a hat.

"We're gonna have to fight this aren't we?" Ky grumbled bearing no excitement for actually committing the act.

"I will not be detained or sealed by anything." Jina vowed as she flipped her staff in front of her body in a fighting stance.

Riftkin suggested. "Why don't we just tell them we don't know where Lili and Will are now?"

"Think you dolt." Byne barked. "That still will not keep them from throwing us in custody to rot in a cell until our inevitable execution."

"Also, if we let them know they're gone, they'll definitely look for them immediately, and if they find them they'll kill them both." Baloe added.

"Not Will!" Ky snapped making sure to stress his point.

The knights looked at Ky with an awful silence lingering around them.

"How do you plead!?" The IO voice bumping out of the tanks' speakers demanded.

"Hold on a second!" Ky yelled back at the army.

"Need I remind you that we are authorized to apprehend all of you by force if need be." The IO illustrated.

"Just...hold on!" Ky persisted with his attention then switching back to the terribly quiet knights. "The IO is NOT going to kill Will if they find him." Ky reformed his statement looking for some gratifying agreement. The group stayed silent and the idea that his assumption was wrong gradually seeped into Ky's thick skull. "Why would they kill Will?"

The dead silence continued for a moment until Byne said. "Do you think she's been drawn to that boy for no reason? Did you ever think Will may be involved?"

"Involved in what!?" Ky shouted.

Baloe admitted. "Lili's plan."

"Crap!" Ky cursed. "So coming clean really isn't an option."

"This is your last warning." The army's speakers wailed at the small group.

"Damn it." A frustrated Ky moaned as he slumped

over to his bedroom. He used the door even though a wall
to his room had just been ripped off and he could have
easily just walked inside. He grabbed something on his
cluttered floor hidden under dirty sheets and clothes. It was
heavy and Ky had to clutch the object with both his well-
built toned arms to lift it. The sheets fell away and Ky
dragged the object out revealing it to everyone. The object
was a giant two-handed gun designed to take down various
spacecrafts. The front of the machine gun was made up of
three separate Gatling gun barrels set circularly on a panel.
As the gun would warm up, the panel would start to rotate
along with the barrels that also spin independently. When
the gun really started going, it would fire abnormally sized
bullets simultaneously out of three different swirling
streams. Even though it was slow to move and wield
because of its weight, the gun's destructive force was
noteworthy. Everyone else wondered how Ky had got such
a powerful and expensive piece of equipment.

All eyes focused curiously on Ky and his flamboyant
machine gun. Jina found it necessary to ask. "Ky, where'd
you get that?"

"What?" Ky defended. "You think Will is the only
one making special purchases with those ripped-off account
numbers? Screw that! I came across this little puppy on the
galactic web and I just couldn't resist. This is a gift to me
courtesy of Bernard H. Wilburn. Sorry Bernie."

"Well it looks like we're all ready to go." Baloe
stated.

"So what's the plan?" Ky strategized with Jina.

"I'll run interference here. Perhaps I can create
enough of a diversion so that you all can get out of the front
line. We should all converge at a location later where we
can decide what to do from then on."

"Got it," Ky assured.

Jina added. "I'll let you know the location later."

"How will we know?" Riftkin questioned. "It's not like we have your number."

"Just follow the path of destruction." Jina instructed. "You'll find me at the end of it."

"Maybe I should run interference now?" Baloe assertively suggested.

"I'll run interference." Jina said in a tone that could not be argued with.

"Everyone ready?" Byne made sure.

"Yeah, let's do this." Ky manned up.

"I know what's going to happen, but it still sounds like fun." Riftkin blathered out of nowhere.

"They will taste the full strength of my club." Baloe swore.

They all slowly walked out onto the front lawn, which was covered in the rubble of Ky's wall. Each warrior, including Ky, took a corner of the lawn looking out at the outrageously huge army. Jina stood in front of them as the closest person to the army. She pointed her staff at the IO in a threatening preparation.

"What is your answer?" The army demanded to know.

Jina whispered. ""No,"

Jina sprinted to the army's front line like a lightning bolt and swung her staff back like a professional batter before the army's high tech gadgets registered her movements. Her long metallic staff whistled forward and crushed in the chest of three IO soldiers. The other neighboring soldiers began to realize they were being attacked at that moment and motioned to surround her, but suddenly a low-pitched tone could be heard. In the blink of an eye, a tidal wave of IO soldiers came crashing down on the rest of the army.

Ky and the knights scrambled to different directions bravely leading their own charges.

The Guider came to a soft landing on an expansive field of long white grass. Inside the craft, Will was using his laptop to pilot the Guider while Lili anxiously waited with him in the cockpit until they arrived at their destination. Will had successfully guided them to where Lili had instructed but something was bothering the boy all morning. He had a recent minor impairment of his vision. He tried blinking and rubbing his eyes countless times but no matter what he did the speck was still there. Will had attempted to stare directly at the speck to get a closer examination, but the speck would move parallel to his pupil and remain in the upper right corner no matter where he looked. The speck mildly agitated the boy, but he believed it was just something in his eye.

"We're here!" Lili cheered as the craft finished landing. "Come on, let's get that beacon." She then skipped to the Guider's exit.

"Hold on!" Will commanded as he tucked his laptop into the satchel and swung it over his neck. He then followed her out of the cockpit.

The craft's automatic door slid open and the children set foot on the never ending field. Lili hastily zipped out into the middle of the field searching for clues to the beacon's whereabouts. Will slothfully stepped into the grass soaking in the entire view of the large field.

"Are these the right coordinates?" An unsure Will asked the overly excited girl. "This place looks familiar." His thoughts searched the rim of his mind until it came up with the correct answer. He didn't recognize it right away because the last time he was there it was dark out. It was the very same field that Jina and the knights fought the silver gilded jaguar.

Too many questions were mounting and the boy approached Lili. "You know, I've been seeing this black dot in the right corner of my eye all morning. Does what happened last night have anything to do with that?"

Lili turned around while still scouring the floor and answered. "You're seeing the Abseninus Void."

"What? How come I see it?"

"When these beacons are being activated, the particles in and around the planet change a bit to prepare for inter-dimensional travel. The phenomenon has too many layered dimensions for normal senses to pick up, but since last night, you can actually physically see the shift."

"How come I can see it since last night?" Will further investigated.

"Because..." Her speech paused and she ran up to Will holding his hand in a sympathetic manner. "...oh Will, you're gonna hate me."

"What happened?"

"I tried to have my knights locate the last beacon last night, but I had to make sure I had the right key."

"What do you mean *key*?"

"Once all the beacons are activated a person's brainwaves are used at the altar to open a path to a different dimension. Different brainwaves lead to different dimensions resulting in hundreds of trillions of different paths. Your brainwaves, the brainwaves which I can't control, are attuned to the Abseninus Void." Lili finally divulged.

"So that small dot is a glimpse of the Abseninus Void?"

"Uh huh," She agreed.

"Well how come no one else is seeing dots to their attuned dimensions?"

"Like I said, I needed to absolutely make sure your brainwaves were the correct ones before I completed the ceremony. I tried to pull out anything I could from your dimension to prove it was the Abseninus Void."

"Like a deadly robotic cat?" Will remarked placing some blame on her as well.

"... I'm sorry." She quoted forming big cute eyes that Will could not stay mad at.

"You pulled a metallic jaguar out of my head." Will restated emphasizing the absurdity.

"Will you forgive me?"

Will cracked a smile and said. "Let's find that beacon."

A wild smirk reformed on her face and they both continued combing the brush for something out of the ordinary. They searched for seven-teen minutes until Lili discovered what she had come for. She was huddled over a big rock imbedded in the ground hidden by the tall grass as she squealed. "Here it is!"

Will rushed over excited to see the entrance to the fabled beacon. The boy was somewhat disappointed when his eyes saw nothing but an average looking rock. "That's it?"

"Watch," Lili gently placed her hands on the stone and the rock slid away like an automatic door. Beneath the rock was a stone staircase spiraling downward. The stairs were carved with expert precision; worthy work for that of the gods. The creepy staircase infinitely spun down into darkness illuminated by white glowing rocks that sat in lanterns.

"Wow," Will gasped as the concealed staircase was uncovered.

"You ready to go?"

"Down there?"

"Are you scared?"

"Of course not." Will huffed as he confidently led the way. The children began descending the spiral stairwell. The staircase must have spiraled downward 4 or 5 stories. The musty staircase led to a large box room. The room was a perfectly symmetrical cube made up of walls, a floor, and a ceiling of equal height and width. The room was made up of the same smooth reddish stone and it also had the lanterns with the glowing blue orbs providing minimal light. All the walls, with the addition of the ceiling and floor, were lined with visually stimulating diamond shaped etchings. All six sides of the cube had the same elaborate diamond pattern as the others. It was a marvelous tapestry of parallel diamonds, concentric diamonds, and diamonds within diamonds that proved fairly taxing on the eyes. A deceiving platform was near the far end wall that just complimented the room's illusion. The red stone platform was formed into oddly angled diamond shapes that blended in perfectly with the wall behind it as someone enters. Upon further inspection, one could see an indentation in the stone platform that was molded to fit a hand.

"This place looks crazy." Just came out of Will's mouth without him thinking too much about it.

"Yes," Lili commented. "Every beacon on every planet looks exactly like this. This is really it."

Will entered the depths of the room in marvel of its detailed design. "I guess when you see stuff like this you know it was made by gods." The boy's eyes darted to the stone platform and the hand-molding in its center. Will skipped over to it and put his hand in the hand-mold. The boy looked around in anticipation for some divine reaction. None came, and he backed away from the platform unsure if he had triggered the beacon. "Did I do it?" He questioned aloud.

Lili didn't answer. She just daintily approached the platform and placed her hand inside it. The entire hand shaped indentation instantaneously emitted a light glow. The glow spread through the engravings on the platform and into the diamond carvings on the walls. Soon the whole room was covered in its white glow.

A sharp pain came to Will's head like a freight train. It subsided quickly but he noticed that the speck in the corner of his eye had grown to a dot.

Lili turned around to face Will with her hands together wearing an achieved expression. "That's it Will. The altar must now be being summoned to the middle of the world." She casually walked by Will heading out of the glowing beacon.

"Do you mean like the core of the planet?" Will inquired as he followed closely behind her.

"Ha ha ha," Lili laughed off. "No silly. It's a location. It's the mapped out center of the world." She clarified as they started climbing back up the steps.

"Wow," Will stated. "I wonder how the gods determined the beginning and end of a planet?"

"I don't know." Lili recited with a hint of interest in the boy's question. "That's a weird point."

They slowly trudged up the stone stairs as Will's list of questions kept coming. "Well, do you know where the middle of the world is?"

"Yup," The princess freely admitted.

"Where is it?"

"Where else? Gohanesse Park."

"What!? That's one crazy coincidence." Will babbled as he continued traversing the steps.

The children made it up to the deceiving rock entrance and it cooperatively slid away to allow safe passage. The kids nonchalantly exited the opening, but what they found as they stood totally erect sent a paralyzing chill down their spines. Their wits were knocked out of them and they froze in place when they saw an IO tank, two IO galactic cruisers, and about thirty soldiers spread around the grassy field. The children were immediately identified.

The soldiers had been sent there to investigate the area where they recorded the knight's facing the jaguar, but what they found was a shocking yet pleasant surprise. As the soldiers realized their golden goose had literally popped up out of nowhere, they instinctively aimed their hand-mounted machine guns at them and ordered. ""Halt!"

The kids then gazed at each other scared and uncertain what to do. Their hearts raced and their breath was flustered as the soldiers steadily advanced to the defenseless children. Lili and Will did what came naturally to them when they quickly ducked under the tall white grass and scampered away undetected.

One of the soldiers in the group commented. "See, I told them. We should have infrared in these helmets."

Another soldier enlightened. "They're gonna try to make their way back to their craft. You two!" The soldier pointed at the two soldiers closest to the Guider.

"Yes sir." The soldiers responded in unison.

"Guard the entrance to their craft." The soldiers promptly jogged over to the Guider's door while the lead soldier delegated. "The rest of us will comb the grass. I want both of them found."

"Yes sir," The rest of the soldiers obliged before they thoroughly began searching through the grass. Their plan was sound and it'd only be a matter of time until they found the kids.

Will and Lili stayed ducked down beneath the grass hoping not to be spotted. They made slow careful moves trying to remain out of view while further confusing the soldiers. They also tried messing with the soldiers by distracting them with the sound of thrown rocks, but with access to their craft blocked, they were just prolonging the inevitable.

Lili whispered to Will in desperation. "Will, can you hack into their crafts and create a diversion or something?"

"We'd need to stay in one spot too long, it's too risky. Plus, the keystrokes might draw their attention." Will calmly and quietly explained.

"So what are we gonna do?"

"I need to think." Will resolved.

Suddenly, the kids could hear legs rustling through the grass and their whispers stopped. The boy could see shadows through the brush of three sets of legs around them. Using nothing but hand gestures, Will signaled to the princess to start heading in the direction he was facing. It ran right between two of the sets of legs and Will thought it was their best chance of remaining unnoticed. Lili gave Will a head nod of understanding and cautiously shifted her body around to point in the direction the boy had motioned. Lili began crawling through the grass making sure not to disturb the delicate blades. Will asserted his body to follow down the path the girl was traveling and he got on his hands and knees behind her.

The boy felt an eerie weightlessness as his hands and legs were unexpectedly separated from the ground. Will had been snatched up by a soldier lucky enough to have spotted the boy. The soldier clasped the ferociously wiggling boy to his body and called out to the other IO agents. "I got him! I located the boy!"

The other soldiers started converging on Will and the boy realized that they hadn't discovered Lili yet. She had frozen in her tracks the moment Will got yanked up. She was mere inches away from the soldiers' ankles and had not been found. Will stared down in Lili's direction giving a few subtle hints for her to stay put and be quiet.

Not thinking twice, one of the soldiers pointed his machine gun at Will and interrogated. "Where's the girl?"

One of the soldiers had hold of Will by the back of his neck. He intimidated the boy by jerking his body around a little then advised. "You better answer us kid."

Will remained quiet.

"I'm not gonna ask again. Where is the girl?" The first soldier repeated.

"I don't know." Stalled Will. "We split up as soon as we hit the deck."

"Just great," A soldier complained. "She could be anywhere by now and it could take hours to search all this grass."

"Shall we keep looking sir?" A duty oriented soldier asked.

The soldier that seemed to have the most authority said. "No. Searching for her now is irrelevant and a waste of time."

"Sir, our objective is to locate the girl and recent reports indicate that the altar has appeared." One soldier reminded.

The main soldier reasoned. "Altar or not, the princess cannot accomplish her plans without the boy, so as long as we have him she'll come to us. Now that we have him, everything is at a stalemate and we have time to breath. Plus searching all this would be like a needle in a haystack."

"Understood," A soldier rang in acknowledgment.

"Should we really just leave her here with that craft?"

"She's just a little girl." The in charge soldier explained. "She doesn't know how to pilot a craft." He then concluded "Let's go."

IO soldiers entered the tank while others walked on to the spacecrafts with Will in tow. The IO abandoned the field leaving Lili alone and with no way to escape the plain.

Meanwhile, an ominous altar smashed out of the ground beneath Gohanesse Park's soft soil. Foundation rattling earthquakes rocked throughout the city as the huge stone brown altar stretched out to the sky. The ancient block towered over the city's tallest skyscrapers and was riddled with inscriptions from the gods. The entire city momentarily froze as all eyes were set on the godly altar rising from the ground. The altar's presence put a feeling that something horrible was on its way in the hearts of Gohanesse citizens.

The all-out battle in the industrial district raged on. Jina had been keeping the bulk of the IO forces busy while Ky and the knights tried to find their own ways out of the district. They were all well aware that the IO was all over the city, but they also knew most of their forces were back at the apartment. They all tirelessly tried to locate a place where they could hide out, but many had already found trouble.

Riftkin was actually covering the most ground. He had chosen a stealthier route than the others. He snuck around taking out unsuspecting IO soldiers when he had to and traveled mainly through unpopular back alleys.

It was one of those back alleys that the insane knight first caught a glimpse of the altar. "The godly altar of realms." He admired. "The conduit to inter-dimensional travel. So Lili finally did it."

Two soldiers making their way to Jina by foot made the mistake of taking a passing glance down that alley. Their eyes found Riftkin and their helmets identified him as one of the fugitives. The knight pulled off two long broad swords from his back as the soldiers went to engage him.

The two soldiers stepped into the alley and aimed their armed mounted weapons at the knight. One yelled. "Stop!"

Riftkin did the exact opposite than what he was ordered. He charged directly at the soldiers releasing a hyped battle cry. The baffled soldiers fired their guns at the knight, sending round after deadly round at the unbalanced man.

Riftkin held his arms high and angled the swords downward as he kept running. The big blades shielded more than seventy percent of his body and the bullets harmlessly pinged off them. Riftkin utilized that protective tactic as he dashed within striking distance of his opponents. He was right in front of their faces when he dipped under their gunfire. Riftkin sent an upward slash at the man to his right that split him in half. His other sword sent another skyward slash that cut off the other soldier's arm at the elbow neutralizing his arm-mounted gun. Even with an arm freshly sliced off, the soldier reflexively performed a spinning roundhouse kick at the maniac's face. Riftkin ducked underneath the kick and beamed a sword up at the soldier. The sword impaled the soldier through the chest and clearly stuck out from his back. The soldier fell to the bloody ground adding to the constantly flowing red mess. Riftkin removed his sword from the deceased soldier as more blood gushed out from the cadavers.

The blood trailed out into the street and had caught the attention of a nearby platoon. Riftkin could hear vehicles rumbling down the road, so he scurried back down the alley. An armored vehicle and eighteen IO soldiers drove up to the suspicious trail of blood and followed it to the dead bodies. That's when they caught sight of Riftkin on the other end of the alley smiling at them with three swords drawn; two were drenched in blood. Eighteen IO arms pointed machine guns at the knight.

One hollered loudly. "Halt where you are!"

Riftkin rapidly unsheathed every blade he had and held them all between his digits. The psycho then carelessly tossed all them up in the air and chanted. "Dance of the guards."

The platoon opened fire on Riftkin but the bullets were soon deflected by a plummeting sword that sunk into the ground at his feet. The rest of the blades followed, each landing in a specific place around the knight until all sides of him were protected. The same sword barrier he had set before was ready to keep him safe from the swarm of bullets, but something was different about it.

Since Riftkin got to the planet, he had been breaking entirely too many swords. One was broke when he tried to cut through the Guider, one was busted by Jina in their bet, and yet another was destroyed by the silver gilded jaguar. He no longer had enough swords to create a tight shield. Riftkin tried spreading the swords farther apart to make up for his losses, but it wasn't enough. There were still little gaps between the blades that a bullet could squeeze through, and that was all the IO needed.

Riftkin's guarding technique required him to crouch and stay absolutely still, because he could possibly be cut by his own swords with the tiniest movement. He kept that in mind the first time he was shot. A bullet sailed right through a gap in his swords and blew straight through his left shin. Riftkin took the shot like a man and didn't move a muscle. Sadly, he did not keep that kind of composure the next time a bullet found him.

A single round whizzed through the knight's defenses and tagged him in the right shoulder. Riftkin screamed and reeled back in pain not remembering that a sword would greet his spine if he did so. As Riftkin's razor sharp sword tore through his nerves, it became impossible for him to get back on his feet. Despite his efforts, his body kept sliding closer to the ground, which was only sinking the blade deeper into his back. He resorted to supporting his back up as much as possible by putting his hands to the ground for stability. With tear filled tortured eyes, Riftkin cried out in agony and pints of blood cascaded from his mouth.

One soldier rushed Riftkin and did a grand acrobatic bound over his sword shield. As the soldier flipped overhead, he aimed his gun straight down at the severely wounded knight. Riftkin's eyes met the soldier pointing his deadly weapon at the only real opening the knight's sword barrier had.

Riftkin's bloodied mouth gargled quickly. "No!"

The soldier unleashed multiple bullets that ripped through Riftkin's body on their journey to the cement below. It truly was the psychotic knight's final dance.

Byne was making his way out of the district pretty fast as well. He chose the roof of a building, then a path to travel, then sniped any IO soldiers he saw along the route. He was making good time until he failed to snipe one in his path and later ended up trotting by right next to the soldier. Byne made it out of the scuffle without being harmed, but by that time he had been spotted by a lot more soldiers. It wasn't long after that when Byne was chased by an IO fleet. With legs constantly pumping, Byne sought refuge in a full warehouse. The army saw him enter the warehouse as they rolled in on its large doors. The soldiers hastily entered the warehouse with their machine guns drawn. Each one was directing their weapon at a different corner of the warehouse, making sure to cover every nook and cranny of the vast space.

The warehouse was loaded with giant wooden cargo boxes haphazardly stacked on top of each other. Narrow paths between the box piles provided limited mobility in such a big room. Their guns searched down every winding path.

Suddenly Byne shouted out from origins unknown. "Ha! You men shall never track me!" Then one of the soldier's helmets blasted off with blood on it. The man dropped dead and the other IO agents hastily searched for where the attack came from. A couple more IO soldiers fell dead, but one eventually found him.

It was the glare of his sniping lens that gave his location away. He was up on the rafters in a high corner of the warehouse. The soldiers turned the flashlights above their machine guns on and pointed at the gunslinger like a spotlight. From then on, there was no more hiding for the gun wielding knight.

Byne immediately dropped his silent sniping rifle and pulled out two guns from the lining of his jacket. One of them was his double-barreled pistol that fires missiles from its second barrel, and the other was the triple barreled mini-Gatling *hand* gun with the enormous clip. The regal knight set his weapons ablaze as his enemies commenced their attack. Even though the knight performed a ballet on the metal catwalk to avoid a lot of the gunfire, there were simply too many soldiers rushing in. Throughout the magnificent gun battle, Byne's gamma shield was going off like a flashlight relaying Morse code.

Baloe hadn't made it far at all. He was wasting a lot of time meeting tanks head on and decimating small platoons of soldiers without receiving a scratch. His pursuit out of the district was far too relaxed as if he wanted to get caught. It seemed like he wished to make one mighty stand like Jina. Baloe got his chance as he briskly treaded over a street and saw that around the corner was choked with IO forces; it was like a parade. Two tanks and a couple hundred IO agents were there at least. Baloe turned to face them.

"Come with us!" Demanded the tank's giant speakers. The robed knight walked within 10 yards of the brim of the massive force. He swiftly raised his powerful club then a golden shine shot out from under his robes before his weapon struck the ground in front of him. The concrete webbed and cracked outwardly and it reduced the ground that he and the army were standing to rubble. Like an avalanche, the entire street crumbled inside itself swallowing up the impressive army. Everything was crushed under layers of cement and chunks of the toxic sewage system.

Baloe's mighty arm came jetting out from under huge cement slabs, his body and cloak ravaged and dripping with filth. He slowly ascended out of the rubble. The giant robed knight knew he would be the only one to weather such an attack. He took his time walking out of the street long chasm.

His ears took to the sky as they picked up on an explosions and gunfire of a far off battle even greater than his. Baloe knew who had to be there.

"Jina,"

The robed knight started walking toward her direction.

Ky was surprisingly becoming a rather huge thorn in the IO's side. He was trapped on top of a three story building gunning down anything that came his way. A burning tank was pressed against the building's entrance making it difficult for the IO forces to get inside. The masked pilot stayed mainly in the center of the roof to drastically lower the chances of being hit from any gunfire or missile coming up from the growing crowd below. Ky would habitually peak out over the rim of the building and pick off some of their forces with his hefty double handed multi-machine gun.

He looked out onto the horizon with his eyes glued to the titanic altar jutting out of the center of the city. "Wow," He reacted in awe of the enormous super structure, "That thing can't be any good."

A spherical galactic cruiser then zoomed over to the building, hovering around and threatening the carefree pilot. The vessel bellowed out of its speaker system. "You must cease immediately!"

"A bit late for that now isn't it?" Ky whispered alone as he asserted the weighty machine gun at the IO craft. The panel housing the rotary cannons heads started spinning around wildly. Soon after that, the barrels themselves started rotating.

The craft's high-powered cameras saw that Ky was readying to open fire, so they launched a missile at him before the pilot's gun could spit out any bullets.

The missile had barely left the craft as Ky calmly readjusted the aim of his gun's rapidly turning heads. The gun blew out three streaming waves of giant bullets while dishing one intense kickback to Ky's chest. Ky had to use all the strength in his well-formed pilot arms to keep the machine gun steady and on target. The gunfire intercepted the missile before it had any time to create a significant distance away from the IO craft and exploded in midair dangerously close to the vessel. The blast instantly caused a lot of the craft's unnecessary functions to be rendered inoperable including its arsenal. The craft took a sudden turn to its side in the sky trying to avoid Ky's gunfire, but it was too little too late.

Ky kept the onslaught of bullets focused on the body of the craft. The galactic cruiser's shell supplied little resistance to the bullets and they continually punctured through the fifty yard long craft. An explosion broke out from where the bulk of Ky's assault was landing and the galactic cruiser began to come down. Ky remained firing even as the craft whistled down to the corner of a two story building across the street. An ear deafening crash blared out followed by the sound of multiple explosions as the craft mercilessly slammed into the top of the building. Both the IO craft and the building were devastated.

"Good job..." Ky commended the gun. The machine gun did indeed do what it was designed to. That day, Ky had used the gun to shoot down four other IO crafts before that one. "...too bad I'm out." He dropped the powerful gun that had finally run out of ammunition.

A soldier had taken it upon himself to get rid of the nuisance that was Ky. The soldier discarded his arm mounted automatic gun to more easily scale the back wall of the building. As he gradually climbed up the wall, he could hear the unrelenting noise of Ky battling the IO craft. It was about the time that Ky had tossed his weapon to the floor when the soldier tirelessly pulled his body over the building's ledge. The soldier was facing Ky's back as he came over the building's rim completely unnoticed.

Ky stretched his arms then put his hand on his back as if he had just finished a tiring day of gardening. He looked back over to the mysterious altar and wondered. "So what do I do now?"

The soldier used that time to stealthily take a bomb-disc from his back and activate it. The soldier then expertly threw the disc at Ky.

Ky heard a sound like a sword chipping away at cement and his eyes were instinctively drawn down to the left of his feet. He put on a curious face under his helmet as he examined a small disc lodged into the floor near him. BOOM! The disc blew up and the building's roof was lost in a blanket of dust and debris. Ky discovered that his body had been slammed against the ledge of the building's east wall. The pilot peeled off the cement ledge and found out that the left side of his body was burnt and aching. He hobbled to his feet in a mind erasing shock. From the cloud of still settling dust, the soldier jetted out and tackled Ky like a raging bull. The impact sent both of them over the side of the building. The tussle escalated as their bodies twisted and knocked against the building while they plummeted down. Ky luckily had his fall broken as the soldier's back collided with the top of a trash compactor in the side alley. The force in which they hit the compactor made them instantly lose their grips on each other and Ky bounced off landing on the ground.

"Oooooo..." Ky moaned with his body spread out on the floor of the alley. Ky was tired of the entire war. He hadn't been severely injured, only really banged up, but he'd been drained by the whole ordeal. At that instant, Ky wished he could sit and have a beer. He took his time getting back up.

Ky didn't have the chance to arc his head up when he heard a pair of feet land on the concrete right in front of him. Ky's masked face jolted up to find that the soldier on the compactor was still ticking and wanted more. Ky morphed into a boxing stance with his fists up like a true champ.

The pilot's fist came in with a right cross that was easily parried off the soldier's defending left arm. The IO soldier jumped into a sweeping dragon-tailed kick that was planted on the left cheek of Ky's helmet. Ky's form spun completely around before his back smacked against the pavement. The soldier swiftly seized the opportunity and straddled the pilot's abdomen while pulling out a battle knife from his utility belt. The soldier came down with a slash to the pilot's chest, but the advancing blade was blocked by a knife Ky had retrieved from his own equipment belt. Pressure on the two knives was increasing as both men tried to force their weapon through the other. Their knives were locked in a power struggle. It took every ounce of strength he had to push the soldier's weapon away from his neck. The soldier changed his grip on the knife to easily come down in a stabbing motion instead of a slash. The soldier thrust his knife down at Ky's masked face. Ky shifted his head to the side and the soldier's knife stuck into the ground only a half inch away from the pilot's helmet. Ky grabbed the soldier's arm that was still clasping the knife and used the man's own momentum and position to pull him down until the agent's chest met the concrete. Ky's other hand still held his own knife and he plunged the blade into the soldier's back. The soldier jerked back and cried out before he went limp and silent.

Ky shoved the soldier's dead body off and sarcastically apologized. "Sorry for that, pal." The beat up socialite brushed his pants off and heard the familiar clicks of countless automatic firearms preparing to shoot. His gaze turned up toward the beginning of the alleyway and Ky realized that the crowd of soldiers that were gathering in front of the building had made their way to him. At least sixty soldiers had their arm mounted guns aimed at Ky. The pilot quickly whipped out his pistol and pointed it back at the army. "Crap."

The alleyway became riddled with gunfire and bodies falling, but none of them were Ky's. The lazy pilot watched in immeasurable relief as a tidal wave of bullets assaulted the soldiers from an unknown source. The army seemed not to know where the bullets were coming from as well, and the confusion resulted in many IO casualties. At the moment, Ky didn't ask any questions, he simply redirected his gun back on the IO and joined in on the slaughter.

A man suddenly leaped out from behind an eight foot stone wall to the rear of the alley.
The man landed next to Ky with two powerful hand guns already drawn from his trench coat.

Ky recognized the man immediately as his optics fell on him. "Lee,"

"I knew you were wearing an IO helmet yesterday." The detective said with words resolving a thought that plagued his mind. "And it's Detective Lee to a slouch like you."

Ky and Lee's firearms lifted up once again and they

fired on the IO's doomed squad until all sixty soldiers fell. Down the bullet-ravaged passageway, G.F.B. soldiers dove out from the already shot-out windows of the alley's east wall. They had been stationed there waiting for the precise moment to get the drop on the IO crowd. Thirty-five G.F.B. soldiers emptied out of those windows.

Detective Lee quickly scanned the heads of all his men to judge, more or less, if all his subordinates were accounted for. "All right," A satisfied Lee voiced. "Let's go."

The large group then hastily ran over the back wall and deeper into the alleys. They navigated its narrow paths using the district's network of alleys to move through the city. Ky and Detective Lee led the pack swapping information.

"Where's Will?!" Lee barked.

"Why!? What's going on!?" Ky shouted back.

"Tell me now!" Lee assertively demanded.

"I don't know. He's been missing since this morning."

"Just my luck," The detective sighed. "I came here to rescue the boy, and when I get here I find the IO crap has hit the fan of the industrial district."

Ky asked. "Do you know where he could be?"

"I think I have an idea." Lee informed. His eyes drifted to the humungous brown altar in the city of Gohanesse; Ky's eyes followed. They stayed silent for a second giving the bone chilling altar a long hard look.

"You know something about all this, don't you?" Ky questioned from behind the IO helmet.

"Let's *just* say, I think I learned more than you were trying to hide from me yesterday." Lee stated.

"Oh you think so do ya?"

"You bet your ass I do."

Rose Star Runners

Wes was in the middle of a control deck on one of the IO crafts overlooking all the details of the war waging in the industrial district. It was a large round spacious room choked with giant monitors and control panels. Soldiers and other IO personnel darted about the screens monitoring all aspects of the battle. The screens were alive with numbers and electronically generated paragraphs that were constantly streaming the developing status of their secretive mission. Wes stood like a titan amidst the bustling room as the other IO agents received orders and yelled facts at him.

A soldier clicking buttons on a console reported. "Our total IO forces are down thirteen percent and climbing."

"What about the fugitive?" Wes inquired, cool as a cucumber.

Another nearby soldier operating his own console said. "It's the same as I said a few minutes before. One has been found and eliminated. We have one cornered in a warehouse. Two are at large. As for Jina...well..."

"Not them," Wes interrupted. "The little girl; have we located her yet?"

"Sorry sir," The soldier answered. "Nothing yet,"

"Damn!" Wes angrily cursed.

"Sir!" A far off soldier abruptly squeaked by a screen installed inside the wall. "We're getting an urgent transmission from the squad investigating last night's events. They are requesting to report to you directly."

Wes sifted through the crowd as he hurried over to the soldier's screen. "Let me see." Wes demanded. He reached the monitor and his eyes fell to the IO soldier's face on the screen. "What do you have to report soldier?" Wes feverishly asked the screen.

The soldier in the frame shot a fast salute to Wes before he informed. "Sir, on our investigation we found the fugitive and her target."

"Where are they now?"

"Sir, we lost the fugitive but we have the target in our custody right now. He is in a holding cell on our lower deck."

Wes' face transformed from a serious leader to an expression of sincere happiness. He removed his sunglasses and the playfulness and sheer glee was evident in his pupils. "Are you serious? That's excellent." Wes praised. "All right, I'm gonna get this craft heading to yours and you start getting yours to mine. We'll rendezvous in the middle."

"Yes sir," The soldier acknowledged.

"Okay, over and out."

"Yes sir," The soldier repeated.

Wes began to head away from the monitor and was on his way to ensure his craft started flying toward Will. He then suddenly stopped in his tracks and stormed back to the console before the transmission was severed. "Did you take away his satchel?"

Fifteen minutes later, Wes and a couple of other IO soldiers were staring down the barrel of an open barren holding cell. Will had escaped from the army's hold right under the IO's nose. The rage that had formed in Wes' gut had swelled like a balloon about to pop. He was furious.

"You idiots!" Wes scolded. "He's a hacker! If you don't take his laptop away it's like handing him super powers!"

The soldiers responsible for Will's escape hung their heads in shame failing to make eye contact with their infuriated boss. Wes' angered face quietly searched for an answer from his subordinates and found nothing.

An empty *sorry* reverberated out of one of the soldier's helmets as their eyes remained to the floor.

Wes threatened. "Yeah well, not as sorry as you're gonna be after I write the report on all this."

"What should we do about it, sir?" Another soldier questioned trying to remedy the mistake.

"There's nothing to do." Wes reluctantly divulged. "The only thing we know now is where they're going. With all the beacons lit, there's only one place they could be headed."

"The altar,"

"We need to increase security on the altar. Expect them." Wes ordered before bitterly storming off.

Jina had proven to the overwhelming force that she truly was a one-woman army. They had been sending wave after wave at her and she consistently beat them back. The intense battle gradually moved a couple of blocks away from the studio/warehouse leaving a short path of ravaged street. The area around her had turned into a war zone, complete with blown-up, flipped-over tanks, piles of deceased broken soldiers, and crumbling smoldering buildings. The IO kept the majority of their force focused on Jina in hopes that they could smother her with numbers alone. They had not been successful.

She stood motionless on a mountain of collapsed cement that used to be a building as soldiers closed in all around her. The troops cautiously neared the femme fatale as if they were planning a strike from all sides. All the soldiers then oddly hit the deck making room for some impending assault.

"Phase 1!" A grounded soldier shouted signifying that the first step of a predetermined plan had been implemented.

Far off in the horizon of the distant blue sky, deadly missiles became visible. A far away spacecraft was answering the call of the desperate army. It fired four missiles at Jina that were designed to take down armored vehicles. The streaming missiles made their long trek across the industrial district skimming over the building tops. The sailing capsules of explosive metal careened toward Jina at a slightly downward angle so that the four probes would slam right into her well-endowed chest. The missiles whistled anxious to meet her but her legs whisked her forty feet into the sky. The missiles were too close to making contact and had no choice but to connect with the ground and blow up.

The scene erupted in flames bearing a shock wave that rocked the entire district. The black smoke of the explosions could be seen even farther than that, but not one citizen noticed it with the giant distracting altar still looming over Gohanesse. The force's numbers were cut in half as everyone who was positioned to Jina's rear was annihilated by the missiles. The remaining IO helmets looked up to the sky searching for Jina's whereabouts. They discovered that she had utterly cleared the blast with her magnificent dive into the heavens.

The helmets' automated cross-hairs locked onto Jina's plummeting body and their machine guns raised up ready to take advantage of the situation. A soldier then screamed out. "Phase 2!" It seemed as though the IO's plan to take out Jina was still working accordingly. Thousands of bullets raced up to her falling countenance.

Jina's powerful staff twirled and danced around her body at an inconceivable rate. To the soldiers, it appeared as though her frame was instantly encased in a shell of her staff's mystical metal. The gunfire bounced off of Jina's rapidly swirling weapon and showered down on the soldiers below. The speeding golden lead rained on the unsuspecting soldiers, dwindling their numbers to only a few. Her feet landed against the smoldering rubble beneath her.

A soldier then bellowed. "At will!" Which is an abbreviation to the command *fire at will*. The IO was supposed to have clinched the bout when they moved into Phase 3 and Jina should have been as good as dead, but something the lady warrior had done before that point had foiled the army's grand scheme. Their best move from then on was to face her as each soldier found fit.

The few remaining soldiers popped up from behind rocky debris with their weapons ready to engage. One soldier chucked a bomb-disc at Jina like a steady soaring dart. The soldier watched his weapon with anticipation as it neared her. Even with the soldier's eyes intently set on Jina, he couldn't detect as she slid her staff with the skill of an expert into one of the disc's slender grip holes. The bomb harmlessly spun around at the end of her staff, and the soldier's sight could still not catch the image as she slingshot the disc back at him. The poor IO agent could only fully comprehend what had transpired as he looked down to find his own bomb-disc had impaled him in the center of his chest. The soldier didn't have a chance to feel the pain before the bomb's charge released blowing the man to pieces. Nothing was left of the soldier except black fiery smog and clumps of frizzled flesh.

The rest of the IO force gazed into the smog trying to gauge their next move, but Jina came sprinting out of the smoke like a glowing arrow from an angel's bow. Her body blurred over to the nearest soldier and she batted him down. She beamed over to the next closest immobile soldier and swatted him unconscious as well. The mere second it took her to take care of them went completely unchallenged. They just stood there in awe of Jina's exceptionally amazing fighting skill.

After the last soldier was crushed, Jina swiveled the head of her staff about to face more of the army, but none were to be found. Finally she had a moment to rest but used it instead to contemplate why the IO ceased their attack on her. The constant swarm of soldiers, tanks, and crafts had stopped coming as if there was something more important for the army to tend to. This thought plagued her mind.

Not the entirety of the army had fled the scene. Two tanks sat side by side on the edge of the battlefield with their cannons aimed at Jina's general vicinity. They had remained stationary for the whole fight so that Jina would have thought them to be abandoned, but they weren't. They simply waited for the exact time for the breathtaking warrior to let her guard down to make their strike. As she pondered with her back turned, the two teams inside the tank silently lined up the cannons to Jina's unsuspecting head. Suddenly the soldiers felt their tanks get pushed into a slant as if a fallen heavy rock had wedged its way between the two massive armored vehicles.

It was the wall-sized knight Baloe who had just arrived, and even though he viewed Jina as a rival, he wasn't going to allow her to be shot in the back. He was in between the two tanks near the front, level with the cannons. He stayed suspended there by pressing his legs against the tanks' walls causing their slight slanting. In one graceful motion, Baloe slammed the club to his left making the cannon's barrel bend an impressive ninety degrees. He then followed through with an upward swing to his right that made the tip of the other cannon point to the sky. He leaped out from between the two vehicles and casually strolled over to Jina.

The soldiers inside heard the banging but didn't care; it was their only chance to do away with the invincible Jina. They took their shots but their cannon's bent barrels made the attack result in backfires. From the exterior of the tanks, they merely seemed to rumble a bit, but the dual explosions that erupted within killed the tanks' operators. Baloe calmly approached Jina as the soldiers' own foolishness led to their demise.

Jina had her head turned to the advancing knight

and she quickly questioned. "Do you know why the IO forces have fled?"

The robed knight neared her and graciously answered. "Lili and Will must've activated this planet's last beacon. They've gone to protect the altar no doubt." His hand then gestured to the great stone altar that had appeared.

"Is it important?"

"Lili and Will must be on their way there now. The IO will kill them once they see them."

Jina ordered. "Then that's where we're going." She readied to head to the ominous altar as fast as her powerful legs could take her but was stopped by Baloe's next word.

"No,"

She faced the knight again determined to set the mild tension between them aside so that they could continue their search for the children. "Don't start this now. I need to protect Will, and if we don't go now Lili will be put in danger too."

"I care not about Lili!" Baloe shouted as a clear declaration of his true goal.

Jina's green eyes formed into suspicion. "What are you talking about?"

"Lili wants to get to the altar, Will wants to help her, the IO want to stop them, and you want to save them. But I... I want to square us away right here right now!" Baloe yelled then held his mighty club at her as a call to fight.

Jina's hand went to her head in frustration. She calmly explained. "Baloe, please stop this foolishness right now. This whole world may be in danger, so we must postpone our rematch until we can get to the bottom of this and straighten it all out. Do you understand?"

"Yes," Baloe revealed. "I understand a great deal. I know exactly what's going on, but we will fight now even if the entire planet is crumbling around us!" With his freehand, Baloe clutched his robe and threw it off his body. Jina's eyes went wide as she got an eyeful of Baloe's new grotesque attire. The clothes were Doc; pieces of him anyway. Baloe had called Doc out early that morning and butchered him. He gutted the poor knight and woven parts of his flesh and skin into his clothes. The remaining skin of Doc's face had been wrapped around his head like a horrifying hat. A psychotic gratifying smile stretched across Baloe's cheeks. He further raved. "I had battled Lili's hold over me with my own will and won. I now have Doc's amplification ability in my possession, and with his remains in such close proximity of me, my speed and strength are boosted to a level you could only dream of."

"Baloe..." Was the only word Jina could form. Baloe's growing insanity had chilled her to her soul.

"With this power, I can crush you. And when I can say that it was I that put you in the ground, I can surely take my place as the strongest in the universe."

Finally accepting that those words came from the knight's blackened heart, Jina's eyes closed and her head fell down in pity. Her face barely made disapproving sways back and forth as she said. "You fool... You're such a fool. I thought of you as an honorable warrior, but your lust for power has blinded you and turned you into a monster not worthy of such praise... You know, you and the other knights kept calling Riftkin crazy, but he has more honor in him than you."

"Your honor is going to be buried with your corpse." Baloe vowed.

Jina stealthily took a fighting stance with her staff at hand and taunted. "That's *IF* you can beat me."

Baloe's free left hand had neared his face directed up as if in prayer. His eyes shut and his head dropped for a moment. Then his body began to glow with a radiance so thick it could be described as bright. The potency of the glow was indeed drastically more intense than when Doc exercised the technique. The deranged knight's glowing face screamed. "You're finished!" He bounded at her with untold speed; that enormous frame moved like lightning that day. Baloe charged at least as fast as Jina had been moving in their previous altercation.

Baloe's gravel club met nothing but the end of Jina's mighty staff as she blocked his attack, but something was different. He could clearly judge her every move; it wasn't even blurry anymore. Baloe felt like they were finally fighting on an even playing field and he confidently unleashed a suppressing barrage of gravel strikes. Each blow fell on her staff as she showcased her true defensive capabilities, but Baloe was certain as the light of day that if he kept going and didn't let up she could be bested. The knight savagely thrashed his club repeatedly at Jina trying to keep pressure on her until her defense slipped. Then Baloe felt a sudden gust of wind followed by Jina vanishing into thin air.

Baloe then realized she was right under his chin as her staff skewered him through the chest in a flash. Baloe's eyes widened and his golden glow faded as his club fell from his hand. Blood began to stream out of his mouth as he asked. "But...how?"

"Like I said before, I thought you were a man of honor, so I didn't want to completely humiliate you in our last match; men and their fragile egos and all. But now, you have proven yourself an animal so I butchered you like one. I told you you were a fool." Jina said speaking her piece. She slowly slid the bloody staff out of the knight's chest and turned around not even facing the falling body.

Baloe's final word was a spiteful drawn out *no* that slowly dissipated like the life force from his body. Baloe died realizing that he could have never achieved his goal as supreme warrior. The blood steadily gushed out of the warrior's chest, but he was already gone.

Jina's eyes then wandered to the altar again as she wished. "Stay alive Will." She then raced to the altar.

The Guider whizzed through the sky heading to the heart of Gohanesse City. Will had already reunited with Lili and they were both aboard on their way to the altar. Will was sitting in the pilot's seat but his tiny hands were not wielding the heavy controls. His fingers were ablaze on his laptop in front of him as he manipulated the craft via the computer. Lili was just lounging over the copilot seat gawking at Will in a deep admiration of what he was capable of.

"You're awesome, you know that?" Lili flattered.

"Shut up," Will reacted with a blush.

A sudden explosion on the side of the craft shook the interior with the ferocity of a severe earthquake. The children instantly tumbled over. Holographic red warning signals started popping up all around the cockpit and wailing a siren of caution.

"Are we okay?" Lili feverishly asked from the floor.

Will stood up and retrieved his laptop, which was luckily not broken, and proclaimed. "We should be fine, but I need to check out what's going on."

An IO craft had snuck up on the Guider and decided at that moment to attack. A soldier monitoring the missile read the information off his screen.

The soldier reported. "Sir, it was a direct hit, but the craft is still flying. It appeared to have caused minimal to no damage."

"Hmmm," The head agent wondered. "Shoot a gang of missiles at it."

"What happened?" Lili gasped getting back into the copilot seat.

Will also took his place in the pilot's chair and

started hacking his way to the answer. "Hold on." Shortly after, he replied. "We were hit by a missile."

"Isn't that bad? Shouldn't we... I don't know, evacuate?" Lili curiously suggested.

Will shot her a reassuring cocky expression. He then said in a sly cool manner as if the words were plucked from Wes' mouth. "It's gonna take a lot more than that to break through this craft's Arlian armor." A passing glance to his laptop's monitor made the boy screech in a terrified urgency. "BUCKLE UP, NOW!"

The children frantically wrestled with their countless straps trying to correctly get them in their harness. In a second they both became a jitter of nerves.

On the outside of the Guider, five missiles were making their way to the craft. They surrounded the vessel from all sides and flew alongside it. The space between the missiles became smaller as they closed in on its target. On contact, the sky was ablaze by multiple tremendous explosions that hid the Guider in its churning fire and flack.

"All direct hits." The soldier manning his monitor informed the captain.

The captain had removed his helmet and was comfortably sipping on a mug of coffee as he received the news. The captain looked to be running a rather lax vessel. "Good," The captain sounded before taking a sip of jo. The porcelain fell from his lips and he said. "Let's see if that does anything?"

The crew of the IO craft anxiously watched their screens waiting to see the fate of the targets and their craft. Masked scowls swept across the control deck as they watched the Guider soar out of the blackened smoke like a rocket's first flight. The craft had remained nearly unscathed.

"Hmmm... this is quite a pickle." The captain commented before taking another drink. The IO craft followed the Guider as the captain nonchalantly assessed the situation. His head tilted back and he called out. "Darnell!"

A rather inattentive soldier trotted over to the captain and said. "Yes captain, what's up?"

"What do you make of all this?" The captain asked the soldier with a mugged hand directed at the screen. "That's the target and I've been sending missile after missile at it and it is just *NOT* going down."

The soldier placed a hand to his helmet's chin in a motion of deep thought. "Hmmm..."

"Do you think shooting at it would do anything?"

The soldier slowly shook his head and stated. "Uhh...nooo... I don't think so. If missiles aren't doing anything, what are bullets gonna do?"

"Right,"

They stood there for a moment as their craft zoomed at incredible speeds toward the fugitive Guider. "Ah!" The soldier sounded in enlightenment. "Their craft must be made out of Arlian alloys."

"You think?" The captain responded.

"Sure, that's the only thing that explains it."

"Well I'll be..."

"Fire a mole at it. That should do the trick." The friendly soldier advised before slumping away.

The captain shifted his head back to the soldier operating the monitor and casually ordered. "Shoot a mole at it."

A mole is a missile type device utilized when their target was either very durable or if it was essential to damage the center of the object. The tip of it was made out of the same metal as the Guider and had the capability of puncturing through it. Once a mole pierces through its target, the tip comes flying off and a powerful drill creeps out of the hole. The drill churns deep into its target's center where it plants a charge. After the mole securely sets the charge, it is detonated and the target blows up from the inside out. The weapon gained the title *mole* due to the way the missile burrows the charge into its target. The IO craft fired a mole at the Guider.

Inside Ky's galactic cruiser, the kids had finally steadied from the ferocious rumbling caused by the multiple missile attack. Will's eyes were stuck to his laptop checking on the Guider's status. Sirens continued to blare inside the cockpit as the helpless children wished they would just go away.

"Is it over?" Lili questioned in a scared tone.

"We seem to be out of danger for the moment but the IO is still right on our butts." Will answered doing everything he could on his laptop. "The IO network is singular and I can't hack in from any normal means. I could use a pulse to virtually locate their crafts' system but not while they're chasing us."

"Meaning?"

"I can't hack into their craft until we both stop."

Will and Lili's bodies jolted as an unexpected impact rocked the Guider. The quake was much more moderate than when it weathered the missile attacks, but the silence it left afterward created an eerie feeling in their hearts.

"What was that?" Lili asked.

"I don't know. It didn't show up on my scanners." Will admitted as he investigated the shock via his laptop.

A new red holographic window appeared more prevalent and serious than the other warning signals. The electronically generated voice of caution was specific with its message. It urgently repeated the message. "Hull breach."

Will's eyes grew wide as he tried to soak in the window's improbable message. He whispered. "Ohhhhh nooooo,"

Alex Benitez

"What is it?" Lili gasped her face a mask of concern.

"They somehow broke through our armor." Will confessed with a voice of disbelief.

"Can't we put a patch over it?" Lili suggested just trying to help.

"Me and you? Lift a patch? Not in a million years."

"So what do we do?"

"Only one thing we can do, come on!" Will commanded as he started unbuckling his harness. On his way out, he clutched his laptop in one arm and Lili's hand in the other. The kids then abandoned the cockpit never to return again.

The mole had indeed punctured the Guider's tough Arlian metal, making contact a few feet to the right of its main thruster. The head of the mole popped off and the drill slowly extended from the bowels of the missile. The drill swirled and churned not caring if it was simply whipping around air or driving through titanium. The drill eventually met with the Guider's inner metal frame and it began tearing it to shreds. Spark's lit up the craft's delicate interior wall as the drill ate through its metal and circuitry. After the drill was imbedded approximately ten feet into the Guider it slowed to a halt. Suddenly the head of the drill detached from the rest of the mole. The separation of drill and mole is what triggers the charge to explode; which is located inside the drill. In midair, the Guider blasted apart like a potato in a science fair project, raining down deadly chunks of the craft onto the populated streets below.

Cheers possessed the IO craft as the flaming galactic cruiser crash landed in the middle of a suburban avenue. Their mission was accomplished, and once they went down and confirmed the identity of the corpses, the entire IO army could finally leave the planet. The IO craft descended and circled around the blazing debris ready to salvage the bodies. Unfortunately, they did not notice a small jet drop out of a chute on the bottom of the Guider right before the explosion. The children were still safely making their way to the altar.

Will and Lili were aboard the small jet replica of Ky's Guider called the Glider entering the outskirts of Gohanesse. It was a small cramped jet housed in the galactic cruiser only big enough to seat two. Since the kids were so young, they actually fit into the vessel quite comfortably.

They could look out the Glider's front windshield and clearly see the giant altar jutting out of the center of the city. They also caught sight of five IO crafts hovering around its crown habitually firing missiles at the altar in vain. They were heading straight into the belly of the beast.

"So that's the altar?" Will said. "It's kinda creepy."

"How's your peek into the void?" Lili wondered.

Will tried to focus on the spinning black spot in the upper right corner of his vision. He replied. "It's still the same size."

"It may fluctuate when the ceremony is underway." Lili warned. "It might hurt."

Will rolled his eyes. "Greeaat."

"What about the IO?" Lili asked in reference to the crafts guarding the altar.

Will assured. "It might take a little time, but I should be able to take care of them... At least they're not moving around too much."

Lili drew a heavy sigh and readied. "Let's do it."

Only a few minutes later, the Glider slid along the side of the altar. Strangely enough, they did not exit the vessel. They just stayed in the small jet for over ten minutes. The surrounding IO craft's definitely realized who they must have been.

One IO soldier leaned over his monitor feeling the anxiety of suddenly holding a lot of authority. This particular soldier was left in charge of protecting the altar, but he never imagined that he'd need to exercise it. He patiently waited there weighing all his options.

Another soldier approached the stressed one in charge. "Sir, they're not answering any of our transmission messages."

The soldier in command just slowly nodded his head up and down in acknowledgment.

"Sir, should we open fire and end this?"

"No!" The soldier quickly responded. "We don't even know it's them. It could be a decoy sent by the target to confuse us."

"Do you want us to contact agent Vega?"

"No!" The soldier yelled with more aggression in his voice. "Wes is a real softy when it comes to that boy. He'd immediately order us to do nothing until he arrived."

"So what are we gonna do?"

With the pressure on, the soldier commanded. "We'll open fire but *AFTER* we visually confirm it's the target."

"Yes sir,"

The hatch to the Glider then opened and the boy stepped out. He had his laptop under his arm and he stared straight up at one of the crafts as if daring them.

"It's the boy but where is the girl?" The stress filled soldier said.

Will took a few steps out onto the brown stone slab before Lili exited the Glider. None of the soldiers could believe it. There she was; well in range and clear for a shot.

"FIRE!" The soldier adamantly demanded on his control deck.

Will's eyes stayed scrolling the surrounding crafts as Lili ventured onto the stone block of an altar. "I wonder how long it'll take them to figure out I locked up their weapon controls?" Will remarked.

Lili just watched Will curious to what she should do.

"That peek into the void is getting bigger. Open the gate." Will instructed.

Ky, Detective Lee, and all his men were hunkered behind a vast granite wall trying to remain undetected from the IO. They were taking a breather and using the opportunity to swap information to ensure they were working toward similar goals.

Lee lounged against the wall and ordered. "All right, tell me what you know and I mean everything."

Ky explained. "Well, it's all about the girl, right? She's some kind of princess from a faraway planet with crazy mind powers. In a nutshell, she ran away from home and that army wants to kill her because they don't like the idea of such a powerful little girl running around."

"Oh man," The detective blurted. "Will must've hacked into the soldiers' data base and not Wes'."

"Who?"

"Ky, Lili is not a princess. She's a god."

"What!?" Ky rang while wearing a baffled face beneath the helmet.

Lee asked. "What buster, you don't believe me?"

"Well, maybe if you were some divine indestructible being, but coming from you, it's a little hard to swallow."

"Believe it or not, it is true." Detective Lee assured before explaining what he knew. "She's the god of the mind, and she's using Will like a key to bust out her old boy-toy, Omega, and meld with him."

"Who's Omega?"

"Omega is the god of power, who was sealed away by the other gods for crimes against the universe."

"Wow," Ky murmured with an astonished look. "I should've shot her in the face when I had the chance."

"Yeah," Lee agreed. "She's making Will fall in love with her so that he'll help her willingly. The gods made the key something she couldn't control directly."

"How's this possible? Where's all this going down?" Ky demanded to know.

Detective Lee pointed a thumb in the general direction of the altar and said. "If Will's the key, then that's the door. They're both probably heading there right now."

"Well we gotta get there and stop that witch." Ky bellowed like a true hero.

"Don't need to." Lee informed. "I'm betting since that ugly-ass altar popped up, Wes is there now trying to talk him out of it."

"Who the hell is Wes?" The pilot forcefully asked.

"Wes is leading the IO investigation...and Will's half-brother."

"Wow," Ky summed up. "So it's between his first love and his long lost brother. Man... Wes doesn't stand a chance."

BOOM! The wall behind them blew apart leaving nothing but two feet of brick at the base. The soldier coughed and wheezed as the broken cinder dust found its way to their lungs. The dust fell revealing a sizable IO force on the other side of the wall. Two tanks accompanied sixty soldiers leaving Lee and his men severely outmatched.

"It's a freakin' ambush!" The detective shouted even before the ringing in his ears ceased.

The G.F.B. soldiers posted against the wall remnants for cover and unleashed flaring gunfire at the overwhelming squad. The IO answered their gunfire with a maelstrom of bullets and the block was deafened with the sound of shooting.

Bullets danced around Lee's crouched body as he cursed. "Damn it," He retrieved two abnormally-sized pistols from his trench coat. "Come on Ky! It's time to nip this problem in door number two!"

"I can't!" Ky answered. "I gotta talk Will out of this

and if he won't come, I'll break his boney legs and drag his ass back!"

"Wes is going to take care of it!"

"Wes doesn't know Will!" Ky reasoned. "But I do! If anyone can get him back, it's going to be me!"

"Then go!" The detective finally concurred. "We'll cover your route!"

"Thank you!"

A G.F.B. subordinate carefully approached Detective Lee and hastily informed. "Sir! Our grenades are having no effect on their tanks!"

"Oh for the love of Pete!" Lee complained before taking action. He grabbed the grenade from the soldier's palm and screamed. "Give me that!" The detective pounced over the destroyed wall and dashed over to a tank knocking out an IO soldier along the way. He jumped onto the armored wheel of the tank then leaped for the cannon barrel and was just able to get hold of it with his freehand. As he hung there, he removed the pin from the grenade with his teeth and chucked the explosive down the cannon's barrel. He dropped from the tank and ran for cover. He almost made it back to the wall as the tank blew into pieces. His war raged eyes met with Ky and he belted out. "Get out of here!"

Ky didn't even respond. His legs just started moving to the altar even though he couldn't possibly get there in time. He slipped on his photon cannon as he ran from the battlefield and let out a shot. The hot photon charge slammed into the barrel of the other tank's cannon. It looked like an invisible ball slamming into a puddle of paint when the blast instantly melted the barrel. The melting metal quickly cooled over the cannon's hole. The shot rendered the tank utterly useless and if they shot a shell it would surely backfire.

Detective Lee witnessed Ky's heroic act and he

boasted. "Good job soldier and, good luck."

Meanwhile, Will and Lili had grown rather comfortable on top of the altar. Will sat on the edge of the titanic monument refining his hold over the army's arsenal. Lili stood in the middle of the altar with her eyes closed and lifted hands like a divine prophet. A flicker of lightning sparked a few feet above the altar's surface and spread open into a tiny portal. The portal was only big enough for a small child to stick a hand through, and inside was darker than closing your eyes at night. Her eyes opened and twisted around to look at Will with a weary face.

"How's your peek in the void doing?" She inquired with care.

The spot in the corner of the boy's vision was rapidly growing and began to take up a quarter of his sight. The swirling vortex in his eye was certainly expanding as the portal inched open. Will informed. "It's getting bigger."

"Does your eye hurt?"

Sweat trickled down his forehead as the boy coped with the increasing pain. "Just finish the portal."

Lili hesitantly shifted her head back around as concern for her friend gnawed at her mind. She wanted to somehow rid Will of his eye aches, but there was nothing she could do, so she continued with the ceremony.

Another IO craft joined the lingering group. That craft was carrying the head investigator Wes Vega whom was none too happy that things had escalated so far. In his busy control deck, Wes demanded to get a line open to the soldier he'd left in charge.

"Sir, we have him on the screen." A soldier reported to Wes.

"Bring me to him." Wes said before a soldier directed him to a holographic monitor. He looked upon the soldier in the screen who was identical to all the other IO troops.

"Status report,"

The soldier in the screen summarized. "Sir, I planned to open fire on the target once visual confirmation was achieved, but it appears the boy has disabled our weaponry."

"Of course he has,"

"I was organizing a party to swarm the altar and take them by force, but then I got word you were coming, so I postponed the order until you arrived."

"They'll be no need to organize a party." Wes declared. "I'll go down there and I'll get him...alone."

The soldier in the screen challenged. "Sir, do you believe that is a wise decision?"

"I think I can talk Will out of it." Wes affirmed. "We still have a chance to accomplish our mission without killing him."

The soldier sighed. "If you say so, sir; over and out." The screen blinked out as the transmission concluded.

Wes turned around and ordered the room. "Get me to the drop hatch."

A few minutes later, Wes and another soldier were in a hangar-like room at the base of the craft called the drop hatch. The room is used to lower soldiers into a certain area with a line while the craft remains in the air. The cold steel room whistled as the powerful hatch door started to slide open from the top. Wes put his left leg in a footing and left arm in a fastened sleeve on one of the drop lines on the wall. The hatch door's opening slowly widened, subjecting the drop hatch to prevailing gusts of wind. Wes' long blonde hair kicked about as he unsheathed an ancient pistol dating back to the 1900s.

The soldier held onto a guardrail with his right hand to ensure that he did not fall out the hatch door. The soldier instructed. "Okay! Keep your arm and leg in the line at all times! On the count of three, you jump out of the hatch and

I'll lower you down to the altar from here! Got it!?"

"Got it!" Wes assured.

"What is that!?" The soldier questioned looking at the rusting gun.

"It's an antique gun! It's called a six-shooter!"

"Oh!" The soldier perceived. "Why aren't you taking a regular machine gun?"

"Hmmm," Wes thought creating an answer in his mind. "I like antiques!"

"Fair enough! Are you ready sir!?"

"Yes!"

"3...2...1!"

Wes bravely hurdled out of the craft as the line fed him down to the altar.

Will was cradling his forehead as the pain in his eye intensified. The boy asked. "How are you doing on the portal?"

The portal had grown to the size that small children could briskly walk through, but it seemed Lili wasn't satisfied. "Almost done,"

"Please hurry," Requested Will who had tears welling up. In a passing glance, Will saw that a man was being lowered to the altar from a wire on one of the crafts. Lili's attention also fell on the man for a moment, but hastily returned to her portal-forming duty. About halfway down the man's descent to the altar, Will could clearly make out who it was.

The furious breeze atop the lofty altar blew Will's hair to one side as Wes landed. With a single tug, the line that lowered Wes to the altar started recoiling back into the craft. Wes aimed his archaic pistol at the children.

Will nabbed his laptop and jogged over to Lili and said under his breath. "Are you finished yet?"

"No, you need to stall him."

"Will!" Wes called out from the other end of the

altar.

Will turned around bearing a heart pumping with fear as he faced Wes. He took a few steps toward the armed agent and tried to buy some time. "I guess you're here to kill us."

Wes pulled out a small single button controller from the back of his pants with his freehand and held it toward the boy. "Not exactly," Wes then pressed the tiny red button at the end of the controller and a most surprising event occurred. All the IO crafts, along with the Glider, suddenly shut down and plummeted to their doom. Each craft fell to the park below in a grand display of destruction.

A confused Will asked. "What just happened?"

"I evened the odds for you." Wes confessed. "I sent out an electromagnetic pulse that turned off all the electronics up here. Your laptop is useless too."

Will let out a little chuckle before he lazily tossed his compact computer off the altar.

Wes explained. "This gun is an antique and has no electronic parts on it. It'll probably break after the first shot, but I still have that one shot. So, let's have a little chat."

"Fine, I see you have no problem killing your own men." Will zinged.

"They were gonna execute you Will, and they will succeed if I can't stop you now." Wes informed.

Lili's hands dropped as the portal reached its maximum girth; big enough for a full-grown man to enter. She said to Will. "It's complete. It's time to go."

"Well, we'll be going now, so don't worry about that. See ya." Will concluded as he motioned to enter the portal.

"She's only using you, Will. When she's done with you, she'll toss you out like yesterday's garbage." Wes attempted to convince.

"I've seen your troops' files, Wes. You guys just fear her abilities so you wanna get rid of her. Isn't that the story?" Will barked back in Lili's defense.

"Will, those files were fabricated so that the soldiers who volunteered for the mission wouldn't be as scared as they should be." Wes claimed.

"I don't believe you." Will then began to head for the portal yet again, but was stopped by the agent's next sentence.

"She's not a princess, she's a god."

"What?" Will instinctively said not fully wrapping his head around the statement. He faced Wes to clear it up.

"That's right, she's the god of the mind." The armed agent restated.

Will's eyes searched Lili's face for resolve. "Lili, is this true?"

Lili's face was wearing an uncomfortable expression of melancholy as if she was seeking a way out. She whimpered. "It's true Will, but I just didn't know how you'd take it."

"Man!" Will screamed not wanting to believe it. His gaze pulled away from her as if he was disappointed. Then his face shot up to Wes. Times of Lili and himself joking and laughing flashed in his head. "Well so what? That doesn't change anything."

"Of course that changes everything. Omega. It's her ex-boyfriend she wants to resurrect. He's the god of power, and she's the reason he's locked away. Along time ago, she used her abilities to manipulate Omega, and together they roamed from planet to planet ruling each one like tyrants. Omega was put to an eternal slumber and sealed in a different dimension for his crimes, but all the other gods knew that she was the puppeteer..."

"These are lies!!" Lili interrupted. "Will don't believe him!"

"Shut up!" Will shouted.

"She wants to meld with him." Wes added.

"Shut up! I don't believe it! I don't believe you!" Will reaffirmed.

"You *NEED* to believe me, Will." Wes eagerly persisted.

"Why!?" Will angrily interrogated. "Why do I need to believe you!?"

Wes somberly took off his sunglasses. He then announced. "Will, I'm your older brother, and I know all this because she tried it on me first."

Lili jerked at Will's arm as she desperately pleaded. "Will, you don't need to listen to this. We can just go right now, you and me."

Will ignored the girl's cries and asked Wes. "What do you mean?"

"When you were real young, these older kids roughed you up one day and I just watched not sure what to do. You ran to your father and our mother and told them what happened." Wes' gaze shifted to the endless blue sky as details of the faint memory came flooding back. "Man did I get scolded for that. I felt so guilty that I made sure it never happened again. The next time the kids tried picking on you, I taught them a lesson myself, but they had big brothers of their own and one day they beat me up real bad."

Vague recollections of the boy's reoccurring dreams played in the boy's head. The connections began to haunt Will's mind.

Wes continued. "I ended up in the hospital with a concussion, and that's where I got this scar on my face." Wes placed two fingers on his scar delicately touching the noticeable wound. "Because of my head injury, Lili couldn't control me either. Do you get it? She got me mixed up with you."

"Will, he's twisting the truth to make you do what he wants." Lili told the boy.

Wes resumed his story. "She came to me as a beautiful young woman; what was most appealing to *my* eyes. She..." Wes became a little choked up before he finished his sentence. "...she made me fall in love with her. She thought she found her key in me because we have such similar brainwaves, but one day she pulled something out of my brain and found out I wasn't attuned to the Abseninus Void."

Memories of the silver gilded jaguar blinked in Will's mind. The similarities between Wes' story and his own chilled the boy.

"Then she was gone, leaving me there to be slaughtered by some monster she summoned. I was saved and recruited by the IO and put in charge of this assignment because of my inner knowledge of the matter, but I couldn't assist them in murdering my little brother... I just can't do it." Wes concluded hoping against hope that he may have sparked a change in Will's heart.

Will stood there like a betrayed man. He didn't move as he absorbed the upsetting news, even as Lili tugged at his sleeve.

"Come on Will," Lili said as if she was trying to erase Wes' words from his mind. "Let's just go."

Wes warned. "Don't do it Will."

The boy then snapped. "Well what do you want me to do, huh!? Run into your arms and let you shoot her in cold blood!? I don't even know you! But you come here and tell me you're my older brother and expect me to stab my friend in the back!? I can't do that!"

Lili opened a hand and held it up in Wes' direction.

"She's gonna cast you aside once she's done with you. I can promise you that." Wes predicted. "She doesn't really care for you, Will. I care for you." The agent's eye started to twitch as tiny balls of sweat formed on his forehead.

"Shut up! You don't know anything about us! Just because she didn't love you doesn't mean she doesn't love me! You could easily be making all this up!"

Wes' head shook as if something was bothering him. "This isn't a jealousy thing, Will. I need you to trust me."

"You had five years to find me and earn my trust. You don't just get it now!" Will proclaimed.

Wes begged as he dropped the controller and put a hand on his head. "Don't make me use this Will. The last thing I want to do is use this." Wes pointed his antique six-shooter higher as if he was preparing to fire.

"You have no hold over me." Will coldly said to Wes.

Wes' body turned shaky and fell to one knee as if he was suffering internally. As the next words escaped his trembling lips it was apparent he was talking to Lili. "Stop it you witch. You know as well as I do that your mind tricks don't affect me."

"Yes," Lili calmly agreed with her hand still in the air. "But as I recall, you would get debilitating headaches if I focused on you hard enough."

"Ahhh," Wes howled in pain. The ancient pistol fell from Wes' hand and his body followed it to the ground soon after. His hands clutched his head in a vain attempt to remedy his outrageously throbbing headache. "Will! Uh-you gotta stop. You must stop!"

The boy watched horrified at the grown man squirming with pain on the floor. Events were occurring too fast for the boy to comprehend. Then a voice sounded that knocked him back into his frame of thought.

"Will," Lili cooed. She grabbed the boy's attention. "You can't believe this guy's web of lies. He's just feeding you whatever he needs to to get you away from me, but I could never let that happen because...because I love you Will."

The children were locked in an endearing gaze searching in each other's eyes for the feelings that were just put into words.

Will was lost in her eyes as he returned her sentiment. "I love you too."

Their lips met briefly.

"Nooo!" Wes cried out from the altar floor. "You need to stop! You can't do this!"

Wes continued wailing his words of caution, but they fell on deaf ears. The children just ignored him as they entered the portal hand in hand. The portal closed up and agent Vega's failure sunk into his head.

"Will!!"

Ky raced through the streets of Gohanesse immediately pumping a photon charge into the chest of any IO soldier who got in his way. He was reaching the end of the industrial district, but he still had a ways to go if he hoped to make it to the altar and save his friend. He felt that the situation had switched to something dire, so strategic combative subtleties were a luxury the masked pilot no longer had. Ky's clunky charge through the roadways thrust him into a rather unfavorable predicament.

Ky directly ran up on five IO soldiers that had no clue he was right around the corner. Ky slid to a halt as he unexpectedly approached the soldiers. Ky was quickly sighted by the soldiers.

"Hey!" One of the soldiers yelled. "That's one of the fugitives."

Five miniature machine guns aimed their sights on Ky, and the cornered pilot aimed his pistol and cannon back at them. Even though Ky's photon cannon may have given him a moderate edge over a single soldier, collectively the lazy pilot was out gunned.

"Before we do this, I wanna let you know what type

of day I've been having." Ky ranted. "I woke up to you guys ripping off a wall from my apartment, and that was the good part. Since then, I've been stabbed at, shot at, blown up, and thrown off a building, so please believe me when I say I'm not to be vexed with right now."

A bullet rang out that neither Ky nor the soldiers fired. One of the soldiers dropped to the floor dead, then another one hit the pavement.

One of the remaining three soldiers barked. "Sniper!" The IO helmets scanned the rooftops in search of the unknown gunman. Whoever released the mysterious bullets made sure to conceal their whereabouts well.

Another one of the soldiers was eliminated before the assassin was spotted. "He's on that roof." One of the remaining two shouted pointing at the one story warehouse to Ky's rear. Out of all the factories, buildings, and warehouses the sniper could have hid, he chose the most obvious location, which coincidentally kept him undetected for so long. The soldier who gave away the assassin's location suddenly had his helmet cave in from the impact of the gunman's rifle. The last soldier aimed his sight at the sniper but failed to fire because a photon charge seared through his stomach and out the other side. Ky somehow made it out of the confrontation alive.

Ky turned around and looked up to the warehouse. He said with a sincere gratitude to the mystery sniper. "That was the second time today my ass has been saved. Thank you."

Byne stood up revealing himself as the sniper. "Do not thank me quite yet." The knight discarded the high velocity sniping rifle he had been using to pick off the IO. Byne used both hands as he hung over the ledge of the small warehouse. Something seemed wrong as he let go of the ledge and his weakened body collapsed to the ground. Byne was over exerted as he rose to his feet and he appeared to be inflicted by some severe exhaustion. "Lili's hold over me is gone. She must be on her way to the Abseninus Void."

Ky commented. "I thought you guys were immune to her. I thought all people from planet Verra had grown some kind of tolerance or what not."

Byne took a few sluggish strides forward and laughed. "Haha, you fool. Planet Verra doesn't exist. We're just some warriors she found along her way, and our overexposure only strengthened her hold over us. Her lies are multi-layered and very convincing."

"I see." Ky acknowledged. "You don't seem to be talking so properly anymore."

Byne rolled his eyes at the brainless pilot and informed. "Take off that helmet, she's not even on this plain of existence anymore."

Ky reluctantly removed the IO helmet from his head showing off the awful moist hat-hair that had formed underneath the mask. His red face asked Byne. "So what can we do?"

"I vaguely remember you defeating me in a gunfight. I can't let that stand, so you and me are gonna have a duel." Byne foreshadowed.

"Are you serious?"

"Yes," Byne affirmed. "And this time it's one pistol, one bullet. No photon cannons involved."

"Fine," Ky agreed. "But that also means no gamma shields."

Byne unhinged the metallic balled band from his left arm and the gamma shield fell off. "I wouldn't have it any other way."

"Then let's do this!"

Byne walked down the rubble and debris-ridden street as Ky took hold of his photon cannon and threw it to his side. Byne halted about thirty paces away from Ky then swiveled around to stare down his opponent. He then clasped a simple small pistol and removed it from his jacket with his right hand and held it down at his side. The gunslinger instructed. "Arm yourself."

Ky adjusted his grip on his own pistol and held it down at his side as well.

It was a showdown of the most traditional fashion. The wind howled, almost taunting the men with the true inevitability; at least one of them was going to die. The skies were striped with slow moving black clouds of fiery destruction. The IO, Lili's plan, and Will's safety all took a back seat at the time as the tense scenario lit a fire deep in their bellies. This was it, and neither of them felt they could afford to lose.

Both arms darted up quick as lightning and two shots rang out, but only one body fell. A look of surprise was on Ky's face as he caught a bullet between the eyes. Ky's lifeless head slammed to the concrete and his arms flung back as his final seconds of vision faded. Byne had won, and the lazy pilot was no more.

The sickly knight collapsed to his knees and began to cough uncontrollably. He placed his empty hand on his mouth as blood relentlessly poured out of it. Byne seemed to still have been hiding his illness, but from that point on, keeping up that facade would be impossible. He was on his last leg.

The portal had nearly closed up behind Will as the boy's last sight of his home dimension was Wes writhing in pain on the altar. Will felt a sadness from then on and an uncertainty that he may not have made the right decision. Will and Lili walked into the room.

The room appeared to be straight out of a medieval dungeon. The place was entirely constructed of dull gray stone blocks and formed an expansive square space. The

edges of the room were broken up by mighty cylindrical columns that stretched up to the high solid ceiling. Between the columns were frightening halls of darkness that seemed to go on for infinity to unknown chambers. The creepy room was dimly lit by eternally burning torches fixed to the columns. A long square stage that nearly took up the whole room was propped up only two steps above the floor. The simple room held sacredness about it, but still seemed rather tiny to be called a dimension.

"This is it!" Lili cheered gleefully running into the unsettling stone room.

"Is this it?" Will asked. "Is this the Abseninus Void?"

"No silly," Lili giggled looking back at the timidly approaching boy. "This place doesn't truly exist."

"Could've fooled me,"

Lili gladly explained. "This very same room is located between each dimension, and it's here where one can get to any dimension...as long as you apply the right key."

"So we're gonna go to the Abseninus Void from here?" Will simplified.

"Yes, but sadly, the portal will only allow one person to enter."

Will quickly did the math in his head and it just added to the mounting doubt that was swiftly forming in the boy's heart. He needed some assurance that what he was doing was the right thing and he searched for those answers in Lili. A lot of the developing story was troubling the boy and he just had to vocalize the one that was bothering him the most. "Lili,"

"Yes Will?"

"Is Omega really your ex-boyfriend?"

Lili turned to Will realizing that that little piece of information was eating at his mind. She touched his face sweetly and her voice rippled with the sound of comfort.

"Oh Will...we were together for a little while, but it's not like that."

Will shoved her hand away and forcefully asked. "Then what is it like?"

"I just need his power, nothing more."

"So you want me to help you bring back your ex?" A flabbergasted Will said. "What about us? Aren't we supposed to be together forever after this?"

"You want to be with me?"

"Of course!" Will bellowed like the answer was obvious. "What did you think this was all about?"

"Will," Lili tried to reason. "Do you actually think we'd work out? I mean, I'm a god and you're just...just..."

"Just a boy?" Will angrily finished for her. "I can't believe this."

"You know Will, as a god, mind manipulation is not my only ability. I can also put people to..." She raised her open right hand an inch from Will's face. "...SLEEP."

The boy's eyelids shut and his body went limp. Lili had instantaneously put the boy in a deep slumber. He didn't even awaken as his body fell. The mind god quickly got to work.

Will awoke moments later at the base of the stage. The large spot in his eye had left him along with the pains in his head. He was face down but he noticed slight wind rustling the hair on the back of his neck. When he looked up, he saw Lili standing in the center of the large stage staring directly up. She was looking up at the ceiling that had completely transformed into a huge portal. The portal was sucking inward like a black hole creating a wind gust in the room. Nothing but misty blackness and the occasional flash of blue lightning could be seen in the portal. The sight scared Will to his soul. It wasn't so much the portal itself that terrified him, but the fact that he had caused all of it. Will stood up ready to face her.

Lili peered around to Will and put on a wider smile than the boy had ever seen her make. She said. "Thank you Will. This is it! The portal to the Abseninus Void. I couldn't have done it without you."

"So what are you gonna do now, huh!?" Will loudly argued at her. "Are you just gonna strand me here!?"

"I thought you'd be happy Will. You helped me realize my dream. Now I can make everyone happy."

"By going back and influencing your planet, right!?" Will cursed not liking the resulting outcome of it all.

"Yes, so I can have the power for my influence to reach the entire universe."

The meaning of Lili's goal suddenly smacked the boy in the face. "You mean control everybody. You just wanna control everybody?! Are you serious!? Didn't you learn anything the day you stopped controlling the planet!? Didn't you see all the pain you caused!?"

"All I saw was billions of people suffering the moment they were released from my influence. These humans don't know how to be happy, but I can make them and I will make them. And this paradise I create is more important than me or you."

"You're insane!" Will wailed.

"I truly don't get you." Said Lili with somberness. "I thought you'd be happy because you made me happy."

"I didn't want this Lili. Not like this...not like this." Will dropped to his knees and his head got lost in his hands. He viciously cried for the love he thought he had was just an illusion. He also cried out of shame of how much of a love led fool he had been.

Lili's feet began to lift from the stage as the portal slowly pulled her to the Abseninus Void. She said with no real sincerity. "I'm sorry for that, Will." Her body flipped around in midair with her front facing the grand portal to the different dimension. Her eyes widened as she could feel the awesome power of Omega within her grasp.

Will pitifully sobbed at the foot of the stage like a helpless puppy until his sadness morphed into anger. He looked up with tears still streaming and the whites of his eyes still puffy and pink, but it was a gaze of rage. He saw red.

Lili's body levitated closer to the portal and nothing broke her gaze of anticipation until she heard a loud *NO*. Her head shifted to the side and saw Will right next to her with a maddened expression.

"Rahhh!" Will grunted as he shoved Lili's body out of the way. Her floating frame was easily pushed out of the portal's pull and she bounced against the floor of the stage. Will then felt a weightless sensation as he started hovering into the portal. He desperately grasped and clutched at air but nothing could help him back down to the ground. With worry on his face, his body drifted into the portal and it immediately closed up behind him.

Lili looked up to what had transpired in absolute shock. All her hard work had been blown away by an upset nine-year-old boy. She couldn't fully register in her head that it was over and there was no way she could get to Omega. Her face changed to one of brewing hatred and a god-like madness that only came to those who held such power. Her dainty fist pounded against the stone floor. "No! No! No! All this time! All this work! I've been at this for more than a millennium and now it's down the drain! Ohhh Will, since I can't get to you, I'm gonna take this betrayal out on your world."

While Will and Lili were breaking up, Wes had passed out atop the altar due to the head pains. He awoke to IO soldiers assisting him up.

"Get your hands off me." Wes quickly ordered as he jerked his arms free and stood up on his own.

The soldiers instantly snatched Wes again. One brutish IO agent said back. "No sir," They forced his hands behind his back. "We're detaining you on charges of treason. You'll be held until your hearing. Then your execution."

They threw his hands in a metallic pipe that acted as handcuffs. It was lined with a liquid nano-memory-steel that would mold to the hands that entered and lock them that way. The soldiers were all strapped to lines from a craft overhead and they connected one to the highly technological handcuffs.

Wes remained silent but cool. He didn't flinch or put on a sour face at the soldier's implication of death. He just accepted his judgment. He accepted it for his brother.

All the lines retracted up into the craft, quickly hoisting Wes to his inevitable fate. Once they were all in the IO cruiser, it left the lonely altar.

At the same time, Byne had just finished his crimson convulsion fit. His hand and the cracked broken pavement beneath him was painted. He started breathing normally and wiped the blood off his face with a cloth. Suddenly, he thought he heard a noise. His head oscillated back to see Jina off in the distance. Byne found strength he didn't have and stood to face her, but it was over. Ky's corpse was about forty feet behind him where she could clearly view and he knew she was going to be steaming pissed about it. He went to move his gun but a long metallic staff was at his neck before he could fully lift his arm.

"Give me one good reason why I shouldn't kill you now?" Jina interrogated like a beautiful reaper.

Byne chuckled. "Good reason? No, I can't give you one of those, but go ahead. Do it. For you see, I'm dying." His left fist opened revealing the soiled cloth and blood stained hand. "That's me." His deteriorating body then collapsed from exhaustion.

Jina caught his frail body before making contact with the road. "Easy," She helped him back up into a slouched position. "It's because of your gamma shield isn't it."

Byne coughed. "I thought I was invincible. I thought I could be that one exception and use it with no consequence. What a fool I am right?"

Jina didn't sympathize with the dying warrior. What he did to Ky wouldn't merit such an act. She just demanded. "Tell me everything you know."

Out of the heavens, a deafening screech rumbled the ground of Gohanesse City. Lili had returned to the planet, but in a completely different form. Out of the sky, from a dark cloud, a monster the size of a mountain range hovered over the doomed city. It formed directly above the park and even with the altar's awe inspiring size, it was just a toy to the grotesque thing. This monster's body was the size of the entire commercial district, and parts of the horrifying sight could be seen from many miles away. The terrifying front half of the monster's form just dangled over the city from the sky, while its back half was hidden behind the black clouds or just not there at all.

It had a demonic skull that was nearly the size of the whole park below. The skull almost appeared human if it weren't for odd symmetrical protrusions on its skeletal structure and its building-long razor sharp jagged teeth. It also had two mantis-like bone pincers the size of mountain sides. The rest of its hideous form was bare muscle and bone making the monster an overly distracting entity of horror.

The monster let out another world-shaking screech before one of its pincers drove down on the mighty altar. The altar cracked and shattered apart under the weight of the monster's grand pincer. As the altar tumbled down, a

death-dealing cloud of stone debris shuttled through the
avenues of the commercial district unforgivably covering all
in a lung-clogging dust.

The beast was a great equalizer. Whether it have
been IO or G.F.B., innocent civilian or galactic fugitive, all
fighting ceased. All that came was a unification of all men
under the crippling terror that was placed in the hearts of
all who witnessed the godly creature. They all knew such a
colossal savage monster could easily make short work of
the planet.

Will walked as scared as a child could be in a reality
of thick tangible darkness. He was lost in the Abseninus
Void; the same place where gods would seal dangerous
galaxy-threatening powers such as the silver gilded jaguar,
Dubius the god of torment, and the god of power Omega.
In the distance, Will could see a small flicker of light and his
fear changed. Whatever the light was, good or bad, the boy
was going to head to it. On the way, his confidence grew.
He figured that the worst thing that could happen was he'd
die, and the release of death had to better than being
stranded there in the darkness for eternity.

He neared the light source until he could make out
what it was. At first glance, Will knew what it had to be.
What he saw could only be titled *god of power*; it had to be
Omega. It was a ten foot entity in the shape of a man asleep
on a black throne that blended into the void. His body was
nothing but churning flaming energy like the most raw and
powerful forces of the universe crammed into one being.
His slumbering head had hair of a twisting inferno like a
bonfire blowing in the wind.

With an aching anger of all that happened, Will
pointed a fury filled finger at the ten foot god. He didn't
care how powerful the god was, it was all his fault, and the
boy was going to deal with him accordingly. "Hey!" He

shouted.

Omega's head grew erect as his eternal sleep was broken. His eyes slowly opened and beamed brightly like two blinding flashing suns in the god's face. Omega's bright star eyes slowly glared down at Will knowing he could crush the frail boy in a single breath.

Will did not care if he was going to be killed, he was going to have it out with the god. The boy furiously shouted. "You and me need to talk!"

With nothing to lose, Byne told the whole story to Jina without holding anything back. They watched as the huge monster crushed the enormous altar like a child's play thing.

"So is that Lili and Omega?" Jina discussed.

"No, that's just Lili." Byne informed. "Something must've gone wrong."

"Is that her true form?" Jina further interrogated.

"No, she has no true form. Just what people think she looks like."

"I'm going to need to put you down now." Jina told.

"Why?"

"I need to try and defeat that thing." Jina confided.

"Don't bother," Byne advised. "You're not going to be able to do anything to it."

"Why not?"

Byne explained. "Because it's not even there. She's just planting that image in the minds of the people and it's their own brain power that is causing the destruction."

"A beast of the mind?"

"Yes, rooted so subconsciously that you'll still see it even if you consciously know it's not real, like us. There is nothing your staff can do against the strength of the mind."

"So we're doomed."

"Yes."

Byne's body jerked forward as the sound of a gunshot was heard. The shirt area around his stomach was hastily turning red and he realized he'd been shot in the back. The dishonorable act filled Byne with a revitalizing anger. With his pistol still in hand, he flipped his body around. He pointed his firearm at the assailant ready to gun down the man that secured the gunslinger's demise, but before he could fire the pistol it was blasted out of his hand. Another bullet slammed into his chest and Byne fell back.

"What...a...good...shot." The gunman praised his opponent as he was spread out on the street. That was Byne's final resting place.

Detective Lee put his gun back in his beaten trench coat with the barrel still smoking. He approached Jina and investigated in an anger filled tone. "This guy killed Ky, right? Why didn't you crush him like the cockroach he is?"

"You didn't need to do that." Said Jina as the detective stood beside her. "He was dying from over use of a gamma shield."

"Well let's just say, shooting him gives me a piece of mind."

"I thought letting him suffer through his vicious illness was more fitting." Jina reasoned. She looked upon Lee's tattered coat and war-scarred face. "What happened to you?"

"I got into a little scuffle with the IO back there. All my men were wiped out. You don't wanna know what I had to do to escape." Lee retold as he casually lit a cigar. "So Jina, do you think you can do your thing on that oversized floating exoskeleton over there?" The detective inquired in reference to the monster that took up most of the sky.

"No, that's a monster of the mind. It's fueled by the fear of all who see it."

Lee simplified. "It's one of those *it's there because we*

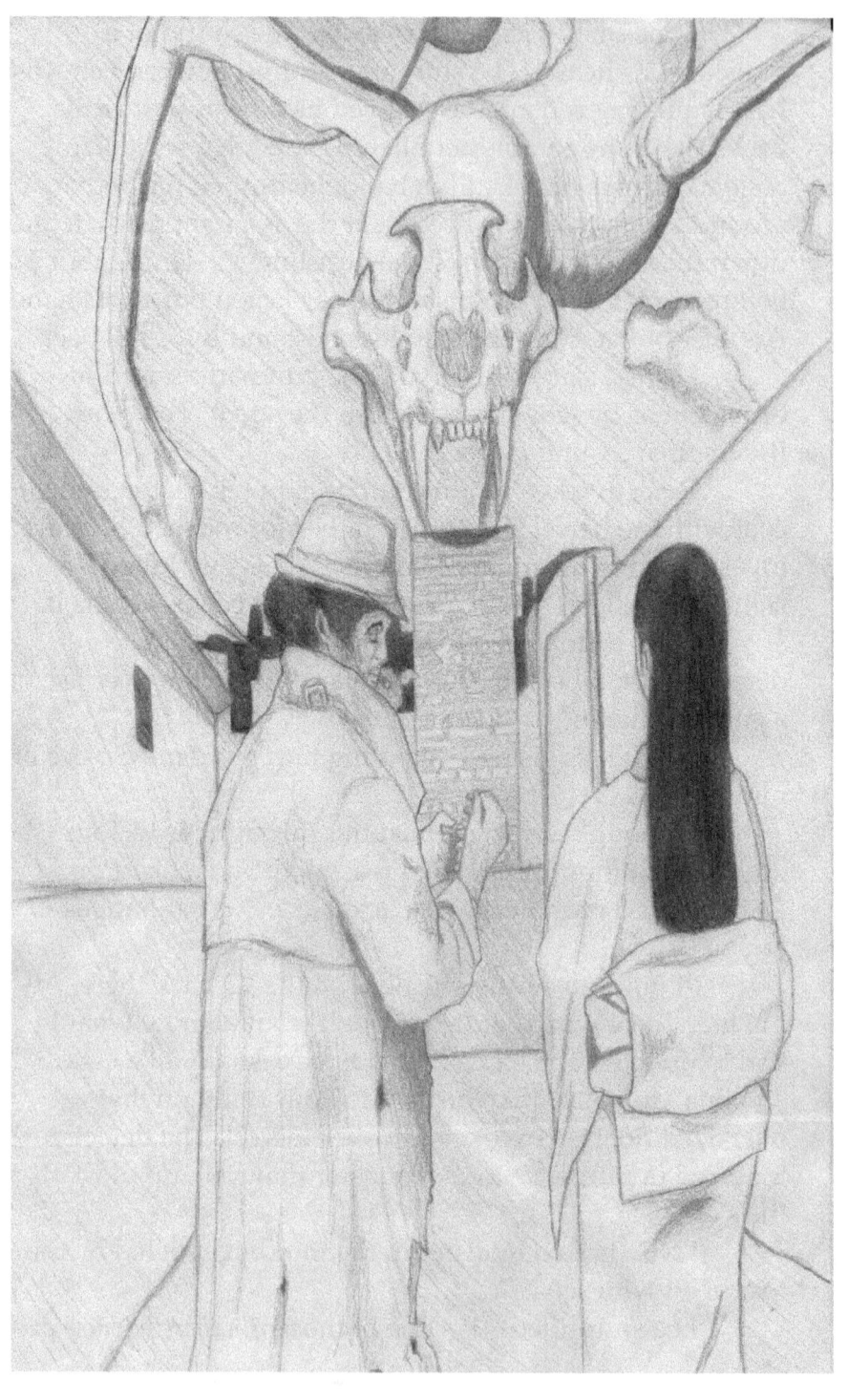

believe in it type deals, huh?"

"Exactly,"

"Damn it," Cursed Lee. "I knew I was going to see the end of the universe. I hate being right all the time."

All four of their brave eyes were set on the demon in the sky helpless to do anything about it.

Wes stood against a wall in an IO craft still handcuffed and with two soldiers restraining him. The ex-IO agent and all the other soldiers on the deck silently watched the huge monitors as another swipe of the beast's gargantuan pincer leveled a building to dust.

With a piling guilt for failing to stop it all when he had the chance, Wes whispered. "This truly is the end of days..."

Out of a portal, something appeared in the sky. It was so tiny and so far up that it went unnoticed. Even if someone did focus on it, it could have easily been confused for a light of a craft or jet. It was in the air on the other end of the city, but still close enough for the god of the mind to sense.

Right when it appeared, the gargantuan monster broke up into building sized ribbons of light that harmlessly vanished and revealed Lili's childish form just the way Will remembered her. As she floated nearly a mile above the ground her face became a mask of absolute loathing. What had arrived had infuriated the god.

"No!" Lili denied. "What I've been told about you three can't be true!"

Floating on the opposite corner of the city was Omega, or was it Will? It had all the signs of Omega, the body made of swirling hot energy, the flaming flailing hair, and eyes as bright as suns, but something was different. For one, he was only four feet tall and a lot of his body resembled Will's. It was both of them put together.

Apparently, Omega was none too happy at Lili for what happened to him. The god of power jumped at the chance to meld with Will and share his immunity from her mind control. As for Will, he just wanted to hurt her as much as she hurt him.

In the busy IO craft, a soldier frantically reported. "Lili has assumed her previous form and there's some mysterious spike of power unlike anything I've ever seen before."

The IO soldier put in charge after Wes' betrayal quickly ordered. "Get it up on the screen!"

The IO camera's located the spike's origin in an instant and a second later the craft's main jumbo monitor was filled with the fusion of the boy and the power god. All eyes in the control deck fell on the screen and they were lost in a quiet baffling moment. Most of them couldn't wrap their minds around what they were seeing.

One soldier remarked. "What is that?"

Wes, still being restrained along the wall, mouthed the word *Will*.

Lili whined like a small girl denied a very expensive doll. "It's not fair Will! You just don't get to have something I worked so hard for!"

Even though Will/Omega didn't hear her, it said back almost like a response. "We loved you."

The gods stayed suspended in the air a moment as the tension mounted. The two gods let out unforgettable battle cries and they projected their forms at each other at speeds that Jina could only hope to follow. They met in a radical galaxy trembling ram of opposing forces. The energy expelled at the moment the two gods clashed immediately ripped a hole into the delicate fabric of reality. A white nothingness began to grow at that spot, and within the first femtosecond, it claimed the entire planet. Jina, Lee,

Wes aboard the IO craft, and even Ky's deceased remains were gone in a blinding white flash. The white nothing broke apart the planet to its smallest molecules and thrust them into its neutral abyss, but it didn't stop there. It spread outwards in all directions as fast as the speed of light multiplied by the speed of light. In ten minutes, the universe was broken down into tiny invisible particles and lost in a white void of emptiness. The universe had been removed and only the neutrality of nothing reigned.

Will is pleasantly surprised as his eyes start to open. He looks down at his body to find he is no longer joined with Omega, but is still not his former self; he's in a different form now. It looks like his old body, but feels more like a projection or a dream. His mind also feels askew. A certain grand acceptance of all things is attached to his psyche that makes his personality seem more sedated. He floats in an infinite comforting light that he does not yet know is me.

I show my face to the boy. It's a warm welcoming face that takes up the entire existence that Will has found himself in. Due to the change in his mind, Will is able to look upon my all-knowing benevolent countenance without his head exploding.

I say unto the boy. "Hello Will. I am EXLA, the creator of all the universes and the gods sworn to protect them."

Will says. "Hi,"

"You have put on quite a show, have you not?" I ask the boy.

Will chuckles. "I guess I have."

"Yes," I explain. "One of the flaws of the gods is that even with their all-encompassing powers, they still fall victim to petty emotions such as greed, envy, jealousy, and so on."

"That's no good." Will comments not fully grasping the scope of the moment.

"No, and it is because of that that I now find myself in this predicament." I inform the boy. "Your encounter with Lili has destroyed my universe."

"Oh snap!"

"Yes, well, the delicate balance of the universes and how they coexist next to each other is dependent on each universe being accounted for."

"Sorry about that." Will apologizes.

"Be that as it may," I continue. "I must create a new universe to replace the one you helped destroy, and since you were the victor of the bout, I summoned you here in this form to help create the universe as you see fit."

"Wow, sweet,"

"So tell me," I graciously request. "In what image shall we construct the new universe?"

"Me? Make a universe?" Will's voice rings with uncertainty. "I don't know if I can."

"You must," I insist. "As the victor of the bout, this is now your duty."

Memories of Lili rush through the boy's mind. Not their tragic end, but the fun times they had together. No matter how hard he tries, he cannot shake her from his head and his heart. He looks upon me and says. "All I want, all I wish for is..."

A boy laid spread out on a grassy field in a park in Gohanesse City. The park was beautiful with acres upon acres of lush green grass and prosperous trees. It had stone trails circling the entire park for the few Gohanesse civilians who enjoyed leisurely walks. The park was dotted with clean ponds that had various ducks and geese sitting on the water's edge waiting for breadcrumbs that the elderly may disperse. Squirrels scurried amongst the trees hastily harvesting acorns and an assortment of nuts before the season became too cold to do so. The park smelt of the sweet scents of pine cones, fresh cut grass, and blooming flowers. The park was a wonderful getaway from the usual hustle and bustle that consumed the overly busy city. It was like a safe haven for the city civilians who appreciate the feel of nature now and again.

The boy was none other than William A. Treyu lying on his back with his face to the sky. His hands were tucked behind his head as he felt the warmth of the sun's rays kissing his smooth youthful skin. The excellently complicated boy was content in his simple moment of calm. He looked up to the skies behind closed eyes, seeing nothing but a pink canvass of light passing through his fleshy eyelids. A tiny smile cracked in the corner of his mouth while a warm breeze rolled through. The wind gradually pushed the thick cotton clouds across the bright endless sky. The day was perfect, and that was the day it all began.

Suddenly, the boy became slightly colder while the pink hue of his eyelids turned black as if someone had blocked his sun. He opened his eyes and saw a cloud obstructing his light. Will arched up in a sitting position and plotted the rest of the day.

"Yeah, I guess I better get home." Will remarked realizing he was being just as lazy as Ky. Will took his time walking out of the park. He waited for the bus around the corner of the park entrance. Once the big silvery bus came, Will gave the park a final departing look as if he had missed something or if he had been in that situation before. The boy had no problem shaking the thoughts from his head before entering the bus.

The bus ride from the commercial district to the industrial district ran as smoothly as it could and promptly dropped the boy off at the bus stop down the street from Ky's large apartment. Will strolled to the front door of the studio/warehouse and opened it. Inside, Jina had her staff resting on the wall beside her as she sipped on a mug of coffee at the round dining table, and Ky was lazily channel surfing on the couch. Will shut the door behind him and stormed in.

"Hey Jina," Will nonchalantly greeted as he bypassed the beauty and headed straight to Ky. Will whined. "Ky!"

"Hey Will," Ky groaned from the couch not pleased with the interrogation he was about to endure. "Channel up." He commanded.

"Did you look for a job today?" Will groaned.

Ky defied. "Nope,"

"And why not?"

"We don't need it." Ky reasoned. "Our accounts are doing all right."

"Yeah, all right but not fantastic," Will commented on his way to the kitchen area to dig up something to eat.

"Hey, can I borrow your laptop for a second?" Ky asked.

"Why?" Will said closing the fridge with a cold turkey leg in hand.

"I wanna check my Headscript."

"Oh brother..."

As the boy's continued to argue, Jina quietly sipped

her mug. Suddenly, her eyes shot open accompanied by a distracting gasp. She quickly grasped her staff and threw it in a straight line towards the kitchen area. The long metal staff appeared to halt in midair and a few inches of its tip disappeared. The staff just hovered in the air for a moment until a little blood started trickling from the tip of the levitating weapon. A shriek of pain sounded before the staff tumbled over still impaled into nothing.

A man who had caught the staff with his chest started flickering into existence. The man was wearing some kind of suit that cloaked him in a perfect camouflage. He seamlessly blended into the background. Ky jetted off the couch in interest and Will jumped back with the body only inches away from him. The guys in the studio/warehouse wondered how Jina even knew he was there, including the one that was dying on the floor. The guys hovered around him as Jina slowly made her way to the victim.

The man's face was graceful and delicate and attached to shiny smooth blonde locks. His suit was highly mechanical and undoubtedly the device in which allowed him to go invisible. With his life gradually fading, the man looked upon Jina.

"Jina," the mysterious man said with a small line of blood coming out of the crease of his mouth. "Is it possible you got stronger since I last saw you?"

"Masala, what are you doing here?" Jina asked the dying man.

Masala said with the only strength he had left. "I came here to tell you that he didn't forget about you. He's coming for you...he's coming soon."

Jina whispered under her breath. "Ehri..."

Ky inquired looking up at Jina with eyes of concern. "Jina, who's he talking about? Who's coming for you?"

Jina reluctantly answered. "My ex-boyfriend,"

What did Will wish in his meeting with EXLA?
He wished Lili never existed.

(TUNE IN NEXT TIME KIDS!)

NEXT TIME;
Rose Star Runners: On Dr. Dougal's Craft

Hello, it's Alex again, one year older and much wiser. After the completion of the first Rose Star Runners, I thought everything was just going to fall into place. I quickly realized that this was not the case and also learned the value of patience. Therefore, this author's corner is going to be a call to spread the word (sorry). If you really enjoyed this story half as much as I enjoyed writing it than you need to let everyone know, and when you see it on TV or on a billboard or in the newspaper, you can have the satisfaction that it was *YOU* that was one of the original true fans and who helped make it big. So please recommend this series to all your book reading friends. Rose Star Runners is now on facebook, twitter, and tumblr, and welcomes everyone to follow and become a fan. Now, back to my post thoughts of Rose Star Runners: and the Universe Princess. I really thought this addition was a good *change of gears* from the first, and now that I no longer had to introduce most of the characters in detail I could focus more on the overall story. I really took it to the RSR limit with the plot, and feel that this installation will be a lot of people's favorite for the cute child love story within. I base a lot of the love aspects on my own personal relationships, and I'm mainly single, so naturally they all come out tragic, but I feel it adds a realistic twist to the fantastic tale. Again, thanks for getting my book and we got a long way to go to the end. Until we meet again, Al out.

Follow Us On

Facebook:
http:m//m.facebook.com/home.php#!/profile.php?id=213
137375375559&_user=100000872053807
(Or just like the title in the book section of your profile)

Twitter:
twitter.com/RoseStarRunners

tumblr:
rosestarrunners-blog.tumblr.com

Pinterest:
pinterest.com/rosestarrunners/